Praise for the DS Max Craigie series

'Non-stop action, breakneck pace, deliciously suspenseful . . . *When Shadows Fall* was my first DS Max Craigie book and won't be my last – I loved it' **Andrea Mara**

'Neil is the master of the crime mystery' **Jeremy Vine**

'Grabbed me from the first page' **Ian Rankin**

'Utterly compelling, ingeniously plotted and incredibly entertaining, this puts Neil Lancaster up at the forefront of Tartan Noir' **Liz Nugent**

'Fast-paced, compelling and deeply authentic' **Jane Casey**

'Neil Lancaster is a thriller writer set to blow up the bestseller lists' **C. L. Taylor**

'Action-packed and lightning-paced with some of the best dialogue I've read . . . Explosive and compelling' **Helen Fields**

'Tight and tense with laugh-out-loud moments. An absolute joy to read' **Marion Todd**

'A masterclass in how to deliver a taut, pacy thriller hot on the page' **Imran Mahmood**

'A wickedly clever and riveting thriller. Lancaster has an innate talent in treating the reader to whip-cracking, deeply authentic stories' **Graham Bartlett**

'Bone-chilling and full of so many twists' *The Sun*

'A good old police procedural . . . I was pleasantly terrified' *The Guardian*

'Deliciously dark' *Daily Mail*

NEIL LANCASTER is the No. 1 digital bestselling author of both the Tom Novak and Max Craigie series. Writing as Max Connor, Neil is also the author of *No Mercy* and *No Way Out*. His first Craigie novel, *Dead Man's Grave*, was longlisted for the 2021 McIlvanney Prize for Best Scottish Crime Book of the Year. The second Craigie novel is *The Blood Tide*, which has topped several e-book and audio charts, and was also longlisted for the McIlvanney Prize and shortlisted for the Dead Good Reader Award. He served as a military policeman and worked for the Metropolitan Police as a detective, investigating serious crimes in the capital and beyond. As a covert policing and surveillance specialist he utilised all manner of techniques to investigate and disrupt major crime and criminals.

He now lives in the Scottish Highlands, writes crime and thriller novels, and works as a broadcaster and commentator on true crime documentaries. He is a key expert on two Sky Crime TV series, *Meet, Marry, Murder* and *Made for Murder*, and appeared on a BBC true crime show, *Big Little Crimes*.

🄷 @neillancaster66
🄵 @NeilLancasterCrime
www.neillancastercrime.co.uk

Also by Neil Lancaster

The Max Craigie Novels:
Dead Man's Grave
The Blood Tide
The Night Watch
Blood Runs Cold
The Devil You Know
When Shadows Fall

The Tom Novak Novels:
Going Dark
Going Rogue
Going Back

The Josie Chapman Novels:
No Mercy
No Way Out

NEIL LANCASTER

The Dark Heart

ONE PLACE. MANY STORIES

HQ
An imprint of HarperCollins*Publishers* Ltd
1 London Bridge Street
London SE1 9GF

www.harpercollins.co.uk

HarperCollins*Publishers*
Macken House, 39/40 Mayor Street Upper
Dublin 1, D01 C9W8, Ireland

This edition 2026

1
First published in Great Britain by HQ,
an imprint of HarperCollins*Publishers* Ltd 2026

Copyright © Neil Lancaster 2026

Neil Lancaster asserts the moral right to be identified as the author of this work.
A catalogue record for this book is available from the British Library.

ISBN: 9780008688387 (HB)
ISBN: 9780008769086 (TPB)

Typeset in Sabon Lt Pro by HarperCollins*Publishers* India

This novel is entirely a work of fiction. The names, characters and incidents portrayed in it are the work of the author's imagination. Any resemblance to actual persons, living or dead, events or localities is entirely coincidental.

All rights reserved. No part of this publication may be reproduced, stored in a retrieval system, or transmitted, in any form or by any means, electronic, mechanical, photocopying, recording or otherwise, without the prior written permission of the publishers.

Without limiting the exclusive rights of any author, contributor or the publisher of this publication, any unauthorised use of this publication to train generative artificial intelligence (AI) technologies is expressly prohibited. HarperCollins also exercise their rights under Article 4(3) of the Digital Single Market Directive 2019/790 and expressly reserve this publication from the text and data mining exception.

Printed and bound in the UK using 100%
Renewable Electricity at CPI Group (UK) Ltd

Dedicated with deep respect to all the men and women in law enforcement who operate in the shadows in order that we might be safe.

1

DR DANIEL SOLOMON stood and waved self-consciously, as he accepted the warm applause in the bookshop in central York. The place was packed to the rafters with readers eager to hear him talk about his inspiration for his new book, *An Iman, a Rabbi, a Priest, and an Atheist Go Into a (Juice) Bar: How Religion and Secularism Can Peacefully Coexist.*

The book was his life's work. A polemic forged by his experiences, beginning in Israel, formed in the University of Alberta in Canada and then crystallised while getting his doctorate at Edinburgh. This was his passion. Social cohesion in a polarised world. Unlike many others, he could see a way out of it, and his driving force was to broadcast it to the whole world.

And how he'd succeeded. Against all odds the book had been an instant, massive success, topping the *Sunday Times* and *New York Times* bestseller lists for weeks and weeks on end. For once, a narrative had been delivered that was not polarising, quite the opposite. He preached to all faiths, and cultures came together with a shared vision, and it had landed on the public like nobody could have foreseen.

He had read from the first chapter, which he had performed with all the vigour of a member of the Royal Shakespeare Company at the Rose Theatre. His voice was rich and sonorous, and had carried to every inch of the space, and into each and every listener's heart, as he espoused his vision of unity amongst all faiths.

His final sentence had captivated the audience, his soft voice accented with a curious mix of Israel, Canada and Yorkshire. 'My friends, this is my message. As communities we must stand tall against the scourge – the pernicious scourge – of the racism and bigotry that we all face. We must do it steadfastly, honestly, with courage, humility and open hearts. How can we succeed? We must unite, as friends and faiths together, whether believers in a higher power or not. We are all the same, friends, and our differences must unite us, not divide us. As one, we can form a world where the overriding agenda is not one of want, of avarice, but is one of service. To serve all by being part of one community of all faiths. We must not fail. We cannot fail.'

The rapturous applause of the fifty listeners could have been a hundred-strong, such was the enthusiasm with which it was delivered.

Daniel was a scholar of philosophy, an academic, and a former soldier, in that order. He had seen evil up close, and knew that there was only one solution to overcome it. Acceptance, cooperation and understanding.

The line of readers, all clutching copies of the book, snaked towards the back of the shop, and Daniel spent time with everyone, shaking hands, posing for selfies, and signing and dedicating copies.

He felt giddy with excitement as the queue began to dwindle and the last customer arrived at the table, book in hand, a wide smile across his face. He was a short and stocky man, with huge eyebrows and thick spectacles, and he wore a heavy raincoat, despite the hot, sultry day. 'Hello, Dr Solomon, I loved your talk. Please would you sign my book?' he said, grinning inanely.

Daniel smiled. 'Sure, what's your name, my friend?' he asked.

'Lionel,' he said, showing stained and uneven teeth that were framed by a wispy moustache and beard. His pale, spotty face was covered with a light sheen of sweat. Daniel enjoyed book signings, but you did attract the occasional odd-bod, and it seemed Lionel was one of those.

A quick squiggle in his book, and a pause for a photograph, and he was done.

'Thank you very much, Dr Solomon. I very much loved your descriptions of life in Israel in the Eighties, very interesting.' His voice was high-pitched, monotone and flat.

'You're welcome, my friend, now if you'll excuse me, I really must get going.'

'Of course, shalom, doctor,' said Lionel, studying the dedication and signature rapturously.

There was a brief pause while Daniel thanked the staff at the shop, and very soon he was emerging into the bright, early evening sun, the rays warming his face after the air-conditioned interior of the shop. He sighed, satisfied about a great talk and a good number of hardbacks sold, which would all add to his chances of staying in the *Sunday Times* top ten.

He was excited to get back to his home in Leeds, where his wife, Abigail, would be waiting, eager to hear all about his first big event. Hopefully there would be something nice cooking in the oven. A story with the kids, and then he had a book he was wanting to finish, perhaps with a nice glass of something chilled.

It was as he was leaving the shop and walking along the narrow, twisty York streets that things changed forever.

His phone buzzed in his pocket. Pulling it out and looking at the screen, he saw it wasn't his wife, as he'd expected, but a private number.

'Hello?'

'Dr Solomon?' A well-educated voice, with shades of public school, tinged with a hint of Scotland.

'Yes, who is this, please?'

'It doesn't matter who I am, Dr Solomon, but you are in danger. You need to hide; you must get away and hide.'

He felt his insides chill as he slowed his pace. 'I'm sorry, but who are you?'

'Never mind who I am. Listen, there are people out there who hate you. They hate you and they want you dead. Your book is the final straw to them, and if you want to live, you must get away.'

Despite the absurdity of the words, he felt the hairs prickle on the back of his neck. Who could wish him harm? He was just a lapsed Jew who preached social integration and peace. 'I'm sorry, I think you have the wrong person, I'm just a writer.'

'No. Look, listen to me, Dr Solomon. You cannot go home, they'll be wait—'

Daniel hung up and quickened his pace, looking behind him. The streets were busy, bustling with early evening revellers.

'Nutters,' he whispered to himself, trying not to break into a jog as he crossed from Parliament Street onto Piccadilly towards the Coppergate Car Park, feeling the colour draining from his face. 'Ridiculous,' he muttered, as he risked a glance behind.

And then he saw him.

It was Lionel, from the shop, his hands buried beneath his thick coat. He was matching the pace of Daniel's stride, about thirty metres behind, head down, his slightly knock-kneed gait giving him a curious rhythm. A cold hand seemed to grip him.

Feeling his stomach clench at the sight, he quickened his pace, pushing the doors to the car park open. He quickly validated his ticket at the machine in the stairwell, hands shaking as he poked the piece of card into the slot, and then tapped his payment card against the reader.

Within a minute, he was blipping the lock on his Jaguar, and sighing with relief as he settled into the cosseting leather. He just sat there, breathing easily, as he regained his composure. He reached down and grabbed his insulated metal water bottle, and took a swig.

It was as he was screwing the lid back on that he saw him again.

Lionel was walking slowly towards Daniel's car, his hands buried in his pockets, head down, a half-smile on his face.

'Oh, shit, no, please,' he said, as he fumbled for the start button, his finger trembling.

Lionel reached the car, his hands moving from his pockets, almost seeming to be in slow motion, a copy of the book in his hand. 'Dr Solomon, you forgot . . .'

As Daniel pressed the car's starter, the world seemed to shift on its axis, and his only conscious sensation was of massive, overwhelming pressure, just for a microsecond before the explosion from the device under the car threw it up in the air, smashing the roof into the low, concrete ceiling, before ripping both Daniel and Lionel into pieces with its devastating force.

2

Almost a year later

TERRY 'STRINGER' DENT smirked as he looked from the dock, in court one of Newcastle Crown Court. The judge, Mr Justice Imran Ahsan, met his gaze, scowling over the top of his spectacles, his wig only just slightly askew. He was a slim man, with heavy eyebrows and thick greying hair. As always, he wore a superior expression, his lips drawn back from his teeth in a permanent sneer.

Stringer had grown to hate the judge with a burning passion. It was the way he fucking stared at him, and the way every single thing his barrister presented to him he rejected, with a sarcastic grin that made Stringer want to smash through the glass in the dock, and wring the skinny fucker's neck.

But not now.

Now Mr Justice Arsehole, or whatever his name was, looked depressed as the prosecution barrister, a severe and stout woman called Mrs Cullompton KC, had offered no evidence after the star witness had failed to turn up at court for the second day running.

This wasn't entirely unexpected to Stringer, owing to the fact that said missing star witness, James McGovern, was currently stricken with a severe case of permanent missing person syndrome, and was in fact at the bottom of the Tyne, weighted down by a twenty-kilogram kettle bell. It had been a bastard to sort from jail, and had almost cost him another six months on remand, with his legal team demanding adjournments for bullshit technical reasons, to allow his people to take care of the grass. It was six months well spent; he sniggered to himself. Six months on an easy remand against a life sentence if the McGovern had turned up in the witness box was an easy call to make.

The judge cleared his throat, faced the jury and spoke in his stupid posh-boy voice. 'Members of the jury, we now find ourselves in a highly unfortunate position. The Crown finds itself unable to proceed in this case, and as such have offered no evidence, effectively ending the trial. However, as you all took an oath promising to fairly try the defendant, he remains in your hands, and as such, only you can clear him. I will soon ask your foreman to stand, and the clerk will ask you whether you find the defendant guilty or not guilty. As the prosecution has unfortunately decided to draw stumps, this case remains unproved, and as such there is only one verdict open to you, therefore I direct that you are to return a verdict of "not guilty".' He nodded at the clerk, who stood and faced the jury.

'Will the foreman of the jury please stand.' A grey-haired woman sitting front and centre of the benches got to her feet.

'In respect of charge one on the indictment, do you find the defendant, Terry Dent, guilty or not guilty?'

'Not guilty.'

'In respect of charge two on the indictment, do you find the defendant, Terry Dent, guilty or not guilty?'

The foreman drew herself to her full height and spoke. 'Not guilty.'

Stringer burst out laughing as the cheers echoed around the public gallery.

He was laughing as he was escorted down to the cell block, was still laughing as he was put in the sweatbox back to Frankland, and he was chuckling as he collected all his shite from his cell. He knew that the smile wouldn't leave his face for quite some time.

*

Stringer was still grinning when he was faced with the pale, bespectacled young prison officer in reception as he was handed a clear plastic bag that contained his few possessions. The same bag, containing the same possessions, that he had handed over when arriving at Frankland Prison almost a year earlier after being remanded in custody to face trial for a single count of attempted murder, and for being involved in the supply of a very large amount of heroin.

'Cheers, Mr Carmichael,' said Stringer, in a tone that managed to convey humour and sarcasm, only just tinged with an edge of hostility.

A diminutive, late-middle-aged prisoner in maroon tracksuit bottoms and a stained white T-shirt was disconsolately pushing a filthy mop around the grimy floor. He was lean and compact, with heavy features, and as he saw Stringer, he leaned his mop against the wall and approached the giant man, without even a trace of nervousness. Crude tattoos covered his forearms, which were tight and corded with sinewy muscle. His hands bore multiple tattoos, including crosses on the knuckles, and the number 88 on the centre of the back of his hand. His face was scarred from the corner of his eye to the corner of his mouth.

'You get out now, Stringer?' he said, in accented English redolent of Eastern Europe. His voice crackled with phlegm.

'That I am, Boggie,' he said, unable to stop a broad grin from spreading across his huge, round face at the sight of the older prisoner.

'You lucky man. Have lady waiting for you, aye?' he said, advancing and hugging the giant gangster. He was so short, however, that his head barely came up to Stringer's chest. Despite the disparity, Stringer returned the embrace.

'Hopefully, Boggie.' He paused and looked at the man, who had slicked-back dark hair and icy-blue eyes that surveyed him with warmth. 'I'll not forget you, pal,' he said, clapping the man on the shoulder.

Boggie stood back and stared up hard at Stringer his eyes burning with intensity. '*Never* forget, eh?'

There was so much emphasis in those two words that Stringer felt a shudder travel down his spine. Stringer met his gaze, his face impassive and full of respect.

'I won't, pal. I'll never forget.'

The Russian pulled himself closer to Stringer, and he whispered, his voice hoarse, 'The cause is everything, my friend. Nothing matters but the cause, never forget this, no?' He gripped Stringer's hand tightly, his eyes damp with emotion. Stringer felt a knot in his stomach as he and Bogdan just stood there in the smelly reception, eyes locked, something tangible passing between them, almost like electricity.

Bogdan had changed everything for Stringer. Before his incarceration he'd been a drug dealer with right-wing opinions, but in his time with Bogdan that had changed. Opinions were like arseholes; everyone has them. It was time for action, and he was here for it.

The officer was clearly unimpressed. 'Bogdan, that floor is not gonna mop itself. Get cracking,' he said, sharply.

Bogdan grinned, tightened his grip on Stringer's hand for a second, before releasing it, shrugging and picking up his mop, continuing to spread the dirt around the floor of the reception area, in half-arsed slow, deliberate circles.

Stringer glared at the screw, before pulling out a plain black jacket from the plastic bag and slipping it on. It was a bit snug across his bulging shoulders. Stringer was well over six feet tall, probably eighteen stone of pure, north-eastern beef. The harsh overhead lights reflected on his shaven scalp that was bisected by a long, livid white scar stretching from the forehead to the crown. His eyes were dark and sunken. Like pebbles, totally devoid of any light or emotion. As he smiled, he showed his stained, uneven teeth that seemed too small for his massive head.

'Sign here for your property, Mr Dent,' said the screw in a wobbly voice, his skinny hand shaking as he pointed at the form. The fear was coming from the pasty-faced dweeb, probably because he had been one of the few officers who had seemed to enjoy subjecting Stringer to the vagaries of the Category A regime. The older, more experienced screws realised that Stringer's reputation made him a man not to get on the wrong side of.

They probably thought he was a man to bear grudges.

And they'd be right. Stringer did bear grudges.

He had resisted the urge not to drop knowledge of the prison officer's address, wife's name, or where his kids went to school into the mix to really shit the little prick up. He'd made it his business to find out everything about him, after his shitty treatment, and almost constant disrespect. One day the little fucker would realise that he'd made a mistake disrespecting Stringer Dent on a regular basis.

Mr Carmichael, the baby-faced screw, would find out to what extent Stringer bore grudges at some point in the future. But not now. Now he had bigger priorities.

Now, he had a cause.

'I'd like to say that it's been a pleasure, Mr Carmichael, but it would just be a lie,' said Stringer, his voice deep, resonant and rich with the tones of the north-east. He took the pen and scribbled on the sheet of paper.

'Well, best of luck. Whatever our differences, Mr Dent, I hope you realise I was just doing my job,' said Carmichael, his eyes darting from side to side and his chin almost wobbling.

Jesus, what a fucking baby, thought Stringer.

'Aye, a shame maybe that you seemed to enjoy it so much, bonny lad. Now, can you show me out of this fine establishment? I'm a busy man, with things to do and people to see,' said Stringer.

He pulled a worn and scratched timepiece out of the bag and slipped it on his wrist. It felt good. Comfortable and tangible and a reminder of who he was. His dad had been an inspiration, and the watch was all Stringer had left of the tough old boy. It was only the fact that his late dad's Omega watch was in that bag that he'd gone back to jail at all.

'Is that it?' he said, staring hard at Carmichael.

'That's you,' said the prison officer.

'Follow me,' said another screw. A more reasonable old chap who understood the rules far better than the pencil-necked Carmichael.

Stringer followed the screw's skinny back towards the exit, and whatever came next.

*

'Bonny lad!' said Jimmy 'Shorty' Shore, as Stringer approached the stocky, wiry man standing by the door of a gleaming black Mercedes G-Wagon.

'Good to see you, brother,' said Stringer, as they hugged.

'Good to be out, man?'

'Champion. Could you have picked a less conspicuous fuckin' car, man?' Stringer threw his bag through the open window and onto the driver's seat. The early afternoon sunlight danced on the car's gleaming paintwork.

'Thought you'd want picking up in a decent motor.'

'Aye, but this is fuckin' mental. Chuck us the keys, I'm driving,' he said, holding out his meaty palm.

Shorty tossed the keys, which Stringer caught, turning them over in his hand.

'Would you've rather I brought a Lada?'

'I'd have cut your bollocks off if you did.'

'Then you're welcome, mate.' Shorty grinned, his teeth too white and too even to be anything other than veneers.

'News?'

'About what?'

'Cozzers hear anything about York?'

'From what I hear, they're still blaming the Islamic fundamentalists, as you wanted. The Cashier was quality, man. Left no clues other than the ones we wanted them to find. The bomb was apparently exactly the same as an Islamic State device, and he even left a breadcrumb trail with phones, and shite that leads right back to some shitty off-shoot of AQ called Sharia 4 UK.'

'Fucking Sharia 4 UK, those bastards couldn't organise nowt, but that's what we need. Angry patriots and Jews. Cashier is a fucking miracle worker, man.'

'Aye, how did your Russian pal get hold of him?'

'He has more contacts than you can possibly imagine, pal. I'll tell you more over a beer, which I'm fucking gasping for.'

'Same,' Shorty said, grinning.

Stringer returned his smile. 'Who was the other poor bugger who died?'

'A nobody. Casualty of war.'

'Not ideal, but cannat be helped. Just the beginning, pal.'

'Who's next?'

'Not yet. I've more plans, which is why we need to keep grafting with the gear. Need money for proper wedge to pay for that.'

'On it. Although we've lost a big customer in the toon who was supplying all the middle men. Revenue has dried up.'

Stringer stopped and stared; his face frozen. 'I heard Digger got nicked. Who's taking over?'

'No one yet. It's still sorting itself out, which is a problem, as the market has to adjust before we can make sure the new dealers take our product. There's another supplier keeping it going, but I cannat find out who. We're also pretty low on people right now. It's costing us a fair amount.'

'Man, not fucking now.' Stringer leaned against the car.

'Just a blip, we need to let it settle before we can be back up and running at full steam.'

Stringer kicked the bulky tyre disconsolately. 'How long?'

'Couple of months before we're back up to the levels before Digger got nicked.'

'Shite. We need money, man. No time to waste. I've things to tell you and things you need to hear about. My time in this shite-hole has changed everything, man.'

'We're okay for now, no panic, Stringer,' Shorty said, his brow furrowing.

'Not with what I have in mind, man. Things are changing, and we'll need money for the cause more than ever. How about Scotland? That was shaping up nicely, big open market there to expand into.'

Shorty hesitated, his mouth pursed.

'Spit it out, man,' said Stringer, eyeing him balefully.

'We may have a problem with our contact north of the border – nasty rumours and that,' said Shorty, opening the passenger door and getting inside.

Stringer rounded the gleaming G-Wagon and climbed in the driver's seat, nestling himself into the soft leather. 'Go on?' he said, picking up a pair of sunglasses out of the centre console and slipping them on.

'A word to the wise was received. Our contact has suggested that someone has loose lips.' Shorty looked at his friend, his face pensive, ready for the inevitable explosion. It didn't arrive. Instead, Stringer's eyes just looked straight ahead, like a viper considering a rodent.

'About what – the business or the cause?' His voice was low and flat, and laced with menace.

'Both.'

'Where is he?'

'Jockland somewhere, but he's coming down tonight for a drink at your do.'

'I hope you've planned something canny, like? Nae "Spoons and slappers"?' He turned his gaze to Shorty, a mirthless smile stretching across his face.

'Aye, man. I've booked the VIP box at the Bandits tonight, and they're laying on a spread for you. I think they were grateful that you continued the sponsorship. Speedway's a fucking expensive thing, lad.'

Stringer just grinned, his heart leaping at the prospect of watching his beloved Berwick Bandits speedway team. 'Champion, man. Fucking missed watching the Bandits. All the lads coming?'

'There's a good few coming. Food's laid on, couple of nice birds available, if you've not been turned by being surrounded by blokes for the last year?' Shorty gave a cheeky smirk.

'You can hadaway and shite.'

'You ready to celebrate?'

'Definitely.' Stringer's gaze stayed fixed out of the windscreen.

'What about you-know-who?'

'Let me think about that,' he said, trying to sound relaxed, despite the familiar fire in his belly beginning to burn hot.

'You sure?'

'Aye, bonny lad, it's been a long fuckin' time in that shit-hole jail, and I know one thing. I'm not gannin back. Let's piss off and get mortal, man. Problems can wait till tomorrow.' Stringer gunned the powerful V8 engine, and roared off.

3

THE GLASS-FRONTED VIP box was hot, sweaty and full of bonhomie, as Stringer held court with his acolytes, each of whom came up to him, shook his hand, hugged him and congratulated him on busting the case.

A couple of fit young girls worked the room with trays of beers. Burgers, sausage rolls and finger foods adorned a groaning table in the corner of the room. The lads were tucking in with gusto, and the shouts and cheers were deafening in the enclosed space as they all gazed out of the window at the mechanical ballet that roared around the track outside.

Stringer watched transfixed as the motorcycles circumnavigated the track, spitting up swaths of dirt as the riders powered around. He loved speedway, always had done since his old man brought him here as a ten-year-old. There was something about the atmosphere, the smell of petrol, the howling engines, the grizzled old northern men, smoking their Woodbines and cheering the local riders on. It was intoxicating, and he had missed it. He just sat there, at the front of the box, taking it all in and feeling a sense of freedom that had almost made the year behind the door in that shite-hole prison worth it.

Almost. But not quite. He looked across the room, and his eyes fell upon the jovial figure of Billy Mac, short, red-headed and freckly, a tough-looking Jock from Edinburgh who had linked him in with the big market in Scotland before he went inside. It had been chaos north of the border, as the cops had destroyed a couple of the big firms up there. First the Hardie boys, and then the Albanians had been totally put out of action, which had been great for business in terms of an available market. They just needed a proper network, which Jimmy had put them onto, even if it was only small time. Now Stringer was out, he could keep on expanding, and get some serious cash moving. Not for him. Not for wealth.

For the cause.

Stringer had no particular interest in wealth, not since meeting Bogdan, anyway. No longer was he a criminal who made money for the sake of it. He had ideals, he had values, and he had something to protect. His watch was modest, his clothes understated, and beyond a nice car, he had no need for the finer things in life.

The cheer in the room rose to a crescendo, as the Bandits superstar, Danny Peters, roared across the line in first place. Victory.

Stringer leapt to his feet. 'Yeees, ya beauty,' he yelled, feeling the familiar fire in his belly as Danny did a lap of the track, doing wheelies, his arm aloft as the crowd cheered.

The shouting in the box subsided as the occupants all cracked open new beers, and the clink of glass on glass became the dominant sound.

'Welcome home, Stringer,' came a Scottish accent from behind him. He turned to see the short, stocky form of Billy Mac, hand extended, a bottle of lager in his other hand.

'Nice one, Billy,' Stringer said, grinning as he clapped the Scot on his meaty shoulder.

'Glad to be out?' said Billy.

'Daft question, lad. Frankland is a shite-hole. You down for long?' he said, eyeing the tough-looking smaller man.

'No. I have to get back to Edinburgh now. I said I'd meet a pal later in Leith for a beer, he's a useful contact, and has access to all the fishing villages up the north-east. Ripe old market, Stringer.'

'Ah, man. Stay. Small fry there.'

'Plenty of junkies, pal. The Scousers were making a packet after the Hardies got weighed off, until the Albanians fucked them off, and then the cops smashed them, so it's all free and easy with just a few local dealers. They'll easily be sorted. Good money to be made, Stringer, and I'll be looking for decent weight from you to keep that going.' Billy grinned, his teeth crooked, but his smile cheeky and cheerful.

'You driving back?' said Stringer, taking a swig from a bottle of beer that had been thrust into his hand by a red-faced bull of a man.

'No, pal. I've had a few too many, and it's less than an hour on the train.'

Stringer's grin widened, as if sensing an opportunity. 'Tell you what, bonny lad. Berwick feels a bit shite for tonight, and I'm up for a big one. I mean, first night out of jail, and what's the options in fuckin' Berwick, eh? Me and Shorty will run you back to Edinburgh in the G-Wagon and we'll all gan and get mortalled in the Jock clubs, how's about that, eh?' He guffawed, a fleck of spittle flying from the corner of his mouth.

Billy opened his mouth, ready to decline, and then snapped it shut, his eyes lighting up with excitement. 'You sure, Stringer?'

'Damn right, mate. We're up for a fuckin' massive night, and Berwick is hardly Las Vegas, is it? We'll get a hotel, not that we'll fuckin' see it before dawn, man. Shorty has some nice pills, be a banger.'

'Stoatin'. I'll show you some mad places, eh?' Billy chinked his bottle against Stringer's.

'Aye, look, give me a couple of minutes to say goodbye to these fucking reprobates, and we'll head off. It's only nine o'clock, and we'll be in Edinburgh just in time for the place to liven up. Meet us in the car park in ten.' He nodded, and began to work the room, pumping hands and slapping backs, the hero indefatigable after beating the system.

*

The sun was lowering as Billy waited by the big shiny G-Wagon, a strange mix of excitement and trepidation fluttering in his stomach. Excitement as he was really in with these boys now, and yet trepidation because he knew just how unpredictable, and frankly almost maniacally violent Stringer could be. Billy had seen him flip from being funny, charming and charismatic, to truly terrifyingly violent, with literally no warning. It was almost as if an internal switch was flicked, and he went from zero to a hundred in a microsecond, as if he deployed adrenaline faster than normal people. And Shorty? Well, despite his comparatively small stature, he could be equally evil, and was possibly even more sadistic.

Billy's phone buzzed in his pocket. An unknown and unsaved number. It was always a new, unsaved number when he received the messages. As always, the message was short and to the point.

Update?

Billy's fingers flashed across the keys. *Heading to Edinburgh on the piss with Stringer and Shorty.*

The dots blipped flashed as the sender typed. *Need new phone numbers for both.*

Billy's stomach began to boil at the sight of the apparently innocuous message, but he quickly replied. *I'll try.* So much unsaid in that message, and its bland response. He felt a bead of sweat trickle down his spine, and he shivered.

A bleep from the G-Wagon made him jump as the vehicle was unlocked. He looked up and saw Stringer and Shorty heading towards him, both grinning widely as they approached.

'You ready?' said Stringer.

'Aye. Buzzing for it, man.' Billy hoped to God that his smile was convincing.

Stringer held up his huge fist and Billy bumped his against it.

'Then let's get gan. The Jock birds will be gagging for it. You take shotgun, Bill. Shorty can ride up back.'

They all got in the big car, and Billy felt a tingle of excitement as the big engine burbled. He settled into the cream leather seat and pulled his seatbelt across him. This was what it was all about, he thought, a grin stretching across his face.

4

JACKIE JAMESON YAWNED, just as the light was emerging above the horizon and casting orange shadows over the tree-lined road. She paused a moment to let Laddie, her ageing collie do his business, just as she came to the break in the shrubbery that offered the view of the River Tweed, a shaft of early sunlight dancing on the surface of the fast-flowing river.

'C'mon, Laddie,' she said, and the collie's ears pricked up. He carried on his slow trot along the grass verge as they descended the slope towards the bridge. She took in a deep breath, enjoying the clean and fresh air, with just the hint of grass and wildflowers.

Jackie always took this route, every morning from her home just up the slope on the English side of the Tweed, heading down to the Union Chain Bridge. She was a local woman to her very soul, and always enjoyed the fact that as she stepped foot on the reinforced suspension bridge, she entered no-man's land until she passed over the 449 feet of tarmac and arrived in Scotland. It made her proud, somehow. The only bridge of its type in the world that was still taking vehicles since its opening in 1820.

She considered herself a local expert on the bridge and was involved in its recent restoration; part of the reason for her early walks with Laddie was to check for any faults or damage.

Occasionally, English or Scottish nationalists would daub a bit of graffiti on the sandstone pier, which was the opposite of what Jackie wanted. She was English by birth, but like some close to the border she felt a great deal of allegiance to Scotland as well. Family members lived on either side of the divide, without difficulty, and a bit of rabble-rousing from nationalists was the last thing that was needed.

As the pair rounded the final bend, Laddie's ears pricked up again, his gait became more alert and he began to pant with excitement. The bridge was clear, the sun casting shadows across the surface. She looked past the sandstone structure, with its simple blue rectangular sign that declared the reader was now in England. She saw nothing. Laddie strained at the lead and let out a little 'yip', and began to pull towards the bridge.

'What is it, boy?'

In a flash, he bucked his head, slipped the lead and took off, barking towards the centre of the bridge and then stopping suddenly, his nose on the ground as he sniffed at the guard rail that had not long ago been replaced. His tail was wagging with excitement, and he began to bark, rhythmically.

'What's going on, ya daft lad?' she said, slipping his lead back over his shaggy, greying head. He just sat, staring intently at the edge.

Feeling a prickle of fear, Jackie's eyes followed Laddie's line of sight. He was just staring at the edge, with burning intensity, as only a border collie can do.

Then she saw it. A slip of blue nylon cord, tied around one of the barrier struts. It looked like the sort of cord her dad used to use to secure tarpaulins over his trucks.

She went to the edge, her breathing speeding up as she looked down. The blue cord was stretched taut and unmoving.

A red-headed figure was there. Just six feet down, the tips of his shoes swaying slightly. His head was at a sharp angle, as the cord bit into his neck and his tongue protruded, swollen, dangling out of the corner of his mouth, his face the colour of bread dough.

Jackie's scream echoed in the valley.

5

DETECTIVE CHIEF INSPECTOR Laura McKechnie sighed as she parked her ageing little Vauxhall by the SCOTLAND WELCOMES YOU sign, just shy of the sandstone pier that held the suspension cables for the old bridge.

She yawned and stretched, the warming rays from the mid-morning sun that streamed through the trees only just cheering her up enough to chase the scowl from her firm-featured face. She looked down at her scuffed lace-up shoes and cursed when she saw that her socks were odd.

She'd got the early call from her DS on the Major Incident Team, the always annoyingly cheery Matt Gregory, just an hour ago, dragging her from her bed at her place just outside Edinburgh, hence the dressing in the dark which had led to the wardrobe malfunction.

'I think it's gonna be a bit of a shite one, boss. Already lots of back and forth over whose bread bin it's falling into, as it is precisely in the middle of the bloody bridge in the middle of naewhere. They've hauled him up, and he's known to us. Billy Mackee from Edinburgh. Drug man who's done a wee bit of time in the jail, hence Northumbria are already looking to chuck it over our side of the border. Metaphorically, like.'

'I take it no chance it's a suicide, Matt?' she'd said, already knowing the answer.

'Hard to say, but looking at the state of him, I doubt it. They only just managed to get him up and on tae the bridge. Needed the fire brigade to help, but he does'nae look too clever. Lucky, I live near enough, so I could get here nice and quick before the numpties from awa' the border made a clusterbourach o' it.'

As always, this ominous news was delivered in his chirpy, thick Glaswegian accent, almost as if he was calling out bingo numbers, which was annoying.

It always made Laura chuckle when she saw cops on TV shows arguing when a difficult homicide was snatched away from them by another agency. If an angry Tommy Lee Jones–type stormed up to her crime scene and said, 'FBI, we're taking over, lady,' Laura's response would have been, 'It's all yours, lads.' But this was real life, and it was probably coming her way, particularly as it looked like it was going to be a sticker. A hanging of a known Scottish drug dealer, right in the middle of the bridge. The English cops would almost certainly peg it as Scottish primacy, and that bampot, Detective Chief Superintendent Miles Wakefield at the Chief's office would certainly want the glory now that he was the Chief's bagman. He'd become more of a pain in the arse since he left his job as boss of the Major Incident Teams, if that was possible. Miles Wakefield would literally step over his dying granny if it meant him getting promoted again.

So, after the call, she'd dragged herself out of bed, had a quick shower, threw on some clothes, and picked up her bag and a scalding tea in a travel mug, accompanied by a slice of toast, handed to her by her husband as she dashed out of the door. And now here she was, slamming the car door shut and meandering towards a murder scene, bullying her long, dark hair into a ponytail with a scrunchy.

She sighed deeply. Another murder scene. This was the third she'd been to in just over a fortnight, on top of a complex trial looming, multiple meetings with the Crown Office, half the team away either at court, or on leave. She swore under her breath, her mood darkening, as she strode over towards the blue tape stretched between the concrete bollards at the entrance to the bridge, where a solitary cop, whom she vaguely recognised, was standing, one hand in his pocket, the other holding his phone which he was studying with interest.

A murder on the bloody bridge. Not quite England, not quite Scotland. Whichever bastard did this had a shite sense of humour. Not just two different police forces, but two whole different legal systems. She knew that the bureaucracy on this one would be a bloody nightmare, and she suddenly regretted her half-pissed agreement to take last night's on-call slot from bloody DI Mikey Hannah.

The cop on the cordon looked up, his eyes widening as he saw who was striding over. He hurriedly tucked his phone back in his pocket, not that Laura really cared.

'Morning, boss,' he said, pulling out his scene log booklet and scrawling in it.

'Aye, morning it is. Is DS Gregory here?'

'Middle of the bridge with the crime scene manager, and some numpty DI from Northumberland,' said the cop.

'Northumbria, I think you'll find, and I suspect that the inspector wouldn't appreciate being called a numpty,' she said, her voice a mix of reprimand and sarcasm.

'Aye, boss,' the cop said, with a touch of the naughty schoolboy, even if his eyes didn't reflect this.

'Right, I'd best join them.' She nodded at the cop, who pushed the cordon tape down with his boot for her to step over.

'They've all suited up, I've one here for you.' He nodded towards a clear bag leaned up against the bollard. Laura sighed, but didn't complain. She pulled out a Tyvek suit, gloves, mask and overshoes, and quickly donned them.

Laura didn't hurry the hundred metres to where the pop-up scene tent was positioned, stark-white against the green backdrop, a lone uniformed cop standing at the open flap.

She held up her warrant card to the bored cop, who just nodded without looking.

'Hello?' she called out, as she poked her head inside the tent.

There were three people inside, all suited up.

'Morning, boss,' came Matt's chirpy voice.

Even with the forensic kit on, she recognised the jade-green eyes of Lucy Kovac, the always cheerful crime scene manager, who seemed to have been at every single murder scene that Laura had been to over the past six months. She didn't recognise the man in the blue forensic overall.

'Morning, Matt, morning, Lucy.' She nodded at the man in the blue overall.

'Boss, this is Inspector Speight from Berwick Police Station, his guys were first on scene,' said Matt.

'Nice to meet you, so what do we have?' she said.

Inspector Speight pulled his face mask down and smiled. He had a clear and open face, and an easy smile, his accent was rich with the tones of northern England. 'Dog walker called it in at 7 a.m. Just hanging there. Got Trumpton down to help us haul him up, but he was well gone,' he said, using the police colloquialism for the fire brigade, after the 1970s kids' programme *Trumpton*.

'Doctor been?' said Laura.

'Nope. No one to send either side of the border, yet. Life pronounced extinct by a paramedic.'

'Pathologist?' said Laura, opening her log and beginning to scrawl.

Lucy spoke for the first time. Her accent was Scottish tinged with a touch of Polish. 'Not yet, although I've spoken to him. He's happy for me to do the necessary and get him in for a special PM. Just about to bag up his hands, but as you're here, you may as well have a look first.' She stepped back, allowing Laura a good look at the body for the first time. The body was laid on its side, hands behind the back, the head lolling, tongue swollen and protruding.

She took a sharp intake of breath. Billy Mackee had not died easily. His face was bloated and brick-red, the blue cord leaving a vivid, deep weal. His face was a mass of blood and contusions, and it was clear he'd had a fearsome beating before he was thrown over the bridge. His nose was misshapen, and blood and snot was congealed in his scraggy moustache. His eyes bulged, the whites a deep shade of scarlet.

'Jesus, he's been fucking battered,' she whispered, hoarsely.

'Aye, but that's not the worst of it. Look at his hands.' Lucy pointed to his back where his hands were out of sight. She moved around the body so she could see, and squatted down. His hands were secured with a set of zip-ties, and each of his fingers was swollen, misshapen and all at angles that would never have been seen in an anatomy book.

'Jesus. He's been tortured.'

'Aye, seems that way, but we should know more at the post-mortem,' said Lucy.

'I think we can all see what's happened, Luce. Jesus, poor bugger. Any CCTV, Matt?'

'Nope. Sod all. No witnesses, nothing. This place is a tourist attraction during the day, but once the sun goes down . . .' He left the sentence hanging.

'Are we sure this isn't a Northumbria job?' Laura looked up towards the inspector.

He shrugged. 'Above my paygrade, but I've spoken to our on-call superintendent, and SIO, and they seem to believe that, at this stage at least, primacy should rest with Police Scotland, as the victim is a known and active Scottish criminal. I'm led to believe that . . .' He paused as he consulted a notebook. 'Detective Chief Superintendent Wakefield has said that you'll take it for now, with our assistance, unless any evidence emerges suggesting that it should move over the border.'

'Mr Wakefield is on-call senior?' said Laura.

'Aye, boss. All week.'

Laura groaned. 'How's he been identified?'

'Driving licence in his pocket. William Mackee, aged thirty-three, from Edinburgh. Checked him out on PNC, a couple of minor convictions for disorder, including a bit of nonsense at a far-right rally, but intel database suggests he was a mid-tier dealer moving north. You know how the drugs market all went a bit mental after the Albanians got locked up. He was trying to take over the rural markets,' said Matt.

'Risky business. Any phone on him?'

'No, but it could be in the river.' Matt pointed at the fast-flowing Tweed.

'Or whoever killed him could have taken it.'

Matt just shrugged.

'I'd best call Mr Wakefield, then.' She stood, moved outside the tent and dialled.

'Superintendent Wakefield,' came the curt voice at the end of the line.

'Boss, it's Laura McKechnie,' she said.

'Ah Laura, what do we have? I've had some dialogue with our colleagues in Northumbria.'

Laura told him.

'Any leads?' said Wakefield.

'Early days, sir. I've only been here fifteen minutes, but my initial view is that it'll be challenging, no witnesses, no CCTV, no phone on the victim.'

'Well, best you crack on then. I'll want a briefing by midday, as the Chief Constable will want to field any questions from the press, particularly as it's cross-border.'

'Well, at the moment. It's just border, boss. Not cross-border. As in it's right in the middle of the bugger. Still nothing to say it's ours.'

'No need for flippancy, Laura. I've taken the decision, as the deceased is our problem as a criminal active in Scotland. If evidence shows that Northumbria need to play a bigger part I've already spoken to Superintendent Levy on their side, and he's ready to assist. We need to bring our A game, here. It's a reputational matter.' The phone beeped, and Laura just shook her head and cursed the fact that the pension changes meant she had ten years left.

'Matt?'

'Aye?'

'How many currently available on the team?'

'What, including us?'

'Of course including us.' Laura felt her irritation rising.

'Then two, although we have Peely-Wally-Sicky-Gordy back at the incident room. He's back off the sick.'

'What, Gordy's back on full duties?' said Laura. Gordy was the longest serving DC on the team, but he was something of an eccentric and a hypochondriac.

'Obviously not. Four-hour days, three days a week.'

'What's up with him this time?'

'Something to do with his arse.'

'Seriously, Matt,' Laura snapped.

'I am serious. Some bahoochie problem, and he's sensitive.'

'What, emotionally, or arse-wise?'

'Both, I imagine.'

Laura shook her head, her lip curling. 'Well, that'll make all the difference, lucky us. Any ideas on when the PM is?'

'Fiscal is on it. Hopefully later today.'

'Okay. Let's crack on then. If Fiscal is happy, we can get the body moved, and see where we are. Get Sicky-Gordy on the intel checks, let's find a vehicle, a phone, and some family for him, okay?'

'Aye, but he's already said he's no feelin' too clever, like?'

'I don't bloody care. Tell him to get on with it, or I'll tear him a new arsehole.' Laura felt her cheeks redden, and she inwardly cursed the new sickness rules. Whatever happened to cops being tough buggers?

'That'd give him three butt-holes, I've heard. But I'll tell him, anyway.'

Laura pulled down her hood, and scrubbed at her face, feeling the tension begin to bubble.

'Seriously, the job really is truly fucked,' she muttered to herself.

6

BARNEY ILLINGWORTH WHISTLED tunelessly as the kettle began to sing on the small gas hob in his campervan. He always did this. Matching his whistle with the kettle's whistle. It made him smile in the same way that he always winked at himself every time he passed a mirror.

He pulled his Leeds United mug out of the box on the floor, popped in a Yorkshire Gold teabag and poured the boiling hot water on the bag, watching as the leaves swirled in their cage, and the tea began to stain the water. He stirred the bag, pressing it to the side of the mug with the back of his spoon until the brew was dark and strong. Then a splash of milk, and boom. The perfect brew.

He slid the van door open and breathed in the clean air that wafted in from the Cairngorms, over Loch Morlich and into his mobile abode. He reached down to the floor and picked up his carbon fibre prosthetic, pulled up his pyjama leg and strapped the prosthesis onto the scarred and pink stump.

Barney had lost the limb many years ago during a covert operation in Iraq, and in keeping with pretty much every aspect of his life before and after, he'd never let it bother him too much. As his old dad had always said, ''Appen don't fret abaat things ye cannat change, lad. Things allus turn aat reyt.'

All that had happened over time was that the quality and functionality of the prosthesis had got better, alongside his ability to walk on it. His limp was now undetectable to the average watcher, and his career had continued firstly with MI5 as a technical surveillance expert, followed by his freelance work for a small, covert unit within Police Scotland. He had initially intended to stop working when he'd been forced to retire from MI5, but he'd soon found himself bored and skint after a lifetime of covert operations in the UK and beyond.

He also had to admit to himself, that because he'd been so wrapped up in his work, his marriage had failed, he'd lost his house and he needed the money. This was all possibly not helped by the fact that he was partial to a flutter on the horses. Or the dogs. Or the footy, or (to be brutally honest) anything that he could have a punt on. He didn't mind too much. He had his van, he had money to buy food, an occasional beer, and enough left over for a pouch of tobacco (or two) a week.

Pulling on his slippers, he stepped out onto the wet grass, breathing the scented air. He reached into his pocket and took out his scratched and worn leather tobacco pouch. With practised ease, he rolled a small, thin cigarette, and lit it with a flame from his battered old Zippo. With immense pleasure, he sucked in the smoke, held it in, and looked out over the glass-like surface of the loch, before letting it wisp out of his nostrils. He picked up his mug again and as he raised it to his lips, he felt his phone vibrate in his pocket. He pulled it out and frowned at the unfamiliar number.

"Ello?"

'Barney?' came the deep, resonant voice. It had a dim and distant edge of a Scottish burr but shot with the unmistakable tones of an expensive public school, followed by an equally expensive university.

'Fin?' said Barney. Finlay Smith was an old colleague from MI5. A case officer he'd worked with on a number of occasions over the years.

'The very same. Where are you?'

'What, now?'

'Yes, of course now.' Finlay was always blunt to the point of rudeness, but he was a reliable and trustworthy man, and a good case officer, who was noted for his abilities in recruiting and handling informants, or more accurately in the world of Security Service 'agents'.

'Loch Morlich, 'avin' a cuppa and a fag.'

'Are you still working with the police?' he barked.

'Aye. A fair bit, but it's been quiet as owt, recently.'

'Anti-corruption, I heard?' A statement, not really a question.

'Summat like that, although I didn't know it was common knowledge.'

'It isn't, but you won't be surprised I've heard some stories. Can we meet? Something I want to discuss, but not over the phone.'

'Business or pleasure?' said Barney, sucking on his roll-up.

'Business, obviously. I'm in Perth, meet in Pitlochry?'

'When?'

'An hour?' His voice was curt and businesslike, and Barney realised that he didn't need to ask if it was urgent.

'I'll be there. Whereabouts?'

'Meet me at the boating station. There's a small café there by Loch Faskally. I'll send you a pin drop.'

Barney looked at his watch. Almost nine. 'I'll be there in an hour and fifteen.'

The three beeps in Barney's ear told him that Finlay had gone. Barney shook his head, took the final drag from his roll-up and drained his tea. Typical of Finlay. He had always been a good agent, but Christ he was abrupt. The buzz from his phone told him that the pin drop had arrived.

'Bloody rude posh spooks,' he muttered to himself, as he turned back to his van. A quick wash, get dressed, and then onto whatever Finlay was looking for. He grinned. This was why he still did what he did, rather than retire and put his feet up.

The only certainty in his life was the uncertainty.

And that was just how he liked it.

7

FINLAY WAS ALREADY sitting on a bench at the edge of Loch Faskally as Barney pulled into the car park. This was unusual.

In fact, it was almost unheard of. Spooks always liked to get to a meet venue before the person they were meeting but they didn't announce their arrival. It was in their DNA to arrive first, then observe from a distance to make sure that the person they were meeting was alone and wasn't followed. It could lead to complex tradecraft dances, particularly if it was a spook meeting another spook, almost like two dominant dogs sounding each other out before deciding it was safe to engage.

Finlay didn't even turn as Barney approached, his boots crunching on the rough surface. He held out a paper cup in his slim hand. Barney took the cup and sniffed it as he sat down next to Finlay, wordlessly.

'Tea, right? Not coffee?' said Finlay.

'You remembered?' said Barney, before taking a sip.

'Coffee is only fit for Yanks or Italians you always said.' He didn't look towards Barney, just stared down, as he tossed another fragment of a sausage roll down towards the eager ducks, who tussled over the crumb.

'Still true today. Not Yorkshire tea, though, is it?' Barney pulled out his leather pouch and began to roll a cigarette. Finlay turned and watched, a wistful look on his slim, angular face.

'Still smoking that crap?' he said, sipping from his own paper cup.

'I only have a couple of vices, Fin.'

'Still keeping bookies in business, then?' he said, with still no trace of a smile. His brow was heavily lined and furrowed, and his eyes had a hunted quality to them that Barney had never seen before. He had worked extensively with Finlay in the past, but hadn't seen him for many years. He'd aged shockingly. His once dark chestnut hair was flecked with silver, and his face was lined and haggard. His eyes were red, and his chin bristled with a greying haze of stubble. He wore a grubby checked shirt and shapeless chinos, and Barney couldn't help but notice that his nails were bitten down to the quick. He looked broken.

'I don't mind a punt, pal. You look tired, Fin. Is everything okay?'

'Roll us one of those, will you?' he said, his eyes not moving from the roll-up in Barney's mouth.

'I didn't know you partook?' Barney unfurled a Rizla, and flaked some of the fragrant leaf into it, before expertly rolling. He held it out and Finlay accepted it, popping it between his thin, dry lips with a trembling hand. He leaned his head forward to accept the light from Barney's Zippo.

'I remember that lighter from years ago. Still going strong?' He exhaled the blue smoke, his features softening and relaxing a little as the nicotine took immediate effect.

'It's a Zippo, mate. Nowt *to* go wrong. Now what's this all about, Fin. You look like shit.'

A wry grin spread across his thin face. 'Life has had its ups and downs, old man.'

'Haven't we all. Now I'd like to say I'm a busy man, but I'm not really, but let's be fair, we're not what you'd call mates, so what's the deal?'

Finlay sighed, took another long pull on the cigarette and shut his eyes as he inhaled. He sat like that, head down for a full thirty seconds, before the smoke began to wisp out of his nostrils. His eyes snapped open, and he turned to Barney, his face hard and fixed. 'They killed him, Barney. He wasn't a good man, but he wasn't an evil man, and he was trying to do right. He was trying to atone, and the bastards killed him.' He paused and sucked on the cigarette again, eyes closed tight.

Barney put his hand on Fin's shoulder. 'Who, Fin?'

'Billy Mackee. He was one of mine. A woman from the Counter-Extremism Forum pushed him to the CT cops in Wakefield a while back, and they introduced him, and her to me, as we've been investigating an emerging white extremist group in the North-East of England called National Force. We'd intercepted some phone calls suggesting they were planning something big. I can't prove it, but I'm certain that they blew up that author in York.'

'That were a nasty one, that. Paper had it down to Islamic fundamentalists, didn't they?'

'Well, they claimed it, and the anti-terrorist police in London and most of MI5 are certain that it's down to Sharia 4 UK. Some chatter and intercepts from GCHQ have persuaded them.' Finlay cast his eyes upwards towards the dappled sky, and his expression was one of doubt.

'I'm sensing you don't buy that, mate?' Barney took a long pull on his roll-up, and looked at Finlay.

'I don't. It's a load of crap. The Defence Science and Technology Laboratory in Porton Down examined the remains of the device that killed Daniel Solomon – it was a sophisticated remotely activated unit – and jumped to a big conclusion that it bore all the hallmarks of ones deployed in Iraq by ISIS. In fact, they were certain enough to tie it to either Abu Al-Ahmed, a well-known bomb-maker in Iraq, or at least a student of his.'

'What was it, TATP?' said Barney, referring to triacetone triperoxide. The peroxide-based explosive was preferred by militants in Syria and Iraq and was created by mixing precise quantities of acetone, oxygenated water and sulphuric, hydrochloric or nitric acid – all easily available in high street stores.

Finlay nodded, tiredly. 'Yeah. With a mobile phone activation. There was nothing on CCTV in the car park, meaning that the device was probably attached well before, and activated for maximum effect once the poor sod left his big book event. Maximum publicity, and all that. Sharia 4 UK immediately claimed the attack as well. So, as CT branch often do, they applied the adage of "if it walks and quacks like a duck", and you know the rest, Barney.' Finlay lifted his cup to his lips, his hands trembling, and frowned when he found it to be empty. He sat it gently down on the bench, and shut his eyes.

'And you're not buying this?'

Finlay shook his head. 'The real chatter didn't really reflect this, and Billy Mac had heard rumours. I'm bloody convinced that it was someone working for, or on behalf of National Force, but I can't prove it, and neither the cops nor my bosses are interested. Billy was sure it was them, and we were working on a strategy to get evidence to prove it. I told him to be careful, but he was slack. It's my fault, Barney. I put him in a situation that he wasn't equipped to handle.'

'It happens,' said Barney, exhaling a plume of smoke.

'I tried to warn the poor bastard, but I was too late.' He turned to Barney, his face stained with fat tears. 'I tell you this, Barney, there's someone, either my firm or the cops, selling secrets. They sold him out to those evil bastards, and they tortured and killed him.'

8

DS MAX CRAIGIE was at the front of the cottage, lying down on a tartan rug staring down the grassy hill and across the farmland that stretched all the way down to the Firth of Forth, a couple of miles away. The sun was gentle and warm, the air full of the scent of a summer in the Kingdom of Fife. A mix of newly cut grass, with a hint of cow manure that drifted from the farmer's fields a hundred metres down from their small semi-detached cottage. His almost one-year-old daughter, Evie, was leaning against him, her chubby little legs extended in front of her as she played with her favourite toy, Postman Pat's van, with the long-nosed character inside. Nutmeg, Max's little golden cockapoo, was stretched out on the rug at Evie's feet. 'Babat,' she said, holding the toy towards Max, 'Babat' being as close as she could get to 'Postman Pat'.

Max then picked up a multicoloured wooden brick, held it in front of Evie's face and tapped it softly against her small button nose. She giggled, her curly blonde hair twitching, as she threw Pat's van onto the rug. She reached her chubby little hand out, grabbed the brick from Max's hand and held it in front of Nutmeg's nose. 'Oof, oof,' she said, in her approximation of Nutmeg's woof. The little dog's tail twitched, and she tentatively opened her mouth to accept the brick from little Evie Craigie, who had very quickly replaced Max and his wife, Katie, as her favourite. Nutmeg had decided that her main job in the house, apart from running with Max, was to look after little Evie. It was a task she took very seriously.

'Nutmeg, no,' said Max gently, easing the brick from his daughter's hand. Nutmeg's ears pricked up, and she looked at Max, disapproval in her hazel eyes.

'No dog slobber, Nutty. You want some lunch, Evie?' said Max, scooping the little blonde girl up in his arms, and planting a kiss on her soft pink cheek. Nutmeg's silky ears cocked up and she let out a little yip, as she sprinted out of sight around the side of the house, clearly off to investigate something she'd heard or smelled.

Evie giggled as Max stood up with her, tossing her in the air with a 'whee!'

'Ga,' said Evie, her sound for 'more'.

Max repeated the action, which resulted in gales of giggles.

'Craigie, if you drop our daughter, you're sleeping in the shed, okay?' Katie appeared at the double doors with a brightly coloured small plastic plate containing some cut-up sandwiches.

'Be the first good night's sleep for ages, babe. Bring it on.'

'Okay, I'll rephrase. Drop our daughter, and I'm sleeping in the shed. Your gym mats will probably be quite comfy, and it's warm enough. You can get up to Evie while me and Nutty get some proper shut-eye. Lunchtime, Evie.' Katie sat on the rug, and patted the space next to her. Max sat Evie down, and she immediately grabbed a square of sandwich and shoved it in her mouth, her cheeks bulging, as she chewed.

'You reckon Nutty would let Evie out of her sight?' said Max, picking up a square of the sandwich and popping it in his mouth. His face registered distaste. 'Jings, what's in these?' he said.

'Tuna,' said Katie.

'It tastes like fish paste. Do they still do that old pish?'

'No idea, but Evie loves tuna, and it's full of omega-3. And no swearing in front of her, Max. Her first words could be a curse if we're not careful.'

'Tastes like it's full of some old shite Nutmeg rolled in on the beach last week.'

'Serves you right for robbing her sandwich, and I thought I said no swearing?'

'Okay, fine. I'm not Ross Fraser, though, am I?' he said, grimacing as he swallowed the fishy sandwich.

'You'd be in bother if you were. Her first word would begin with an "F" if he was around more than he is. I had no idea what an absolute softie he was about babies, and he's insisting on being called "Uncle Ross". Doesn't go with his red-faced anger act, at all.'

'I think he said "Uncle Fucking Ross",' said Max, grinning, just as his phone started buzzing on the rug.

'I'm gonna chin you, Craigie,' said Katie, returning his smile.

'Speak of the devil, I'm pretty confident Uncle Ross is about to lambast me about something.' Max picked up the handset and pressed the answer key. 'Uncle Ross, how are you?'

'Fucking lonely in the office and wondering where my bastard half-arsed, workshy team is. I bet you're sunning yourself in this very un-Scottish weather, eh?'

'Aye, sitting in the garden with Evie, giving her a terrible fish paste sandwich that her mum insisted is good for her,' said Max, popping a small piece of sandwich into Evie's mouth. She chewed, cheeks bulging.

'Tuna, not paste,' said Katie, shaking her head.

'And she'd be right, pal. Nothing wrong with a bit of paste. My old ma always used to give me bloater paste sandwiches. You millennials are bloody soft, that's the problem. Anyway, enough pleasantries, where the shagging bollocks are you?' His voice went from that of the soft-hearted uncle to the angry, sarcastic boss in a heartbeat.

'I told you. In the garden.'

'You know what I bloody mean. Why aren't you here, ready to accede to my every whim, eh?'

'Can I remind you that you said, just twelve hours ago,

"Work from home tomorrow, Max. Spend some time with my goddaughter." Not that we've had, or are planning to have, Evie christened so the title isn't justified.'

'I know, you couple of bloody heathens. I just made the assumption that were you to have that lovely wee toot christened, I'd be first in line.'

'You would, Ross. You definitely would.'

'Bollocks. Right, enough sucking up to me. Police Scotland's elderly answer to Q has some very disturbing news from one of his spook contacts, and we need to chat it through, but he won't talk about it on the phone. I almost told him to get tae fuck, but then it occurred to me that the most unflappable and tightest human known to man being concerned enough about something to use his own petrol money was probably in itself a cause for concern. Get your arse weaving, and get in here now. Janie is on her way, and Norma is already moaning that there are no cakes in the office.'

'On my way.'

The phone bleeped in his ear. Max dropped it on the rug, a grin across his face.

'I'm assuming that was Uncle Ross wanting you to respond in an indecently fast time?' said Katie, bending down and picking up Evie, who giggled.

'Aye. Barney has had a call about something. Best get in, I guess. Do we have any cakes?'

'I think there's a pack of Tunnock's in the cupboard. Is this going to be a long hours situation?'

'Who knows, babe?' Max stood up, and stretched, just as Nutmeg tore around the corner, with Amber, the neighbour's new puppy in hot pursuit. Amber was another cockapoo who looked like a smaller version of Nutmeg. They whizzed by, both barking furiously, and disappeared as quickly as they had arrived.

'God, Nutmeg just loves that puppy,' said Katie, laughing at the look on Evie's face as she stared, open mouthed, at the departing blonde dogs.

Max chuckled. 'I'd best head off.' He kissed Katie, and then Evie in turn.

Within ten minutes, Max had grabbed his bag, ready as it always was for the urgent, and usually foul-mouthed, call from his boss, Detective Inspector Ross Fraser.

9

MAX PARKED HIS car at Tulliallan Castle, the headquarters of Police Scotland, and got out, slinging his bag over his shoulder and picking up the box of teacakes from the passenger seat. He was locking the door when he heard footsteps crunching on the gravel.

'You took your time. Ross will be giving you pelters when we get in.' Janie's voice was laden with amusement, as Max turned to see her at the boot of her Volvo, pulling out a large, clear bag full of documents. Janie wore a wide grin, and her normally short chestnut hair was a little shorter and streaked with blonde highlights.

'Not in a good mood?' said Max, slamming the door.

'Ach, he's okay, but I think Barney's call has dragged him away from his rose garden, and he's scunnered about it. He's on his way, apparently. Barney, I mean. Do you know anything about the job?'

'He didn't say anything, and cut me off before I got a chance to ask. Nice hair by the way, was that your achievement for yesterday?'

'Aye, it took bloody ages sitting there, looking like metal micky with foils in my hair. I'm not used to shite like that, reminds me why I like uncomplicated haircuts. That, and the fact that it cost me eighty quid.'

'It suits you. You look like a member of a 1980s boy band.'

Janie stopped and stared at Max. 'Sounds a bit homophobic to me, sergeant.' Janie's potentially concerning comment was only partially tempered by the puckish smile on her face.

'W-what?' said Max, unsure what else to say.

'Well, just because I'm currently in a relationship with a woman, you're using the boy's haircut on a girl stereotype. Microaggression, or what?' Janie's voice was without inflection.

Max opened his mouth to answer, but then paused. 'Oh, shut up,' he said, his smile widening.

'Had you for a moment, didn't I?' She giggled, throwing the bag over her shoulder.

'Not even a bit. How is Melissa?' said Max, feeling a touch of relief in the unconscious unclenching of his stomach muscles.

'Bonny and ditsy as ever. Come on, we best get in. He's already had a go at me because I didn't bring all the stupid unused material in from the last job. They've managed to get Baz off the MIT team to volunteer to schedule it all.' Janie's grin widened.

'That's a lot of unused material, is Baz off his nut?' said Max, nodding at the bag.

'It was a big job, but Bazza is a disclosure nerd. Up for trial soon, but the whisper is we're getting a plea offer imminently.'

'That'll be a result. Where's Barney been?'

'He was up in the Cairngorms in his van, but got a worrying call from an old spook pal. He didn't want to talk about it on the phone, apparently. Being cagey.'

'Well, as Barney isn't prone to hyperbole, we should probably listen.'

'I think "prone to hyperbole" is something of an understatement. I doubt his pulse would go over sixty bpm even if he was putting a tracker on Vladimir Putin's limo, under the nose of the FSB.'

'That'd be before lunchtime, before moving onto whistling as he bugged Kim Jong-il's car, deep undercover in Pyongyang.'

'Un.'

'What?' said Max, eyeing his friend balefully.

'Kim Jong Un is the current supreme leader, although Barney is probably old enough to have worked against his dad.'

Max shook his head and sighed, and then grinned. 'You're such a pernickety geek. Come on, let's get in there, and get the swearing over with.'

*

Max pushed open the chipped and scuffed painted door that bore the dog-eared, laminated A4 sign declaring the small office to be the home of Policing Standards Reassurance. The door creaked alarmingly to reveal the depressing interior. The windows were small and dusty but wide open, one of the lighting tubes flickered. And then the smell hit them. A faint, yet pervasive odour of sewage, deep, noxious and cloying.

'Jesus, what the hell is that stink?' said Janie, wrinkling her nose, as she pushed the nearest window open to its maximum.

Ross had a phone clamped to his ear, and his face was brick-red as he muttered into the handset.

Norma had a handkerchief held under her nose, but her eyes sparkled with amusement. 'Morning, team, I like your hair, Janie. Do I spy teacakes?' she said, eyeing the box under Max's arm.

'Indeed, you do.' Max laid them down on her desk.

'So, what is the stink all about?' said Janie.

'Something unpleasant with the soil-pipe upstairs, I'm told. Ross is getting very angry with building services, as usual,' she said, unboxing the Tunnock's and beginning to peel the foil off.

'How can you eat? It's bogging. I hope they can sort it out pronto, or I'm gonna boak,' said Janie.

The phone slammed down on the desk, and Ross scrubbed his face with his large, calloused hands. 'I know, it fucking reeks. I'm on the case.'

'You sounded almost calm and empathetic, boss,' said Max.

'Aye, Mrs Fraser has been impressing on me the need to not lose my shit with people who push me, and I almost managed it with that weapon of a building services manager.'

'You called him a "useless, incompetent roaster", Ross,' said Norma.

Ross's eyes narrowed. 'I thought I was being subtle, like.'

'Subtle. You?' said Norma, her eyes wide behind her statement spectacles.

'Well, I had my voice lowered, and I didn't know you could hear me, so that's a start. Anyway, stop fucking eavesdropping on important managerial phone calls. I've sorted it, the bog-squad are on their way, and it's all down to bloody you lot blocking toilets again with your big jobbies in the ladies khazi. Now I cannae work in these putrid conditions, it stinks like the Portaloos at a Grateful Dead outdoor gig in 1980.'

'I didn't know you were a Deadhead, Ross. I bloody love them, what's your favourite period of their work?' said Janie, her eyes brightening with the enthusiasm of a dedicated music fanatic.

'I'm not, it's a load of dull hippy shite.'

'Nonsense, their early work was seminal, and particularly the early albums beginning with *Anthem of the Su*—'

Ross shot Janie a glare, his eyes narrow and flashing. 'Dinnae give a toss about your weird music bollocks. Come on, Barney's got the kettle on, and bring those Tunnock's.'

'What about me?' said Norma.

'Aye, you too. Let's reconvene in old Father Time's campervan in the car park, where he's setting up a Wi-Fi link. A bit of al fresco crime busting is just what we need on a lovely day like this, and Janie?' Ross looked across.

'Aye?'

'Your hair looks bloody weird. You look like that mannie from Wham in the 1980s before he went bald.'

*

Barney had set up a trestle table on the grass outside his VW California camper van, just in front of where he'd parked at the immediate front of the Police HQ. A long wire snaked from the side of the van and into an ajar window. The kettle was singing, as they all sat on folding camping chairs, and Barney poured boiling water into a battered old aluminium teapot and filled five mugs.

'Well, this is nice,' said Norma, as she unwrapped another teacake and dipped it into her tea. Norma was the team's analyst whom Ross had poached from the National Crime Agency. She was capable of unpicking the most complex piles of raw intelligence and condensing them into charts and summaries better than anyone Max had ever worked with. She also had an insatiable desire for cakes and biscuits.

'I note that, as fucking usual, you're choring leccy from the Chief Constable,' said Ross, with a half-smile and pointing at the orange hook-up cable that snaked into the building.

'Borrowin', I think you'll find.'

'Aye, right.'

'You want the tea that the kettle has provided?'

'Isn't it a gas hob?'

'It needs leccy to spark the gas.'

Ross just shook his head. 'Why have you dragged us all in?' said Ross, without sarcasm or anger, probably because he was about to take a big bite of his own teacake.

Barney told them. He told them everything that Finlay had told him. When he'd finished, there was a brief silence before Max spoke.

'I heard about this. A body found hanging from the bridge. It made the BBC News. South MIT have picked it up, I hear.'

'I heard as well, but does it feel likely that a load of far-right football casuals have moved from smashing up shops to bombings, to hanging MI5 agents from a bastard bridge?' Ross said, his eyes narrowed.

'Well, National Force had apparently been written off as a bunch of hooligans who were behind a few protests at hotels where asylum seekers were housed, certainly before Dent got remanded for a year on the murder case he's just beaten.'

'A year? How did they get over custody time limits?' said Janie.

'At defence requests, strangely they asked for extra trial prep time, but a cynical man would assume that Dent was giving himself enough time for the main witness to not show up.'

'Missing?' said Max.

Barney shrugged.

'So let me get this straight. Your man, Fin. You trust him, right?' said Ross.

'He's a bit of a funny bugger, but he's dead honest, and he had a real knack with agents. According to him, he'd been running Billy Mackee, the dead man, for a couple of months. He was a decent level drug dealer, who had moved into the space probably created by us after we busted the Albanians and Hardies before him.'

Max shrugged. 'That's the problem with the war against drugs. Bust a network, create a vacuum to be filled by a possibly worse network.'

Barney just raised his eyebrows. 'Anyway, he was apparently supplying all the old fishing villages on the north-east coast, and had a big piece of Inverness, but then he started working with a crew from the North-East of England. Two blokes called Stringer and Shorty, one of who's just got out of jail, and that's when things changed. Stringer and Shorty run a firm that are starting to take over a lot of the markets in the north of England, and wanted to move into Scotland. Billy Mac was gonna be their route in.'

'So, what made him want to clipe on Shorty and Stringer?' said Ross, licking a shard of chocolate from his lips.

'Billy was a drug dealer, but he apparently wasn't a bad bloke. Not violent, was good at building bridges, and he discovered the real problem with Stringer and his crew.'

'And?' said Norma, licking her lips and eyeing the remaining teacake.

'They are horrible, evil racist thugs. They're part of an emerging far-right group called National Force. They initially thought that they were just like English Defence League or National Action. Then it went a bit odd, as they stopped any of the more typical yobbery a year ago or so, and then they went very quiet, possibly because Stringer was on remand. Billy told Fin that he reckoned they're linked to the bomb in York almost a year ago, and the rumour is, they're planning summat else bigger. Like proper big.' Barney slurped at his tea, and raised his eyebrows.

'I remember the car bomb. Killed that lovely author, didn't it? I read his book afterwards, and it was really thought provoking. I thought it was linked to Islamic terrorism,' said Norma.

Barney nodded. 'Aye, they scrambled a big old team to run it, led by a superintendent from national Counter Terror. Apparently the IED bears a very strong resemblance to those used by ISIS in Syria and Iraq, and the folks at Porton Down are rarely wrong,' said Barney.

'I had some input on this when I was in the Met at the time of 7/7 and 21/7. Bombs are almost like fingerprints. Each bomb-maker has a unique style, so I can see why the CT team would dig their heels in. Or are we suggesting that National Force employed an Islamist bomb-maker?' said Max.

'Fucking typical. "When I was in the fucking Met, guvnor, strike a light, my old man's a fucking dustman,"' Ross said, in an appalling cockney accent.

'Well, that's hardly likely, is it? Far-right terrorists using Islamists to make their bombs?' said Janie, shaking her head at Ross's typical bumptiousness.

'Aye, well, that together with the fact as usual every bugger, including Sharia 4 UK, tried to claim it, as they often do, but Fin's man was convinced that it's connected to these two bastards. Hard to prove, I guess, particularly as one of them was in jail when the bomb went off.' Barney took a swig of his tea.

'Okay, but why us? Why not farm it out to the cops over the border?' said Janie.

'Here's the thing. Billy didn't go straight to the cops. Have you heard of CEF?' said Barney.

'Counter-Extremism Forum, right?' said Janie.

'That's the one. They're an online blogsite that tracks racist activity, a bit like Hope Not Hate. Well, that was Billy's first stop. He met with one of the investigative journos there, a woman called Juliet McNamara, and after a load of toing and froing, she put him onto Police Counter Terror North-East team in Wakefield who in turn handed him over to Fin. Seems it were going okay, but—' Barney left the sentence hanging.

'Does this sound to everyone like no one was taking Billy seriously, or Fin for that matter?' said Norma.

'It does a bit, but then I think the link to the bomb emerged a little later. Who knows? Let's not forget just how bloody incompetent some police are. MI5 are worse,' Barney said, shrugging.

'But then Billy wound up hanging from a bridge over the Tweed, having first had the shite battered out of him, which adds to the mix,' said Max, shaking his head, sadly.

'Tortured, and hung, to be more accurate.'

'It's hanged, not hung,' corrected Janie.

Everyone turned to look at her, her face frozen and reddening, as if she suddenly realised what she'd said. 'Sorry, it's my weird thing, isn't it?'

'Really, Janie. Now's not the time for pedantry,' said Max.

'Aye, lass. Nae time for pedantry, whatever that actually means. Anyway, one question remains, Barney,' said Ross, turning to the ex-MI5 man.

Barney just raised his eyebrows.

'Why us? Or why you, anyway?'

'Looks like there's a bent bugger, either in the cops, or in MI5. Fin doesn't know who to trust. Whoever they are, they sold out Billy Mac, and he wound up tortured, and dead. Christ knows what he told them.'

'But Fin trusts you?' said Ross.

Barney shrugged. There was a long, pervasive silence that enveloped the space, the only noise being the soft wind wafting through the trees.

'I need to ask the unavoidable, Barney. Do you trust Fin?' asked Max.

'He's a funny bugger, and he hasn't always been popular with the bosses. He's not averse to jumping in with his big clod-hoppers, which doesn't do well with the management at my old firm.'

'So, that's a no?' said Ross.

'I didn't say that. I'd say he's an honest fella, if a bit odd. I have to say, that for some reason he was one of the best agent handlers I met during all my years with 5.'

'So, is that a yes?' said Ross.

Barney just nodded, and sipped his tea.

'Right, get going on this, team. I want a strategy, pronto. It could be that in light of what the old goat has told us, the anti-terror cops may want to re-evaluate their conclusion on National Force and the York bomb, and we have a bent copper to find,' said Ross, his brow heavy.

10

JULIET MCNAMARA WAS sipping a coffee in a small café on Exchange Street in Jedburgh, as she absent-mindedly switched between her WhatsApp screen and her news feed. They didn't have an office. Clem always felt having a fixed locus just made them vulnerable. An address was just a target for the type of people that they were trying to disrupt, dissuade and, if necessary, dismantle. (By legal means, of course.)

She looked at the time. He was late. Bloody late again. Clem, her colleague on the Counter-Extremism Forum, was always late, always digging, and always looking for the next big job. He was never satisfied, never happy, but he was utterly committed to their objectives of exposing, and tackling extremism.

She dialled Clem once more, and was almost surprised when he answered. 'Jules, sorry, I totally forgot the bloody time, and I'm stuck in crap traffic, with a dying phone battery, sorry.'

'You're bloody useless, man. Where are you?' she said.

'Kelso.'

'Kelso? God, you're gonna be ages, and I really want to get home,' she said, feeling her cheeks flush.

'Aye, I know, sorry. Can we do it tomorrow? We really need a catch-up. Are you supposed to be meeting your contact?'

'Yes, and he's sodding late. I wanted you to meet him.'

'Look, I'm sorry, but I'm not gonna make it, Sally is coming home from school early unwell, so I'm going to have to mind her at her mum's. You do the meeting, and we'll catch up tomorrow, okay?' he said.

She felt the heat rising from her. 'Fine,' she said, and hung up, exhaling hard.

She took another sip of her cooling, bitter coffee, and sighed, feeling desperate for a cigarette but resisting the urge. Six weeks since her last, and she had no intention of yielding, but the constantly unreliable Clem made her anxious, and anxiety made her want a fag. She ran her hand through her short, choppy hair, her hand not quite trembling, but not quite still, either. She dialled the number for Billy. Nothing. Not even a ring tone. Just dead. 'Shit,' she muttered. Where the hell was he?

'Want a top-up, love?' said the smiling barista.

She just shook her head and began to idly fiddle with her phone. Juliet navigated to the BBC News app, and a headline made her skin begin to tingle and face flush.

A photo of the Union Chain Bridge, with a headline in bold letters.

Identity of Bridge Hanging Victim Released

Police confirm they are treating the death as a murder and are appealing for witnesses.

Juliet gasped as she looked down at the small photo on the screen, the breath almost knocked out of her.

It was Billy Mackee.

The Billy Mackee that she had been with just a few weeks ago, whom she was waiting to meet, right now.

The Billy Mackee whom she had introduced to the cops on the anti-terror team, and to the slightly mysterious Finlay in a grimy greasy spoon in Melrose.

The same Billy she'd assured would be safe and could trust her.

She felt the blood drain from her face, and her lips went numb.

She dialled Clem again, but it went straight to voicemail. 'Clem, call me back, urgent,' she said, her voice crackling.

Juliet's brain felt like a cog had been removed, and she felt suddenly dizzy and sick at the same time. They'd killed Billy, because of her.

Then it hit her. These bastards were evil. Would they have tortured him? Had he told them about her? She began to shake. She had to get out of here, she had to get away.

Grabbing her bag, she shot to her feet and made for the exit, feeling her heart beating in her chest and sweat breaking out along her spine, as she emerged into the sunshine. She looked left and right, but saw nothing other than a few pedestrians on the street, mostly with their heads bowed looking at their phones. Exhaling with relief, she crossed the road and began the short walk to Canongate Car Park, just a couple of minutes away.

She walked at a pace just below a run along Exchange Street towards the High Street, her eyes roving as she broke out into a jog. She halted as she reached the junction, the heavy traffic causing her to halt. Feeling a prickling between her shoulder blades, she turned her head as far as she could, looking behind her. Her heart leapt as she saw him. She didn't recognise him, but she still saw him, closing in on her, just twenty or thirty metres behind.

A small, wiry man, dressed casually, striding purposefully towards her, the sun reflecting off his shaved scalp and mirrored shades. Panic consumed her as she saw the hard look on his angular face. He was focused, and he was looking straight at her. He was coming for her, she knew it.

Without another thought she stepped into the road, her desire to be far away in the safety of her car overwhelming her road sense.

Tyres screeched as a car skidded, but she didn't stop to look. She broke into a run, crossed the High Street and into Market Place, the breath escaping her in rasps, desperation overcoming the pain in her legs as she sprinted up the narrow street towards the car park.

She slowed, and looked over her shoulder again. 'No, no, no,' she gasped, as she saw him there, thirty metres behind her, his pace not increased, just determined and steady, his head down, and arms swinging in time with his steps, the sun dancing on his mirrored sunglasses.

She sped up, tears spilling down her cheeks, her chest heaving as she turned into the car park. She sprinted along to where her car was parked at the far end of the space in the shade of the trees. She was scrabbling for her keys in her bag as she reached her ancient Ford Fiesta, blipping the car locks open. She turned and looked behind her again, heart pounding in her chest. She stood, her hand resting on top of the car.

He was gone. The car park was totally empty. She exhaled, relief flooding through her body.

'Bastards,' she sighed, almost sick with relief as she scanned the car park for her follower. Nothing. Just an empty space with a few cars dotted about. She exhaled, and her hand found the door handle.

She needed to speak to Finlay, urgently. She pulled out her phone, and dialled, listening to the ring tone in her ear. 'Come on, Fin,' she said, her breathing rapid and shallow.

There was a sudden scrape behind her, and a shadow flickered as a face appeared reflected in the car's window. Her heart froze just at the point that the world turned black owing to the massive, unimaginably devastating impact that smashed into the back of her skull. She fell to the scrappy tarmac, like a puppet whose strings had just been cut. Her vision was fading, the blackness creeping in. Her follower was there, sneering, as he raised the small wooden bat, the type she used to use when playing rounders at school. She opened her mouth to scream, but nothing came. When the bat landed again, there was nothing.

11

'I DON'T LIKE this, Ross. I don't like it one little bit. The CT briefings I read were clear that the main line of enquiry was Islamic terror in the guise of Sharia 4 UK?'

Ross nodded. 'That's the received wisdom, boss, but Barney's contact at MI5 is adamant that the murdered Billy Mackee was one of his, and he was certain that it was National Force.'

'Wasn't the forensics on the device clear that it was Islamic?'

'Apparently so, but then . . .' Ross left the sentence hanging.

Macdonald exhaled, his eyes worried. 'I've been briefed on the Billy Mackee murder – is it right he was tortured prior to his death?'

'Seems so.'

'This is really serious. We're talking about a group that killed two in a racist terrorist bomb almost a year ago, that the National Counter Terror teams seem to be struggling with. A murder that's currently unsolved. Do we think that this guy Fin Smith is genuine?' Chief Constable Chris Macdonald eyed Ross across his battlefield-sized desk.

'Barney swears he is, and much as it pains me to say it, the old buffer isn't one to exaggerate or to engage in speculation. Much as he annoys me, when he says something is important, we all tend to listen.'

'I'm minded to agree. He's been a real asset for us, despite his unconventional lifestyle. Is he still living in his campervan?'

Ross grinned. 'Aye, well, since you kicked him out of your

grace and favour flat.' Barney had spent some time in the Chief Constable's unused police-provided flat, but had been forced to vacate when the auditors asked what exactly a freelance contractor was doing living rent-free in a valuable piece of Edinburgh real estate.

'Is he over that?'

'Like everything, boss. He didn't really give a shit. He just shrugged, and hooked up his van to the police power supply, and put the kettle on.'

Macdonald snorted in amusement. 'I'll sneak him back in there when winter hits. So, we are taking what Smith says as genuine?'

'I'd say we have to. Fin Smith is apparently an expert agent handler of many years standing. Some of it doesn't makes sense, though.'

'How so?'

'Dent and his crappy bunch of Newcastle football casuals with a habit of shouting at immigrants in hotels moving to blowing up a leading journalist and an unfortunate passer-by, and then torturing and killing an MI5 asset in their organisation. I think we'd call that an unexpected acceleration of offending, boss.' Ross's face was grave.

'That's an understatement and a half.'

'Who's picked up Billy Mackee's murder?'

Macdonald sighed. 'Laura McKechnie has taken the case, but it looks like it's going to be a tough one. Do you want to link in with her?'

'I think that we need to firm up what Barney's pal has to say, first, or, you know—'

Macdonald sadly shook his head. 'I hate to say it, but I'm minded to agree.'

'I take it you're not going to approach anyone from MI5 or the police Counter Terror team just yet?'

'What, you think I shouldn't?'

'Not until we know what we're dealing with. It's possible someone is leaking info, that's for sure. Maybe Barney could give us a steer about who to talk to at MI5. He worked with them long enough, and he's a good judge of character.'

'Last time I was with you all, you called him a useless fud.'

'Just joshing. He's a solid man, but I don't think it's wise to approach until we have a clearer picture.'

Macdonald nodded, gravely. 'So, a more detailed debrief of Fin Smith, and then we can take something solid to the MIT. Do we think he'll cooperate with us? I know what spooks can be like.'

'I can't see why not. He came to Barney because he knew he was working counter corruption. I'll get it set up, get Max and Janie on him, and see where we are. Norma has already begun to work her magic. It doesn't look great, Billy Mackee getting strung up on the same bloody day that Dent is let out of the jail.'

Macdonald nodded again, and paused, his eyes pensive and thoughtful. 'I want this sorted, Ross. An agent at the heart of an embryonic, but wildly accelerating terror movement being tortured and murdered in the most brutal and emblematic manner isn't the endgame.'

Ross shook his head, his eyes mirthless. 'No way. It's just the beginning.'

12

MAX, JANIE AND Barney were all crowded around Norma's monitors as Ross burst into the office.

'Jesus, smells like a hoer's handbag in here, what the fuck have you been spraying?'

'Better than the smell of shite, though? Building services have fixed the leak, and Barney had a nice can of air-freshener in his van,' said Norma, peering out from behind her monitors.

'So why does he always smell of Old Holborn, then?'

'I don't use it much. I pinched it from the Chief's flat, as it sometimes gets a bit musty in't van.'

Ross scowled. 'Not surprised it's foosty with you living in it. Anyway, enough fucking levity. We have a working office again, thanks to my diplomacy, but you lot need to piss off. Chief wants you to go and meet your spook pal, Barney, for a full debrief. Is he up for it?'

Barney nodded. 'Said he would.'

'Also, do you have names of any managers you'd trust at MI5? It's going to be hard to not include them if this develops.'

'I have a couple I trust, but maybe let's see what Fin has to say first.'

'Where's he staying?'

'Stirling. Big place on the outskirts, being a posh Scot, who sounds like he's English, he has a family pile. Want me to set it up?'

Ross nodded. 'Always the same with posh Scots. They go to

English schools and have surnames for first names, like Finlay or Crawford. As soon as possible, eh?'

'On it.' Barney reached for his phone.

'Any updates from the world of intel, Norma?' Ross rubbed his face with a meaty palm and looked at the analyst.

'On it like a car bonnet. I've been chatting with a pal who's an analyst on the MIT and they're struggling big time. No immediate evidence to link to Dent. The victim's phone is missing, and there's no live number known for him. I'm just working everything up on Dent and Jimmy 'Shorty' Shore. Both linked to serious drug dealing in northern England, and they've been moving into Scotland, which is where they have had dealings with Billy Mac. Strong, but not admissible intel that they are eyeing up the fragmented Scottish market.'

'Fragmented?' said Janie.

'Aye. Just that. Let's be fair, we've taken out loads of networks in the last couple of years, so it's never had a chance to get nailed down to one OCN, since the fall of the Hardies. It seems Dent and co want that market, as well as northern England. Seems the Scousers think it's too much bother, and there's only a few small firms from Birmingham making some inroads.' Norma paused to sip her tea.

'How about Billy's market?' said Max.

'He was making modest progress in Perth, Dundee, and up the coast, which it seems is why he was linking up with Stringer's firm. Look where that got him, eh?' she said, shaking her head, sadly.

'Anything else notable about Stringer? Family, friends, accomplices?'

'Stringer's brother, Charlie Dent, seems to be something of a black sheep,' said Norma.

'More of a black sheep than a large-scale drug-dealing and murderous racist?' said Janie.

'Well, kind of. Serial recidivist thief. Always in and out of the jail, apparently has a bigger habit than Mother Teresa's frock. Heroin and crack, and he's never lasted more than a couple of days of rehab, even with Stringer footing the bill.'

Max stroked his chin as if digesting this new piece of information.

'Right, we're on. Early tomorrow morning. He wants to meet at the Star Pyramid in the Old Town Cemetery,' said Barney, simultaneously rolling a cigarette.

'How early?' said Max.

'Early enough that I'm driving up tonight and kippin' in me van. Might 'ave a cheeky pint in the Golden Lion first.'

'Typical bloody spook. Why can't he just meet in the bloody pub, or a café at a normal time? It's not a bloody John le Carrier-bag spy novel, you know.' Ross sat down with a grunt in his chair, causing a minor eruption of dust particles from the tatty fabric that caught a shaft of sunlight that had managed to pierce the grimy windows.

'It's an impressive edifice, that. Laid in recognition of all those who suffered martyrdom in quest for liberty in Scotland. Did you know they used to hold jousting tournaments there?' said Janie, her face lighting up.

'No, Janie, because we're not all insufferable swotty nerds. We were all having fun chasing girls, smoking behind the bike sheds or necking bottles of Buckfast in the school tennis courts. You are so bloody geeky, it's no wonder you were on the high potential development shite,' Ross said, trying to suppress a smile.

'Chance would be a fine thing. I'm on a final warning about getting my thesis on qualitative evaluation in to my assessor. You keep me so busy I've not had time to start it, let alone complete it.'

'I don't even know what that bloody means. Isn't "qualitative evaluation"' – Ross mimed the quotation marks – 'something the government does when they print money, or some such bollocks as that?'

Janie shook her head, a smile creeping into the corners of her mouth. 'No, Ross. That's quantitative easing.'

'Aye well, whatever, it sounds shite. Now piss off, you've an early start in the morning, and Craigie needs to tuck my goddaughter in before her bed.'

'Not your goddaughter, Ross. She's not anyone's goddaughter. She's not getting christened,' said Max, shaking his head, and grinning towards Janie.

'Bloody heathen. Now sod off. I expect a forensically detailed debrief of this bloody toffee-nosed spook first thing.'

13

FINLAY SMITH FROWNED and stared at the phone in his hand. His finger hovered over the call button, but then he withdrew it, and dropped it to his waist. Why had Juliet tried to call him? He felt the hairs on his neck stand up. This wasn't right. He decided that he had no choice, he'd have to call her back. He didn't like to just call like this: as a lifelong intelligence agent it went against all the tradecraft lessons he'd learned over many years.

'Sorry, the person you're calling is not available. Please try later.'

He sat down on the bench that overlooked the lake at the front of the large, rambling house on the outskirts of Stirling. A knot of ducks paddled in the water, suddenly silhouetted against the dipping sun that danced against the glassy surface of the small body of water. He sighed, his instinct rarely let him down, and he'd been in the intelligence game for a long, long time. Something was most certainly wrong. First Billy brutally murdered, then a call out of the blue from Juliet, and *she* now wasn't picking up.

The number wasn't even listed in his phone as Juliet, rather it was saved as John Plumber. Direct contact was only supposed to be used in extreme circumstances. This meant only one thing. Something was wrong.

His mind turned to Juliet's partner at the CEF, the rather lively and slightly scatty man he knew as Clem, whom he'd only met twice. Again, all his instincts told him not to, but he didn't see he had a choice. He went to the contact listed as Charlie Electrician, and dialled.

'Hi, it's Clem, sorry I can't take the call, leave a message.'

Stomach churning, he jumped up from the bench and passed through the large farmhouse kitchen and into the hall where there was a long, sleek sideboard. He pulled out the SIM from his phone, and discarded it on the top of the unit. He slid open the top drawer and picked out a brand-new SIM card, from a small Tupperware box containing a stack of identical cards, all in small plastic cases. Taking one, he snapped the case open, and popped it into the handset, dropping the small plastic case next to the discarded SIM.

His stomach knotted, and he held a breath in his lungs as he dialled.

Thankfully, this call was answered immediately. 'Ayup?' said Barney.

'Barney, are we good to go for tomorrow?' said Finlay, trying to keep the wobble from his voice.

'I'm on my way now in't van. Max and Janie are coming up early tomorrow. You okay, mate? You sound a bit odd.'

'I just got an abandoned call from one of my contacts at CEF, and now I can't get through to her, or her co-worker. I think something is wrong, and we need to accelerate. Can we meet sooner?'

'Like how much sooner? I'm about an hour away, the others have gone home.'

'I need to meet now, Barney.'

'I'll make a call, where?'

Finlay paused, wondering who he could trust, and considering for a moment if he could even trust Barney. He shook his head, trying to shake the thought from his mind. He'd meet Barney and the cops now, but not out here. Not in private. He needed the safety net of bystanders.

'You know the Golden Lion?'

'Aye, middle of Stirling, funnily enough, I was planning a pint there in a bit.'

'When can your colleagues get here?'

'I'll call them, and get them running now, pal. Anything you can enlighten me with?'

'Not over the phone. Text me on this number when you know a time for all of you getting there.'

'Righto. I'll call them now.' Barney rang off.

Finlay tucked the phone into his pocket, and headed out towards the back garden, pausing to grab a bottle of beer from the fridge. He snapped the top off, and took a long swig of the cool lager. It was instantly soothing as it slid down his throat, and he sighed as he leaned against the fridge and pressed the bottle against his forehead, enjoying the cold glass against the hot skin.

These bastards wouldn't win, they'd crossed too many lines and done too much damage. He'd make sure of it. In all his years in the Security Service, he'd never gone against the bosses. Never gone rogue in the face of a threat, but this was different. Someone, somewhere was telling tales, and until he found out who they were, he wasn't putting his head over the parapet.

He trusted few people, but he trusted Barney more than most. He was an odd character, but he was as straight as they came, and his link into the anti-corruption cops meant he was useful. He'd heard good things on the grapevine about the small and shadowy team based out of Tulliallan. Worked directly for the Chief Constable, kept themselves away from court cases, and had chalked up some notable successes. Hopefully they'd know what to do.

His phone buzzed in his pocket. It was Barney. *With you in an hour.*

Finlay nodded, happy that things were underway. He was gonna blow the bloody lid off it. He didn't know who the bent bastard was, but between him and Barney's lot they'd get them. He'd get them all, and he'd finish them, once and for all, if he could stay alive long enough. Finlay squared his shoulders, and walked over to one of the kitchen cupboards. He knelt down and pulled at one of the plinths, where there was a small space underneath. He reached in, took out a compact plastic box and opened it, revealing a Glock 19 pistol. Wrapping his hand around the cool polymer handle, he lifted it from the box. It felt comforting, and comfortable. He pushed the box back under the cupboard, returned the plinth and stood up, tucking the pistol into the back of his waistband.

If they'd got to Juliet, they could be coming for him and no fucking way was he ending up like Billy.

He sneered. He'd faced the IRA, Al-Qaeda and the worst of the worst in his time in the service.

He'd be ready.

14

'IS IT DONE?' said Stringer.

'Yep. Got the bitch with a baseball bat across the head in the car park in Jedburgh, easy as. Took her purse, phone and some shite jewellery, to make it look like a robbery. No one saw me, not that it matters if they did.' Shifty's accent was pure, unadulterated Belfast. Shifty was a true believer, and ex–Ulster Volunteer Force who'd moved into the private sector, where he deployed his talents partly for money, but mostly because he was there for the cause. A white supremacist. A true patriot.

'Any other loose ends you want me to deal with?' he said, still feeling the excitement of the hit. Shifty really did love his job, and not just because the cash was good.

'Nah, we're all sorted, man. You get yourself away, the cops are gonna go mental when this breaks, and you need to be well gone.'

'I'm on it, don't fret. I'll be gone before the Peelers even realise I'd been over.'

'We need her phone. We need to see who she's been messaging and calling.'

'I have it. She was dialling when I did the business. I wrote the number down, want it?'

'Aye gan on.'

Shifty read the number out from the handset.

'Got it, I'll get it checked out, anything else on the phone?'

'Haven't had chance to look yet, but it's full up. May be something on it.'

'Okay, deal with it as per normal, and I'll get them picked up. Have you bypassed the PIN?' said Stringer.

'Yeah, it's PIN free.'

'Good man. Right, are you off now?'

'Aye, ferry from Stranraer later on. I'll deal with the car over the water. I'll be long gone before the cops even know what's actually happened.'

'Right. Nice one, Shifty. Money dealt with as usual, eh?'

'Of course.' And then he cancelled the call.

Checking his watch, he realised that the ferry was leaving in five hours, and it was well over three to the port. He needed to get going. He smiled, an easy drive, with his favourite podcast, and then a couple of pints on the ferry to Belfast. Before he knew it, he'd be tucked up in his cottage in Dungannon with a nice few quid in his off-shore.

15

MAX, JANIE AND Barney pulled up just along the road from the Golden Lion in the centre of Stirling. It was a handsome old coaching inn in the middle of the one-way system of the old city. They'd left the Volvo on the outskirts and had all jumped in Barney's van at his insistence.

'Nice place this, I stayed here a few years ago for a literary festival. Dates back to late 1700s. Rabbie Burns stayed here in 1786, and scratched a verse on a window pane. *"Here Stuarts one in glory reigned, and laws or Scotland weal ordained . . ."* Something like that, anyway, I don't admit to perfect recall.'

A heavy silence descended in the van, and Barney eyed Janie balefully in the rear-view mirror.

Janie furrowed her brow, as Max sniggered.

'It's me saying things like this that makes everyone think I'm weird, no?' Her voice sounded almost perplexed.

'So old Rabbie was a bloody criminal, damaging windows, eh?' said Max, with amusement.

'Well, it got worse, because he was scunnered at the state of the castle and bust the window in disgust . . .' Janie suddenly looked embarrassed. 'I'm doing it again, aren't I?'

'It's why we all love you, pal. Come on, let's avail ourselves of Barney's snidey blue badge, and get inside.'

'Cheeky bugger. It's not snidey at all. I'm an injured veteran after serving country, blah blah,' said Barney, tossing the badge onto the dash of his van.

'Barney, you barely limp, and you're definitely fitter than Ross, and he doesn't have a badge.'

'Well, that's nowt worth sayin', is it? My old mum is fitter than Ross.'

'Wait a minute. Are you saying your mum is still alive?'

Barney nodded, with obvious pride. 'Aye, she's a tough old Yorkshire bird, she's ninety-two and still lives on her tod in Leeds.'

'I can't believe you never mentioned this,' said Janie, eyes wide.

Barney shrugged. 'You never asked. Come on, Fin should be in there, and I'm right famished, me. Your company Amex can buy me a fish supper.'

The hotel interior was just as expected, as in it appeared that the furnishings and decor hadn't changed for many years, but the place reeked of slightly shabby charm, with nods to the past wherever you looked. The bar at the front was compact, and seemed empty.

In fact, it was empty, beyond a lone barman sitting on a stool scrolling his phone, yawning.

'Well, unless the barman is Fin, I'm saying he's not here yet,' said Max.

'If I know Fin, I suspect he's just watched us arrive from somewhere out the way and is making sure we've not been followed. Fancy a bevvie?' said Barney, nodding at the bar. The barman returned his nod, and put his phone down.

'What can I get you?' he said, his accent pure central belt.

'Heavy for me, Max?' said Barney.

'Oh, cranberry juice, please.'

'You have dangleberry juice, mate?' said Barney to the barman.

'Aye, course we do. Ice?'

Max nodded.

'Janie?'

'Just water.'

'Christ, last of the big spenders. A pint, a dingleberry juice and a water. Sorry, mate, my friends don't appreciate being in a nice bar.'

'I'll bring them over,' said the barman, and began busying himself pouring the drinks. They all moved over to the stools surrounding a small, high table at the far corner.

'Is he always late?' said Janie.

'All spooks are. Tradecraft, in't it?' Barney smiled with anticipation as the barman wordlessly placed the three drinks down on the table. Barney nodded in thanks, and took a sip of his dark brown pint, smacking his lips in appreciation.

Max's phone buzzed on the table. A message from Ross.

What the fucking fuck is happening? You numpties are supposed to keep me in the shitting loop.

Max sniggered and showed the message to Janie and Barney, who both grinned.

'He's right, though. Where is the bugger? I get the staking the locus out, and watching us arrive before he comes in, but come on. I've places to be, guys,' said Janie, sipping at her water.

'I'll call him,' said Barney, reaching for his phone and dialling. He grimaced, and then redialled.

'What's happening?' said Max.

'Voicemail, I'll try again.' Barney pressed the key again, and raised the phone to his ear. His face remained impassive. 'Same. Bugger.'

'Keep trying. May be a crap signal,' said Max, his voice tense.

Barney tapped at the screen again, put it on loudspeaker and lay the phone on the table. *'Sorry, the number you are dialling is not available.'*

No one spoke, they just looked at each other in turn, all the subtle noises from the bar faded.

'I'm ringing Norma. She's on standby, and Ross authorised a ping on his phone in case of unforeseen issues. I'm callin' this unforeseen.' He dialled again, holding the phone to his ear.

'Norma love. Can we get a ping on that number, last activity, and last cell site?' he said, his voice low. He waited a moment, and then spoke again. 'As soon as you hear, love.'

'Is she on it?' said Max.

'Aye, all pre-authorised, and out-of-hours single point of contact is on standby. Should get a response fast.'

Barney laid his phone down on the table, and took a long sip of his pint, the silence between them thick and tense. Something was wrong. They all knew it.

The buzzing of Barney's phone on the table seemed extraordinarily loud. Barney picked it up and looked at the screen, his face grim. 'Let's go.'

'Where?' said Max.

'Fin's place. Last activity was my message, cell-sited nearby, and the azimuth puts the phone at his place. There's nowt else nearby.'

'Cell-sited there now?' said Janie.

'Nope. Phone's not active, now. Switched off just after my message. Summat's wrong.'

16

FINLAY SMITH'S HOME was a large, substantial place, but Barney stopped short of the drive, and tucked his van in to the side of the entrance to the driveway. A small woodblock of tall conifers was to the side of the entranceway. Max had brought up the Google Map of the area and had zoomed in on the satellite image of the property, noting the small lake to the rear of the property, and the woodblock to the side. The other side was just a wide-open field that looked like it was planted with barley.

'Are we calling the local cops?' said Janie, strapping her body armour in place.

'No time. They could be bloody hours, and it's not like we can call for an emergency response, can we? A bloke has just missed a meeting at the pub,' said Max, as he pulled his own armour into place.

'Fancy checking out the back?' Barney said to Max.

'Aye, no armour, Barney?'

'Nah. Not my style, pal.'

Max nodded, and disappeared towards the back of the property.

'How'd you want to play this?' said Janie, checking her harness that contained her PAVA incapacitant spray, rigid cuffs and extendable baton.

'Give Max a moment to get to the back, then we just go up the drive, and bash on the door, I'd say,' said Barney, reaching into his pocket. He pulled out a small brass knuckleduster, and slipped it over his fist.

Janie's eyes widened. 'Barney? Those are bloody illegal,' she said, pointing at the knuckleduster.

'Oh, give over. We may be outnumbered in there, and I'm an old sod. This is what I call my equaliser, so any bad bugger in there is getting his 'ead brayed in. You ready?' Barney said, his jaw firm, and all the relaxed, affable Yorkshireman gone.

'Come on, then,' said Janie, and they both set off towards the house, feet crunching on the immaculately raked gravel drive. The large, double front door came into view, and there was a BMW X5 parked at the front of the house.

Janie put her hand on the bonnet as they headed for the door. 'Engine's stone cold. This hasn't been driven any time recently. Do we just knock?'

'Any other suggestions?' said Barney.

Janie shook her head.

Standing in front of the impressive, solid old wooden door, Barney was raising his brass-clad fist and was about to knock when his phone buzzed. He accepted the call. 'Max?'

Barney's eyes closed, and his head rocked backwards. 'We're coming.'

'What?' said Janie, tension in her voice.

'Round the back.' Barney set off towards the side gate, unlatched it and headed around the back of the house.

Janie knew. She just knew what they were going to find.

Max was standing on the terrace at the back of the house where a figure was slumped in a wooden garden chair, head lolling back, a pistol clutched in his right hand on his lap.

A small black hole was slap bang in the centre of his forehead, rimmed with red, and a solitary trickle of blood traversed his nose, onto his lip, staining his shirt.

The back of the head was very different. The back of his head barely existed anymore.

'Ah, bugger it,' said Barney, in barely a whisper.

17

'TOO LATE, WE'RE too bloody late,' said Janie.

Max said nothing, his stomach roiling as he looked at the slumped figure on the garden chair. His back was damp with cold sweat, and his fingers tingled as he breathed in deeply, held for a count of ten, and then eased out the breath. Square breathing, calm the nerves, steady the heart rate, focus the mind. Max always reacted like this at death scenes. A hangover from an incident in Afghanistan, years ago.

'You okay, Max?' said Janie, concern in her voice.

'Aye,' said Max, without turning to look at Janie. He slowly eased out another breath, focusing his mind, and took in the scene. The pistol dangling from the right hand, the expensive-looking watch, the mouth open in shock, eyes wide but cloudy, and the small, neat hole, as dark as pitch, ringed by red.

The skin around the wound was as pale as alabaster. Max took a further deep breath, feeling the hairs begin to tingle on the back of his neck, and walked to the rear of the body. The exit wound was large and ragged, the white of the skull jarring starkly against the pink and red gore. The nausea began to rise, thick and acrid at the back of his throat, so he breathed in again, counting silently as the bile settled. The smell arrived in a sudden wave, rich and coppery. The paving under Fin's head was covered in blood, and gore, and Max didn't linger on. He'd seen enough.

'Is this supposed to look like a suicide?' said Barney, his craggy face sad, as he stood there, rolling a cigarette.

'You can't smoke that here, Barney. Local cops on the way, Janie?' said Max, looking at his partner, who nodded.

Janie shrugged. 'Fifteen minutes, not priority as it's an apparent suicide, with no evidence of suspects nearby.'

Max turned away from the body, shut his eyes, and just stood there for a moment, gathering his thoughts and clearing the fog.

'Well, I guess he isn't going to get any more dead. This is definitely not a suicide, though.'

'Cops may think it is. It looks like it was his pistol, as well. The box is on the table over there. What kind of killer leaves a pistol, together with its box behind at the scene of a murder?' said Janie, pointing at an open box, just visible through the open kitchen door.

'It's a half-arsed attempt at best. They know we'll know, as well, they're just trying to slow down a full response, so they can get away before roads start getting closed.'

'How can you be sure it's not suicide? I mean, I don't think it is, either, but Fin looked proper depressed when I saw him.'

'His watch.'

'What's his watch have to do with it?' said Barney, his brow furrowing.

'Pistol in his right hand, watch on right wrist. I'd say he was left-handed. Who shoots himself in the head with their weaker hand? If you're killing yourself, you don't take chances, do you?'

'I can barely pick me nose with me left hand,' said Barney, tucking the roll-up between his lips.

'Nice image. Thanks, Barney,' said Janie, grimacing.

Max ignored the exchange and continued, his voice low and flat, 'Plus, there's no scorching or stippling around the wound, and of course the main problem.'

'Who shoots themselves in the centre of the forehead?' said Janie.

'Bingo.' Max scrubbed at his face, and sighed. His phone buzzed in his pocket. 'Ross?'

'Janie told me what's happened. Suicide sounds like a load of shite to me, am I correct?' Ross's voice lacked any of his usual sarcasm or bumptiousness. He just sounded worried.

'Very correct. He's been executed, Ross. A cold-blooded execution.'

'Aye, I agree, even without seeing the scene. We've a problem.'

'Well, that's not up for discussion, but I'm sensing you have more.'

'Fin's contact at Counter-Extremism Forum, Juliet McNamara, has been murdered, found dead in a car park in Jedburgh. Bashed over the head during an apparent robbery.' Ross's voice was laced with a mix of sadness and anger.

Max felt like he'd been punched in the guts, the breath knocked out of him. 'What?'

'MIT deployed,' Ross began, 'and scene secured. I'm waiting for an update, but shite . . .'

Max just stood there, unable to find the words.

'Craigie?' said Ross, his scant store of patience clearly wearing out quickly.

'Aye. I heard you. You know what this means, right?' Max's voice was tight, and hard, as the anger began to bubble. 'Three people murdered to protect some evil, racist scumbags.'

'Yeah. These sick, racist bastards have just taken out everyone who knew about what they were up to. We are back to square one. We have bloody nothing.'

'It's worse than that, Ross.'

'How?'

'They knew what we were planning. Someone has told them what we were doing, and they killed them all to stop us finding out. If we were only concerned there may be a rat before, I think we can be certain now. I've no idea where from, and no idea how, but I damn well know one thing. We're gonna find out.' Max ended the call and turned to face Janie and Barney.

'I don't like the sound of that,' said Janie.

'Fin's contact at CEF murdered in Jedburgh. Apparent robbery, but that's bullshit, as we all know.'

Barney just stood there, the roll-up in his mouth flipping up and down, his eyes half closed and his nostrils flared. He looked different, very different from the usually relaxed, unflappable and unemotional man, but something had changed.

'Barney—'

The ex-spy stopped Max from continuing by slowly turning away and retracing his steps towards the front of the house.

Max tried again. 'Barney, where're you going?'

Barney didn't turn around, he just carried on sauntering away. 'I'm going to smoke me fag, and put the kettle on in't van. Nowt I can achieve here.'

But Max had seen it. He'd seen the shift in the implacable old MI5 agent's eyes.

Barney was angry.

'Janie, stay here, I'm gonna take a quick look around the house, just on the off-chance.'

'Not want to wait for backup?' Janie looked worried, her face pale.

'They could be ages, just a quick look. There's no one here, mate. This is the work of a pro, and they won't have hung about,' he said, and headed off into the house.

As he passed through the kitchen, the first thing he saw was the pistol box open on the table. The kitchen unit plinth had been pulled out, leaving a gap underneath.

Max reached for his extendable baton, racking it open as he moved into the hall, his ears straining. All his instincts told him that Fin's killer had gone. It looked professional, and no way would a pro hang around after an unsilenced pistol shot, even in a remote area. Moving into the hall, his eyes were drawn to the sideboard, the solitary SIM card and discarded case. He reached into his pocket and pulled out a pair of nitrile gloves, and snapped them on. He slid the drawer open, noting the small box filled with identical SIM cards. Obviously, Fin had been habitually careful with his phone discipline, as one might expect from an experienced intelligence agent. He pulled out an evidence bag from the front pouch of his body armour, and dropped the SIM and case inside.

He moved on to the comfortable living room, and then quickly cleared the rest of the property. It was, of course, empty, with no evidence of searching, rummaging or clearing up. One thing was clear. This was a cold, efficient and professional hit, not a burglary gone wrong.

As he descended the stairs, he heard the faint wail of sirens. This place would soon be locked down tight for forensic examination, and the SIM cards in his hand offered an opportunity.

He dashed down the stairs and out the back of the property, where Janie was still waiting. 'Sounds like local cops are close. Anything notable?'

'Looks like it was Fin's own Glock. Box is on the table, and I'd bet it had been hidden under the cupboards. I found this SIM, and I suspect he'd changed it to call Barney. Once this place is locked down, we'll get bugger all. Let's get Barney to download it now.'

'You sure? Kinda goes against crime scene management.' Janie's brow was furrowed.

'It'll be fine. I'll cover in a statement later, but whoever he's called using that SIM could be in danger as well. Come on, let's go and see Barney.'

Barney was in his van, smoking his roll-up, his eyes half closed and his face impassive.

'Barney, do you have your SIM reader?' said Max.

'Aye, all in the van, what d'you need?'

Max held out the bag containing the SIM and box. 'This was

on the unit in the hall, when he called you was it on a familiar number?'

Barney shook his head. 'He never called on a familiar number. He was a serial SIM switcher. Give it here.' He held out his hand. Within a minute, the SIM was slotted into a reader, which had in turn been plugged into his laptop.

'Did we locate a phone?' said Barney.

'I didn't see one, but it may be in his pocket,' said Max.

Barney scrolled through his own phone, before setting it down and squinting at his laptop. 'Well, this isn't the number he called me from. Limited data on this, but from what I can see it was just used to call two numbers, recently. I'll forward them to Norma for checks, but I suspect this would be the card he used to call his CEF contacts, unless he changed again. Either way, it needs bottoming out.'

They all looked up as the sirens grew louder, and there was a crunch of gravel as the first of the local police arrived.

'Okay, do it, then put the kettle on. We could be here a while,' said Max.

18

DCI LAURA MCKECHNIE tore off her face mask and pulled down the hood of her Tyvek suit, as she rounded the side of the house and approached Max, her face a mix of confusion and frustration.

Max was steeling himself for a huge bollocking, but instead, she just sighed, and shook out her hair from the confines of the back of the white suit.

'We've not met, have we?' said Laura, unzipping her white suit and slipping her arms out of the garment to allow it to flop around her waist. Underneath she was wearing a plain sweatshirt with some kind of stain on the front. She looked down and cursed.

'I don't think so, boss.'

She continued to stare at the orange mark on the sweatshirt, and shook her head. 'Can you tell I came from home, midway through making a spag-bol for my kids?'

Max smiled, but didn't say anything.

'Well, I know of you, but very little. Some kind of review team working directly for the big boss?' she said, pulling the suit down and stepping out of it. She was wearing worn jeans underneath.

'Something like that, boss.'

'Laura, please. I can't be doing with all that nonsense. Look, Max, I'm up to my neck in the murder of a professional drug dealer found swinging under the Union Chain, and now I find myself here looking at the body of a man who has apparently killed himself. Miles W. assured me that there was a strong link between both, but he didn't manage to tell me exactly what. Any chance you can elaborate?'

'I can tell you why we came, Laura, but background-wise we're a little in the dark.'

'Anything is better than nothing, Max. One cat A murder is bad, two is way worse. Fortunately, Miles is swelling my staffing levels exponentially, as before I just had one cantankerous DS, and a DC who can rarely get through a shift without having to go home with a sore backside. Added to that we now have another murder in Jedburgh that thankfully my colleague is dealing with.'

'Not to ruin your day any more, Laura, but that is going to be connected as well.'

Her eyes widened and mouth gaped. 'Tell me,' she said, flatly.

Max told her everything he knew, from Barney's first call from Finlay, through to all their research and work to this moment. He even, slightly apologetically, admitted to downloading the SIM card.

She sighed, and pursed her lips, and Max could almost see the cogs turning. She was pale and looked tired.

'Okay, well no doubt this is a link we can't ignore, especially as that's the worst staged suicide I've seen. I'm not sure that you downloading that SIM card before we even got here is strictly in line with the murder manual, but as a realist, I appreciate it, especially as he suspiciously doesn't seem to have a phone on him, or in the property.'

'As we had Barney here, it seemed opportune.'

'As long as you document it all clearly, I'm relaxed, and I'm just glad we have a lead. Let me get this straight. He had been dealing with Juliet McNamara, and Clem South from CEF?'

'That's what he told Barney.'

'And then today, his SIM was called by Juliet, presumably around the time she was murdered, and then he tried to call her back, and when that was unsuccessful, he tried to call Clem South?'

'That's about the size of it. Phone records back that up as well.'

'Blimey, you got the data fast.'

'We have a well-connected analyst back at Tulliallan.'

'But we know no more than that?'

'That's it. It looks to me like this is a clear-up operation to cover up whatever Billy Mackee was telling Fin, Juliet and possibly Clem,' said Max.

'Has anyone tried to call Clem?'

'Aye, just before you got here. Voicemail. His data shows that his phone powered down while cell-sited in Kelso, just after he received a call from Juliet. I sent my DC to his home address in Cumbernauld to check on him, as it's less than half an hour away.'

'How long ago did he leave?' Laura asked.

Max looked at his watch. 'About half an hour ago.'

'Can you call him?'

'Her. DC Janie Calder. Aye, I'll call her now.' Max pulled his phone from his pocket and dialled.

Janie answered almost immediately.

'Max, we have a problem,' she said, and he could hear the tension in her voice.

Max pulled the phone away from his face and activated the speaker. 'Janie, I'm here with DCI McKechnie, the SIO. Carry on.'

'I've just got here, and his door's been forced open. I've called the locals for some support before I go in,' she said, tightly.

'Can you see anything at all?' said Max.

'No. It's a wee detached bungalow on Castle Court. No lights on, no car on the drive, I've been around the back, and nothing to see. Net curtains up.'

'Okay, hold off going in until you get support. I'm on my way.'

'Don't hang about, Max.'

'On my way.' Max hung up.

'I'm coming with you. Do you have a car?' said Laura.

Max pointed at Barney, who was sitting outside his van, a glow of a cigarette in his mouth, and a steaming mug in his hand. 'Just Barney's van.'

Laura looked slightly confused at the old spy and shook her head.

'Right, I don't need to be here anymore, CSM is here, and the scene processing will take all night. I have the on-call DI's car, and it has covert blues and twos. We'll both go. It's only twenty minutes away. Let's go, your Barney can follow.'

19

THE CASHIER WAS feeling satisfied as he drove the anonymous, slightly dull Vauxhall along the A9 south towards Glasgow. As always, he drove carefully, a touch under the speed limit, in the typical salesman car, the image strengthened by the suit jacket on a hanger, the shitty laptop case and the sales booklets for double glazing. Even if the cops did stop him, he'd just be taken for what he looked like. A struggling rep, on a busy motorway full of other struggling reps, all chasing the same shitty business in a cost-of-living crisis. It wouldn't matter if they checked the brochures online as they'd find the basic website he'd created to authenticate them. Modern camouflage, of which he was an expert.

Even if they searched the car, they wouldn't find the pistol secreted in a hide contained within the seat cushion. If he was stopped, he'd be polite, smile and cooperate all the way. The car was taxed, insured, and he had his driving licence in his pocket. In reality, the car was a clone, registered to a shell company in Halifax, with a named driver that matched the licence in his pocket. Of course, the driving licence wasn't actually his, either. The name had been taken from a gravestone of an unfortunate individual who had died many years ago, who fortunately had been the same age as the Cashier, and apparently lived in a modern semi-detached in Hartlepool, where the car was also registered. Well, by registered, in reality the genuine number plates were currently hidden under the rear seat, and he planned to replace them once a little farther away from Stirling. He'd switch them back before he got home.

The Cashier was an expert at this, having received training from the best while serving his country over many years. But that was another life, in another era. Now he was a ghost. A chameleon, capable of blending into any terrain, and passing as part of whatever environment he was operating in.

The job had gone way smoother than he'd imagined it would. The incompetent spook hadn't noticed him hidden behind a large shrub as he'd tucked the Glock he'd just pulled out from under the cupboard into his waistband. It was a simple enough task to take him out of the game. The Cashier was expert in many martial arts, so a silent approach from behind, followed by a standard rear-naked-choke had been enough to put the stupid man to sleep. Then it was a simple job of yanking him outside, sitting him on a garden chair and popping one in his head with the Glock. He stood far enough away to avoid any blood spray, and much of the gore had come out of the exit wound, which was the size of a man's fist. He then just left him there, Glock in the corpse's hand, head lolling back, as the unfortunate spy sat slumped, inert and lifeless. He was pretty sure that the tableau he'd left wouldn't fool the cops for very long, but it'd mean that it would be less of a response, with road blocks and the like, until he was well out of the way.

He hadn't hurried after the job; he'd used the woods as cover to make his way to where he'd left the car in a concealed spot not visible from the road. He'd stripped off his gloves and windcheater, removed the overshoes, and secreted them in a small plastic bag under the boot lining. He'd dispose of those in the wood burner when he got home. He had then driven off at a leisurely pace towards the motorway, and had headed south.

He used the car's hands-free setting to dial. Never pick up a phone on a job. Being caught on a phone while driving was a very fast way to get a tug from the police. He made sure that the voice-disguising app was initiated on his phone.

The Cashier never met a client in person, and they never heard his real voice, and his contracts came through via the draft folders of a dormant email address. All tradecraft techniques learned during many years of covert work.

'Is it done?' said Stringer, his thick north-eastern accent crackling out of the car's speakers.

'Yes. He had a Glock under the kitchen cupboards, so I used that. I made it look like a suicide, that'll slow the cops down a bit, at least.' The Cashier's voice was like his car. Anonymous, and unremarkable – its mild Cumbrian accent removed by the app on his phone.

'All loose ends tied up, good work. Your reputation is justified.'

'Of course. Once I take on an assignment I deliver. It's why I'm expensive.'

'I thought you'd be doing it for the cause?' said Stringer, his tone not wholly serious.

'I don't care either way for your cause. When can I expect payment?'

'Any time. Shipment is due very soon, and once it's in, we're taking over. Billy Mac being a grass was a bump in the road, as he was our route into Scotland, but we're still rocking.'

'Not sure I care about the state of your business, as long as I get paid. You know how I operate, half upfront, half securely lodged electronically until after the job, to be automatically sent to my Bitcoin wallet, unless you cancel. I don't want to wait six weeks after the job is done. I need it within a week.'

'It's almost like you don't trust me, man.'

'You're correct, I don't. But that's not the reason. Should you or your colleague come to a sticky end or get arrested, I don't want to forgo my full fee because you're not around to pay me, with the money just sitting in your Bitcoin wallet. We're both protected.

I don't do the job, you can cancel the payment, but I still get paid if you get topped or jailed.'

'What if you top us first, eh? Don't do the job, no risk, and get paid anyway?'

'My reputation is everything. It's why people pay me so well.'

'All about the money to you, isn't it?'

'What other reason could there be?'

'You'll get paid, but I may need you again in the not-too-distant future. A more significant target.' The hardened criminal's voice suddenly had a pensive edge to it.

'Significant?'

'Okay, let's say notable.'

'Are we talking about a publicly notable figure?'

'We are.'

'It'd be reflected in my fee, which isn't negotiable. Same principle. Automated full fee unless you cancel. If the subject is notable, the risk is higher, and I'd need to go fully off radar once it was done. For a while, at least.'

'Like you did after York.'

'Indeed.'

'You know I'm good for it.'

'Who else knows about this?' The Cashier was a careful man, it was why he'd stayed out of jail. He wasn't going to get careless over the phone with a two-bit gangster, even if he was a good client.

'Just me and Shorty.' Stringer had an edge to his voice which the Cashier didn't care for.

'You really need to look at your security, you made a big mistake with letting someone get into your organisation, it makes me nervous to be working with you.'

'Aye, I knaa, and we won't make the same mistake again of trusting anyone without a proper recommendation. We'll be back up and running soon.'

'Quite frankly I don't care. Just get the money transferred, and if you want the other thing doing, let me know by the usual means.'
'What will you need?'
'Photograph, and a name if I wouldn't recognise them.'
'Fine. I'll be in touch.'
'Acknowledged.' The Cashier hung up.

He grinned as he reached down, popped the SIM out of the cheap phone, opened the window a crack and tossed it out onto the motorway. He navigated into the car's phone settings and deleted the burner from it. He was far too experienced to keep using the handset. He knew the police investigative tactics well enough. If they got hold of the phone, a simple search on the handset number would reveal all the SIM cards, and therefore telephone numbers that had been used. It was the sign of an amateur.

He looked at the car's clock, and smiled. A nice, early finish. It wouldn't take long to get back to his modest home in Cumbria, then it'd be a hearty meal, and maybe a decent glass of wine in front of a film.

It wasn't a bad life being a contract killer.

20

CASTLE COURT WAS a small street of bungalows on the outskirts of Cumbernauld. The daylight was fading away, and the lights from the other houses cast a glow on the unlit street.

'There we are,' said Max, pointing at the Volvo, which was parked next to a marked police vehicle outside one of the houses. Janie was on the pavement talking to one of the uniformed cops. Max and Laura got out of the car and joined them on the pavement.

'Janie, this is DCI Laura McKechnie. Laura, Janie Calder,' said Max, and both women nodded at each other.

'Nice to meet you. House is clear, and what looks like a bit of a stramash in there. A few drawers turned out, wardrobes opened and the like, but nothing mad.'

'Any blood, or other suggestions that something bad has occurred?' said Laura.

'No, boss.'

'I'll have a look.' Laura headed off into the house and disappeared out of sight.

'Jesus, this doesn't look good, two killed within hours of each other. Is this a kidnap?' said Janie.

Max just shrugged.

A set of headlights illuminated them on the pavement as a car swung into the close. The car sped up as it drove towards them, engine screaming.

'What the hell,' said Max, getting ready to dive out of the way, but the car kept coming before screeching to a halt diagonally in the road in front of the property. It was an ancient-looking Citroën. The burbling engine note suggested that the exhaust could probably do with a bit of attention.

The door flew open, and a short, stocky man with sandy hair jumped out, his face bleached pale in the twilight, mouth open in shock at the sight of a cop car outside the house.

'What the hell is going on?' he said, voice trembling.

'I'm DS Craigie, who are you?'

'Clem South, this is my house.'

21

STRINGER CHINKED GLASSES with Shorty, as they sat on the heavy cast-iron chairs outside the Queen's Head pub in Berwick. They both took deep draughts from their pints and grinned at each other as they put the glasses back on the table. They were the only people outside the pub, as the summer sun announced that it was about to disappear for a few hours.

'All in all, a good day's work, eh?' said Stringer.

'Aye, bonny lad. Cops will be going mad.'

'I take it no whispers?'

Shorty shook his head. 'They've found the daft bint's body in Jedburgh, which is being put down to a robbery gone wrong, at the moment, but that won't last long. Word is that they have nada. No witnesses, no CCTV, nowt. How about that bastard spook in Stirling?'

'Cashier did his job perfectly, as you'd expect. The cops are all over it, but reports coming in say that it's being treated as suicide at the moment, although no way will that last. Doesn't matter. The two contractors are both pros. Shifty will be over the water before they've even got the forensic team there, and the Cashier never leaves any trace. He's far too clever.'

Shorty narrowed his eyes. 'Do we know anything about him?'

'Who, Shifty or the Cashier?'

'The Cashier bastard. Shifty is just an ex-UVF psycho who likes topping people. He was fine for the woman, but no way would I use him to take out a pro, hence the Cashier. Have you met him?'

Stringer shook his head. 'No one meets him, apparently. I'd never have been able to use him if I hadn't been vouched for, he only takes new clients from existing ones. He doesn't meet face to face, and once he's accepted the job, he guarantees it will be done. It's why the fucker is so expensive. They'll never get close to him.'

'The York job was a masterpiece, String. Cops are still convinced it's fucking ISIS, as the bomb bears all the hallmarks of one of their bomb-makers. Perfect for our purposes. Gets the Jews riled up, so we just need to get the Muslims mad next. Before we know it, they'll be at each other's throats.' Shorty's smile should have been chilling, bearing in mind the subject matter, but Stringer just matched his expression.

'I think we can safely say we wouldn't want to make an enemy of the Cashier, eh?'

'Damn straight, man.'

There was a pause as both men took swigs from their pints.

'So, are we all good personally with Billy and the other two?' said Shorty.

'We're well away from it all, man. Even if they do look at us, our alibis couldn't be tighter. I was at a fuckin' boxing gym with some kids I've been working on, and the coach there is an ex-chief inspector.' Stringer laughed.

'I was with my probation officer. All phones ditched, nothing to link us to anything. Heads down for a bit like, eh?' Shorty chinked his glass against Stringer's again.

'I wish, but we need funds fuckin' pronto. I've some product about to land from the Dutchman with a short line of credit. Newcastle is a bit warm, and I don't want the grief right now. We need a new buyer, sharpish.'

'That's a big consignment, mate. Without Newcastle, how are we gonna shift it?'

'We have to. Firstly, the Dutchman isn't known for his patience, and we need to make some cash quickly if we're to move forward with the next phase of the cause.' Stringer's face darkened at the mention of 'the cause'.

'Meaning?'

'A new proper target. Someone who deserves it more than anyone. Daniel Solomon was a big success, with it being put down to Islamists. The next one will be something different, with someone else getting the blame, or taking the credit, whichever way you look at it. The result will be the same. More anger, more hatred, and we're further down the road. We'll have the Cashier take the bastard out, but using a totally different method. A precision attack. No innocents getting hurt.'

'Why the change? You weren't bothered about the twat from CEF, or the spook.'

'That's a totally different ballgame. That was housekeeping, nothing else. It wasn't for the cause. Billy had somehow cottoned on about York and was mouthing off to the CEF do-gooders. If we hadn't taken them all out, the whole plan would have fallen down.'

'So, what's next?'

'Bogdan put me right, pal. Precision attacks, on strategic targets. Key players, with no collateral, if possible. We're holding the strings now, Shorty. We're shaping the agenda, stirring up division, making people hate each other more. Bogdan has all the contacts, and it's getting noticed in the right place. Once we get the jobs done, they just reap the rewards. Bots on social media, Facebook algorithm, all stirring it up. I wish you could meet Bogdan, mate. He was fucking inspirational. Russian mafia, hard as nails, but clever. He knows what's what, and we just need the money to get the jobs done. This isn't work for National Force anymore, that was just a smokescreen to make the cops underestimate us. Bogdan showed me the way, mate. I've been reading all about it in the jail, stuff that Bogdan gave me. The west is fucking finished, and we need to play our part in hastening its demise.'

'If he's Russki mafia, can't he have us sorted out for cash to get the jobs done?'

Stringer shook his head. 'No way. The fucking Jewish illuminati track the money moving from Russia like a hawk, we do it with good old-fashioned drug money, then it can't be traced. The trail starts from nowhere. It's perfect, Bogdan explained it all to me, lad. Once the job is done, then the world changes, but we need to get the funds in pronto to get things moving properly.'

'Are you gonna tell me then, brother?' said Shorty.

'Soon, man. Soon. We really jack it up, and make the bastards take notice, eh?'

Shorty paused, his pint midway to his mouth as he looked at the fire in his old friend's eyes. 'What you talking about?'

Stringer grinned, fiddled with his phone and held up the screen for Shorty to see. A face filled the screen, in lurid colour.

Shorty looked at the instantly recognisable face on the phone's screen, and he gasped, his eyes as wide as saucers. A face he'd seen every day until very recently. A scumbag, with traitorous opinions. Shit, if they pulled this off, they'd go down in history. It would change the country forever.

22

CLEM SOUTH'S FACE was still pale as alabaster, as he sat on the sofa in the bungalow, a mug of tea in his hand, his face stained with tears.

'I can't believe Juliet is dead. We were supposed to get together earlier, as she'd wanted me to meet Billy, and now you tell me that he's the poor man who was hanged from the Union Bridge?' he said, in an accent tinged with shades of Belfast.

'I'm sorry for your loss,' said Laura.

'You think it's a robbery?' he said, his voice shaking.

'I didn't say that. I said that at first glance it appears to be a robbery, but enquiries are ongoing.'

'Do you think it's a robbery?' he said, eyeing Max.

'I'd say that we're all keeping an open mind,' said Laura.

'We've been working together for five years now. I can understand why Billy would be a target, I mean it's a risky world for the people we deal with, but who would want to kill Jules? She was the kindest, most tolerant and driven person I ever met.'

'Why didn't the meeting go ahead?'

He wiped at his face with a tissue, before answering, his hands trembling. 'I got waylaid, as always, during a meeting in Kelso, and then I realised that I'd forgotten I'd promised my ex-wife that I'd pick up our daughter from school, so I bailed on the meeting with Jules. Why? Why did I bail? If I'd have met her, just maybe this wouldn't have happened.'

'Your phone's been off all afternoon,' said Max.

Clem reached into his pocket and pulled out a scratched and worn smartphone. He pressed the side buttons, but it remained inert. 'The bloody thing died just after I spoke to Jules, and I don't have a lead with me, not that it would have worked in my old heap of a car, anyway. Shit, I'm an idiot, why didn't I bloody meet her?' He paused, while he swallowed, before his eyes widened. 'So, she was trying to contact me?'

Laura nodded.

'Oh fuck. She called, but I wasn't there for her. All because my bloody ex-wife couldn't sort out our daughter.'

'Your ex can confirm this?' said Max.

'What do you mean?' His eyes widened.

'Clem, this is a triple homicide. We need to verify everything.'

He shook his head, as if clearing it. 'Yes, of course. I'll give you her details.'

'Do you know why Juliet was engaging with Billy?' said Laura.

'He'd come forward about a newly emerging far-right group he was on the periphery of, who he was concerned were getting much worse, and who he felt were planning serious violence. She'd got him to a point where he was willing to assist the authorities, and I think he'd met our contacts from the police, and the Security Service.' He slurped noisily at his tea.

'Do you know who?'

'Cop would be one of the CT team in the North-East, not sure who, but they'd have records. She also facilitated a meet with our contact at MI5. We're usually reluctant to deal with the authorities, but sometimes needs must.'

'Do you know who from MI5?' said Laura.

Clem hesitated, colouring immediately. 'I'm not sure I'm supposed to say.' He cleared his throat, nervously.

'Fin Smith?' said Max.

'I still don't think . . .' he began.

'Clem, Fin is dead, we know it was him. We also knew that he tried to call you when your phone was off,' said Laura, flatly.

Clem's mouth gaped open. He trembled and began to weep again, head in hands, shaking like a leaf.

'Clem . . .' began Laura, but Clem removed his hands, and his eyes snapped open.

'Oh Christ, no, no, no. Fin was a weird bugger, but he was honest, and decent. What's happening, here?' he sobbed, the tears flowing down his cheeks.

'Who was the cop she dealt with?'

'I genuinely don't know. The liaison team is led by a Detective Inspector Nick Ord, but I'm not sure who they met with.'

'What did you know about National Force, Clem?' said Laura.

'Nothing. Really, barely anything. They were Jules's project, while I've been concentrating on the de-radicalisation programme we run. I know almost nothing about them other than they were an emerging threat, and I understood that the main man was in jail, Stinger, or something like that.'

'Stringer?' said Max.

'That's it. Jules was going to introduce me to Billy so I could start doing some de-radicalisation with him, as he'd apparently been captured to some degree by the ideology, even though Jules thought he was rescuable.'

'What type of work?' said Max.

'I'm lead for the Desistance and Disengagement programme, and I wanted to see what I could offer. He was helping the cops, and Fin, but he really needed help to pull back from it all mentally. I'm part of the Violence Prevention Network, whereas Jules mostly dealt with initial approaches and intelligence dissemination. God, it's so sad.' The tears began to well in his eyes, again.

'Clem, do you have anywhere else you can stay?' said Laura.

'What? Why can't I stay at home?' he said, his eyes widening.

'Look, they came looking for you tonight, they searched your house looking for you, and anyone else connected to this case is now dead.'

'But I know nothing. I never met Billy, I only met Fin once or twice, and Jules was just a colleague, and our work rarely crossed over. Anything she told me about National Force, little though it was, was just hearsay.'

'Clem, you're all we have,' said Laura.

The silence in the room was thick and unpleasant. 'I could maybe stay with my ex-wife and daughter.'

'You think that's wise?'

He opened his mouth to argue, but then snapped it shut, again. If anything, his pallor lightened a shade further. 'I guess not. I can't put them at risk, can I?'

'I wouldn't if I were you. Anyone else?' said Laura.

The silence returned in the room, as Clem sat, looking at the carpet, massaging his temples. His head snapped up. 'Look, no offence, but it's just occurred to me, but it was only Fin, Juliet and I who really knew about this. Doesn't this mean that one of your lot has leaked the information?'

'We're looking into all possibilities,' said Laura, but the discomfort on her face was clear.

He looked between Max and Laura repeatedly before wiping his eyes, and shaking his head. 'I can't stay here, I know that, but now I'm not sure I know who to trust. I'll sort myself out.' He stood, and walked over to the sink, where he splashed water over his face.

'We can arrange a safehouse for you, Clem?' said Laura.

His demeanour suddenly shifted, and the tearful grief became something else, entirely. 'I'm sure Billy thought he was safe with you lot. Jules thought she was safe, and I dare say Fin did as well.'

'Clem . . .'

'No, fuck this. I'll sort myself out. Give me a card, and I'll call you from a new line once I'm settled, but I'm taking care of myself.'

'This is madness,' said Laura.

'That's possible, but perhaps the only way I can stay alive is if no one knows where I am. Not even the police. In fact, especially the police.'

23

BARNEY AND MAX had barely spoken on the half-hour trip from Cumbernauld back to Max's cottage in Culross. Janie had taken the Volvo home to Edinburgh, and Max had offered Barney an electrical hook-up for his van at home.

'Sure, I can't offer you a spare bedroom, Barney?' said Max, as Barney parked the campervan outside.

'Nay, lad. I'm all good. Don't want to impose.'

'You're not.'

'I'm fine in Sybil.'

'Sybil?' said Max.

'It's what I call the van.'

'You never mentioned it before.'

'You—' began Barney.

'Never asked,' Max interrupted, in a terrible Yorkshire accent.

'I love old Sybil. Never lets me down, until she does occasionally let me down, but I can normally fix her.' Barney shrugged.

'Well, at least come in for a cuppa. Katie will still be up, and she'd like to say hi. We may be able to stretch to a cheese sandwich as well?'

Barney grinned. 'I never say no to a bit of free snap, lad.'

'Well, you are a Yorkshireman.'

'Eat all, drink all, pay nowt. Come on, I'm starving, and van needs a charge. It's flat as a pancake from making you all cups of tea.'

Within a minute they'd snaked Barney's electric hook-up into the garage and were entering Max's cottage. Katie looked up and smiled as they entered the living space. Evie was on her lap, looking utterly delighted about the new arrivals, and Nutmeg treated Barney as if he was a long-lost relative, fussing around his work boots, her tail lashing.

'Ayup, pup,' said Barney, as he patted her shaggy head, and Nutmeg collapsed on the floor in ecstasy of having her tummy rubbed by Barney's calloused hand.

'Hey, Barney. Long time no see,' said Katie, standing and passing Evie over to Max, and then hugging him warmly.

'Now then, love. You're looking well, and look how big little Evie's got,' he said, grinning at the little girl and ruffling her dirty blonde hair. She giggled.

'Why are you up, little lady?' said Max, sitting on the sofa with Evie on his lap.

'She wouldn't sleep, I think she wanted to see you before she went off, but now Barney is here, you may not get a look in, Craigie.' She nodded at Evie who was struggling to get to Barney from her dad's lap.

'Come on, then, love. Come and have a hug with Uncle Barney.' He held his arms out, as she crawled off Max's lap and onto Barney's. She immediately pulled herself up and grabbed at his nose.

'Don't let Ross hear that. He's still convinced he has an absolute right to be Evie's godfather,' said Max with a grin.

'Tea?' said Katie.

'That'd be lovely.'

'Cheese and ham toastie?' Max said, jumping to his feet.

'You spoil me, I'll just sit here and 'ave a natter with Evie.' Barney grinned at the little girl, his eyes creased and sparkling with mischief.

'Uncle Barney is a natural,' said Katie, as she flipped the kettle on, smiling as she looked at Barney and Evie giggling away together.

'I know. Very odd for an undemonstrative Yorkshireman who lives in a van.'

'Is he staying here tonight? I could make up the spare?'

'Nah, he's happy in his van. He's hooked up, and we have an earlyish start in the morning. Tough day.'

'Anything you want to talk about?' said Katie, a worried look appearing on her face.

Max shook his head. 'It's all good, you know the score, babe.' He smiled as he assembled a couple of toasted sandwiches and pressed them into the scorchingly hot press.

'Best not to know, I guess. I did hear a few concerning reports about some suspicious deaths in Kelso, Jedburgh and Stirling, but no details.'

Max leaned in and kissed Katie on the mouth, briefly, hoping that it would stop the line of questioning. He wanted to forget today's sights. The images from the garden in Stirling flared in his mind, vivid and raw. The pink of the gore, the open, sightless eyes, and the single neat hole in the centre of Finlay's forehead. He shook his head to chase the unwelcome memories away, feeling the familiar nip of anxiety, almost like butterflies. But butterflies with sharpened steel wings.

They cut, and almost hurt.

'Max?' said Katie, sensing his discomfort.

'All good, nae bother, babe.' He flicked open the sandwich toaster, a waft of smoke emerging. It smelled savoury, cheesy and delicious. He plated both sandwiches and took them over to the sofa, where Evie was fast asleep in Barney's arms, her face buried in his raggy, old blue fleece jacket.

Katie grinned widely, as she placed two steaming mugs of tea on the coffee table.

'You're a miracle worker, Barney. Let me get her off you and into her bed,' Katie said, squatting down and picking Evie up, shushing her with a whisper and a kiss.

'No idea how you do it, Uncle B,' said Max, as Katie headed off towards the bedrooms.

'I've plenty nieces and nephews.'

'I didn't know that.'

Barney grinned, his eyes twinkling. 'You never asked. That looks grand, I'm as hungry as a stoner with the munchies,' he said, smacking his lips as he took the plate off Max.

'You up for an early start tomorrow? We've lots to be getting on with, and Ross is gonna be under the cosh.'

'As long as Police Scotland keep paying my exorbitant day rates, I'll keep turning up, pal.'

'I guess you will. You'll need to earn it, though. This is a triple murder now, with all sorts of suggestions of bent cops, and maybe bent members of your old firm. I suspect your wage bill will climb exponentially.'

'I'll drink to that, lad.' Barney offered his mug, and Max tapped his against it.

24

THE TEAM WERE sprawled around the office, yawning and sipping coffee that Norma had already prepared before they all arrived. There was a sense of lassitude and pensiveness in the stuffy room.

'So, what's the news from the MIT teams?' said Max, as he drained his coffee and ambled over to the drip machine to pour another cup. 'Moneypenny Miles phoned me in great delight this morning to tell us we were being kept away from any further active role in the reactive murder inquiries of Billy Mackee, Finlay Smith and Juliet McNamara.' Ross shook his head, slightly.

'Really? I'd have thought they'd be grateful for extra bodies,' said Max.

'You'd think. Apparently the SIOs think we're too close to the lead in to it, and they "need some distance". Like I give a shit about that, eh? Three separate murders in a couple of days are way too much for politicians not to bloody notice.'

'I bet the Chief is getting pelters from all concerned,' said Janie.

Ross almost grimaced. 'Aye, but you know how parochial SIOs can be. The only one of them I don't bloody viscerally hate is Laura McKechnie, who is decent enough.'

'She seemed smart to me in her dealings with Clem South.'

'Aye, she's a smart cookie. What did you think of him?'

Max shrugged. 'Genuine enough. Seemed really shaken up, and clever enough to realise that having the cops sort out his secure accommodation isn't such a good idea. Laura says she's keeping an open mind.'

'She's no choice, she's so much on her plate. The poor bugger has copped the murder of Fin and Billy, as the link is so clear, and they're bringing in resources from all over to form a big team. There's a management meeting this afternoon to get a handle on the peculiarities of this case, and our presence is requested. The SIO for the Jedburgh job is John Macrae, and he's an A-grade walloper, who isn't happy that Laura has been put in overall day-to-day charge of all three under Miles.' Ross removed his glasses and tossed them carelessly on the table.

'How about the York bombing?' said Max.

'Yeah, there's another thing. The intel from Fin was sanitised and sent to the Counter Terror SIO, but he's having none of it, and is being a typical secretive cockney bastard. The DCS running the job politely thanked Miles for the intel, but said that all the chatter and the forensics on the bomb strongly point to Islamic extremist methodology that was being actively progressed.'

'Was that it?' said Max.

'Aye. You know what CT are like. Secretive, and they don't want to listen, and they don't want any assistance from us, and they won't tell us fuck all for "security reasons". Obviously, they've been asked to be kept in the loop, and will send a representative to any future meetings.'

A gloomy silence descended on the room for half a minute.

'So, what are *we* doing, then?' said Janie.

'Chief wants us to, and I quote . . .' Ross fumbled for his reading glasses, and perched them on his nose as he read from his laptop. '"Thematically investigate, prepare and promulgate a proactive strategy to investigate any connection, direct or indirect, of the Dent family, together with the OCN known as National Force to prove or disprove corrupt involvement of any law enforcement, or intelligence agency."' He sighed and shook his head. 'I've read the bastard email six times and I'm still not sure what he means, although I assume it's to make a plan to see if there are bent cops or spooks feeding the beast.'

'That's quite broad,' said Max.

'Aye, that's what I bloody said. We had witnesses, but now they're all fucking deid. We don't even have a starter for ten.'

'How about linking in with MI5, now Fin is dead? We have to bring this out into the open, right?' said Janie.

'I agree. Being secretive is all well and good, but if we're to flush out who the bastard is, we need to give them something to latch onto, right?' said Max.

'Chief is in sensitive negotiations with the buggers, and they're sending someone to the meeting, as well as someone from the Counter Terror investigation team.'

'You know who's coming from MI5?' said Barney.

Ross flicked through a sheaf of papers, balancing his glasses as he squinted at one. 'David Stafford, who is some kind of boss-level spook.'

'Dave Stafford, you say?' said Barney.

'Aye, that's what's on here.'

Barney shook his head slightly, and smirked.

'What?' said Ross.

'I remember Dave. Pencil pusher, with an inability to even begin to make a decision.'

'Trust him?'

Barney just shrugged. 'He'll go out of his way to say bugger all while talking a lot. I once heard him say, "Even if our decision is to *not* make a decision, we still have to be decisive, and not make the decision."' His apeing of a public-school accent was not impressive.

'Sounds familiar. By the way, that's the shittest impression ever,' said Max.

'Aye, from the Dick Van Dyke school of accents, eh?' said Ross.

'I think we're missing the bigger problem, here,' Barney said, thoughtfully.

'What?' said Ross, sharply.

'Well, Billy was apparently killed because he was a grass, snitching to the CEF people and then to the cops and Fin. And then Fin and Juliet get murdered. Would they do this to protect whoever they're protecting? I mean, you're never getting out of jail, ever after that, are you? Are they protecting something much bigger?'

'The man makes a good point,' said Max.

'Look, despite the bomb in York being as big as it was, there was never any evidence to link Stringer and Shorty to it, especially as Stringer was in bloody jail. There's zero chance of them getting caught, especially after it was being put down to Islamic terrorists, as the IED make-up was right out of the AQ textbooks. We've heard what CT are saying. They're convinced it's Islamic terror, not far-right, and I can't see them changing their minds now. Seems really bloody extreme to kill three innocent people over that. I mean, what are they actually protecting, beyond a bit of mid-tier drug dealing?'

'Carry on,' said Ross, narrowing his eyes.

'They're protecting someone or something else significant. Something bigger than drug dealing or racist thuggery. It makes no sense to kill three people for that alone. No sense at all,' said Barney, his eyes cast to the ceiling in deep thought.

As a deep, enveloping silence descended on the office, everyone felt the frustration crackling like static electricity until Ross broke the silence. 'I know bugger all about how MI5 work, but how would Fin have handled this once the cops handed Billy Mac over?'

Barney pursed his lips, as he considered. 'He should have been handled like a regular agent. Same rules that apply to cops apply to spies handling covert human intelligence sources, as far as I'm aware. Then again, I'm a bug man, what do I know?'

'So, there would be Fin as the handler, probably another spook as a co-handler, and then a controller authorising the meets, paying rewards, or lifestyle payments, and the like?' Ross looked at Barney over his spectacles.

'Aye, I guess. Fin was a stickler for the rules. It should all be recorded in the agent files. See if we can get Dave Stafford to give us anything at the meeting, although he may be a bit reticent. People like him often are.' Barney yawned.

'When's the meeting?' said Max.

Ross looked at his watch. 'In an hour, in the conference room here. Chief is attending, so everyone's coming here for a change, and unfortunately, I have to go. The rest of you get cracking running ideas up flagpoles, or whatever you millennials do.'

Max stood up and stretched. 'Norma, wasn't there something about one of the Dent crew being a serial thief and a drug addict?'

'Yeah, Charlie Dent, younger brother of Stringer. Revolving door inmate, apparently. Lives at home with his mum, but always getting arrested for thieving to fund his habit, particularly when Stringer was in jail.'

Janie, shifted in her seat, and her face lit up. 'Can we work that intelligence up, alongside packages for Stringer and Shorty? It may offer something.'

'Like what?' said Ross.

Janie shrugged. 'Options open, and all that.'

'Aye, you'll need to be more specific. Chief is offering intelligence support. Hold up.' Ross scrolled at his keypad on his laptop. 'Jesus, where are my fucking glasses?' he grunted, searching around his desk, which was piled high with files, mugs and empty biscuit packets.

'On your face,' said Janie.

Ross's expression darkened. 'Cheeky bastard, in your bloody face back.'

'No, I mean your glasses are on your face,' Janie said, trying to suppress a giggle.

Ross coloured as the other members of the office giggled. 'You can all piss off. Look, we're doing no good sitting here. Let's go our separate ways for a bit. Run bollocks up fucking flagpoles, and do some blue-bird thinking. There's a plan out there somewhere.'

'I may have a bit of an idea, but it's probably a bit too mad, and it'd take some resources, and maybe a bit of time,' Janie said, tentatively.

'Spit it out, then.'

Janie sat and looked at the wall for a moment. 'Max, let's take a walk, I need your perspective, and I'll buy nice coffees for us all from the machine in the hall. I may have a vague plan, but I'll need to make some calls first.'

'Aye, good idea,' Ross said. 'I'll have a hot chocolate, and get the cakes in, but don't go missing. Meeting in an hour, and I want a proper briefing with some dazzling ideas on getting to the bottom of this bloody job. It feels to me like we're nowhere.'

25

THE WOOD-PANELLED CONFERENCE room at Tulliallan was modest with a long, pale wooden table surrounded by chairs, and a spider phone in the centre. The walls were corporate blue, and the flat-screen monitor on the wall was inert. There were a few people around the table, none of whom were speaking, and most looking at their phones, or fiddling with A4 notebooks.

Chief Constable Chris Macdonald, who sat at the head of the table, flanked by Detective Chief Superintendent Miles Wakefield, spoke first.

'Okay, everyone, this is our first Gold Group meeting for this case, which is a little unusual owing to the nature of these terrible offences. I genuinely believe that to move this complex inquiry forwards, we really do need some open sharing of intelligence, so thank you all for coming. Firstly, I think it'd be helpful if we introduce ourselves, as we do have a couple of guests with us from outside the organisation. I'll start, Chris Macdonald, Chief Constable. Miles?' He looked towards his staff officer.

'Detective Chief Superintendent Miles Wakefield, I'm overseeing the three homicide inquiries of William Mackee, Juliet McNamara and Finlay Smith.'

Wakefield nodded at a female officer with long dark hair, who cleared her throat before speaking. 'DCI Laura McKechnie, I have overall SIO responsibility for the murders of Billy Mackee, Juliet McNamara and Fin Smith, primarily because of the strong anecdotal link established. John is my deputy, handling day-to-day activity in Jedburgh for Juliet. John?' She turned to look to the man to her right.

A short, stocky officer with thinning red hair and wearing a sharp suit spoke. 'John Macrae, SIO of the murder of Juliet McNamara in Jedburgh.' He turned to the Chief, and nodded.

Macdonald looked across the table at an immaculately suited man. 'Nigel?' he said.

The man, who was in his forties with short greying hair and heavy-rimmed spectacles, cleared his throat. 'DCS Nigel Barr. I manage the North-East Counter Terror teams, and I'm leading the inquiry into the Islamist terror attack in York last year.' His eyes had a bored expression to them, and his voice made it clear that of all the places he could be, a meeting room in a historic castle in Scotland was the last of them.

Macdonald moved his gaze to another pair of plainclothes men.

'Dave Stafford. Senior case officer, MI5 northern office, responsibility for liaison, and I'm also in control of a number of case officers involved in intelligence gathering and agent handling.' He was a small, middle-aged man, with thick, dark hair, wire-framed spectacles, and a pudgy nose. He wore a shabby grey suit and a lurid floral tie.

The man to Stafford's right cleared his throat. 'Detective Inspector Nick Ord, Counter Terror North-East. We work closely with Dave and his team in intelligence development and liaison with the Security Service.' He was tall, dark-haired, good-looking and sharply suited. His accent was richly north-east England.

The final person spoke, a lean, expensively dressed woman, with neat grey hair and an NCA badge around her neck. 'Charlotte O'Neill. I'm Scottish lead for the National Crime Agency Protected Persons Unit, I've been advising Miles and Laura on witness protection issues bearing in mind the nature of the inquiry.'

'Thanks to all. Now, you've all seen the briefing document that was circulated relating to the murders, which I don't think we need to go into in any level of forensic detail. Any updates?' said Macdonald.

Macrae spoke first. 'Not much in Jedburgh, boss. Scene gave us nothing. Murder caused by blunt force trauma with a heavy object. Recent CCTV shows the victim leaving a café in Jedburgh, but the quality is very poor. No obvious suspects, as yet, but my team is ploughing through CCTV and house to house. No family issues, lived alone, and was a founding member of the Counter-Extremism Forum looking to tackle radicalisation.'

'I understand that there's another founder of CEF?' said Wakefield.

Laura nodded. 'Yep, Clem South, who we've interviewed, and a witness statement has been taken. He is cooperating, although somewhat reluctantly.'

'Can we blame him, bearing in mind what happened to the others?' said Ross.

'I don't personally. We've offered assistance, and Charlotte at the NCA is ready to advise more specifically if he takes us up on the offer of protection.'

'Full cooperation I hope?' said Macdonald.

'To a degree, he is, and he's provided a witness statement. He says he knew Juliet was meeting Billy in Jedburgh. He was initially due to be present at the meeting as lead for de-radicalisation. Claims he didn't know much about Fin Smith. In fact, he's somewhat perplexed by the whole thing, and he has a cast-iron alibi for the time of Juliet's murder, and the phone data corroborates his story.'

'Is his security being addressed?' said Macdonald.

'As far as we can, but he's suspicious of cops, now, understandably. He's currently in hiding somewhere, under his own steam. I tried to get him to let us find some secure accommodation, after his place was broken in to, but he wasn't having it. He has mine and Charlotte's numbers.' Laura, looked down at her A4 book and frowned.

'That's not ideal, to say the least,' said Wakefield.

'Aye, I know, but we can hardly force him, can we? I've also flagged him nationally, so if he pops up anywhere, or his name is searched on PNC, or other police databases, I should get to hear about it.'

'Sensible. Look, I want to move on. Dave, what can you tell us about Fin's dealings with Billy Mackee?' said Macdonald.

Stafford shuffled his papers, and looked over the top of his glasses. 'This is where we have a problem, I'm afraid,' he said.

Macdonald's eyes narrowed. 'Sorry, I don't understand.'

'Billy Mackee wasn't a registered agent with us. I believe he was introduced to Nick by Juliet McNamara, but he wasn't an active agent with MI5.'

There was an audible gasp in the room.

'I thought that Billy being an informant was what this was all about?' said Macdonald.

'Not with us, he wasn't. His file certainly didn't hit my desk, and there's something else.' He paused to sip his water. 'Fin Smith wasn't an active agent handler. We'd recently removed his privileges, and his vetting status had been downgraded. He was effectively on gardening leave.'

It was almost as if the air had been sucked out of the room.

'Had he ever met Billy Mackee?' said Ross.

'Not with my authority, although he may well have done and just not reported it in as required,' said Stafford.

'So, are we saying that Fin Smith had gone rogue?' said Laura.

'It seems that way,' said Stafford.

'How about the Glock he was shot with?' said Ross.

'Not one of ours. Are we sure that it wasn't his killer's?' said Stafford, turning to Laura.

'Only Fin's fingerprints on the gun, and his DNA was in the bullet casing expelled when he was shot, and also on a number of the rounds left in the magazine. I'd say it's inarguable that it belonged to anyone except him, but are you now saying it wasn't issued to him?' said Laura.

'I can say that with all confidence. Fin Smith had never even trained in firearms. Despite what you see on the TV, the vast majority of our staff never go anywhere near guns.' A trace of a smile touched Stafford's face.

'Why was he on gardening leave?' said Laura, turning to face Stafford.

'It's unconnected to anything to do with these events.'

'Care to elaborate?' she said, her hackles clearly rising.

'Afraid not,' he said, with a little too much enthusiasm.

'Really?' she said, looking to Macdonald, and then back to Stafford.

'Afraid so. Sorry, I can't breach protocol, it's not relevant to this case.'

Laura was opening her mouth to argue, when Macdonald cut in. 'Okay, this is a conversation for another day, perhaps. DI Ord, anything to add?'

'Not a great deal, I'm afraid. I have had dealings with Juliet McNamara on a couple of occasions, and she did introduce Billy Mackee to us. I met him once after this, and then several weeks ago together with Fin, but didn't progress to registration as an official informant. I never saw him, or Fin again, after that initial meeting.'

'What did he tell you?' said Laura.

'Not much. Mostly rumours about some far-right yobbery, but nothing we were that interested in.'

Macdonald turned to DCS Barr. 'Nigel, any observations? You guys were at the forefront of the car bomb in York?'

Barr paused for a moment, almost a look of mild amusement on his face. 'I'm afraid that your man, Billy Mackee, correct?' There were nods around the table. 'Well, God rest his soul and all that, but I think I can say with confidence that he was very much barking up the wrong tree. We have solid forensic evidence that the bomb was either built by a specifically identified and well-known bomb-maker, or at the very least one of his students. The remains of the device have been subject to the most diligent scrutiny, and the experts are convinced.'

'How can they be so sure?' said Macdonald.

'Well, as I'm sure you're all aware, most IEDs have a set of identifiable similarities, in the mix of the precursor, the fuse, the initiator, and the way the things are put together, which is almost as distinct as a fingerprint. Boffin evidence from the Defence Science and Technology Laboratory at Porton Down is strongly suggestive that the make-up of this specific device bears all the hallmarks of an Iraqi bomb-maker who we understand has visited the UK in the last year or so. He must have slipped in undetected, but intelligence from covert sources makes it clear he's been here, both instructing, and building for a fairly new group, Sharia 4 UK.'

'So, you haven't considered far-right ideology as motivation?' said Ross.

Barr shook his head, with a slight, condescending smile on his narrow mouth. Clearly, he had little respect for the other members of the meeting.

'You're certain of this?' said Macdonald.

The detective sighed, dismissively. 'We have significant evidence of the fact that Sharia 4 UK are planning further attacks, so this is our focus. Not to belittle this meeting, which of course is very significant in Scotland, but my priority has to be my current live investigation.'

There was a long pause, and a sudden chill in the room, as the condescending nature of Barr's demeanour rankled. Ross's face darkened, and his mouth opened, but Wakefield jumped in, clearly eager to move the conversation on.

'Nick, did you know that Fin shouldn't have been handling sources of intelligence?' said Miles.

'No. I had no idea. I know he was under some pressure, and he seemed quite stressed, but he said nothing to me.'

'Is that it?' said Ross.

'Pretty much, plus we really thought Billy Mac was too risky to bring on board.'

'Why?' said Ross, eyes narrowing.

Ord sighed. 'He essentially wanted a free hand to deal drugs in return for giving low-grade intelligence on far-right activity. We weren't willing to acquiesce, he didn't like it, so we dropped him. Billy Mackee was a drug dealer, and we wanted nowt to do with him.'

There was another long silence in the room, as all the occupants considered the information they'd just been given.

'Let me get this straight, are we saying that if Billy was speaking to Fin, it was unsanctioned, and off books?' said Laura, brow furrowed with confusion.

'As far as I'm concerned, yes,' said Stafford.

'Same here, and I had no idea Fin was effectively suspended. We do share some degree of intel with our colleagues in MI5, but we like to keep sterile corridors between each other,' said Ord.

The silence descended again, until it was broken by Macdonald. 'Okay, folks, thanks for coming in, it's been helpful. If we can all share full contact details on the sheets in front of you, we plan on having a WhatsApp group in case of any urgent dissemination requirements.'

Ord frowned. 'That's a little unusual, boss?'

'I agree, but in a cross-border, inter-departmental operation like this, with differing email systems I'm concerned that things may accelerate, and may do so out of normal working hours, and with double-ended encryption, I think it would be at least as secure for non-classified, information sharing. I think that fast-time means of communications will be vital, don't you agree?' Macdonald looked hard at Ord.

'I guess so.' Ord shrugged.

'DCS Barr?' Macdonald raised his eyebrows looking at the detective.

Barr smiled, the insincerity dripping from every pore. 'Of course, sir.'

'Miles, over to you and your people on the reactive inquiries. Whatever resources you need, just shout and you'll have them. Dave, Nick and Charlotte, thank you, but could you hang about with Laura for a while just to make sure we've captured everything? Ross, hang back, will you? I need a moment.' He nodded as chairs scraped and the room emptied, leaving just him and Ross, who had been uncharacteristically quiet.

'Go on then,' said Macdonald, as the door closed.

'What?' said Ross.

'You're not convinced, are you?'

'Well, it does'nae sound right, even a little bit, does it? Firstly, Fin speaks to Barney, and alleges that Billy was topped because someone sold him out for being a snitch, and now we find out that he wasn't an active, official informant, or agent if you use the spook vernacular.'

'It all sounds very wrong, so what do you suggest?'

'Something a little more irregular, I'd say. My guys are working some ideas out now, are you open to all suggestions?'

'Of course, as long as they're legal.'

'They will be, but you may need to put your brave boy pants on, boss. It could get complicated.'

'It's already complicated, Ross. I have a call with the Justice Minister soon, and I'm expecting pelters. When can you let me know a plan?'

'Give me a couple of hours. Craigie and Calder were planning something, I'd best go and see what it is.' Ross stood up, nodded at the Chief and left, his jaw square, his shoulders back.

26

A couple of days later

STRINGER AND CHARLIE were sitting around the dinner table in the family home on the modest council estate in Alnwick as their mother, Marjory, set the plates down in front of them with a clatter, an angry expression across her lined, fleshy face. Her hair was dyed blonde and styled in a halo of curls, which didn't match the heavily made-up lips and blue eyeshadow. When it came to her, Stringer could never remember anything other than that vivid blue make-up against her orange-hued skin from a fake tan. She wore a printed dress, covered by a full-length, gravy-stained house coat.

'Looks champion, Mam,' said Stringer, as he stared at the dry-looking chicken, soggy vegetables, wrinkled, pale potatoes, and gravy that still had the remnants of the flaccid skin from being repeatedly heated, refrigerated and reheated. Stringer reckoned it was probably this particular gravy's third (and hopefully final) outing.

'Should be, took me long enough to cook. Now eat it all up, both of yous.' She sat down, her lips tightly pursed and as wrinkled as a dog's backside.

'Tasty, Mam,' said Charlie, as he tucked into the full, flabby roast dinner. The same flabby roast dinner that they were forced to endure every Sunday, without fail. Stringer would always struggle to eat the tasteless mass, whereas Charlie, having probably spent the last few days not eating, and out of his box on skag, would hoover the whole lot up with relish.

Stringer would also eat the lot, with less relish, but no way would he leave so much as a fossilised pea, nor a thrice-cooked carrot. Incurring the wrath of Mam wasn't worth the bother.

'When can I expect me housekeepin'?' said Mam.

Rather than answer, Stringer dug into the pocket of his jeans and pulled out a wad of notes. He handed it over to his mam, who just looked at it, and sniffed.

'What? There's two grand there, Mam,' said Stringer.

'Used to be five, minimum. You've slacked since comin' out of jail, boy. Need to step up the pace. I need a new washin' machine, and the carpet needs changing. I'm runnin' this place all alone, you know.' She sighed, and took a sip from the glass at her side. It was a clear liquid, but both Stringer and Charlie knew that it was pure vodka. Their mum drank only neat vodka, starting at noon, and steadily continuing for the rest of the day, not that either of them had ever seen her in any way intoxicated.

'I'm working on it, I'm only just out of Frankland bloody jail, so it takes a moment to get things moving again.' Stringer was, as always, disgusted with himself for his whining tone.

'Shorty hardly even kept me straight while you were away. And me a poor widow, all on me own, eh?' She dabbed at a damp eye with her handkerchief, and took another sip on her vodka.

'Mam, he gave you a grand a week, and there's no mortgage on this place. Look, we're all getting up and running again, I've a shipment coming in, and we'll be operating soon, coining it in, eh?' Stringer took a swig from his bottle of Newcastle Brown, and sighed.

'The both of yous have been too much focusin' on this political shite, constantly on the bloody internet, and angry wi' immigrants and the likes.'

'What, you think what's happening to the country is okay, Mam?' Stringer said, feeling his blood begin to fizz with anger.

'I've no idea about any of that, but you and Shorty are spendin' your money on nonsense that doesn't affect me. Your father would be disappointed.' She sniffed, and cuffed her damp nose with her sleeve.

'Mam, it's importa—' he began, but she cut him off, her thin lips pursed.

'Well, if you're happy to keep your own mam short, that's just fine, then. I guess I'll be eatin' from Aldi this week, when that Margo Johnson shops at Waitrose. And at my time of life, eh?' She pursed her lips even tighter, and they compressed until they were as tight as a rubber tea-towel-holder.

Stringer sighed again, and opened his mouth to argue, but she cut him off with an icy glare, the glare that could halt him in his tracks at a hundred metres. Yep, he knew it, and he was ashamed of it. Eighteen-stone Stringer Dent, boxer, MMA fighter, doorman, and all-round evil, ruthless, nasty gang leader who'd killed on multiple occasions was scared of his seven-stone, skin and bone, alcoholic mother, Marjory Dent.

'I'll have to tell Chubby Patterson not to deliver the washin' machine, the shame,' she said, dabbing at her eyes again.

Stringer rubbed at his face with his calloused hands, and his face suffused with blood. 'Na, man. Not Chubby Patterson, imagine the fucking jibes.'

'Well, if you spent more time graftin' than trying to change the bloody world with your stupid cause, then I don't know what to say. Chubby won't be happy, like.'

'Mam, what I'm doin' is fuckin' important. The country is going to the dogs, and I have to act.'

'I divn't wanna hear it, man. I'll phone Chubby now and cancel 'im.' She reached for the phone on the arm of the chair.

'Ah, Jesus fuckin' Christ. Don't do that. Charlie, do you have your car here?' he said.

'Yeah, why?' said Charlie, his face smeared with gravy.

'Drive over to my gaff. Box under the sofa has three grand in it. Go get it for Mam, eh, man?' He grinned at his little brother, who just scowled.

'Why me?' he said, his eyes wide.

'I've had a beer, and the cops will always be over me, the bastards. I cannat lose me licence straight after coming out of jail. There's a fifty in it for you?' he said, plucking the notes out of his pocket.

'What, now?' said Charlie, his rheumy eyes wide.

'Aye, now. Mam needs it for the washer and carpet, come on, bro.'

Charlie sighed, and pushed his empty plate away, eyeing the notes in Stringer's hand. Everyone in the room knew that he'd take it, and that he'd go and get the money. Charlie would do anything for fifty quid.

'Gan on, then,' he said, standing up.

27

CHARLIE DENT SWORE as he drove into Berwick-upon-Tweed in his scrappy old car. He quite liked Berwick, he spent lots of time here, particularly recently when Stringer was in jail, keeping an eye on his house in one of the nicer bits.

The fifty quid was burning a hole in his pocket, and much as he tried to tell himself he wasn't going to, he knew he was lying. He was probably going to spend it on a decent hit of skag and get totally out of his box once he'd delivered the cash to Mam. He wasn't quite at the withdrawal stage yet, but he knew it wasn't ages away, and the fifty from Stringer would keep him out of the shit for a bit. Charlie was a thief, and he'd steal from wherever to fund a hit when he was clucking, but he'd never robbed his big brother. Family loyalty only went so far, and they were close enough, but Charlie knew that his brother would kick the shit out of him if he stole from him. His brother had always been a scary bastard, but he'd got much worse since he'd got out of jail, and he was obsessed with the dumb politics thing, now. Worse than that, he'd tell their mam. No way was he risking that.

He was just about to turn in to Stringer's road when sirens behind him almost caused him to jump out of his skin. He looked in the rear-view mirror, and swore. A fucking cop car with lights on. He breathed a sigh of relief that he wasn't carrying and, maybe they weren't even giving him a tug? Maybe they were going to an urgent call somewhere else?

He sighed again, knowing that was bullshit, reinforced by the cop in the passenger seat pointing to the side of the road. At least he wasn't carrying any gear, and at least he hadn't got Stringer's dosh on him yet. They'd have had that away in a flash. All he had was fifty quid, and a packet of gum.

'Yes, officer?' he said after the hi-vis-clad cop tapped on the lowering window.

'Going a bit fast, pal,' he said in a broad Geordie accent. He was a square-shouldered older cop, with silver hair, and an open and friendly face, unlike most of Northumbria police.

'Aye, sorry,' said Charlie, who had learned years ago, that getting gobby with cops in the north-east often got you battered.

'Charlie Dent, right?' he said.

'How'd you know?'

'Car's registered to you in Alnwick. We checked on the mobile data terminal in the car. You aware you're on a recall to prison?'

Charlie felt his bowels turn to water. 'Ah no, man, there must be some mistake.'

'Missing probation appointments, it says on the computer. Come on, you're nicked.'

The cop leaned in, removed the keys and opened the door, and Charlie leaned forward, softly butted the steering wheel and cursed his stupid luck. Fucking jail again. He'd only been out two months from a short sentence.

Just why hadn't he gone to his bloody probation appointments?

The car door was opened by the cop. 'C'mon, fella. Cell waiting at Berwick nick.'

28

CHARLIE SIGHED AS he looked at the scratched surface of the many times painted cell door, portions of which had flaked off like blue scabs onto the worn concrete floor. It wasn't the decor that made him sigh, he'd seen it a million times, it was the fact that the door was locked, forbidding and immovable as every other cell door he'd been behind.

He'd been in many cells during his thirty-five years on this planet. He'd seen them all, from sleek and shiny purpose-built custody bridewells, with flat-screen monitors on the freshly painted walls and lots of staff and health care professionals on tap, to shit-holes reminiscent of the Victorian era, with the ever-present stench of sweaty feet, piss and microwave curry.

And this place, Berwick Police Station in the far reaches of north-east England definitely fell into the second category. He sighed again and felt the familiar shudder ripple through his painfully thin frame. He knew what this was, alongside the equally familiar rising nausea and suggestion of a banging headache. He massaged his temples and closed his eyes. He knew it was coming.

Cold turkey. Withdrawal. Clucking. More accurately, and exactly how the stern-faced police doctor arsehole had diagnosed, opioid withdrawal. He was a miserable bastard, and all he'd been willing to prescribe was a single, manky Valium that wouldn't even scratch the surface of what was already bubbling. Not even a bit of methadone. 'You're not going to die, young man. It's an addiction, not an illness.'

All this added up to one thing. He was going to be suffering very soon. He'd most likely be going to court tomorrow, and then on to prison. He'd be able to score once there, but he had no chance before then. He shuddered, violently.

His mind swam as he imagined a hit. Just a small nub of that pale, golden powder on a sliver of foil, the acrid, vinegary smoke into his lungs, and straight into his bloodstream, and the subsequent caress of the opioid. It was terrible stuff, but that first hit was something he'd never forget. Like being wrapped in a warm, soft blanket and cosseted into the deepest of dreamless sleeps.

He hadn't smoked any brown since last night, and now here he was, in this crummy, stinking cell with its stained, foul-looking fucking toilet, with the knowledge that things were just going to get worse.

He needed a fix, and he needed it very soon, or he was going to be climbing the fucking walls. His heroin habit was long and distinguished, and he had no interest in getting off the stuff. It could be a wretched existence, only made bearable as his brother gave him enough money to keep the demons at bay, but even he couldn't get him any in here at this particular moment, and there was no way he was calling him until he knew what was happening, particularly as he was expecting a load of cash from him. His stomach broiled as he realised that he would inevitably have to call him should he end up back in Frankland jail, where, coincidentally his brother had just been released from, having just bust his big case after a year on remand. He'd go fucking doolally if he knew that Charlie had been nicked again.

The rattle at the door made him look up, and the cop who'd nicked him peered through the wicket.

'Right, get your shite together, bonny lad, you're on your way oot, man,' he said in a Newcastle accent as broad and recognisable as the Tyne Bridge.

'What, to court?' said Charlie.

'Not unless you want to. You're ganning yem, man.'

'What, no court?'

'Nope. Some fuck-up on the computer, and you've got an appointment ye cannat miss, not unless ye want banging up for a year. Howay, we've things to do, and you're cluttering up the place.' A trace of a smile played across his beefy features, but it had no mirth behind it.

'I should fucking complain about youse lot,' he said, as he leapt to his feet, a sudden surge of energy chasing away the impending nausea. He knew enough dealers, and he knew exactly who his first call would be to as soon as he got his phone back. Berwick-upon-Tweed, the historic walled city, had its dealers, like every other town, and Charlie was like a truffle pig in sniffing them out. Drop Charlie on the surface of the bloody moon, and he'd be sorted for gear within ten minutes.

'Aye well, don't forget to file it in the fucking bin on your way out, bonny lad, now hadaway, clocks ticking, and I've places to be.' The cop spun on his heels and walked out, his rubber-soled boots squeaking on the scabby, stained and pitted flooring.

The custody office was busier than when he'd been booked in, what felt like ages ago, although looking at the old clock, askew on the wall, he saw it was only two hours. It had felt like years, being on the edge of turkey, as he was. If he was high, he'd have not given a shite.

A prisoner was being booked in by the friendly, matronly female sergeant who'd dealt with him earlier. She was stout, with a huge bust, and hair that reminded him of Princess Anne. She looked up and smiled apologetically at Charlie. Her name badge read, SGT JAQUES.

'A big mess-up, I'm afraid, Charlie pet. Not our fault, bloody probation service cocked it up, give us a couple of minutes and I'll get your property back. Let me just finish up with this fella, so take a seat on the bench while PC Shaw gets your stuff,' said Sergeant

Jaques, turning back to the silent prisoner who stood in front of the plexiglass shield.

Charlie muttered as he sat on the worn and shiny bench scarred with cigarette burns, a throwback to the days when a custody office such as this would have been seen filled with the omnipresent haze of tobacco smoke. He sighed, the longing for a tab almost as strong as that for some gear.

He studied the prisoner being booked in. He was tall, lean and anonymous, but it wasn't that which caught Charlie's attention. It was the pile of money that was being counted out on the desk. A huge stack of twenties all in the familiar hundred-quid folds drug dealers habitually used. Charlie narrowed his eyes and looked at the man with renewed interest. He wore Gucci trainers, expensive-looking jeans, and he couldn't help but notice the patch on the arm of the thin, dark jacket. Stone Island. Whoever this was, he was clearly successful.

He stared ahead at the custody officer, who was busy at her keyboard.

'Watch, please, Robbie,' she said, a demand, not a request.

Robbie said nothing, just removed the watch from his wrist and laid it carefully on the desk. Even from his position on the bench, Charlie could see it was a Rolex.

The custody officer turned her attention to the officer standing next to the prisoner, a young-looking, skinny female plainclothes cop. 'Any other offences, or just money laundering?'

'Just the money laundering, and a cash seizure,' said the cop.

'How much are we talking about?' said the custody officer, nodding at the banknotes.

'Not fully counted it, but we've weighed it, and we're estimating almost ninety thousand quid,' she said.

'Jesus, that's double my bloody yearly salary, man,' said the custody officer with a wry shake of the head.

'Should get a better job, then,' said Robbie quietly.

'Cheeky bugger. Right, any other property?' she said, her face hardening and turning to the cop.

'No, that's it,' said the detective.

'Right, we'll call your solicitor. As you've been arrested for a recordable offence, I'm authorising that your fingerprints, photo and a DNA swab are taken, and they'll be subject to a speculative search, okay?'

Robbie nodded. If he was nervous, he wasn't showing it; in fact, he almost looked bored.

'Right, pet. Take a seat on the bench next to Charlie over there, and when it rings pick up the phone on the wall so you can chat with your brief.' Sergeant Jacques nodded to an ancient-looking, bright red telephone that was secured to the wall above the bench, the curly flex snaking down against the scuffed wall.

Wordlessly, Robbie spun on his heels and walked over, and sat next to Charlie. He was lean and fit-looking; his face was tanned and he wore a small diamond stud that glinted in his left earlobe. The baseball cap on his head was a Lacoste.

'You all right, mate?' said Charlie.

Robbie turned and looked at him, his eyes blank and devoid of even a trace of fear. 'I'm fine.' His voice was flat and quiet, but he seemed utterly unbothered by his situation.

'No talking please, this isn't a bloody social centre. Charlie, you'll be pleased to know that as soon as PC Shaw comes back with your stuff you can sod off without any new stains on your already slightly grubby character, for this bit at least.' She bowed her head and began to tap at the keyboard, as the female detective began bagging the stacks of cash.

'Fucking lot of money to lose, pal,' said Charlie.

Robbie just smiled. A tiny uptilt in the corners of his mouth. His face was angular but not memorable, and his total absence of even a tiny vestige of fear was impressive. Charlie mused that if he was about to lose ninety K he'd be shitting himself inside out.

'Are you getting out now?' said Robbie in barely a whisper, bowing his head and scratching at his stubbled face, the rasping sound, almost, but not quite drowning out his voice.

'Yeah, why?' said Charlie.

Robbie looked up at the desk, as did Charlie. The custody officer was tapping away, her face a mask of concentration, and the cop was still busy with the banknotes.

Robbie said nothing, just smiled again, and turned to face him, his dark eyes suddenly glinting. 'Charlie, right?'

'Yeah, why?'

Robbie's smile widened and he extended his hand, which Charlie took. His grip was dry and firm, but with no trial of strength.

Charlie felt it immediately. A small slip of paper into his palm, and he balled his hand into a fist as Charlie released his grip.

Almost without moving his lips, and so quietly that Charlie could barely hear Robbie speak, he said, 'Call the number, and tell them Robbie is here. There's a nice drink in it for you.'

'Now didn't I say no bloody talking?' barked the custody officer, her eyes angry and hard just as the old phone on the wall burst to life with a shrill tone.

'Sorry, sarge, but I'm just telling your man here about the amount of compo I'm fucking getting after your boys falsely arrested me, eh?' said Charlie, feigning an aggrieved tone, as he felt his synapses fire. Charlie knew that he wasn't the greatest villain out there, but he recognised an opportunity when it fell into his lap, or more accurately, into his hand as he felt the scrap of paper nestling in his palm.

'Ah hush, man, you know the score, so take it up with probation, not us. Robbie, that's your solicitor on the phone. Charlie, your property is here, letter here for a new appointment with probation. Don't bloody miss it. Now sign here, and bugger off.' She nodded at the cop who had suddenly appeared, clutching a plastic bag containing his property.

Within two minutes, Charlie was exiting the side gate into the bright afternoon sunshine, already ripping into the property bag and pulling out his phone, which he powered up. Ignoring the predictably abusive text from Stringer, he tapped in the digits that were on the slip of paper that Robbie had handed him and pressed 'call'. The phone was answered immediately, by a voice with a soft and easy-going Scottish accent.

'Who's that?'

'My name's Charlie, I've just got out of Berwick nick, and your boy Robbie is in there.'

'Sorry, who?' came the retort.

'Robbie. He's been lifted with a pile of cash, he asked me to call, so I'm calling. He said there'd be a drink in it for me if I tipped you the wink?'

'Charlie, you say?' said the voice.

'Yeah.'

'Are you staying in Berwick for a bit?' The light Scottish accent was comforting and familiar, not harsh like in Glasgow, but soft and gentle. It was the sort of accent you'd expect your friendly old grandpa to have. A pipe-smoker's accent. He felt himself relax.

'For a while. My brother's place is here.'

'You know the Brewers Arms?'

'It's just five minutes away.'

'Okay, I'll meet you there in a wee while. How will I recognise you?'

Charlie looked down at his T-shirt, a garish, if grubby, yellow Nike top.

'I've a yellow Nike T-shirt on.'

'Right, sit at the very back on the leather bench, and I'll be there in thirty.' The phone beeped three times to indicate that the call was over.

*

The man's appearance didn't match his soft, easy-going voice. He was huge. A fucking behemoth of a man, almost a match for Charlie's brother, and his dark Armani hoodie couldn't disguise the massive build as the fabric stretched across huge biceps and boulder-like shoulders. He nodded as he sat in the chair opposite Charlie, who had been nursing a pint on the leather bench at the back of the almost empty pub.

'Charlie?' said the man, as he appraised him with piggy eyes that looked too narrow for his swollen frame. He had tightly shorn hair and his ears almost seemed as if they were in the process of being swallowed by the fleshy head.

'That's me. And you are?' said Charlie. He was a little nervous of the bullock who sat opposite him, but being used to criminals and crime almost all his life, he wasn't going to show it.

The small eyes of the newcomer assessed Charlie for a full thirty seconds, seemingly taking in his skinny arms, greasy hair and slick, spotty complexion. He shook his head, just a tiny, brief gesture, but the meaning was clear. He'd sussed out Charlie in a heartbeat. 'You can call me Jed, what's your full name, Charlie?'

'Charlie Dent.'

'Where are you from?' said Jed.

'All over the north, but mostly Berwick.'

'So, Charlie, what got you nicked in Berwick?'

'Some nonsense about probation appointments. Cops fucked up, and I reckon I'm up for compo,' he said, sipping his lager.

'Charlie Dent, you say?'

Charlie just nodded, as he swilled the cold lager around his cheeks.

'Any relation to Stringer Dent?' Jed narrowed his eyes and looked at Charlie with renewed interest.

'He's my brother, you know him?' said Charlie, stifling a burp.

'Only by reputation, I thought he was behind the door,' Jed said. The fact that he used the phrase 'behind the door' for being in prison, suggested that he too had experienced being in custody.

'He was, but he bust the case and was released a short while back. Some witnesses decided they didn't fancy giving evidence, and it seemed like a juror or two had differences of opinion on the evidence, you know how these things go. Sorry, how've you heard of him, then? He keeps his head down.'

Jed grinned, showing even white teeth. 'Similar area of business, mate. You know how it is. We know people who know other people who buy goods and services from other people on both sides of the border.'

'I guess so. Interesting. Now you want to hear about your man, Robbie?' Charlie decided that he needed to get the initiative back a little.

'Assuming we know Robbie, what can you tell us?' Jed's huge Teutonic brow creased.

'I was told there was a drink in it for me.'

'Depends what you tell us.' Jed's eyes didn't leave Charlie's.

'He passed me this.' He handed over the slip of paper, which Jed studied with interest, before smiling.

'What?' said Charlie.

'Robbie has shite writing, like a bloody six-year-old.' He sniggered and seemingly relaxed a little. 'Why's he in Berwick nick?'

'I heard money laundering, and there was a fucking big stack of readies on the desk. Cop said ninety K.'

If he was feeling any emotion, Jed didn't show it. 'He seem okay?'

'Cool as a cucumber, mate, cooler than I'd have been if I'd lost a wad like that, anyway.'

Jed nodded, as if this was all he needed to know. He reached into his jacket pocket and pulled out a fold of banknotes. Charlie felt his stomach tighten at the sight of the money. Jed peeled off a few from the sheaf and slid them across the table. 'There's two hundred there, in appreciation for services rendered, pal.' He nodded and stood up.

'Is that all?' said Charlie.

'Aye, what else?' said Jed, his face quizzical.

'What's gonna happen to Robbie?'

'We'll find out soon once the lawyer gets to him, but you've given us time to make sure our decks are clear in case the cops start searching. We've a business to protect, and we can make sure we're squeaky clean. If it's just money laundering, he'll be out soon enough, they'll never get enough on him now. It's just money, Charlie. It's not illegal to have money if there's no crime.'

'Aye, but I'd like to check in with Robbie, he seems a good bloke, can I call again?' Charlie said, trying not to gabble. Two hundred quid, just for making a phone call, meant that the big bullock of a bloke in front of him may present further opportunities.

'I'm ditching this burner in a few days, but you could send a WhatsApp, and we'll get the message. I'll talk to Robbie when he gets out and maybe he'll call you. Is your brother looking for business?' Jed stared hard, seemingly studying Charlie. It wasn't a comfortable feeling.

'Depends on what's on the table. You know his rep. He's big time, man.' Charlie hoped he wasn't overcooking it. These really did look like proper people, and it was a chance to show his brother that he wasn't just a useless junkie.

'What do you reckon we are, Charlie?' Jed lowered his head, and looked across his eyebrows at him, his face as hard as granite.

Charlie felt a shudder of fear begin to tickle the nape of his neck. 'You look serious enough to me, man. Stay in touch, eh?'

A huge grin spread across Jed's face, and it wasn't reassuring, and it wasn't comforting. It was hard, harsh, and no part of it reached the big man's eyes. Charlie had seen eyes like that before, and always on the faces of serious, dangerous people. Killer's eyes.

One thing was for sure, no way was he underestimating Jed. There was a long silence, that in reality was no longer than ten seconds, before the big man spoke. 'Be lucky, Charlie, stay out of jail and spend the two hundred wisely.' Jed nodded, stood, turned and strode off, his huge back almost blocking the light out, as he loped off, his legs having to circle slightly as his thighs were so huge. Clearly someone not to mess with. His fingers played with the banknotes, and his stomach quivered knowing what was next. He picked up his phone and composed a text to his brother.

Sorry man, got waylaid. Fucking cops tugged me. Just got out of Berwick nick, all some bullshit.

The reply was instantaneous. *Tell me you weren't carrying the money? Mam is going mental.*

Charlie's fingers tapped a reply. *No, it was before I got to yours. I'll get it now.*

Hurry up, man. She's being a fckn nightmare.

Charlie's fingers hovered over the keys, wondering if he should mention the meeting with Jed, and Robbie. He nodded to himself. Here was an opportunity to look good. Maybe an intro of a decent-looking firm. He tapped out a message. *Just had an interesting meeting with some jock in a boozer in Berwick. Big money men. I've got a number, we need to have a chat about them, you wanted a Scottish connection?*

The reply was instantaneous. *You need to watch your trap, man. Busy now, meet me later on this evening in the Wick.* The message clear. A meeting later on in Alnwick.

Charlie grinned; his brother would love this. Some smart-looking chaps from Scotland, maybe this would get him some respect, which was usually sadly lacking from his brother.

He looked at the scratched and fading fake Omega on his wrist. He had plenty of time. He dialled a number from memory, which was answered immediately.

'Charlie, man. You okay?' said the croaking, droney voice.

Creaky was a heroin dealer who had a trap house just a mile away from where Charlie currently was.

'Creaky, I'm in Berwick, can you sort me out?' he said, feeling the desperation begin to ratchet as it always did once he knew he was about to score.

''Course I can, man, 'course I can. Come round now.'

Charlie grinned with relief. A quick score from Creaky, maybe a livener, then back to Mam's with the dosh. After that, oblivion beckoned.

29

ROBBIE YAWNED AS he sat down onto the wafer-thin mattress, taking an exploratory sip of the tea that the chirpy jailer had handed to him as he had ushered him into the cell. It was weak and lukewarm. He grimaced and laid it gently down on the sticky, worn flooring. He sighed and arched his back, feeling the ache in his lower back muscles, probably the result of an excessively tough deadlifting session the previous day.

Despite his predicament, Robbie felt no nerves, in fact he was almost enjoying the brief moment of silence after a hectic twenty-four hours. He knew it wouldn't last long, the way things were progressing, and he suspected that life was about to get very interesting, and probably a lot more demanding. He was ready for it.

His fingers went to his wrist, feeling the skin where his watch would normally be, now that the Rolex was tucked away in a property bag in a police store, no doubt being ogled by the cops that had booked him in. Rolexes had that effect on people. The fact that a small timepiece on a gaudy bracelet could be worth more than a cop earned in a year was always intriguing to Robbie.

One thing was for sure. There was no way he was getting that watch back. The cops would be very keen to keep hold of it. He smiled at the prospect. A watch could be as much camouflage as the ridiculous Stone Island jacket, fancy trainers and cheap jeans made expensive only by the Armani label on the back pocket. An image created with sweat-shop-produced designer wear that only really differed from Primark because of the price tag.

But it served a purpose. People like him had to dress as the customers expected. To dress in supermarket clothes was akin to wearing a sign around your neck that said 'no mark loser'.

And Robbie wasn't a loser.

Robbie was a mid- to high-level narcotics trafficker, shifting kilo numbers of high purity cocaine and heroin from northern England into Scotland, ostensibly to fill the vacuum that was left when another network of top-level drug dealers were taken out by the cops in Scotland.

Footsteps in the corridor made him look up towards the cell wicket, which rattled and shook as whoever was on the other side of the door tried to work the sticky, old-fashioned mechanism that had probably been in place for close to a hundred years by the look of the thickness of the chipped and peeling paint.

A voice, shot through with frustration, was just audible outside the door as it muttered muffled expletives in a hard-edged Scottish accent. 'Fucking bastarding shite of a thing. This place is a bollock of a bawbag cop shop.' The wicket rattled and clanked. A smile stretched across Robbie's face at the familiar voice.

There was a brief pause, and then a thump from the bottom of the door as the person the other side delivered a swift kick, followed by a muted grunt of pain. 'Ach, my fucking foot, piece of shite thing,' rang out as the voice got louder.

Robbie's smile widened, and he had to stifle a chuckle, just at the point that the voice went from an angry mutter to a bellow. 'Will some bastard come and open this total fud of a fucking door? It's pushing me awa' the fucking line, man.'

There were more footsteps squeaking down the corridor, followed by a jangle of keys, and then the heavy cell door swung open with an arthritic creak.

A hefty man, with untidy hair, wearing a shabby, ill-fitting suit, and a grubby and creased white shirt filled the doorway. His shiny blue tie was managing to be both askew and too short, and his meaty features surveyed Robbie with a scowl. A silence filled the cell.

'I cannae believe you've dragged me down to this bastard shite-heap of a polis station on a shagging Sunday, in the fucking middle of bloody nowhere, you utter dobber,' he said, his twinkling eyes betraying his furrowed brow, bristling eyebrows and angry demeanour.

'Hello, Ross,' said Robbie.

'You look like a ponce, Craigie. What's with the bloody earring? Think you're David bollocking Beckham, eh?'

'Camouflage, boss. Has it worked?' said DS Max Craigie, hitherto known as Robbie, the drug trafficker.

'Aye, like a bastard spider to a flame.'

'Moth to a flame. It's spider to a fly,' Max said, a smile spreading wider on his face.

'Ach pish off, numb-nuts. The surveillance team picked him up as he left. Straight on the phone to the number you gave him, and he met up with big scary Jed in the boozer a wee while ago, then scored. He's name-checked Stringer already. Hook, line and sinker, pal. Bloody good idea of mine, eh?'

'I've a distinct memory that it was mostly Janie's idea, but it's looking good. Now what?'

'Bollocks, she heard me discussing it with someone, and then stole it, the bloody thief. Typical "high potential development" behaviour, that is, ripping off someone else's idea as your own.' Ross furrowed his brow, but his eyes told the usual tale.

Max shook his head. 'So we're looking good?'

Ross nodded. 'The wee junkie is two-hundred-quid richer, so I imagine he'll be out of his box on skag by now. We'll give him a day or two to spaff all his cash, and then we'll make contact, dangle a carrot and see what happens. You ready to get out of here?'

'Aye, place stinks of pish and sweaty feet, and I told Katie I'd be home tonight in time to tuck wee Evie into her bed.'

'Damn straight. You look after that wee toot, you don't get a second chance at this stuff, you know.' Ross's face softened.

'I'm trying, but my DI is a bloody slave-driver,' said Max, standing up.

The soft and sensitive look immediately changed to his usual scowl. 'Aye, well, there's a bloody job in Traffic with your bloody name on it if you like?'

'Hours would be better.'

'You'd be shite at it. Right, let's piss off then. Custody office is fully cleared, apart from the lovely Sergeant Hattie Jaques, who knows the score, unlike all the rest of the woolly suits. We've done it all above board, so anyone looking at the paperwork will see that audit trail and will see that Robbie fucking Oliver, or whatever your stupid cover name is, was in custody for money laundering, and was bailed out. Once this job is done, we'll cancel the bail and it'll be like you were never here.'

'So, no further action like all your other cases.' Max chuckled.

'Piss off, I have a great charge record and anyway, Janie is on the custody sheet for this so it can be her failure. Come on, Hattie is waiting to "bail you out", and we can all go home.' Ross mimed quotation marks with his fingers.

'Hattie Jaques? Are you on first name terms?'

'No. I've no idea what her first name is, but she reminds me of Hattie Jaques. You know, "Ooh, matron".' Ross guffawed in a terrible impression of Kenneth Williams, but then stopped when he saw Max's blank face.

'Tell me you know who Hattie Jaques is?' said Ross, his eyes hardening.

'No idea. Is she an ex-lady friend?'

'No, you fud, she was the portly matron in the *Carry On* films.'

Max just shrugged. 'Not a clue, Ross. Remember how much younger I am than you.'

Ross just exhaled. 'I can't bloody stand working with millennials. *Carry On* was the basis of everything that was great in British humour back in the day. Come on, let's go. Janie's in the car in the yard.'

'No, I'm not. I'm here,' said Janie Calder, appearing in the doorway, grinning.

'Are we all clear?' said Ross.

'Aye, just your bird Sergeant Jaques there, and she's all set. Want to hear the news from Norma back at HQ? She's been monitoring Charlie Dent's phone.'

'Go on, and never refer to her as my "bird" again. Mrs Fraser would give me fucking pelters if she heard you. Anything from the office?' said Ross.

Janie smiled. 'As soon as he split from big scary Jed he sent a text to a number that was cell-sited in Alnwick. It replied straight away. Want to know the interesting thing?' Janie smiled.

'Why do you always do this? Is it a fast-track fud thing to pose daft questions? Of course, I want to bastard know.' Ross exhaled in exasperation.

'Well, it's a brand-new burner, bought just a few days ago. Want to know what Norma found out?' Janie grinned.

'I'm definitely transferring you to the bloody Outer Hebrides, you soppy mare. What?'

'It was bought with a bank card registered to a Mrs Marjory Dent.'

'What, as in scary matriarch of the Dent family, the only person that Stringer claims to fear?'

'Aye, the very same.'

A big grin stretched across Ross's face. 'Nice. I'm glad I had the genius to poach that cake-eating analytical ninja from the NCA, despite her petulant gobbiness. Looks like we're on, and all set up in a day and a half, thanks to my inspired bloody leadership, and can-do attitude. You ready for this, Max?'

'Damn right I'm ready,' he said, trying to ignore the nagging feeling of unease that was beginning to rise in his gut.

'How about you, Janie?' said Ross, staring hard at the detective.

'Aye. Why not, if it becomes necessary. Have to break my undercover cherry, eh?'

'You did a bit up that Munro last year,' said Max, stifling a smile.

'Aye. Walked up a hill and nothing bloody happened, a great top-level infiltration, that was.' Janie shook her head, smiling sarcastically.

Max clapped his partner on the shoulder. 'This one will be different, that's for sure.'

Ross nodded, his face firm. 'Then let's get on with it. Operation Sentinel is go.' Ross made a chopping motion with his hand.

'What, like *Thunderbirds*?' said Max, his eyes wide in surprise at Ross's excited outburst.

'Eh?' said Ross, his brow furrowed.

'Like "Thunderbirds are go!"' Max mimicked Ross's chopping hand.

'Piss off, Craigie. Come on, let's get weaving. Operation Sentinel is now active. Is that better for you, you soulless bugger?' Ross's smile was full of sarcasm.

'Aye. Let's go.'

30

'**SO, WHO THE** fuck was he, then?' Stringer glared at Charlie, as they sat in the front room of Mam's place.

Charlie shrugged, shifting his elbow on the crocheted arm protector of the floral armchair he was in. 'Some rich-looking Jock.' His stomach was roiling, a mix of nerves, and the need for a fix growing stronger by the minute. He'd allowed himself a quick toot of the brown at Creaky's place, but it hadn't been enough. It was telling that he hadn't smashed the lot, but such was his fear of his big brother that he'd stopped after the first hit of the acrid smoke. He'd do the lot once Stringer was finished with him. His brother wouldn't notice, as he'd probably be knee deep in some mental dark-web load of shite, convincing himself about Jewish bankers, or the great replacement theory. He'd tried to get Charlie interested, claiming the reason he was addicted to skag was the Jews. Or maybe the Muslims. Or possibly the WEF (whatever that was). Whatever. Charlie didn't really give a monkey's.

'How'd you know he was rich?' Stringer's steely voice dragged him from his skag-induced reverie.

'What, apart from the ninety grand on the table?'

Stringer glowered at his brother. 'May not have been his, man. How else?'

'Rolex, Armani jeans, Stone Island jacket. He was minted, man. And the way the big unit in the pub went on, it was like ninety grand was fuck all. He knew you by reputation, and he knew you'd been behind the door.'

'Who?'

'The big guy in the boozer. I only exchanged a couple of words with Robbie, like I said, but he looked the real deal.'

'What was his name?' Stringer said with a sigh.

'Jed.'

'Jed what?'

Charlie shrugged.

'See his car?'

Charlie shook his head.

Stringer let out a snort of irritation. 'Fuck's sake, man. Think he's a player?'

'I'd say so. Robbie was cool as a cucumber, like it was all no bother, being nicked with ninety bags. Not a massive fella, but he looked hard, Stringer. Proper hard. All in the eyes, man. And the big bastard in the pub looked dangerous.'

'What'd he say?' Stringer's eyes didn't move from Charlie's and were like two laser cutters, boring into his.

'He said that if we WhatsApp him, they'll get the message, although he also said he's ditching the burner, so I don't know how.'

Stringer narrowed his eyes, as if considering this fact. 'He sounds careful. I like that, but not as fuckin' careful as me. Let me think about it.'

'From what he said, they had lots more bunce hidden away, and me giving them the lowdown meant they could secure it. Maybe there's another drink in it for us, Stringer?' A wave of nausea gripped Charlie's stomach, vice-like and intense, but other than a tensing of his cheek muscles, he gave no sign of unease. Stringer would go fucking nuts if he knew.

Stringer leapt to his feet, his face darkening, and he loomed over Charlie, his face hard, and jaw tight. 'We don't need a fucking drink, man. We've a shipment coming in, and we need fucking wholesale customers who are gonna buy weight.

I've a fucking huge debt with some very bad bastards from Amsterdam, and I need to turn fifty keys of Charlie into bunce very bastard quickly, and a decent price on the key so I can pay them for the line of credit we have on the shipment, you understand me?'

'Defo, Stringer, man. They looked serious.' Charlie nodded, enthusiastically.

'Any photo of him?'

'Not in the cells.'

'Not him, you muppet. Jed, the bloke in the pub,' Stringer almost shouted.

'I couldn't. He was a big, scary bastard.'

'Why didn't you get a more info, or at least a photo of the bastard I could show around? We've no idea who they bloody are, and the names could be shite, for all we know.' Stringer's face had reddened, and his eyes had become hard and steely.

Charlie looked downcast, his eyes focusing on his stained Converse. 'Sorry, Stringer.'

'You fucking let me know if the bastard calls.'

'Are we calling them?'

'I don't fucking know. I'm gonna ask around and see if anyone's heard of them, that's a first, but you need to watch your bloody mouth, brother.'

'You want the number?'

'Of course I want the number. Send it to me, and then delete it from your phone, last thing I want is you bloody texting them while ripped to the tits on brown.'

Charlie nodded, and quickly sent the number to Stringer, who looked at his handset when the phone pinged.

'Now fuck off, and stay off the skag. I cannat deal with Ma moaning to me about you.' Stringer leapt to his feet and stormed out of the room.

Charlie sighed with relief when he heard the front door slam, and the big burble of the Mercedes spark to life. His hand went to his pocket where the wrap of brown was, and he felt the familiar tingle of anticipation in his stomach. Maybe just one little hit, just to calm the nerves.

31

MAX WAS SITTING at the kitchen table in the cottage in Culross, holding out a spoon on which there was some unidentifiable mix of potato and something brown. It could have been Bolognese sauce, or it could quite easily be chilli. Or maybe just mince. Whatever it was, Evie was not interested, and shook her head as he offered her the spoon of questionable food.

'Come on, sweetheart. It's delicious,' he said, miming eating it with accompanying appreciative yummy noises. Evie was clearly not impressed; instead, she looked down at Nutmeg's shaggy head. 'Oof, oof,' she cooed, in a fair impression of a bark.

Max proffered the spoon again, and she reluctantly opened her mouth, allowing him to shovel the slop in. 'That's better, is it nice?'

Evie just scowled and picked up her Postman Pat van. 'Babat,' she said, holding it out to Max, her mouth full of slop.

'She's fussy, our daughter,' said Max, as Katie walked into the room, a big pile of washing in her arms.

'I know. She's done half of it, so that's fine. It was a huge portion,' she said, dropping the washing down on the sofa and stroking Evie's curly blonde hair.

Max spooned a little into his mouth and grimaced at the bland slop.

'Don't pull that face. It's nutritious ragu, full of blitzed veg.'

'It tastes of actual nothing. I didn't realise that nothing had a taste, but it does, and this is what nothing tastes like,' he said, stirring it into a vague brown sludge.

'Well, then you cook her food,' said Katie, without irritation.

'I would, but I'm always at bloody work,' said Max, standing up and walking the leftover food to the bin, where he spooned it in.

'Been nice to have you home today. Has Ross discovered a sympathetic gene?'

Max laughed. 'Strangely, he has. He's always telling me to go home and see his goddaughter.'

'Still banging that drum, eh?' Katie chuckled, and wiped Evie's mouth that was smeared with orange-red slop.

'Aye. Should have seen his face when he heard how much Evie loves Uncle Barney.'

'I can imagine the language. Is there nothing going on, then?' Katie began to fold the washing.

As Max pulled Evie out of the high chair and cuddled her tightly, a familiar putrid smell wafted up. 'Oh-oh, we have a code brown situation,' said Max, ignoring the work-related question. He wasn't keen to tell Katie at this point that he was on the cusp of a major undercover infiltration into a murderous criminal gang with far-right extremist sensibilities.

'Your turn, and you didn't answer my question about work,' said Katie.

'A few things bubbling. It may get busy soon, or it may not. We'll see.' He pulled out the change mat from behind the sofa, and deposited the giggling and wriggling Evie on it.

There was a vibration in his pocket; it was the phone they'd set up for the undercover operation. A plain, simple Android. He pulled it out and looked at the screen, his stomach tightened as he saw the message.

It was from Charlie Dent. They'd bitten. The message was brief and to the point. *My brother wants to meet you.*

Max just sat back looking at the six innocuous combinations of vowels and consonants, but each one carrying way more potential than they had a right to. His fingers hovered over the keyboard, but then he hesitated.

Not now.

Not yet. No need to appear too eager.

Katie's voice made him jump. 'Whose phone is that?' The words carried an edge.

Max looked up at his wife, who was looming over him, her expression a mix of curiosity and suspicion.

'Work phone, babe,' but he knew his voice wasn't as confident as he'd intended.

'No, it's not. Your work phone is charging on the bedside table, and your own phone is on the table, covered in ragu sauce.' She folded her arms and cocked her head to one side, a look Max knew well.

'I should have been clearer, it's an extra work phone. For a specific job.'

'What job?' Katie unfolded her arms and put her hands on her hips, the right side of her mouth tilted upwards. He knew it then. He'd been rumbled.

'Just a wee thing we have bubbling.'

'Tell me it's not an undercover job, Max?' she said, her eyes showing a touch of fear.

Max said nothing, he just turned to Evie, who was happily on her back with Postman Pat in her hand. He began the process of changing her nappy, but his stomach was churning, and not because of the ripe smell his daughter had produced. Previous undercover deployments while in London had been long, difficult and intense, and Katie had hated them.

'Max, don't think that changing Evie's crappy nappy will get you out of this. Is it an undercover job?'

Rather than answer, Max carried on the task at hand. When done, he stood Evie up and kissed her on the top of the head. She took a few faltering steps, before sitting down with a bump, and crawled away towards a shape sorter that was a few feet away.

Max smiled, looking at his wife, as he balled the nappy up. 'It's nothing at the moment, babe. Just prep work, may fall at the first hurdle.' He tried for 'bright and breezy' but he knew she wasn't buying it.

'So, what was the message?'

'Come on, babe, you know the score, it's nothing. I may just have to go to a meeting with some people.'

'Is this connected to the big headlines about murders in the Borders and Stirling that I saw on telly?' Concern had crept into her normally warm Yorkshire-tinged accent.

'Can we change the subject, and enjoy the rest of the day? It's lovely and warm. We should take Nutty for a walk,' said Max, dumping the dirty nappy into a bag, and then into the bin.

'Max, please not undercover, again. It was bloody hateful last time you did it. Interminable hours, constant worry about a knock at the door, or a phone call. You're a dad, now.' Katie's eyes were dampening as she spoke, and Max felt his heart breaking, but he knew.

He knew it was already too late. The die was cast, and the roadmap to infiltration was now wide open. All he could hope for was a quick resolution, or at the worst, a quick exit strategy. But this case was now too serious, too important, and it had way too much riding on it.

It was going to happen. The question was, how much did he tell Katie?

He sighed, walked over to his wife, hugged her tight and kissed her on the top of the head. It smelt clean, and fresh. 'It's just a quick one. A short job. I'll introduce someone else, and I'll withdraw. A week at most.'

Katie looked up at him, eyes sad. 'You'd better not be lying to me, Craigie.'

Max grinned. 'Come on, let's go for a walk.'

So, they went for a walk. A small family of three, with their little dog scampering in the beautiful countryside, and Max wore an almost seraphic smile.

But his thoughts were on the images that flooded his mind. Memories of Fin Smith, dead in that garden chair, his brains decorating the patio, his eyes open but empty.

He knew that something had changed within him, as he looked at his daughter in the pushchair, her beautiful face shining in the sun. Normally he'd be full of excitement about an undercover deployment.

As he looked at Katie, she smiled and grabbed his hand, entwining her fingers around his. 'Don't you go sodding off for weeks on end, Craigie,' she said, before reaching up and planting a soft kiss on his cheek.

'I won't, I promise.' But even as he said the words, he wondered if they were true.

He tried to immerse himself in the scenery, and the comfort of being with his little family. But he couldn't drag his thoughts away from Daniel Solomon, Fin Smith, Juliet McNamara and Billy Mackee.

A new emotion pushed the others away, and it was familiar, and almost comforting. Justice.

He wanted justice.

32

MAX LOOKED AT the massive form of DC Joe Blair, and nodded as they sat in the BMW X5 that was parked up in the station car park in Inverness. Joe was a behemoth of a man, and his huge, hulking form was only saved from being intimidating by the glint in his friendly eyes. His shaven head, football casual gear and Omega watch completed the image of a successful drug dealer. Despite the hard exterior and massive build, Joe – also known as Jed – was a sharp character, and a kind-hearted man with a wife and two kids who lived not far from Perth.

Joe was usually a DC on a CID team in Perth, but was on the level 1 undercover index, and was now seconded to Policing Standards Reassurance. No longer a standard detective investigating robbery, burglary and assault, he was now playing the part of a minder to a successful drug courier. He certainly looked the part.

'Different from our last job, eh?' said Max.

'Aye, Midlands when you were still a Met cop?'

'That's right. Contract killer case. Scary Bosnian bugger. I take it he's still in the jail?'

'Bloody hope so. This one's looking good, though. A classy plan for a cold infiltration, which is much better than an informant introduction. I hate bloody trusting snouts.'

'Aye. Good idea from Janie. They contacted us, rather than the other way round.'

'You all ready for this, Joe?' said Max, who was dressed in designer jeans and an Armani Polo shirt, his usual G-Shock replaced with a hideous Rolex. The gold ear stud and gaudy rings completed the look.

'Aye, *Robbie*. Ready as I'll ever be.' Joe winked and held up his fist, which Max bumped his against. His phone buzzed on the dashboard. Max read the message and then deleted it. His personal phone was with Janie who was in a support car in another car park just off the town centre. Just his cover phone that had no messages, or numbers stored on it. A burner. As Stringer would expect Robbie would be carrying and what he'd find should he happen to look at it.

'Surveillance team have reported that both are already there, ground floor just to the right of the door, just Charlie and Stringer, with no sign of any counter-surveillance in place. In fact, they're currently in the middle of a bit of beer pong.' Max chuckled as he set the phone down on the centre console.

'Beer pong?' said Joe, his voice not in keeping with his physical appearance, being as it was soft and lyrical.

'Aye. One of those activity boozers with beer pong, foosball and axe throwing. A decent place to use, nice and busy for a first meet. You'll recognise Charlie, yeah?'

Joe nodded. 'Skinny wee gadgie, I can't believe that Stringer will want to talk business with him present, so maybe we'll go and play foosball whilst you big boys talk big deals. I'll be all deferential to you, like, boss.' He sniggered.

'Cool. Is your legend all tight?' said Max, referring to the backstory that they'd been imprinting on themselves over the two days since Charlie sent the message to Max's operational 'burner'.

'Dead tight, but I'll just play the muscle. Strong and silent,' he said.

'That's good, because your pleasant central belt accent doesn't fit the hard case image,' Max said, grinning.

'You can talk, ya teuchter bastard. I'm ready as I'll ever be, how much you looking to get them to supply?'

'As much as possible. Let's see how big time they really are, eh?'

'Nice one. I love this bit, don't you?' Joe looked at Max, his eyes twinkling with excitement.

'Which bit?' said Max.

'Pre-deployment. About to leave the car, right into the lion's den to meet up with some proper mad, bad bastards, and try and convince them that we're equally bad, and that what they really want to do is sell us a stack of class A drugs. It's a buzz, man. Way better than neighbours' disputes about dog shite on the pavement.'

'I think you're more up for it than me, mate. My wife isn't happy I'm undercover again. She always hated it.' Max's stomach felt curious, and he realised that he was more nervous than he had thought.

'Mine knows sod all. She thinks I'm on a course at Gartcosh. She panics like crazy, which in turn makes the kids jumpy.' The big man's huge forehead creased with worry lines.

'I'm surprised they agreed to come up here from Berwick, they must be desperate for new territory,' said Max, changing the subject as he fiddled with his phone.

'A good test, offering them a meet here. Plus, it limits their reach and puts us in the driving seat. They clearly want a piece of teuchter land, and this is the place to be. Is the phone working, okay?' Joe nodded at the basic-looking smartphone in Max's hand.

'Aye. Ross has just messaged saying we're loud and clear.' The phone in question had a few extra features. It had a mic fitted that would transmit all conversation within reach, irrespective of whether the handset was powered up. It also had a panic button on the side in case they needed urgent backup. Max had made the call that he wouldn't wear a concealed recorder, or earpiece, in case he was searched.

Max looked at Joe. 'We ready, then?'

There was a moment of silence between the two men as they locked eyes, their faces impassive. Something passed between them. Something intangible, and unfathomable to those who hadn't done work like this. Stepping into the lion's den with a savage, murderous criminal.

Max broke the silence. 'Let's go.' They got out of the car, and walked towards the station and through the concourse before emerging onto Academy Street in the bustling capital of the Highlands. The bar was almost opposite the station. A fairly new building over several floors.

Max looked at his watch, the stark gold metal glinting in the early afternoon sun. 'We're appropriately late, let's go.' They crossed the road heading towards a sign above a door that read, PLAYBACK. DRINK. EAT. PLAY. INVERNESS.

33

STRINGER AND CHARLIE Dent were either side of a huge foosball table, in the open-plan bar that was all exposed industrial fittings, ducts and polished concrete flooring. Graffiti art adorned the concrete walls, and music played. It was nothing like the boozers in Berwick. Charlie spun his handle and the ball went shooting up the table and past his brother's goalie. Stringer scowled, feeling his face reddening, and his forehead creasing.

'Hard luck, bro,' said Charlie, resisting the urge to laugh, knowing the total absence of humour his brother had when it came to his proficiency in physical pursuits.

'Bollocks. Stupid fucking game,' he said, spinning the handle with venom.

'Another game?' said Charlie.

'Another fucking pint would be better, where are these Jock bastards?' he said, as he almost stomped back to the high stool and sat down, grabbing his half-finished beer and swallowing the cold lager in one go. 'Fetch the beers then, man,' he said, tossing a twenty-pound note at Charlie.

'Keep the change?'

'Jesus, you're a fuckin' disgrace. Keep your bloody eyes open while you're there. Only reason you're here is because you've met them. Once they're here, I want you out of the way, yeah?'

'Might want to give the beers a minute, and I may need another couple of quid, we have company,' said Charlie, nodding towards the door. Two men had entered the pub, one massive, with a shaven head, enormous chest, boulder-like deltoids and the familiar walk of a bodybuilder: arms away from the chest and the typical loping gait of someone whose quadriceps were big enough to impede normal walking. He was accompanied by a much smaller, but physically fit man, with a shaven scalp that reflected the harsh overhead industrial lighting. His face was blank, but his eyes shone with intelligence as he surveyed the bar. The gorilla nodded in their direction.

'Is that them?'

'That's Robbie and Jed,' Charlie said in a whisper that would probably have been heard from the far end of the vast space, even over the music that was playing out of the hidden speakers.

'Shut up, man.' Stringer's whisper was coarse and full of venom, as he watched the gorilla named Jed nod towards Charlie. Stringer locked eyes on the smaller one, like a cobra fixating on a rodent. He was a predator, and this was his prey.

Stringer got off his chair, and stood, arms away from his body, his chin up, as he surveyed the two men like an alpha dog getting ready to meet a newcomer to the pack.

Robbie and Jed approached the table and stopped about a metre away from Stringer and Charlie. A tense, frigid silence hung between them, despite the background music in the bar.

'Welcome to the Highlands, I'm Robbie.' He extended his hand, and a smile stretched across his face. Stringer was used to people being intimidated by his very presence, so it was a strange situation to see Robbie, who was several stones lighter than him, clearly totally unmoved. He looked as relaxed as you'd expect someone to be if Stringer were a double-glazing salesman.

Stringer offered his hand, eyes locked on the newcomer. Robbie's handshake was firm and confident, but with no attempted display of machismo; probably because he could see that Stringer could have crushed his hand with ease. Stringer's eyes didn't move from Robbie, who didn't flinch and didn't avert his gaze. Despite the size disparity, Stringer could tell that Robbie was not to be underestimated. A nose that had clearly been broken, a firm jaw, knotted and corded muscular forearms, and a shaven head that bore a couple of small scars. But it was his eyes. Clear, open, full of intelligence, but totally devoid of fear. Stringer let a smile creep onto his face. 'Stringer,' he said, as he pumped the newcomer's hand, and grinned. Robbie returned the smile and sat on one of the vacant stools.

'Glad to meet you. I've been asking around. You have something of a good reputation, Stringer,' he said, in a soft Jock accent.

He eyed Robbie some more, before turning to Charlie, another banknote in his hand. 'Gan and get the beers in, Charlie, maybe see if the big man Jed here fancies a game of foosball?' He jutted a thumb at the huge Jed but didn't look at him, making the point that he wasn't intimidated by the size of the bloke. Stringer was a big guy himself, but Jed was fucking enormous, and again, didn't look daft. He concluded there and then that he was probably more than just a minder to Robbie.

'Fancy a game, Jed?' said Charlie.

'Aye, why not,' said Jed, in a soft accent, not looking in the least bit put out at what could have been taken as disrespect.

'What are you drinking?' said Robbie, pointing at the half-drunk beers on the table.

'Some weird IPA he ordered. Grapefruit shite.'

'Thought you'd be drinking Newky Brown.'

'I'm not a Geordie, man.' Stringer felt his hackles rising a touch, but smiled anyway. He was a Northumberland boy, not a Geordie, but he decided to let it pass.

'We'll have the same,' said Robbie, picking his phone out of his pocket and laying it on the table.

'Phones-off type of convo?' said Stringer, eyeing the phone, suspiciously.

'Aye, if you like, as long as you do the same.' Robbie made a big show of picking up the phone and powering it down, holding up the screen for him to see.

Stringer grinned, and did the same with his phone, placing it next to Robbie's on the table. It flitted through his mind, the incongruity of a newish-looking boozer having worn tables. He made a bet with himself that the scratches and gouges were made in the factory when the table was manufactured, probably just a few months ago.

Both men remained silent, nodding at Charlie as he deposited two amber-coloured beers on the table. They then watched as Charlie joined Jed at the foosball table.

'Cheers,' said Robbie, offering his glass to chink.

Stringer accepted the salutation. 'Cheers, so where are you from, then?'

'All over, but mostly Highland.'

'I've asked around, nobody's heard of you.' He sipped at his beer but didn't remove his eyes from Robbie's.

'That's good. I like to stay under the radar. It's how I've kept out of jail. I've heard of you, though. You have a reputation, Stringer.' Robbie had a glint in his eye.

Stringer tensed, and felt his brow furrow. 'Meaning?'

'Not to be messed with. Just out of Frankland on remand after you beat a case. Congratulations, nice lucky result.'

Stringer grinned. 'No luck involved, man.'

'I also heard that. Jurors got cold feet, and the Crown's biggest witness decided he did'nae fancy it?'

'Summat like that. Who's telling you this?'

'It was in the paper, pal. Plus, I keep my ear to the ground.'

'So, what are you looking for?' said Stringer. He'd had enough of the pleasantries.

'I hear you can supply what I need?' Robbie sipped at his beer and pulled a face. 'Grapefruit? Tastes of bloody grapefruit?'

Stringer felt himself relax, just a touch. 'It's a thing. Grapefruit

IPA, I think the brewers do grapefruit, passionfruit and all sorts of shite. What's your market?'

'Inverness, and beyond.' He took another sip and raised his eyebrows.

'Sounds small time. I've been selling into Newcastle, Middlesborough, Durham and beyond. I want to make inroads into Scotland, but I'm only interested in shifting weight, man.'

Robbie chuckled, and shook his head in a way that made Stringer want to punch the daft Jock. 'What makes you think I'd want less? This looks like a backwater, pal, and to some degree it is, but the market is busy for brown, decent for Charlie, and disco biscuits are starting to jump. And that's before we talk about the old fishing towns up the east coast, Fraserburgh, Peterhead, Cullen and the like. Brown and white is mad up there. We also have the old smelter towns like Alness and Invergordon, heading up towards Wick and Thurso. Plenty big market, mate.'

'I thought the Albanians had it sewn up?'

'"Had" being the word. They did for a bit, and the Scousers before them, but cops took all the big players out, and now it's just a few neds slinging shite, heavily cut product. They're all easy pickings for someone with the contacts and network, or at least who can supply a decent bit of quality gear. Trust me, the brown up north is shite, and the crack may as well be crushed Murray Mints, there's that little coke in them.'

Stringer sat back in his chair and appraised Robbie for a full thirty seconds. He seemed smart, but there was something that made him uncertain. 'Who've you worked with in the past? Not being funny, mate, but you're a nobody to me. You could be a fucking cop, as far as I know.' He hardened his voice and firmed his jaw, feeling the muscles in his arm tense, reflexively.

'A cop. You think I'm a fucking polis?' If Robbie was intimidated, he didn't show it, his eyes flashing with anger. Despite their size disparity, he clearly had a pair of bollocks.

'Just thinking out loud, man. Who knows you? Who've you worked with?'

Robbie visibly bristled, his eyes suddenly hardening. 'Listen, firstly, call me a cop again and I'm fucking out of here. I don't need to be fucking disrespected like this, on my own turf. You're not the only person selling product, you know.'

'Aye well, as may be, man. I want to know what you've been doing, and where I can get you vouched for, eh?' He leaned forward, bringing his face much closer to Robbie's. The smaller man didn't flinch. Not even a bit. He looked at Stringer, his eyes steady, with a glint of amusement in them.

'Looks like I'm wasting my time here. Look, if you don't want the business, I can go elsewhere, man. I've been about, but I keep my head firmly down, and away from the polis. You know the Hardie family, I take it?'

Stringer felt his eyes widen at the mention of the legendary Scottish gang. The Hardies, headed up by the fearsome Tam. Scary bastards that ran Scotland for decades. 'Aye, I've heard of them. Who hasn't?'

'Well, I used to look after all the north-east coastline for them. Since old man Hardie was killed, and the others jailed, I've been overseas, as it was so fucking hot around here. Now I'm back. I'm back, and I'm ready to make Inverness and the Highlands mine, but I need a reliable source. Now that can either be you or I can go elsewhere, but don't take the fucking piss, man.' Robbie's eyes were flint hard.

'How much?' said Stringer, feeling himself relax at the mention of the familiar names.

'As much as you can give me. It all looks small town, but the appetite is here, Stringer. I need weight every week. Can you handle it?'

The room seemed to go quiet, and even a hoarse cheer from Charlie didn't pierce Stringer's thoughts. Multiple kilos a week.

That'd do it. He'd make serious money very fast. Way faster than if he had to get Newcastle back, and without all the fucking hassle. More than enough for the cause. More than enough to fund the objective.

'White or brown?' said Stringer. Cocaine or heroin. Coke was fairly cheap, but heroin was expensive right now, and massive profits were there to be made if it was cut right.

'Just white to start with, but we'll want brown at some point,' said Robbie.

'How much?'

'How about we get a couple of keys to start with? I want to check purity, and make sure you can deliver. I don't want product that's been cut to shit.'

'Two fucking key? Wasting my time, man. I thought you were a big-timer not a two-bit street dealer.' He sat back in his stool and exhaled.

'Chill out, pal. Who takes a big fuck off consignment from a new supplier? If this goes well, and it's sound gear, I'll be wanting a decent number up front, and then weight every fucking week after. Jesus, it's you wasting my time.' Robbie jumped down from his chair and picked his phone up from the table.

'Where are you going?' Stringer said, also jumping to his feet.

'You seriously think I'm taking multi keys on first meet? So, I hand over a few hundred grand for untested product, and you fuck off? You must think I was born yesterday.'

The gorilla, Jed, materialised by the table, his chest puffed, jaw set, his eyes narrow. 'All okay, Robbie?' he said, his feet apart.

Stringer bristled. 'Look, you don't need your fucking steroid man, here. We can do a deal, but we need to stop pissing about. It's fucking good gear, man. Ask around. You'll hear no complaints.'

Robbie turned to Jed and nodded. The big man turned, and walked back to Charlie, and leaned on the target table, his eyes not leaving either of them.

'I just don't want to be pissed about, Stringer. Time is tight, and the market is there to be exploited.'

'Three keys minimum. You can test each brick as much as you like, but I'm not taking the risk running across the country with just a lousy key. That'll allow you to get your dealers running on it, properly field test and see how you go, but we'll not be holding on to the rest for long, you ain't the only dealer in the business, mate.'

'You run your own gear about?' Robbie looked surprised, and once again, Stringer wanted to knock the smug bastard's grin off his face.

Robbie narrowed his eyes as he looked at Stringer, and he could almost hear the cogs turning. Three was good. Three would net them enough to get things moving with the Cashier. There was no time to waste. This wasn't just about moving product, they had bigger objectives. They also had the matter of repaying the Dutchman's line of credit in plenty of time. He wasn't to be underestimated.

'How much for three, then?' Robbie exhaled, and the tension seemed to dial down a little.

'Thirty on the key, so ninety K?'

Robbie chuckled. 'Man, I thought you said thirty on the key for a second. Maybe my maths is wrong, but thirty a key?' He snorted with amusement.

Stringer felt his hackles rise and face flush again. 'Test price, we'll renegotiate when you take a proper amount.'

Robbie shook his head. 'Twenty-five on the key, and that's fucking expensive, man. Prices are low right now. You know this. If we take any more, I'll definitely want a better price than that.'

Stringer felt himself relax again; thirty was a piss-take, he knew it, and Robbie knew it, which was reassuring. It confirmed that the bloke had done this before, no dealer worth his salt would take a first offer. Surest sign of a cop or snitch was taking a daft offer.

'Seventy-five grand then.' He extended his hand, and after a heartbeat of a pause, they shook. Robbie tried to pull his hand away, but Stringer held on, not crushing the smaller man's hand but just gripping it. Letting him know. Letting him feel who he was dealing with. Stringer grinned, and spoke softly, but his eyes were pure iron. 'Robbie, don't forget who you're dealing with here, eh? Did you know Billy Mackee?'

Robbie didn't remove his gaze from Stringer, and the total and complete absence of fear was not something that Stringer was used to. He was used to scaring and intimidating people, but if this bloke was intimidated, he wasn't showing it. He felt his brow furrowing in confusion.

'I'd heard of him, sounded like he crossed the wrong people, eh?' said Robbie, a glint of amusement showing in the crinkles of the corner of his eyes.

'Aye well. Maybes you should wonder how he got in that situation, eh?'

'What are you saying?' Robbie cocked his head, his eyes full of fascination as he locked eyes with Stringer.

'Saying nowt, mate. Just remember what happens to folk who cross me. Billy crossed me, by talking to the wrong people, and I found out.'

Robbie narrowed his eyes. 'How did you find out?'

Stringer raised his eyebrows and touched the side of his nose. 'Let's just say that I have friends in all kinds of places, bonny lad.'

'I'll be in touch,' said Robbie. He nodded at the gorilla and headed for the door, the bigger man almost blocking out the light.

'All good?' said Charlie as he rejoined Stringer.

'Aye. All good.' He picked up his phone and dialled.

'Now?' said Shorty without preamble, the sound of traffic was faint in the background.

'Yeah, he's left the boozer. Follow him to his motor, get the number plate and a decent photo of the both of them.'

'I'm on it. Looking promising?' said Shorty.

'I'd say so, but I want to check him out more. He's no mug, that's for sure, but after Billy Mac, I'm taking no chances, man. Let me know when it's done.'

'I can see them now. Give us a minute.' Shorty rang off.

Stringer sat down again and picked up his half-drunk beer, which he necked in one.

'Now what?' said Charlie.

'Now you get me another beer, but one that tastes of fucking beer, not a fruit salad,' he said, not looking at his brother.

Stringer's phone pinged in his hand, a photo message from Shorty. He looked at the image of the two men, the big brute towering over Robbie as they were captured in the weak sunshine. Not a perfect image, but definitely good enough for them to be recognised.

He sat there, staring at the image, his thoughts whirring. All his instincts told him to be careful. Billy Mac had almost brought the whole house crashing down, and it had taken a lot of effort, and a lot of money to tie all the loose ends, and he didn't want to be burned again. There was too much riding on this, and there's no way that Bogdan would approve.

It was time to seek a little more reassurance. A bit more effort to ensure Robbie was who he was. The fact that he wasn't the usual aggressive type almost made him more concerned. Bogdan's old Russian proverb rang in his ears: 'In a quiet lagoon, devils dwell.' He'd had to ask the Russian what it meant, and the answer had stuck with him as being a little profound. 'Never underestimate the quiet man, Stringer my boy.'

One thing was for sure, if Robbie wasn't who he said he was, then he and his muscle-bound pal were both gonna end up the same as all the others. No more pissing about.

The stakes were too high, and the cause was too just.

He took a long swig from the fresh pint that Charlie had

deposited at his elbow, and then forwarded the message on to a contact that was saved in his phone as 'Dougie'. He followed it up with a message. *Smaller one says he used to work with the Hardies back in the day, can you ask around? Drink in it for you.*

'All good?' said Charlie.

Stringer clapped his brother on the shoulder and grinned. 'All good, bonny lad.'

34

MAX AND JOE both crossed Academy Street, heading back towards the car park where they'd left the BMW.

Max looked straight ahead, his mind racing as the pent-up adrenaline began to dump into his bloodstream. His heart was pounding in his chest, and he felt himself flushing as they entered the warm, stuffy air of the concourse. It had been a long time since deploying undercover, and his emotions a mix of euphoria and relief, as they had always been after a job. The dopamine hit was intense and addictive, and he wiped his sweaty palms on his jeans. He tried to suppress the feelings, his thoughts turning to Katie and Evie. Little, perfect Evie. Was this the right call? There were other undercover officers who could have done this, so why had he pushed himself forward?

It had been a long-term undercover deployment against a team of sex-traffickers in Gloucester that had caused his and Katie's separation a few years ago, and his memory of those dark days were sharp and unpleasant.

'No more,' he murmured under his breath.

'What?' said Joe.

'Nothing,' said Max, suddenly desperate for a bottle of water and some mints to take the taste of the beer away. The first time alcohol had passed his lips in almost three years. The taste was dank and bitter, but it had stirred something in him. A memory, of a sensation. He shuddered. Altering his course, he veered towards the small branch of WH Smiths.

'Just getting some water, that beer was rank,' he said, forcing a grin towards Joe.

'I thought it was okay, but then I'm easy pleased.'

'Want anything?'

Joe shook his head.

Max picked up a bottle of mineral water from one of the fridges, and a pack of gum at the till. As soon as he'd paid, he cracked the water and necked the whole thing, following it with a piece of gum. He felt his heart rate slow as the water and minty gum chased away the dank, odd taste of the beer from his mouth.

'How'd that go?' said Joe, as Max rejoined him outside the shop.

'Interesting to say the least. Stringer has agreed to supply three keys of coke, so we'll need authorisation for a buy-bust op. I also think we have a partial admission to the murder of Billy Mac, and a suggestion of a rat. He may be a big villain, but he's daft. He was just bloody bragging to show how big his bollocks are.'

'Sounds promising. Charlie is a bloody wreck, man. He's clucking for a hit as far as I can see, and he tried to ponce twenty quid from me.'

'Pretty sure his only role was to point us out. I just hope to God that Barney got it all captured. It was noisier in there than I'd have liked.'

'What, he confessed to bloody murder?' Joe's jaw dropped.

'Not quite, but it's gonna chuck the cat in with the bloody pigeons, and I suspect they'll be looking for a quick arrest strategy. You drive, and I'll call Ross.' Max tossed the car key to Joe and they climbed in after Joe blipped the lock.

Max reached into the glove box, pulled out his work phone and dialled, as Joe was starting the car and moving off.

'Craigie?' said Ross.

'Tell me you heard all that?'

'We did. Music was a bit of a ball-ache, which Barney is

filtering. You know I'm no' one for giving praise, but you nailed that negotiation. I'm just gonna need to persuade Miles to release seventy-five grand in cash for the buy bust.'

'I hope you heard the partial confession,' said Max, raising his eyes at Joe.

'I heard the comment about Billy Mac, I don't think it's enough to be considered a confession to satisfy the Crown Office, but it's on the right track, and it's certainly grounds to justify an arrest. I'm sorting a meeting with the Chief to discuss, but I can't see a way we won't have to tell the MIT. They are investigating Billy Mac's murder, after all.'

'Did you hear "the friends in all kinds of places" quip?'

'Aye, although it could be discounted as him being a bullshitter. Still worrying, though. We have to keep this tight as we can, but the pressure will be huge to act, Max.'

'How do we do that? We have to disseminate the intel to the MIT, but if we reveal an undercover operation is in place, and it leaks . . .' Max left the sentence hanging.

Ross's exhale caused the phone to crackle. 'I know. It's a worry, but maybe we can release it in a sanitised fashion that won't lead back to you. We can't completely withhold this from the MIT, Max. It's a partial admission to a murder that was preceded by a fucking torture, and almost inevitably to the other two murders, including an MI5 agent. I have a nasty suspicion they'll want us to act, and if I was a betting man, I suspect they'll be wanting to nick Stringer and his crew for the homicides, sooner rather than later.'

'Ross, that'll be disastrous. What if they find nothing evidential to link them? Stringer will be back out on the road, and will be cleaning up all the evidence that may be out there. If he's nicked, we need to make sure he gets locked up properly.'

'I'm just telling you what I think is gonna happen. Pressure on the MITs is huge. Three fucking murders, all professional hits. We may get a few days, but that'll be it. Look, get back here, early doors tomorrow, and we'll chew it through. I'll try and persuade the Chief to give us a little time, eh?' Ross sounded far less caustic than usual, and Max could hear the frustration in his voice. Despite the bumptious persona, Ross was a skilled and experienced detective and leader, and this would be as difficult for him to swallow as it would be for Max.

'Aye, okay. We'll head off, but we do have an advantage here, Ross. If we can just at least do a couple of buys, we'll have enough to take them off the streets for a decent amount of time and give the MIT enough time to get the evidence, without them out and about. We must be able to do this, just a few more days.'

There was a long pause at the other end of the phone.

'Ross?' said Max.

'Aye, I'm here. I'll go and see the Chief, but get this deal set up for the test purchase of the three kilos. If I know the boss, he won't want to look a gift horse in the mouth. I'll go now.' Ross hung up.

'I got the gist of that,' said Joe.

Max shrugged. 'Three unsolved murders. Patience is going to be wearing thin, but if we're to get to the bottom of who Stringer's source is, anything we do will leak straight back. We need more time. Lots more time.'

Joe looked across at Max. 'Think we'll get it?'

'I doubt it. You'll be back in the main office in Perth before you know it.'

'More's the pity. I'm enjoying this deployment.'

'Maybe a few more days, but not much more.'

Max's phone buzzed, it was a message from Ross. *Meeting at Tulliallan with Chief at 9am tomorrow.*

35

FRANKIE HARDIE BLINKED as he emerged into the early morning sunshine, feeling the familiar sense of freedom as he left the grand exit of His Majesty's Prison, Castle Huntly. His hand went to the mobile phone that had been handed back to him ahead of his weekend home leave. After the regime at Shotts, getting his own phone back as he left the estate for his weekend leave still felt unreal. He only had a year left to serve, which still felt like a long time, but he knew he was on the downward slope. A new life awaited him, and that made him happy.

While Castle Huntly was still a jail, it couldn't have been more different to HMP Shotts where he'd been a year ago. The last year in the only Scottish open prison had been a breeze. Mostly friendly screws, and most of the other cons kept themselves to themselves. No one wanted to get shunted back to the closed estate, probably into the digger for some daft infraction or stupid fight. By comparison, it was a holiday camp.

'Be lucky, Frankie man, have a nice weekend,' said Mr Jarvis, the reception officer from behind him.

'Aye, thanks, boss.'

'Anything nice lined up?'

'Nah, weather looks grand, so just some walks, and a pub lunch or two,' he said, feeling the smile stretch across his face at the prospect. Two days with Sarah in her nice wee place in Dundee. Two days doing normal stuff. Two days away from the stink of men all holed up in Wallace Hall. It was okay at Castle, and some of the lads were decent, but it was still the jail.

He felt the familiar frisson of excitement at the prospect of seeing Sarah again. His heart softened at the thought of her honey-blonde hair and kind smile. He'd met her a while ago during a work placement at a coffee shop in Dundee, and their friendship had developed to what it was now. She was kind, non-judgemental and strong-willed. She made him happy.

'Aye well, enjoy, but don't forget, back here by ten Monday morning.'

'Can't wait, boss.' Frankie chuckled, revelling in the late afternoon sun bathing his face.

He climbed into the waiting cab, strapped himself in and sighed as the car moved off.

'You okay, pal?' said the driver.

'Aye,' said Frankie.

'Home leave?'

'Aye.'

'Must be nice.'

A buzz in his pocket tuned out the driver's inane ramblings. He reached into his pocket and pulled out the scratched and worn old Samsung, the same phone he'd had since getting jailed. The only difference was being at Castle Huntly, he was allowed it back while on home leave. The message was a blast from the past. Dougie Campbell. His stomach gripped. Dougie was an old family associate and something of a criminal concierge. He knew everyone in the business, a bit of a *Yellow Pages* of crime. What the hell did he want? he thought.

He felt his face flush as he looked at the WhatsApp message. It came with a photo attached and had only been sent a couple of hours ago.

Alright, Frankie mate. Not sure if you have this phone behind the door, but worth a shot. Do you know these two? Robbie and Jed are the names. Stringer D is looking to do business with them, and one of the fuckers name-checked your old Pa. Recognise him? Bit of canteen dough on your account in it for you.

Frankie clicked on the photo and watched, his heart pounding, as the message downloaded, the image crystallising as the blue circle completed.

Two men, one a huge great boy, hard and dangerous-looking, whom he didn't recognise.

He gasped audibly. The other man was Max Craigie.

Detective Sergeant Max Craigie.

Max. Fucking. Craigie.

Frankie had changed since being in the jail. Before his incarceration, he'd been a member of the family that had ruled the criminal underworld for over half a century throughout Scotland. He was the only Hardie left. His father was dead, almost disembowelled in a graveyard in Caithness. His brother, Tam, had been missing for almost two years, believed dead, and his other brother Davie was dead, having had his head blown off by a sniper while escaping from the jail.

He sighed and scrubbed at his face, feeling the tension in his muscles and the unease in his stomach as his fingers hovered over the screen. This was not a conversation for over the phone.

He composed a message.

You have a big problem. We should meet.

The reply came back immediately. *When and where?*

Frankie looked at the handset, long and hard, before replying. This couldn't wait, but he didn't see why it should fuck up his weekend.

How quick can you get to Dundee?

Again, an immediate response. *Soon.*

Frankie typed his reply. *Waterfront of the V&A. As soon as you can.*

He looked up. The driver was looking at him in the rear-view mirror, his eyes questioning. 'Usual place?' he said.

Frankie breathed deeply, wondering if he wanted to get into this. He only had a year left in the jail before he could get parole. A new life in Dundee with Sarah. He could just not go. Not go to the V&A, and ignore the meeting. Fuck all of them off, but something was stopping him.

He was what he was. He was a Hardie. He was the *only* Hardie. Could he be anything else?

He scratched at his scalp, his head itching badly as it always did until he'd showered the prison stink off him.

'No. Take me to the V&A. Someone I have to see before I go home.'

36

FRANKIE HARDIE WAS sitting on a concrete bench, in the shadow of the Victoria and Albert Museum, just a few feet from the metal barrier that separated the esplanade from the River Tay. He breathed in the air, which despite being Dundee central was clean and fresh, and tinged with the saline tang of the sea. The sun was lowering but still warm and soft as it bathed his face. It felt good, despite the gnawing anxiety that gripped his stomach.

He looked up at the huge building with its weird, angular façade that seemed so at odds against the backdrop of the city. Sarah loved it here, and they often visited during his home leave, and she enthusiastically tried to interest him in the staggered architecture. To Frankie, it just looked weird, but he never said anything. He was just happy to be in Sarah's company, and they had a nice café. So, he'd tag along happily, pretending to be impressed by the massive Dundee Tapestry. At least he recognised many of the images on there: Desperate Dan, Dennis the Menace, and Minnie the Minx. Sarah was so proud of the heritage of her hometown that he didn't have the heart to tell her he'd rather go to the pub. Or for a walk at Broughty Ferry Beach with her wee dug, a cocker spaniel called Lucy. It was relaxing, and most important, it was simple, simple, uncomplicated, and without consequence, and it gave him more pleasure than he had believed possible.

He'd gone from being a member of Scotland's top criminal firm, and now it was just him. The last Hardie. It sounded like a title for some shite gangster movie. Would there be a happy ending for him? He was broke, the polis having taken any cash they'd had, including seizing all the properties, and the bank accounts had all been frozen. His lawyer had laughed when he'd asked whether there was any chance of them being thawed out. So, he had nothing.

But he was alive, and he had Sarah, and he had a chance at a new life when he got out of the jail. Would that be enough?

He looked out across the river and sighed, almost desperate for a pint. But that could wait.

A shadow was suddenly cast across his position. A break in the early evening sun. He looked around, and there he was. Smiling that easy smile, eyes twinkling with humour, as he sat next to him on the uncomfortable concrete slab.

'How you doing, Frankie?' he said, the voice familiar with the soft Scottish vowels prominent.

Frankie turned to the newcomer and returned his smile.

'Hello, Max.'

37

STRINGER AND SHORTY were sitting in an anonymous old Renault van outside a rickety old barn, in a clutch of agricultural buildings just outside Low Cocklaw, a tiny hamlet just 500 metres away from the Scottish border. Rather than their usual smart designer gear, both were dressed in crappy builders' clothes. Stringer wore plaster- and paint-encrusted jeans, a scummy old fleece that was similarly splattered, and an old baseball cap. His work boots were worn and covered in dried mud. Shorty was similarly clad.

The van was a twenty-year-old Master with a zillion miles on the clock, and faded, milky red paint. Despite its shabby appearance, it was taxed, insured and road legal. One thing they didn't want was to give the cops any reason to give them a tug. Not with the cargo they were planning on loading up, as soon as their contact turned up, anyway.

The phone on the dash buzzed, Stringer picked it up. A message from Dougie. *I've spoken to Frankie Hardie in the jail. He recognises the bald one, apparently used to graft for his brother back in the day. Says he's sound.*

Stringer held up the phone so that Shorty could see.

'So, he's legit?'

'Seems that way, if Frankie Hardie says he knows him, he must be stand-up.'

'Dougie knows everyone, eh?' said Shorty, grinning.

Stringer nodded.

'Let's get off the road, man. How far away is the Dutchman?'

'Any time. Get the barn open, and get all the shite out of the van.'

Shorty nodded, opened the door, and stepped out of the van and onto the cracked concrete in front of an old corrugated-iron-clad barn. He went to the door and slid it to one side, it creaked open on arthritic-sounding rails. Once fully open, he nodded at Stringer, and he eased the van inside the open and cavernous space.

'Get the door shut, Short.'

Shorty nodded, and within thirty seconds, the door was shut, plunging the barn into gloom. Shorty flicked a switch, and a solitary strip light flickered, bathing the depressing space in a sickly, flickering yellow light. The type of light guaranteed to deliver a blinding headache within ten minutes.

Stringer jumped out and opened the back of the van, which was full of paint pots, rollers, brushes, stepladders and dust sheets. All the trappings of a painter and decorator. Quickly he unloaded the van, leaving just a length of stained carpet covering the floor. Within a second, he'd peeled back the carpet, revealing a ply floor. He grabbed hold of the edge, and pulled hard, his face contorting with the effort, and slid the sheet of ply out, revealing a recess about four feet wide and six feet long. A small duffel bag was nestled in the corner of the space.

The sound of an engine outside made them both look towards the door. Stringer reached into the waistband of his work trousers and pulled out a small, compact pistol, which he held down by his side. 'Check it out, man,' he said in a hoarse whisper. Shorty went to the door, and peered through the crack. He turned and nodded. 'It's the Dutchman,' he said. Stringer exhaled with relief. He'd been in this game for a while now, but this was the vulnerable time. Once they were on the road with the consignment in the back of the van, he was always much happier. The reason for the hide in the van, covered by all the detritus of a painter and decorator, is that he knew from experience that cops were lazy bastards. If they stopped him with the load secure, they'd never be arsed to shift all the crap in the back of the van, as sure as God made little chickens. He tucked the pistol back into his waistband, and nodded.

Shorty slid the door open, blinking in the harsh sunlight that flooded the space.

A small Ford drove into the barn and pulled up alongside the Renault. The door opened, and a grinning man alighted. He was compact and wiry, and had collar-length dark, wavy hair that was streaked with grey. Despite the chippy appearance, his eyes were hard, and he had a quiet, steely determination in the way he carried himself. He radiated utter confidence.

'Hey, boys,' he said, his accent unmistakably Dutch.

'Hendrik,' said Stringer, extending a hand, which the Dutchman accepted and shook.

Shorty slid the big barn door shut.

'All is well, yes?' Hendrik said, almost bouncing on the balls of his feet with enthusiasm. This was typical Hendrik. He was short, enthusiastic and amiable, but also, he was a mid-ranking member of a sadistically violent, incredibly effective cartel, running high purity Colombian cocaine between Amsterdam and northern England. Hendrik was the main man, who unlike many organised drug traffickers, liked to take personal responsibility for the final leg of the journey, from the port at Newcastle, through to the end user.

'All's fine, mate,' said Stringer.

'Excellent. You ready to receive product, no?'

'We're ready, when are we not ready?'

'Excellent, now the line of credit on this is as per usual terms. You have the deposit?' he said, eyebrows raised.

Wordlessly, Stringer went to the back of the van and reached for the duffel bag. He handed it across to Hendrik, who opened it, and peered inside.

'Okay, two hundred K down, we need the balance in a month, okay?'

'You don't want to count it?' said Shorty.

'Ah no, my friend, I never count the money, and I think you know why, yes?' He smiled, but not even a tiny bit of it managed to get close to his eyes.

Stringer returned the mirthless smile. 'Aye, the last person to top-slice you ended up top-sliced themselves, eh? Like with a bloody bacon slicer.'

'Business is business, gents. Now, come. Product here for you to test.'

'We trust you, Hendrik,' said Stringer.

'No, you don't, Stringer, nor should you. Never trust anyone. Please, test. I always insist on a test.'

'But you trust us?' said Shorty.

'Not particularly, but you by no means are our only customers. You rip us off, and we kill you both, very publicly, and photos of your terribly ruined corpses will be circulated on all the Telegram channels, which will serve as a timely reminder not to ever bacon slice us. We are always happy for an occasional rip-off, Shorty my friend. We call it the price of doing business.' The statement was delivered with such an icy disdain for the fact that the diminutive Dutchman was outnumbered, that it caused a slight shiver to travel along Stringer's spine. He'd seen similar pictures on other Telegram channels, after a Somali gang ripped off Hendrik's organisation. The images of the tortured bodies, ears and fingers removed, all having been burned with blowtorches was not something that Stringer wanted to see again, and he was no stranger to violence. His version of violence was a little more agricultural in nature. Where the Dutchman used knives, he preferred kicking the shit out of those who upset him.

'Fine. We'll test one at random if it makes you happy, Hendrik.'

He chuckled, but went to the back of his van, opening the back door and pulling out two large black holdalls. He let them fall to the compacted dirt floor.

Stringer unzipped the first, revealing that it was stuffed tight with parcel tape-wrapped bricks, all identical in size, and all stamped with the indented outline of a rat, with razor sharp teeth. The producing cartel's calling card. A guarantee of purity.

Stringer nodded at Shorty, who produced a small craft knife. He stooped down and made a cut in a brick in the middle of the bag. He dug the knife in and prised a tiny amount of the flaky white powder out.

'Look at that flake, boys. Sign of quality product, no?' Almost as if he was selling apples at a fruit and veg market.

'Aye, looking fine, pal,' said Stringer.

Shorty took a small piece of the powder, on the tip of the knife, and tipped it into a plastic bottle that was half full with a clear liquid. Shorty shook the bottle and held it up to the light.

The silence in the barn was thick and turgid as they watched, the atmosphere taut and unpleasant.

'There she goes,' said Shorty, as the liquid turned a sky blue.

'Looks great, let's get loaded up,' said Stringer, holding out his hand, which Hendrik accepted.

'Nice doing business with you, my friend, how soon for re-up?' said the Dutchman.

'Soon. We're opening a new market in Scotland, and demand is high.'

'Excellent. Let's load up, and get gone. Places to go, people to see, I'll even help you, this is how much of a colleague I am, eh?' said Hendrik, grinning. His English was almost flawless, but there were some peculiarities. To the uninitiated, it sounded endearing, to those in the know, it was chilling.

Within ten minutes, each of the fifty bricks of cocaine had been stacked into the hidden space in Stringer's van, the false floor secured into place with a nail-gun, and all the paint, ladders and dust sheets returned. Now, if stopped, they were just two painter and decorators on their way to another job.

'Good doing business with you chappies, don't be strangers,' Hendrik said out the window of his Ford. Shorty opened the door, and the Dutchman drove off.

'We're in business, man,' said Shorty, clapping Stringer on the back.

'We are. Let's get on with this.' He pulled out his phone, and composed a message to Robbie. *We're ready. Let's do this.*

The reply came back almost immediately. *Tomorrow afternoon?*

Stringer grinned. 'We're on, man.'

Shorty nodded. 'He's hot to trot, mate. We'll turn this consignment round in fucking no time, and then we have enough to pay the man for the job, eh?'

'Damn right, mate. No time to piss about. We're gonna shake the country to its fuckin' foundations. Let's get it on.' They bumped knuckles.

He tapped out a response. *Where/when?*

The response came back immediately.

Pitlochry. Salmon ladder car park. 2 p.m. There was a pin drop attached to the message.

38

'NOT GONNA LIE, I'm surprised, Frankie,' said Max, as he looked at the last remaining member of the Hardie family as he tucked his phone away.

'Aye, I'm surprised myself, but I've changed, Max. I don't want to be part of this world anymore, and if I grassed you up, you'd be bloody dead, and I'd be right back in the thick of it. No more, Max.' His eyes were clear, firm and determined.

Max grinned, although he felt like he'd been punched in the guts. This could have ended up really badly. His thoughts suddenly were full of Katie and Evie. His thoughts were whirring, and not totally connected. He opened his mouth to answer, but then stopped, unable to know what to say next.

'As soon as I left the jail, they'd be back onto me. I'd be back into it, up to my neck, and I'm done with it. I'm the last Hardie, and if I go back to the old life, I doubt I'll last a year. There's something else, as well,' he said, turning away from Max and staring out onto the river.

'Go on.'

'You're a decent man, Max, and you were as good as your word last year. I've not always been a good man, and I need that to change. Despite everything I've done, you supported the transfer to Huntly, and because of that I met Sarah.'

'Sarah?' said Max, narrowing his eyes.

'She's special, Max. She doesn't care who I was, just who I am now, and she's willing to wait for me. We've a life together.' He turned to face Max, and his face was earnest, open and honest. A total transformation from the young man he had first met a few years ago in the Hardie family kitchen, all suspicion and hostility.

Max couldn't help but chuckle. 'Blimey, have you found God, or something?'

'Hardly. I just don't want my old life anymore. Look what it cost my family.'

'I assumed you'd blame me. At least partly, I mean, I did lock you all up.'

'Aye, well, we did bad stuff, Max. You were doing your job, but you did it fair, and you did it straight. You remember I called you the only straight cop in Scotland?'

'I remember. I'm not the only one, you know.'

'You're the only one I'll deal with.'

'I'll take that as a compliment.'

'As soon as I saw the photo, I knew you were undercover, and if I said I'd never heard of you, or worse, grassed you up for being polis, you'd have been killed. Sure as eggs are eggs, Max. Stringer Dent is a mad, bad bastard, and he wouldn't bloody hesitate to wipe you out. In fact, he'd be willing to wipe your whole life out, so you need to take care.' Frankie looked genuinely concerned.

'Frankie, I'm going to ask you a question, and I need you to be honest with me.' Max stood up and walked to the river's edge, where he leaned against the rail. The river was turning grey as the sun was suddenly covered by dark clouds. It felt warm and sticky, and the smell of ozone suggested a storm may be coming.

Frankie joined Max at the rail, staring at the river's surface. 'Go on, then.'

'What do you want out of this? Money, early release from the jail?' Max turned to look at the former gangster, a onetime key member of a gang that had almost cost him his life, had bugged his home, and had almost killed Janie.

Frankie paused, and looked down at the dark and foreboding water, an uneasy tension settling like the suddenly sticky air. He looked at Max, his eyes hard. 'Nothing.'

'Nothing?'

'Nothing. I want my freedom, but only when I've served my time, and can truly stop being part of that world.' He opened his mouth to continue, but the words seemed to catch.

'Frankie . . .' began Max, but Frankie held up a hand as he fixed him with a gaze that was full of pain, his eyes brimming with tears.

'Max, I've done some bad shit in my time. Things that wake me up at night, and then keep me awake the rest of that night. I've done things that make me ashamed, things that haunt my dreams, and make me wonder who the hell I even am, anymore. I want the ride to stop, so I can get off, but that's not all.' He stopped and wiped at his eyes.

'What else can you do?'

He took a deep breath in, and looked at Max, his eyes clear and determined. 'I want to make things right.'

39

MAX, JANIE, ROSS, Barney and Norma were all sitting around in the office clutching mugs when Chief Constable Chris Macdonald entered the room, with his staff officer Detective Chief Superintendent Miles Wakefield a few paces behind. Both wore smart dark suits, and Miles clutched a preformatted decision log.

'Don't be bloody ridiculous,' said Macdonald, as they all moved to stand.

'See what a crack, respectful team ethic I'm fostering here, eh, boss?' Ross chuckled.

'I'm always conflicted, or at least wondering if you're taking the piss,' said Macdonald, sitting down in one of the vacant chairs at the end of the dark and depressing office.

'As if. Tea or coffee?' said Ross.

'Coffee for me, it smells nice in here. I heard you had drain issues.'

'With my customary tact, I got them resolved. Building manager is now my best buddy.' Ross stood with a grunt and made his way to the drip machine, where he poured two mugs. He handed them to Macdonald and Miles, who accepted them, sniffing appreciatively at the brew, which Norma had produced just before they arrived.

'You discovered that he likes a Macallan Gold single malt, then?' said Miles, sipping his coffee and nodding, appreciatively.

'Aye. He was grateful, and our office no longer smells of sewage, so a win-win. He's also promised to replace my knackered chair and have the windows cleaned. I take it you want a full briefing about where we are?'

'It's why I'm here, Ross. I have some very anxious SIOs looking for a break in their cases, and I also have the Justice Minister giving me pelters about what's going on. Understandable. Three professional hits within a day or two of one another.'

'Well, thanks to my inspired leadership, we have an opportunity. I'll leave it to Max to give you the lowdown.'

Max briefed them, quickly, succinctly, but leaving nothing out.

There was a long pause while Macdonald drummed his fingers on the desk, his handsome face pensive, his eyes downcast.

'As I see it, we do have an opportunity, and we do have some evidence on tape thanks to Max, but I'm not sure it will suffice for the Fiscal.'

Miles Wakefield sat up in his chair, his face alight. 'It won't. No chance, but it does give us grounds to arrest, and search all properties, seize all devices, take clothes for forensics. I don't see how we have a choice. The verbal suggestion from Dent that he either killed Billy Mackee or had him killed is irresistible evidence that should prompt an arrest strategy immediately. I need to brief the SIOs as soon as we can. This is an enormous break, despite the issues. We arrest straight away, and we get to make our own luck.'

'With respect, boss, that's a bad idea,' Max said, his voice low.

Irritation flashed in Wakefield's eyes at this display of apparent insubordination. 'Care to elaborate, sergeant?' He managed to convey an enormous degree of sarcasm in the short rebuff.

'If we nick them now, before the drugs change hands, we're totally relying on luck that we find some forensics, tech or other evidence to get them remanded, and off the streets. All we have is a half-arsed suggestion that he killed, or had Mackee killed. He could easily explain that away as bluster, as well as the supplying of drugs. He could claim that he had no intention of supplying drugs, and was planning to just rip us off for cash. In short, I think he'd walk, even if he was charged, which is an outside chance at the best. We're also ignoring the big issue here.'

'Meaning?'

'These look very much like professional jobs, evidenced by the absence of leads, if what we're hearing is true.'

'So, what do you suggest?' said Macdonald.

'Let it run for a few days. They want to do the deal quickly, so let's do the deal. A big old undercover buy-bust operation that'll catch them red-handed with a great big pile of cash having just flogged us seventy-five grand worth of cocaine. Then they get locked up for that until trial, which the way things are right now is probably a year. We then get as much time as we need to dig into the whole thing. Who tipped them off, National Force, all the murders, the whole shebang, all while they're locked up in Saughton, not shooting anyone else.' Max sat back in his chair, and sipped his coffee.

Ross leapt to his feet, suddenly animated. 'The other bonus is, boss, we get access to all their communications, and we can even look at all the tactical options when they're in the jail. Phone intercepts, mail intercepts, and with a bit of tactical jiggery-pokery, how do we fancy them both in the same jail cell, which we've got our ancient old MI5 spook to bug up first? The options are endless, and all while they cannae kill anyone else. It makes total sense.'

Macdonald looked at Wakefield and shrugged. 'This makes sense to me, Miles. Opinion?'

'I get it, sir. I truly do, but we're going to take serious heat from the press about the lack of arrests on the murders.'

'Ross, any reason we can't arrest for the murders to keep the press at bay?'

'I'll encourage team opinions, but it's a balancing act. We just need to be a hundred per cent certain they won't get bail on the drugs alone.'

'Agreed, and I've another suggestion,' said Max.

'Go on, Max,' said Macdonald.

'They're looking for a serious transaction quickly after the initial trial purchase of three kilos. I say we buy the three keys, and then tempt them with an almost immediate purchase of a much larger quantity.'

'Christ, that's a risk. Seventy-five grand handed over, which we may never see again,' said Wakefield, stroking his eyebrow nervously.

'Max is right, Miles. Two buys are a massive tactical advantage. We could get their car, maybe get a tracker on it, or better. We let Barney jark the cash bag which will hopefully lead us to unknown properties, stash houses, tech and the like. Big opportunity to get the evidence to link them to the murders. This guarantees they'll be treated as an organised criminal network, and it also allows us to get the next link in the drugs chain who, let's not forget, are part of the reason three people were murdered.'

'I've another idea,' said Janie.

'Go on,' said Macdonald.

'We have the current phone number for Stringer. If we keep him properly onside, with the promise of a major purchase of cocaine he'll keep the phone live. I say we go to the First Minister for authority to get his phone intercepted. It's not evidential, but if we dangle enough carrots, it may lead us to the corrupt individual, be it a cop or a member of MI5.'

The silence was deep and penetrating in the dusty office, as they all looked at each other in turn.

'Getting an intercept in that timescale would be almost unprecedented,' said Miles.

'They're expecting us to meet to buy three kilos of coke for seventy-five grand tomorrow at 2 p.m. in Pitlochry,' said Max.

'That's mad quick, can we delay?' said Macdonald.

'I can give it a shot. Stringer will no doubt moan, but he's champing at the bit to sell,' said Max.

'Okay, make it happen, people. Time is very tight. Miles and Ross, back to my office, and we'll discuss getting a meeting with the First Minister to authorise this interception warrant. Her staff officer is rigorous in controlling her diary, so no doubt I'll have a battle getting an audience, thankfully she should be at Bute House this evening. Max, you need to get really going on getting the phone line attributed to Dent, and make sure that collateral intrusion and proportionality are dealt with in the warrant information, okay?' The Chief's brow looked damp with perspiration, clearly the prospect of an urgent interception application before the notoriously ferocious First Minister, and her rottweiler-like Chief of Staff Michael Kovac, was uncomfortable, even to the normally unflappable Macdonald.

Max nodded, and then grinned as he caught Ross's eye. 'Best get your best suit to the dry cleaners, Ross.'

Ross's brow furrowed and his bushy eyebrows bristled. 'Piss off and get typing. Norma, you'll need your funny old Anacapa charts to make this make sense. If I'm presenting this to a bloody politician, you'll need to use wee pictures, and no' many words.'

'On it like a car bonnet, Ross-Boss,' said Norma, grinning.

Soft chuckles reverberated in the small office.

40

STRINGER WAS SITTING in the floral armchair as his mam looked at the TV, her eyes half closed against the smoke tendrils snaking from the cigarette dangling from her thin lips. A half centimetre of ash trembled at the end of the cigarette, before dropping onto her housecoat.

His phone buzzed in his lap. He looked at the display, raising his eyebrows when he saw who was calling. Robbie.

'I gotta take this, Mam.' He stood and made for the kitchen. If she'd heard him, she didn't show it.

'Yeah?' he said, as he answered the call.

'Stringer, it's Robbie,' came the familiar soft Scottish voice.

'Yeah. What?' he said, his voice hard.

'Slight issue for tomorrow. I need a bit more time, can we delay until the next day? Same place?'

Stringer felt himself flush, and the familiar adrenaline surge of anger that felt like a sudden heat in his gut. 'Fuck's sake, man, why? We're all set.'

'Wedge is laid up, and I just need a few more hours to get hold of it. Remember the cozzers still have ninety of mine at bloody Berwick.'

'I don't want to be pissed about, man. Day after tomorrow, ten thirty, no fucking later, or I'll find another fucking customer.'

'What, ten thirty in the morning?'

'Nah, fuck that. Night. Never gets dark up there, but there'll be no tourists, at least. Last chance, man.'

'Thanks, man. I appreciate it.'

'Be thankful I'm not putting the fucking price up by ten grand. In fact, if you're a minute late that's what I'm doing, understand?'

Robbie gave a chuckle, which made Stringer's teeth itch but he said nothing. 'Aye, that's fine, man. I'll even chuck in a good bottle of malt to sweeten the deal, eh?'

'Just bring the bloody dosh, and don't be bastard late.' He hung up and leaned against the fridge in the chintzy kitchen. He dialled another number from memory.

'Yo?' said Shorty.

'Delay on the job, man. Jock bastard is delaying until the next day at half ten at night.'

'Fuck's sake. Why?' Shorty said, his voice tight.

'Money. Needs to collect the rest of it from up north. Daft bastards, I've told him I'll fine him ten grand if he's a minute late.'

'How much do we have in the Bitcoin wallet?'

'A hundred, but it'd take a while to turn that into cash, and the Dutchman only wants readies.'

'How much will the Cashier want?'

'I dunno, I can ask, but it'd no doubt clear us out.'

Stringer stared at the photo on the dresser of his mum and dad, taken forty years ago. His dad was a big strong man, and he stared at the camera with that unrelenting, steely gaze that he habitually wore. 'Ask him.'

'Ask him what?' said Shorty, his voice uncertain.

'How much, and how soon?'

There was a pause before he answered.

'Okay. I'll message him.'

Stringer walked back into the lounge where his mam was asleep in the chair, her cigarette smouldering on her housecoat where it had fallen from her lips. He sighed and picked up the almost burnt-out fag that was beginning to melt the nylon garment.

'Fancy a pint? Mam's doing my nut in, man.'

'Aye, the George in fifteen?' The phone clicked.

41

'BINGO, THAT'S THE attribution evidenced for that phone number,' said Max, as he put his undercover burner down on the desk. Joe was sitting next to him, his massive body making the chair sag alarmingly, as they bumped fists.

'You get that, Barney?' said the huge cop.

'I've got it all recorded, and timestamped,' said Barney, looking up from his laptop and nodding.

Attribution. The most important aspect of a phone intercept. Being sure that the subject of the intercept warrant was actually in possession of the phone, now Max could provide that evidence, beyond reproach, having just spoken to Stringer, backed up by Barney recording the conversation.

'Good little team this, Max. Need another member?' said Joe, grinning widely.

'You fancy commuting here every day from Dunkeld?' said Janie.

'Probably not, but it has to be better than bloody main office at Perth. Assaults, disputes and a DI I have to stop myself from chinning every morning.'

'I can speak to Ross, if you like?' said Max.

Joe just shrugged, but his eyes were wide with anticipation.

Norma cleared her throat, and looked up from her desk, holding a phone to her ear. 'Phone spoc confirms a call straight to another number after he hung up that's currently cell-siting in Berwick-upon-Tweed. Just running it through the databases, hold up a second.' Norma tapped away at her keyboard, her eyes rapt with concentration, lips pursed. 'It's a pay-as-you-go phone, but it's getting topped up remotely with a bank card in the name of Georgia Shore, who I am fairly confident is Shorty's wife.' She paused briefly as she tapped, before nodding enthusiastically. 'Yep, that's her. I think we can call that double attribution, and I don't think that'll cause us any collateral intrusion issues. We're good to go. Boom! God, I'm good.' Norma punched the air with a fist.

'Nice one, well done, mate. Everything else looking good for the application package for Ross's presentation at Bute House?' said Max.

'Bute? Is Ross having brekkie with the First Minister? They normally use the government offices at St Andrew's House,' said Janie.

Max chuckled. 'Aye, I can't wait to see his choice of attire. Then all we have is a simple purchase of three kilos of coke the next day. Piece of piss. Normal day on Policing Standards Reassurance, eh?'

'And to think my last job at Perth was an argument over dog shite in a less than salubrious neighbourhood, and now it's all breakfast meetings with the FM, and major drugs purchases,' said Joe, shaking his head.

'You fancy a quick recce of the salmon ladder, Joe? I can drop you home after, Dunkeld isn't so far from Pitlochry,' said Max.

'Aye, that'd be grand. I've been a couple of times, but it'd be good to operationally scope it out properly.'

The office door swung open, and Ross walked in, yawning, his eyes red-rimmed and his suit dishevelled. 'I'm ready to be dazzled. Team?'

Max updated him.

'So, we're good to go?'

'Yep. Hopefully you get the intercept warrant signed off in the morning, they should be both hooked up by the afternoon, ready for the drugs buy the following day. Me and Big Joe are off to recce the meet plot before we head off home.'

'Plot? What is it, a fucking house build site or something, or is "plot" some shite old Met cockney bastard term that you're showing off with?'

'Plot, as in locus.'

'Well, why didn't you just say shagging locus then. Joe, don't listen to this fud, he spent too long in London. You all set?'

'Aye, guvnor, I'm ready, it's a good job. Way better than any I've done before,' said Joe, respectfully.

'Guvnor? Jesus suffering fuck, you've been working with the ex-Met walloper here, and his shite vernacular is infecting you, as well. Go on, piss off, both of you. Right, sod off.'

42

SHORTY SAT BACK from the iPad as he sent an email to the address which was a simple combination of numbers and letters suffixed by @gmail.com.

Shorty had just typed a hashtag in the subject line and left the body of the email blank. The Cashier would know what was required. He'd know to go to the draft folder on the other account. Shorty knew that the Cashier would be there within a few moments. This was how he took contracts. An empty message to an unused Gmail inbox.

Shorty opened the draft folder and refreshed it.

There was a new blank message open with just a question mark in the subject line. Shorty typed in the email body.

Hi, Cashier. Job we spoke about. It's on. We're ready to transfer Bitcoin to wallet. How much deposit for the contract?

He waited a moment and then refreshed the page. And the words magically appeared.

50 up front. 50 once task completed, as before. Any request for method of despatch?

Shorty chuckled. The Cashier really was a pro. He knew that sometimes a subtle execution was required, or sometimes a fake suicide. But not in this case. They wanted a big, splashy, spectacular event. One that would be all over the news, and social media. One that no one would ever forget. He knew the Cashier wouldn't let them down, but this was important.

Spectacular. As spectacular as Daniel Solomon, but maybe a different method. Brains all over the pavement would be nice.

Acknowledged. Identity?

Shorty smiled. Normally the Cashier would require detail: name, age, address and a photo, at the very minimum. But not today. Today would just require one thing. A photograph. Nothing else would be needed.

His mouse clicked on the image from a news page, highlighting the photo, which he then pasted into the blank space. It was just a thumbnail, but clear and obvious. And instantly recognisable.

He refreshed the screen again. There was just one word.

Acknowledged.

Shorty deleted the draft email from the folder.

Nothing sent. Nothing to intercept. Just a few 1s and 0s in the deep memory of an old, knackered iPad. Almost irretrievable. He'd smash the thing to smithereens at the end of the job, but right now it was his sole means of communication with the Cashier.

It would just take twenty minutes to sort the finances out. Move half the fee to the Cashier's Bitcoin wallet, and then set up the automated transaction to pay in the usual timeframe. They could always cancel the transaction if the Cashier didn't deliver, but the prospect of that happening was tiny. The Cashier never failed.

It was on.

He picked up his phone and dialled.

'Is it done?' said Stringer.

'Aye, it's done.'

43

MAX AND JOE sat together in the car park of the salmon ladder. The deep-blue sky had suddenly been covered by a wave of bruise-coloured clouds, and the air that wafted through the windows was thick and damp. It was clearly going to piss down any time soon. The midges seemed to realise this, and a few began to stray into the car, before Max raised the windows on the BMW.

The car park was half full, with space for about fifty cars, mostly visitors for the dam and salmon ladder, which was a fairly popular destination for walkers and sightseers. It was surrounded by mature trees and shrubs, all of which cast a thick shade from the shaft of sunlight that had pierced the roiling clouds.

An elderly couple sat on a nearby bench, holding hands, both with disposable cups of tea in their other hand. It was peaceful and quiet, but not so quiet as to be risky. Stringer wouldn't want to cause a scene with potential witnesses nearby, and three kilos of coke was small enough to be handed over discreetly.

'Problem with this location being close to the water, midges love it. Are we sure about this place?' Max looked across at Joe who was slapping at a couple of the tiny insects that had landed on his face.

'It's perfect for a buy bust. I come here with the missus and kids occasionally, for a dog walk. They love throwing a line in the water, hoping to catch a salmon.'

'How many kids?'

'Three, twin boys and a wee girl.'

'Ever caught one?' said Max, grinning.

'Aye, every time one of my boys climbs on the bloody slide?'

'No, a salmon, ya dafty.' Max snorted.

Joe sniggered. 'Nah. No chance. It's a decent venue, though. It's why I suggested it, equidistant between Berwick and Inverness. Only one way in and out by car, enough cover for the surveillance team, and not busy, but not deserted. Will we have firearms support?'

Max nodded. 'There's enough of an intel picture to suggest that they've been in and around guns in the past. I wouldn't want to do the buy without having someone nearby, at least.'

'Aye. I guess they may be suspicious enough to not want to pitch up with a big bag of Colombian marching powder without something. Remind me why we're not taking them out here, red-handed with seventy-five K of public money?' Joe scratched at a small red mark on his cheek, grimacing.

'All about the murders, pal, and why this place is perfect. Surveillance team can hang back, and pick them up after the exchange. Once the intercept is on, we can use that to get new tactical options of getting new assets in and get irrefutable evidence linking them to the murders.'

'Risky, no?' Joe's big face wore a worried expression.

'Calculated. Nick them now, and we just have what we have. Plenty to remand them for a three-kilo drug supply, but no further forward on the murder inquiries. No way could they have killed all of them personally, so we're looking for others, as well as them. If we give them a few days, with them on the hook hoping for a much bigger deal in a week or so, we have all the opportunities available. Lump up their car, tactical options on their homes, more meetings with them, all with the backup of an intercept on their phones, so we can stay ahead of them. It's a big advantage.'

'We can't use that as evidence, though,' said Joe, making the point that in the UK, intercept conversations were not admissible in court.

'No, but once they do say something incriminating, we know what we're dealing with, and can work to parallel prove it by other means. Right now, we're totally in the dark about the murders. MIT have nothing. We give them a rope, and hopefully they hang themselves. If it doesn't work, we organise another buy bust and take them out with a much bigger package.'

'Fair enough, I'm not complaining, it's keeping me away from the bloody main office in Perth. You should see my caseload, Max.'

'Ugly?'

'Pug-ugly. Thirty open crimes. Assaults, frauds, domestics, the whole shebang. Scunnered with it,' he said, shaking his head ruefully.

'Well, see where we are after this job, but we could probably do with another DC. I can speak to Ross again. It's a bit management heavy on the Policing Standards Reassurance team.'

Joe turned to face Max, his eyebrows raised. 'You serious?'

'Aye. Why not?'

Joe scratched at his shaven scalp and grimaced. 'I'm not sure my DCI at Perth would release me.'

'Joe, man. We work direct to the Chief. If Ross convinces him, it'll happen. Come on, let's have a walk around, and get the lay of the land, and then I'll run you home. It's gonna get very busy once the intercept is running.'

*

'Just here,' said Joe, as they pulled up outside a nice detached house on a quiet street on the outskirts of Dunkeld, a pretty town on the banks of the Tay. The garden was well-tended, with a swing in the centre of the small lawn.

'Nice place, been here long?' said Max.

'Perthshire born and bred. Lived in Edinburgh for a while, but after I met the missus, we moved back. Look out, here's trouble,' he said, a big smile stretching over his face.

The red-painted door crashed open, and three kids, aged between about three and seven flew out, sprinting down the path towards the gate. Joe jumped out of the car and was instantly mobbed by two kids, of which there could be no doubt were Joe's twins. Like their dad, they were stocky and solid-looking. They danced around him, giggling and hugging his huge legs. 'Dad, Dad, where ya been?' they chimed. His daughter was much smaller, and just stood, grinning, as she clutched a small stuffed cat. Effortlessly, Joe scooped her up and planted a kiss on the girl's cheek. She giggled and buried her face in her dad's neck.

'Cracking kids, man,' said Max, getting out of the car.

'The best, man. You have any?'

'Aye, a wee girl. Just a year. Evie.'

A small blonde woman appeared in the doorway, a big smile on her face as she watched Joe being mobbed by his kids. 'Max?' she said, as she reached Joe.

'That's me,' said Max, returning her smile.

'Joe has told me all about you. I'm Hettie.' She extended her tiny hand, which Max took. It was smooth and dry, but she gripped firmly. She had sparkling blue eyes and choppy blonde hair, her face open and shining as she looked at her husband who now had all three kids in his arms.

'Pleased to meet you, Hettie. Sorry we've been keeping him from you,' Max said.

'Ach, we need the overtime, Max. Come on, kids, it's bathtime.' She started divesting her husband of the kids.

'Fancy a beer, Max?' said Joe, his face red and flushed.

'I'm good, thanks. Best get off, I'd like to see Evie before she goes to her bed. I'll call you tomorrow, but maybe take the day off, I'll get Ross to cover for you with your bosses at Perth.' Max clapped the big man on the shoulder.

'Man, you're a star, and Hettie'll love you.'

Max grinned, got in the car and left, catching all the kids waving in the rear-view, as he drove away.

As he sped away, the undercover phone buzzed in its cradle on the dash. He pressed the WhatsApp icon. It was Stringer. *Still on as agreed? No pissing about, eh?*

Max just sent a thumbs-up emoji and continued to drive.

The game was truly on, now. His thoughts shifted to Katie and Evie, and he couldn't shake the feeling of disquiet that was fluttering in his gut.

44

MAX WAS SITTING in the office scanning through the rest of the document, with a network of i2 analytical charts, timelines, photo montages and pages of text all assiduously collated over the last few days by the ever-efficient Norma.

'This looks great, pal,' said Max.

'So it bloody should,' said Norma, next to him. 'It almost killed me getting it together in this timeframe to support an intercept warrant. I'd never have got bloody near it in the NCA with all the daft layers of middle management.'

'You're a genius. Tea?'

'Obviously.'

Barney was in his usual scruffy armchair, fiddling with an anonymous-looking electronic box, a micro-screwdriver in hand, his tongue protruding from his mouth.

'What you doing, Barney?' said Janie, looking at him from her desk.

'Just getting ahead of the game. A new tracker I've been working on for their car. I've been looking at G-Wagons, and I wanted something bespoke for when the moment comes. I'm also designing an audio bug. I found a G-Wagon on a forecourt in Edinburgh, and the bloke let me have a poke about. I think I could get a listening bug in easy enough if I had five minutes with it. There's a couple of nice hidey-holes. I'd love a tea, as well, Max.'

'Yeah, and me,' said Janie.

Max's phone buzzed in his hand, and he looked at the screen.

There was no number, just a collection of unusual characters. Ampersands, hashtags and stars.

His stomach clenched. He knew what that meant. 'Give me a minute, just going to the gents.' He walked out of the office and let the heavy old door slam shut before he took the call. 'Hello?'

'Max Craigie, how're you doing, pal?' came the familiar voice. Deep, authoritative, resonant and full of the lyrical vowels of Caithness.

'Hello, Bruce, I was wondering when you were going to call.'

'That obvious?' said Bruce, a touch of amusement in his voice.

'Anything involving a Hardie always piques your interest.'

Bruce chuckled, a low gravelly sound.

Bruce Ferguson had first featured in a case a few years ago when his brother was murdered during an inquiry into the Hardie family. Tam Hardie had ordered that his brother be killed, and Bruce was not a man to forget. An ex-Special Forces senior NCO, he was now head of security to a billionaire Russian oligarch. One of the few not internationally sanctioned following the invasion of Ukraine. Bruce had access to data, intelligence and resources worldwide that most national security agencies could only dream of.

'A wee birdy tells me that you went to see the remaining member of the Hardie family, Max. Anything to report?' Despite the jocular tone, there was steel in the words.

'He's a changed character, Bruce. He was calling to tip me the wink about something that's going on right now. How did you know? I'm always curious.'

'I'm sure you can imagine, Max. My boss owns two very large telecom multinationals, and as his beef with Russia's president has insulated him from sanction, I can continue to keep my watching brief on Hardie with ease. He's been living the life of Riley in Castle Huntley, eh?'

'It's still the jail, Bruce. He deserved his move after helping us out last year. I genuinely think he's wanting out of the life of a criminal.'

There was a long pause on the line, and Max could almost hear the cogs turning.

'Bruce?' said Max.

'Aye, I hear you. Look, I always said that as long as he plays the game, completes his sentence, and stays out of his former life he'd get no quarrel from me. Despite my background, Max, and despite what his family did to my brother, I believe in rehabilitation. How long does he have left to serve?'

'A year.'

'And he's helping you to cut that short?' His tone carried an edge.

'No.'

'What, genuinely?' He sounded surprised.

'Aye. He wants to do his sentence, and face the parole board. He wants to leave it all behind, Bruce, I'm sure of it.' Max leaned against the scuffed, overpainted wall, and scratched an itch on his scalp.

There was another pause before he spoke again. 'What's prompted this, you think?'

'Love of a good woman, Bruce. Look, I have to dash, there's lots going on, here.'

'So I hear.'

'I hesitate to ask how you hear.'

'I like to stay abreast of developments. We look at all the variables in the countries my boss has interests in. He likes regular threat assessments, particularly about areas of concern that may be considered helpful to the Kremlin. I have heard that Stringer Dent is a very bad man, however. Dent has been recently influenced by someone connected to malign forces who are looking to sow real discontent, which the powers that be in Moscow are encouraging. You need to stop him, Max.'

'We're on it.' Max felt his hackles rising at Bruce's tone, which carried the legacy of a regimental sergeant major gently chiding an underling.

'I hope so. The drugs are just a small part of the problem. I take it you know about the link to the terrorist bomb in York a while back?'

'Aye.' Max didn't elaborate.

'They were keen to put the spotlight on AQ for that, but our analysts don't buy that for a moment. Right now, they're just fundraising to do the bidding of the Kremlin. Stringer Dent and Shorty Shore are both just useful idiots, Max. I'll be in the UK in the next few days, maybe meet for a coffee?' Max could tell that Bruce had more. He sighed, not now. There was too much at stake.

'Does it change anything that we may be planning, Bruce?'

Max looked up as the office door opened, and Janie stepped into the corridor. She looked at him, her eyes full of suspicion. He scratched at his scalp again.

'Well, as I don't really know your plans, I couldn't possibly answer that, could I? Maybe stay in touch, eh? A bit of quid pro quo?' Bruce's tone was genial, but backed with some steel.

Jane raised an eyebrow and tapped at her wristwatch.

'I have to go.'

'Fine, but I'll be watching and listening.'

'Glad to hear it.' Max hung up.

'Who was that?' said Janie.

'No one,' said Max.

She narrowed her eyes at him. 'It didn't sound like no one. And you're doing that nervous thing.'

'What nervous thing?'

'Thing where you scratch your bald heid. Come on. First Minister has signed the interception warrant, and it's about to be reviewed by the independent judge. The line room is getting it set up now. We should be live later on this afternoon.'

'Authorised? Jeepers, that's quick going.'

'Aye, three dead bodies in a couple of days will do that, come on. Briefing time, then we're testing it works. Fancy calling Stringer later?'

'Aye, why not.' Max held up his fist, and they bumped knuckles.

45

STRINGER WAS IN the gloomy barn in Low Cocklaw, humping and dumping all the detritus from the ageing Renault van, to reveal the false floor. It just took another ten minutes before the floor was lifted, revealing the fifty kilo bricks of purest Colombian marching powder, all tightly packed in the space. He selected three at random, and dropped them into a small rucksack by his feet.

He was replacing the false floor when he felt his phone buzzing in his pocket. He pulled it out and looked at the screen. It was Robbie. He felt a small blip of nerves. This was a big job, now. They needed the cash, urgently. A mad Dutchman was waiting for a great deal of money, and he needed to balance the books to make sure that the Cashier's Bitcoin would arrive properly.

'Yeah?' he said casually, as he answered the phone.

'Stringer, it's Robbie.'

'I know that. We all good?'

'Aye, just checking you're still okay for tomorrow.'

'Yeah, of course. We're heading up in the afternoon, same place?'

'Aye. We'll be in a dark X5, what you driving?'

'Why do you need to know that?' he said.

'Mate, we'll be in a public car park, and we don't want to be pissing about. It's quiet enough there, but not so quiet that we'd attract attention if the polis swing by. The car park gets about half full this time of year, even later on, so you can spot us, or we can spot you depending on who arrives first.'

'Why can't we do the job in a fucking hotel room, or something?' said Stringer, already knowing why. First time deals, with no track record, who'd trust walking into a private hotel room with a big bag of cash? It'd be the easiest rip-off ever, whereas no one wants a confrontation in a public place, despite what you see in films.

'No disrespect, but we don't know each other. We have no reason to fucking trust each other, so we do this as we say, or we go somewhere else. I'm not going somewhere out of public view. I'm not a fucking newbie, man. I've been ripped off before. If this goes well, the next job can be somewhere much quieter over a cup of coffee. Now, can we get this done? I've a fuck ton of cash burning a hole in my pocket, pal.'

Stringer thought about this for a moment. Not the G-Wagon. Way too flashy, and guaranteed to attract the attention of the bizzies. It wasn't like he didn't have access to other cars. He mentally ticked through the other possibilities, remembering the images of the car park he'd studied on Google Maps Street View.

'Stringer?' Robbie's voice was tight.

'Aye, fine. We'll be in a grey Mondeo. A 59 plate. Just me and Shorty, is it just you and the Gorilla?'

'If by Gorilla you mean Jed, then yes.' Robbie sounded amused.

'Far-right side of the visitor car park closest to the trees, by the bin. Find two empty spaces and wait for us there. Text when you arrive, and we'll be there within five minutes, as long as there are no cozzers about, okay?'

'Got it.'

'You have the readies?'

'Of course, unless you take American Express?'

'Fat fucking chance, bonny lad. Don't fuck us about, and remember who you're dealing with, eh?' Stringer said, his voice hardening. He hung up and immediately redialled.

'Yeah?' The rough Berwick accent.

'Shorty, we're on. Get the Mondeo ready for tomorrow, the one with the hide under the rear seat.'

'Right, I'll call Jimmy J. to fetch it over to mine, and I'll pick you up early, how far is Pitlochry?'

'Just over two and a half hours.'

'Shit, why are we doing it up there?' said Shorty, sounding indignant.

'Halfway for both of us. We won't always do it this way, but we want this one to be quick, we're committed with the Cashier, and he needs his dough. I don't want to risk pissing him off, do you?'

'No bloody way, man. Right, pick you up at seven. One thing?'

'Aye?' said Stringer.

'Are we strapped?'

Stringer paused, considering the options. It was only three key, but Robbie was an unknown. Would it be a rip-off? He pursed his lips and scratched his itching scar.

'You know the answer to that. I'm not risking getting rolled by no bastard. We need this wedge, and we need it now.'

'Whey-aye. I'll sort it,' said Shorty, as calm as if he was talking about collecting a loaf of bread, not two nine-millimetre pistols.

'Canny. It's on, lad.' Stringer hung up, feeling a surge of energy in his chest. Despite only getting out of jail a few days ago, here he was. Back in the thick of it, making money, but this time for a genuine cause.

Things needed to change, and they needed to change now. The only way to bring the country to its senses was chaos. Chaos followed by the reset.

And he was here for it, one hundred per cent.

46

ROSS WAS IN the office, staring at his empty cup, hoping that it may magically refill with tea, as it seemed like no other bugger here was going to make one any time soon. He looked at Barney, who was pretending to fiddle with some stupid bit of tech, when in reality he was trying not to nod off. Max was just staring at his phone, and Janie was leafing through a magazine about some stupid martial art. Only Norma seemed to be working, tapping away on her computer.

He opened his mouth, intending to indulge in some abuse relating to who was making the tea, when his phone began to vibrate on the desk in front of him. The display read, 'Private number'. He knew, or rather hoped he knew who it was.

'Ross Fraser,' he said, answering the handset.

'DI Fraser, it's Maggie in the line room.' Ross sucked in a breath. The line room. An independent and isolated unit in a secret location somewhere in Scotland. Or maybe London. Ross didn't have a bloody clue. All he knew was they were the ones listening, and they stripped back the information to its component parts, sanitised it and relayed it in the most anodyne fashion possible.

'Aye, that's me.'

'We have recent intelligence that subjects known as Stringer and Shorty are leaving his home address at seven tomorrow evening in a grey 59-plated Mondeo to travel to the car park at the Pitlochry dam. It is believed that they will be in possession of three kilos of cocaine for supply to another. The car is being supplied by Jimmy J., and has a hide under the back seat.'

'Excellent, thanks, Maggie. Anything else?'

'Yes, for a separate intelligence sheet. It is also suspected that they need the funds to pay an individual known as the Cashier, who they seem to be in fear of.' Her delivery was brusque and matter-of-fact.

'Hmm, right, okay,' said Ross, scribbling in his A4 day book, a brand-new item he'd started specifically for receiving these intelligence reports from the line room. Once finished, the intelligence in the book would be transposed onto intelligence sheets, graded and evaluated. At the conclusion of the job, it would be destroyed.

'That's it for now. Stay tuned for further updates.'

Ross ended the call, looked around at the team, all of whom were staring at him expectantly. 'We're on.'

47

Three months earlier

STRINGER WAS SITTING in the association hall of Frankland jail, his eyes down and taking in the chessboard in front of him. There was no doubt about it. He was screwed. He only had four pieces left, to Boggie's five. He'd been getting excited as he'd picked off the Russian's pieces nicely, and he really thought that the time was now. He genuinely thought he'd beat the bastard for the first time.

He was very wrong.

He looked up at his opponent, the skinny Bogdan, who showed his crooked teeth in a wolfish grin.

He looked down at the black and white pieces, and sighed. His king was pinned in the corner with Boggie's rook and knight, and he pretty much had nowhere to go. Take his rook, and his knight had him. He had nothing else. He reached over, and knocked over his king with a forefinger.

Bogdan let out a throaty cackle, his rheumy eyes glinting.

'You cunning old bastard,' Stringer said, grinning widely. He and Bogdan had become close soon after Stringer's remand almost a year ago. The little Russian was quiet and aloof, and rarely spoke to any of the other inmates, but after a week sharing a cell with Stringer, he'd opened up. Stringer had been moved to a single cell shortly after but they'd remained close, and religiously played chess at every association session. He'd told Stringer his life story, and what a tale it was. Born into poverty in Moscow, he'd started out picking pockets, before moving to burglaries, and then robberies. The inevitable happened, and he was jailed in Siberia. This left only one option. Join the gangs, or die.

He joined the Solntsevskaya Bratva, the feared Russian crime syndicate, and entered the world of organised crime, enduring battles with the Chechen mafia, and spending time in New York, before he was deported back to Russia. He'd ended up in the UK after he'd been sent to London with a new identity, in order to represent the interests of his boss, who in turn was heavily influenced by forces deep in the Kremlin. He'd been in the UK only a year before he was jailed for shooting a Russian journalist in the head, netting him a life sentence. He was an intense man, full of quiet passion, and when he spoke, Stringer listened. He listened intently to everything the man said, and he was captured by those hard Baltic blue eyes, and the fervour with which he spoke.

And when they realised that their worldview aligned, the deal was done. They discussed it all, endlessly. How Europe was being poisoned by the Jew and the Muslim. How the Aryan race must fight back and must stop the pollution of the white majority. The '88' tattoo – as in the eighth letter of the alphabet, H – told its own story.

'Heil Hitler.'

Bogdan was a dyed-in-the-wool Nazi. And Stringer was here for it. He was captured by it, and a new desire was planted deeply in him. Sow division, create havoc and spread hatred. 'Hatred is powerful weapon, no? UK is divided, left or right, black or white, gay or straight. Our paymasters make Brexit happen, it make NATO look weak. Only by destroying can we rebuild, you understand me, Stringer?' His burning eyes bored into him. Well, that was that. He was captured. No more just dealing drugs for nice watches and cars. Now he had a purpose.

'So, you don't see Arabian checkmate? I knew four move ago, and you took bait.' He chuckled, a crackling and harsh noise, as he began to reposition the chess pieces.

Bogdan was in his sixties and was a husk of a man compared to the hulking bulk of Stringer. But Bogdan had something intangible. Bogdan had presence. He was the only Russian in the jail, but he was given a very wide berth by all the other prisoners. Memories of his attack on a tall, young inmate known as Legs was a thing of legend in the jail. It had been an argument over nothing more than access to one of the prisoner phones in the association hall. The young con, who was in for a nasty murder of a fifteen-year-old, had pulled Bogdan away from the phone when he felt he'd had long enough. Bogdan had done nothing initially, just smiled at the younger man's back as he had dialled.

A day and a half later, during a violent disturbance on the landing between a number of cons, Bogdan had struck. While the chaos was happening, the young con had been blinded when chlorine gas had been sprayed directly into his eyes. It seemed that Boggie had knowledge of rudimentary chemistry, aware that mixing vinegar and bleach would create the horribly corrosive substance.

Of course there were no witnesses, and Legs certainly wasn't grassing. A visit to his mother in Newcastle from one of Bogdan's associates had made it very clear that giving evidence wasn't an option.

'Another game?' said Bogdan, lining up the board with the cheap plastic chess pieces.

'Aye, gan on. Although I'm shite.'

'You improve, my friend. You improve every time. It good to play chess. Chess is all tactics, and you need to know and learn tactics, yes?' The diminutive Russian stared hard at Stringer, his eyes deep set and icy blue. Eyes that seemed to see into your very soul.

'Aye, I guess.'

'Not guess. Know. Always know.' His eyes went to the tattoo on the back of his hand, the two digits, 88.

Stringer was entranced as he looked into his friend's eyes.

'You must be smart, my friend. The Jew writer was a good operation, but he is small time. Better targets available, my friend. Much better. Most of world not even know he exist. You are a soldier, no?'

'Soldier?' Stringer felt his insides freeze at the man's delivery. The short staccato sentences, the blazing eyes, the hard face. They were mesmerising.

'Yes. Leader and a soldier, Stringer. Soldier uses tactics, planning, and think ahead like in chess, no?'

Stringer held the man's gaze. 'Like chess, aye.'

'Just like chess. In chess, you go for the king. You may take out a pawn, or a knight, you may even sacrifice a rook, or a bishop, but objective is always the king.'

Stringer couldn't find the words, so entranced was he by the diminutive Russian.

'I'm lock in here for many time, and I'm an old man already, Stringer, but you,' he tapped a finger on Stringer's massive chest, 'you are powerful, you are young, and you make a difference, when you get out, and get out you will, because you smart.'

Stringer's mouth opened and closed like a fish as the words seemed to physically strike him in the face with Bogdan's tobacco-laced breath. He felt a surge of energy. He knew now. He knew that it was his destiny. He had to make a real, proper difference.

'Stringer, my friend. You now like a son to me, so make me proud, but make me real proud for real reason.' His head snapped down, looking at the chess pieces.

'Boggie?' he began, but the words died in his mouth.

The Russian looked up, a smile stretching across his face. 'Let's play chess. You beat me, and I tell you how to make the world shake like never before.'

48

THE UNUSUALLY CLEMENT Scottish weather had disappeared to be replaced by a more typical set of affairs. The rain lashed down in warm sheets as Joe steered the BMW along the A9 heading north towards Pitlochry, the big tyres kicking up a deluge of spray, and the steering wheel juddering as the car aquaplaned in the ribbon of water that ran down the edge of the tarmac.

'Looks like summer's over, then?' said Joe, grinning as the windscreen wipers fought against the deluge.

'We've had it too good, pal. If it was always like it's been over the past couple of weeks we'd be bloody flooded by tourists. Rain will make some of them re-evaluate.' Max was fiddling with his phone. 'You getting all this back there?' Max said, ostensibly to no one. A ringing tone erupted through the BMW's speakers. The display declared that the caller was 'Profane Pete'.

'Aye, and if the rain doesn't put them off, the midges surely will once this does clear. Still warm, like. Wee shites would love this.'

Max snorted in laughter, as he answered the call. 'Ross?' he said.

'Yes, we can hear you, shit for brains. The old codger seems to have done well with the fit-out. We have imagery inside the car, and he's done something clever with the front and rear cameras so we can see out of those. Pishing doon, I can see.' Ross's voice crackled a little through the car's speakers.

'Aye, not so great. How far behind are you?'

'Not far, but slow up a bit. Tac firearms adviser has handed over to Joey Daglish who is the operational commander. His boys have already recce'd the meeting site, and we have an ARV shadowing us, ready to intervene if we decide to dynamically intervene.' Ross's usual jocular tone was modulated, and he almost sounded professional.

Max didn't ask where the firearms officers would be. It was better not to know. If he knew, or even suspected where they were, or whether they were actually watching, there was a risk he'd act unnaturally, almost by instinct. Max had to think like the part he was playing. It wasn't enough to pretend to be a major drug trafficker, with links to international crime syndicates. He had to *be* a major drug trafficker, and international criminal.

There had been a full briefing a few hours ago, at a nondescript building just outside Perth, with only limited information given to the surveillance and firearms teams. Max's and Joe's phones were adapted with mics, and the BMW had been fully fitted with a tracker, and internal and external cameras and microphones.

'Have you ever dynamically done anything, Ross?' said Max, grinning at Joe.

'I'll dynamically kick you up the arse when I see you, ya fud. Now drive careful, and don't forget the trigger word if you need help?' The uptilt at the end of a sentence sounded Australian, framing the comment as a question.

'Aye, "bloody beemer",' replied Max, giving the emergency shout line. The *get me out of here* message for the benefit of the monitoring team, designed to be inserted easily into speech without arousing suspicion.

'And the visual signal?' Ross's voice was that of an authoritative teacher testing a pupil before an exam.

'Rub my right hand across ma bald heid twice. Your words, Ross.'

'Aye, only because it made me laugh. No messages from the subjects, I take it?'

'None. No line activations?' said Max, referring to the intercept.

'Just a quick phone call from Shorty to Stringer when he arrived to pick him up, but we wouldn't know about WhatsApp. We can't access those at all,' said Ross, referring to the double-encryption on WhatsApp.

'Aye, I know. We'll be good. Right, we need to go. Moving to operational mode now, no further contact from us, unless the shite hits the fan, okay?' Max said, having had enough of the talking. The time for planning and talking was done. It was game on.

'Where are they?' said Max.

'Phones are cell-siting close to Pitlochry, so it looks like they're ahead of you. I guess they're off for a fish supper before meeting you buggers. Unfortunately, we had no time to ID and put a lump on the car, so we're relying on phones only.'

Max relaxed his shoulders, and exhaled, trying to get the tension to dissipate before he answered. 'All good. Speak soon.'

'Stay safe,' said Ross, and the phone beeped three times out of the speaker as he hung up.

Max looked at the BMW's clock. It read 10 p.m. Half an hour before they were going to hand over £75,000. He looked down at the rucksack between his feet in the footwell containing £75,000, in twenty-pound notes, all in hundred-pound bundles with the fifth note folded around each small stack. Each of these was secured with nine similar bundles and made into small stacks of £1,000. Each of these was then added to a larger bundle to make a small brick-sized wedge amounting to £10,000. There were seven of these in the bag, and one half the size. Seventy-five grand. Seventy-five 'bags of sand'. A year's salary for two new police constables. Max's stomach clenched at the thought of it. These were big-boys' games.

Max had signed for the cash from a dour-faced civilian worker at Gartcosh, and was given dire warnings about 'getting it back here, toot-sweet, pal'. Max failed to mention that they had every intention of handing it over to some very serious criminals, in the bag that contained a very discreet tracker. A risk. A big risk, but with three bodies still barely cold, it was a risk they had to take.

Max and Joe had then spent an hour folding the cash so it would be exactly as Stringer and Shorty expected to find it. The quickest way to blow an undercover job would be just to hand over a load of neatly stacked money fresh from the bank.

That was asking to get shot.

49

'WHERE ARE THE buggers?' said Shorty, as he sat next to Stringer in the driver's seat of the Mondeo that had been delivered to them just a few hours earlier, one of a fleet of cars they had laid up ready for business. The Mondeo was perfect, as it was almost invisible, being as dull and commonplace as it was.

'Cannat believe we're sitting here in this shitty car park in the stupid Jock weather,' said Stringer by way of an answer.

Rain was running down the windscreen in rivulets and bouncing off the tarmac of the car park's surface.

Stringer looked at his watch, a plain black digital, his old Omega being left at home. He never wore it on a job. It was way too precious for him to lose if the police lifted him, or worse they got robbed. His hand went to his waistband where the old, worn and scratched Smith & Wesson revolver was tucked. It was almost an antique, but he was attached to it, being as it was part of his dad's legacy. An old piece from the halcyon days of bank robberies, and cash-in-transit raids, which was now a total mugs game. High risk, low reward.

The Smith & Wesson had a big advantage over the more fashionable automatics. It didn't leave spent cases lying about, and was totally reliable, with far less chance of a stoppage. It only held half the amount of ammunition of your average automatic, but he always felt that if six bullets weren't enough you were probably in the shit so much that it didn't matter anyway.

He looked at his watch, 10.28. 'They'll be here soon. What I mean is, the buggers better be here soon, or I'm fining them, like I said,' he muttered, as he squinted through the rain cascading down the windscreen.

'Heads up, mate.' Shorty nodded towards the car park entrance as the halogen lights of a BMW X5 pierced the rain-soaked gloom heading towards them. It rounded the almost empty car park, stopped, and then drove forwards into the space directly next to them. The passenger's window slid down, and Robbie grinned at Stringer. The gorilla was sitting hunched over the steering wheel.

'Nice Scottish weather for us, eh?'

'It's hardly any better in Berwick,' said Stringer, grinning at Robbie.

'How you doing?' said Robbie, showing his teeth in an easy smile.

'All good. I was just about to issue you with a ten grand fine, man.'

'Always on time, pal. Punctuality is the politeness of princes, or so my old ma used to say,' he said, enunciating each of the *p*s theatrically.

'What the fuck are you talking about, man?' he replied.

'Nae idea. Some old shite she used to say. Are we all good?'

'Canny. Light's just fading, bollocks weather, and there's no bugger about. Shall we do this?' Stringer wanted this job done, so they could get back down the road with enough time to go and celebrate.

'Fancy stepping into my office? I'm sure we don't want to do this transaction in the rain,' said Robbie, jabbing a thumb at the back of the BMW.

'You want to test the product?' said Stringer.

'Of course we want to test it.'

'You don't trust us?'

'Nope. I'm assuming the feeling's mutual.'

'You're bang on, bonny lad.'

'Sensible. You want to count the cash?'

'Whadda you think?'

Max chuckled. 'Pal, if you didn't, I'd think you were polis.'

'Then we're on the same page. I'll bring the product to you, you can test in your car while Shorty counts the notes in ours. If we're both happy it's a done deal, okay?'

Robbie nodded.

'Let's do this, then.' Stringer nodded at Shorty and opened the car door, heaving his bulk out into the pouring rain, the rucksack sagging as he picked it up from the footwell.

Simultaneously, the big gorilla heaved himself out of the driver's seat of the BMW, rounded the front of the car, climbed into the passenger seat and slammed the door.

Stringer went to the back door of the BMW, and climbed in, shuffling across so that he was behind the passenger seat. Robbie swivelled around to face him, his expression one of amused boredom.

Without a word, Stringer threw the bag over the passenger seat, where it landed on the leather upholstery. 'It's all there, mate. Top quality stuff, test one brick, test 'em all. Makes no odds to me. High purity, and plenty more where that came from.' He swiped his hand over his head, wiping the rain off.

Robbie reached across and opened the bag, pulling out one of the packing tape–wrapped bricks. Stringer began to relax when Robbie reached into the glove box and tugged out a small electric scale. Balancing it on the centre armrest, he put the brick on the scales and nodded. 'Nice one, bang on a kilo,' he said, eyeing Stringer in the rear-view mirror.

'Of course it's bang on. Test it.'

Robbie pulled out a small folding knife, extended the blade and made a small nick in the packaging. Using the tip, he scooped out a small amount, and studied it closely, holding it up to the light. 'Nice flake to it.'

'Straight off the boat, mate. No cutting in there.' He relaxed even more, this guy had spent time amongst cocaine, he could just tell. Rubbing a bit on the gums was a load of bollocks, only done by amateurs. If it was cut with lidocaine, or novocaine, you'd still get the same numbing, but it wouldn't be coke. It could be baking powder just cut with a bit, and the gum rub wouldn't help you at all.

Robbie pulled out a tiny clear plastic bottle, the size of a typical eye-drop dispenser. He flicked the lid open, and tipped the powder in. He folded the knife, and tucked it back in his pocket. Vigorously, he shook the bottle, and placed it on the dash, grinning at Stringer in the mirror. 'Now we wait a moment.'

'It'll turn blue, I guarantee it.'

'If it doesn't, we're leaving without it, and with the cash, pal.'

Stringer looked across at the Mondeo, through the tracks of rain running down the glass. Shorty had his head down, a look of intense concentration on his face.

'Bingo,' said Robbie, reaching forward and picking up the bottle which he shook again. The liquid inside had turned a vivid sky blue.

'Told you, didn't I? Now shall we do this? Places to go, people to see, and all that.'

'Aye, let's do it.' Stringer gave a thumbs-up towards Shorty, who held up two fingers. The meaning was clear, two more minutes to finish counting the cash.

'Two minutes, Shorty's just finishing counting.' Stringer sat back in the plush leather of the BMW, the silence cloying and uncomfortable. Robbie looked at him in the mirror with amused eyes, apparently totally relaxed.

The buzz of Stringer's phone in his jacket pocket almost made him jump. Plucking it out, he glanced at the screen.

He froze.

A WhatsApp group message with three members. Stringer, Shorty and another number.

He didn't recognise the number, but he recognised the words. The words could only have come from one source, it could have only have come from *the* source. That source was never wrong. The words made his stomach turn to ice.

UC COPS. GET OUT NOW!

Robbie was still looking at him in the mirror, one eyebrow slightly raised, and suddenly appearing a little less relaxed. He glanced out of the window to see Shorty staring at him, eyes hard. He nodded at him, his jaw firm.

50

MAX FELT IT. It was like someone had suddenly turned the temperature in the car down ten degrees. He looked in the mirror again and saw that Stringer wasn't staring at him. His eyes were fixed on Shorty who was in the driver's seat of the Mondeo, staring straight back, his face hard. Even through the driving rain, there was something in that stare that made a chill settle on him like a damp sheet.

'Everything okay, Stringer?' he said, keeping his voice relaxed despite his roiling stomach.

Stringer turned to Max, face pale, and his eyes instantly hostile.

The silence returned, and somehow it was thicker and more turgid than before, as Stringer held Max's gaze, the heavy brow fixed and the jaw muscles pulsating.

A bellow from the Mondeo made Max's stomach lurch. He snapped his head to the right where Shorty was out of the car, a gun pointing in towards Joe. 'You fucking pig bastard,' he shouted, his voice full of hatred.

Max was reaching for the door handle when he felt it. Cold steel pressing into the back of his neck. He flicked his eyes to the mirror, Stringer's arm was stretched out, his hand clutching a revolver, his teeth bared and eyes flashing.

'Move one muscle and you're gonna have a hole in your fucking head,' he hissed between his teeth.

'Stringer, what the fuck?' he said, surprised at the sudden calm that had descended on him.

'You know, you fucking pig bastard.'

'Stringer, I've no idea, man. We're just sitting here in our bloody beemer, and you jab a fucking pistol in my neck. I told you, man, we're not cops.' Max was almost astonished as to how calm his voice was as he delivered the trigger word, hoping to God that the backup team had heard.

Stringer almost growled, pressing the pistol tighter into Max's neck. 'Right, listen. Here's what's gonna happen. You're gonna open the door, and step out. I can cover you from here, so one bad move and I'll put a bullet in you, even if you try and slam the door, I'll just shoot through it. If I even suspect for one second that you're thinking of legging it, I'll shoot you in the back. If you shout, I'll shoot you in the back. If you try anything at all, I'm gonna blow you the fuck away. Do you understand me?' he said, his voice tight and malevolent.

Max flicked his eyes to the right, Joe was out of the car, his hands on his head while Shorty had an automatic pistol trained on him across the bonnet. The pistol was held in both hands, in a decent stance, and Max knew immediately that he knew how to shoot. He'd been trained, no doubt. He flicked his eyes back to Stringer, the pistol moved back a few inches, as he eased the back door open.

'When I say, step out of the car, okay? Hands on your head, and stand perfectly still, facing away from me, towards the trees. If you think I'll miss, you're wrong. I won't miss, I'll blow a hole in your bastard cop back, you understand?'

Max just nodded, not taking his eyes from the mirror. Katie and Evie suddenly appeared in his consciousness. His beautiful family. He had to stay alive. He knew he was in no position to do anything, if he dived for cover, he'd be shot. If he tried to retaliate, he'd not get anywhere close. He had to play for time, to allow the backup to arrive. He had no choice.

'Stay chilled out, Stringer. I'm getting out of the car now, and I'll nae do anything, okay? But you're wrong, pal. I'm no polis.' Max knew something had happened. Something had changed when Stringer had looked at his buzzing phone.

But no way would he admit to being a cop. You never admit to being a cop.

Ever.

'Get out now. One fucking move wrong, and you won't be going home tonight. Am I fucking clear?' A vein was visibly pulsating in his temple.

'Right. Stay chill, Stringer, I'm opening the car door, now.' Max reached down and flicked the car door handle. It opened with a *thunk*. He pushed it open, swung his legs out and stood up, glancing towards the Mondeo as he did. Just a flick of the eyes to where Shorty stood, six feet from the huge form of Joe, who had his hands on his head, his face as pale as bread dough. The rain was bouncing off his scalp and running in rivulets down his face. Shorty looked calm and in control as he stood there, pistol levelled at Joe, his eyes focused on him like a viper about to strike.

'Face the fucking trees,' shouted Stringer, who had opened the rear door behind the passenger seat, the pistol pointing directly at Max as he jumped out with a speed that belied his huge size. Max did as he was told, turning away from Stringer, the rain hosing down on his head, drenching him almost immediately.

He heard heavy footsteps on the hard car park surface, and flinched when the cold steel of the pistol was pressed into the nape of his neck again. He shuddered involuntarily.

'On your knees,' came the barked command.

Max closed his eyes. He was going to get shot.

Here, in a car park in the Highlands, in the pissing rain, he was going to be executed. Someone had betrayed them. Someone had grassed, almost certainly knowing that there would be an inevitably fatal outcome.

No way. Not like this. Not on his knees. He remained motionless, and closed his eyes.

'I said, on your fucking knees,' said Stringer, as he pressed the muzzle of the pistol into his neck even harder.

A sudden bellow erupted to his right, and he heard Joe roar, an animalistic howl of fury. The pistol pressure on his neck slackened, and he turned his head. Joe had Shorty in a bear hug and was raining headbutts into the much smaller man, as they engaged in a furious tussle. There was a sharp crack of a pistol shot, but they continued to struggle. With a burst of energy Max dipped his shoulder, dropped his knees and swung around, his forearm crooked to knock the pistol away from his bodyline, but not far enough. The weapon bucked, the roar of the fired weapon was deafening, and there was a sudden, hot searing pain in the side of his head. The world slowed, and nothing else mattered, as Stringer's arm continued its slow, sweeping motion until his muscles took over, his face scowling, and he halted the momentum and swung the pistol back towards Max.

Then everything changed.

Shouting, yelling, blue strobing lights and chaos from all around them. Laser dots appeared on Stringer's chest, to be immediately replaced with bullets smashing into his torso, stomach and face. He fell to the ground like a puppet whose strings had been cut.

Max was briefly aware of more explosions to his right, and then it was all over.

Armed officers, clad in Kevlar helmets and body armour, all brandishing carbines or pistols.

He reached up to his throbbing temple, and it came away wet and sticky with hot blood, rapidly being diluted by the pouring rain. His head swam, and he dropped to his knees, the rain bouncing on the tarmac. He stayed there for a moment, trying to clear his swimming head.

Chaos was everywhere, and Max looked around through the

stair rods of rain, his mind racing as more cops turned up. Max remained still as he looked at the scene. Stringer and Shorty were flat on the ground, Stringer's arm extended, covered in slick blood, twitching on the ground. Shorty wasn't moving at all, as the armed cops approached, guns trained on both men. Both still a threat.

The whole scene swimming around him, Max felt dizzy.

A pair of feet in Timberlands was just visible at the front of the Mondeo. Fear gripped Max as he stood up and approached them. Joe was flat on his back. He raced over to the big man.

'Joe!' he yelled, as he knelt down next to him.

His pale shirt was saturated with blood that was rapidly spreading in the unrelenting deluge. Joe's eyes were wide open, and his chest was moving up and down as he gasped, trying to suck air into his lungs. He turned to Max, his eyes full of fear, wide, but somehow vacant. His mouth moved but only a gurgling noise came out, accompanied by bright red blood.

'Joe, hold on, man. Help's coming.' He looked around at the thronging cops in the melee that was all round him, and he yelled, 'I need some help, man down. Man down.'

Max assessed Joe's blood-soaked chest, and his heart sank as he saw the almost black hole at the centre of the bloom of blood.

Then it happened. The look of terror on Joe's face eased, he shuddered as he tried in vain to suck air into his ruined lungs.

'Joe, man. Look at me, pal,' Max said, grabbing hold of the man's huge hand. It was cold. So cold, and so wet.

Joe turned his head, just a fraction, and looked straight at Max, his saturated face pale, his eyes fading and terrified.

Total, unmitigated terror in his friend's face. 'Joe, man, hold on, pal. Please hold on,' Max said pleadingly, his voice cracking.

Then Joe's eyes emptied, and he was still. His eyes were open, and staring, but devoid of any vestige of life.

Max knew immediately. As the rain cascaded down his face in thick rivulets, he knew.

He knew that it was too late. In that moment, everything changed. The world stopped, and Max had no awareness of the ensuing chaos as the blue lights strobed around him, armed officers swarmed, with the stink of coppery blood in his nostrils.

He didn't even acknowledge the throbbing pain at the side of his head, the warm blood that was trickling down and being cooled by the rain.

Max raised his head to the darkening sky, the rain battering into his face, and roared. He roared animalistically until the blackness began to infiltrate his vision, and he fell. He welcomed the velvety silence, even with Janie calling his name, over and over again.

51

THE DREAM ARRIVED, almost immediately. Afghanistan. Helmand Province, Max sucking in the hot, dusty air as blood pulsated from Dippy's stumps onto the dry, desiccated sand. The stench of death in Max's nostrils as his friend's eyes relaxed and filled with confusion, before clearing and becoming . . . Nothing.

Just empty.

Max cried out again, his eyes snapping open, as he sat up rapidly, sucking in a breath. He was saturated, but not like he usually was after one of his dreams. Not sweat. He was slick and cold with rain, and he could taste blood in his mouth.

'Max,' came the voice, full of concern, but familiar and comforting. He opened his eyes, and looked to where the voice was coming from.

It was Janie, gripping his hand tightly, face pale, her eyes full of tears. He looked around him, in the brightly lit space, a burly, young green-uniformed paramedic was shining a torch into his eyes.

'You're okay, pal. The bullet just grazed your temple. You'll be grand, but we need to get you checked out,' he said, as he sprayed saline water onto the side of his head. It stung like a bitch.

'Janie . . .' Max tried to find the words, but she just gripped his hand tighter.

'Just relax, we're on way to the Perth Royal, you need that sorting.'

'Janie . . .' He tried to sort through the thoughts and emotions that were bouncing around his head, images of Katie came into his mind, then of Evie, and then of Joe.

'Janie, what about Joe?' he said, turning to look at her, unable to properly focus.

'Just relax, Max. You need to relax.'

Max knew. He knew, but he needed to hear it. 'Janie, for fuck's sake. What about Joe?' Max bellowed, his throat cracking.

Janie's eyes brimmed with fat tears, and she shook her head. 'He didn't make it, Max. Paramedics tried, but it was too late.'

Max felt as though his head was about to explode, such was the pressure throbbing at his temples, his eyes feeling like they were going to escape from their sockets. He wanted to scream, to curse, to get out of this fucking ambulance.

'Those fucking bastards, where are they?' he stuttered, looking pleadingly at his partner and friend. His vision swam, and his head felt like it was being pumped with air.

Janie nodded. 'Both gone. Multiple shots from the ARVs.'

Max's vision began to fade again. Of the four of them who went into that encounter, he was the only survivor, and it was with that thought that the darkness returned.

52

Breaking News: Three Shot and Killed in Police Drugs Bust in Pitlochry

Sources confirm that a police officer is amongst the dead.

THE CASHIER FROWNED as he saw the news story flash up on his phone. He knew immediately. There could be no doubt that Stringer had failed, and that he and Shorty were now dead.

He switched to his Bitcoin wallet. The money was there. A single Bitcoin, worth just over £50,000, had come via a circuitous route from Stringer. Untraceable, and anonymous. The other £50,000 was all set, ready to automatically transfer in a month, unless it was either cancelled, or paid early, by the person who put it there. Well, it looked like he'd be waiting for a month for his other half of the payment. A smile stretched across his lips.

He felt nothing for Stringer, or Shorty. He couldn't give a hoot. They played big-boys' games, with big-boys' rules, and they had lost. Such was life. They were a couple of morons, and he was thankful that he'd never met them. No links to him in any way. As always, he was thankful for his standard operating procedures. It just showed how important self-discipline was in his line of business.

But he'd complete the contract. The Cashier always completed his contracts.

His clientele were very discerning, and he only worked from

personal introduction, on this occasion via the Russian. Only a former client could refer a new client. That was just how it worked. The world was small, and reputations were hard to acquire, but very easy to lose. His reputation for a hundred per cent reliability was everything to him.

He refreshed the newsfeed, but it hadn't been updated. He moved to WhatsApp and tapped at the screen.

Pitlochry?

The response came back quickly. *Stringer and Shorty, plus a cop killed. Undercover sting gone very wrong. I didn't hear until late, tried to warn them, too late, it seems.*

Now was the perfect time to get on and fulfil the contract paid for by the now deceased Stringer. The police would be so busy with recent events, they'd have almost no capacity for anything else.

A target as notable as this one would take exacting research.

He was almost looking forward to it.

53

ROSS WAS SITTING in the Volvo next to Barney, as the rain lashed down against the windows. The place was full of cop cars, vans and armed response vehicles, all with lights strobing. Forensic tents had been erected over the bodies of Stringer, Shorty and Joe by the local CID team that had responded to the incident, all being directed by the duty inspector, a small, nervous man who looked totally out of his depth.

His phone began to buzz on the dash. Ross looked at the display – it was Norma.

'Aye?' said Ross, his voice flat.

'What the hell has happened? Everything is going mental, I'm hearing people have been killed,' she said, her voice full of panic.

'Both suspects down, and tragically Joe was shot by Shorty. He didn't make it, pal.' Ross struggled to get the words out.

'Oh, God, no. Poor Joe, he was so lovely.' Norma began to sob.

'Aye.' Ross didn't know what to say, feeling the same pressure in his chest that always came with grief. Not now, he thought. There was work to do.

'What about Max?' said Norma, her voice full of fear.

'He's got a wee graze, but he's gonna be fine.'

'Oh my God – like a graze from a fucking *bullet*?'

'Aye, but it's minor, just needs patching up, and he'll be right as rain.'

'God, this is just fucking horrible.' She began to weep again.

'Norma, listen to me now, I know it's fucking horrible, but we still have to do our job. There are still dirty bastards out there who are responsible for making this happen.'

'You're right, there is. I was about to phone when it all went crazy.' She paused to blow her nose, her voice cracking up.

'What for?' said Ross. 'We had no line activity on the intercept.'

'I've been monitoring both suspects' phone data, live. Just before it all kicked off both Stringer and Shorty had data activations, at precisely the same time.'

'What, calls or texts?' said Ross.

'Neither. Data. Specific data activations. Both phones hit exactly the same 4G mast in Pitlochry, with the correct azimuth, at precisely the same time, having been totally silent all day. I don't think it was browsing, I think they made or received messages to or from someone, and that person has to be dirty. Right while they were in that car park. We need to secure those phones, now. If they were WhatsApp, Wickr or similar they may have the auto delete function on them.' Norma's voice was thick with emotion, but her underlying professionalism still shone through. No doubt, the analyst wanted what they all wanted. To catch those responsible.

'How long?' said Ross.

'Depends on the app. WhatsApp is minimum twenty-four hours, I think, but other platforms can be much quicker. I'd say we need to get into them right bloody now,' she said, her tone as hard as iron.

'Right, we're on it.' Ross hung up and looked across at Barney. 'Can you do it?'

'Aye, I can 'ave a look at the very least. If it's proper PIN protected it may take a while, mind, and I'd say you'd need to be persuasive to get past that bolshy-looking inspector.'

'Leave that one with me, get your kit from your van. All we want now is the number that called into them both. Whoever has that phone is the dirty bastard, I'm willing to bet.' Ross began to dial as Barney stepped out into the rain.

54

MAX AND JANIE were sitting silently in a cubicle, both staring into space, the sounds of the busy A&E ward had faded to almost nothing. A flat-screen TV was on the wall, set to a news channel. Max looked at the screen without really seeing it. First Minister Ria Choudhary, along with her entourage, was opening a new hospice in Arbroath. He turned away from the TV screen, immediately uninterested.

They just sat there.

Janie looked across at Max, at the scorched and blackened wound on the side of his head where the bullet had burned as it skimmed his temple. About the size of a fifty pence piece, it oozed; the harsh lights bounced off the moist wound.

'I think that'll leave a scar,' said Janie.

Max said nothing. Just sat up on the trolley, staring straight ahead.

'It won't affect your looks, though. You're already hacket enough.' Janie let a slight smile touch her lips.

Still Max was silent, but his lips twitched, just a little.

'Max?' Janie spoke a little more firmly.

He turned towards her, his face pale and eyes dull.

'You know this isn't your fault, don't you?' she said, gently.

Max turned away from her but spoke, his voice cracked and hoarse. 'Stringer got a text, just before he pulled the piece. He and Shorty were eyeballing each other. We need to get into the phones, urgently. Some bastard was grassing on us.'

Janie nodded. 'Ross texted me. It's in hand, and Norma is on standby. Both their phones were active at the time. Irrespective of that, you know it's not your fault, right?'

Max just nodded, then looked back towards her, his eyes widening. 'What about Joe's wife?'

'Police in Perth are going to see her now to deliver the message.'

The message. Known in policing as a 'death message'. All cops dread delivering death messages, of shattering a person's life with a few words.

But this was different.

This was one of their own.

'I need to go and see her. She needs to hear what happened from me, I owe her that.' He closed his eyes tightly, creasing the wound and causing it to seep.

Max's thoughts were crashing into each other, like dodgems at a funfair, and his ears rang with tinnitus after the gunshot, so close to his ear, but then, out of nowhere, his mind cleared.

The curtain pulled back, and a smiling doctor in scrubs entered. 'Hi, guys, I'm Dr Sharma. X-rays look fine, no fractures, nothing sinister. I think we can call you very lucky.'

'Aye, right,' said Max.

'We just need to clean you up properly, get a decent dressing on the wound, and you can go. Dawn is coming in now, and she's way better at deep cleans than me.' He smiled, and then was gone.

Max sat upright and swivelled his legs off the bed. 'I need to get out of here, Janie. This job hasn't died with those two scumbags, and I need to speak to Katie.'

'Max, you need to rest, you've been shot, for God's sake,' said Janie.

'No, I don't. I need to catch the bastards behind this. For Joe. We're doing it for him, Janie.'

55

ROSS AND BARNEY were both dressed in full forensic kit as they approached the car park, which had been totally encircled with blue scene tape. Uniformed cops stood on each side, and temporary lights had been erected. Three forensic tents were in place on the tarmac, alongside the BMW X5 and the Ford Mondeo.

It hadn't taken much persuasion to get Miles Wakefield to authorise access for Ross and Barney to retrieve the phones from the bodies of Stringer and Shorty.

The scene guard lifted the tape, and they ducked underneath it and headed towards the cars.

Firstly, they rounded the Mondeo, looking in each of the windows for any phones. There were none immediately obvious, but there was an old-looking iPad. Ross leaned in and grabbed the tablet. 'We'll take this. By the time the MIT team get to it, someone could have wiped it remotely.' He handed it to Barney, who opened his rucksack and pulled out a square pouch, dropping the iPad in.

'Faraday pouch, no signals in, no signals out,' he said, winking.

A quick walk around the BMW yielded nothing else. No phones, no computers, no tablets. They headed for the closest of the forensic tents, and Ross pulled the flap to one side and stepped in.

The huge form of Stringer was laid flat on his back, and his soaked body was riddled with at least seven bullet holes. Ross looked at the previously formidable gangster. All muscles, intensity and bravado.

Now he just looked dead. Empty. A hollow shell. His eyes were open, a look of confusion on what was left of his face. A bullet had caught him under the chin and had blown a portion of his jawbone away, revealing white shards of bone that shone out vividly against the gore. His T-shirted torso was studded with red-rimmed holes, and the entire barrel chest was saturated in dark, diluted blood. The smell in the tent was fetid with a mix of coppery blood, and shit.

Stringer hadn't died well.

'Right, where's the bastard's phone?' said Ross.

Barney squatted on his haunches and pointed to the right-hand side of the big man's jeans. An oblong outline was visible. 'There we go, in his pocket.'

'I'll get it, you're still a contractor, while I'm the cop. Best it's me that writes the statement,' said Ross, squatting down with a muffled groan, his knees cracking as he reached for the pocket. He eased his gloved fingers into the sopping wet, tight pocket, and in a moment had pulled out a basic-looking smartphone. He pressed the button on the side, and the phone woke up, requesting a PIN.

Ross handed the phone to Barney, who pulled out a tablet computer. He plugged a lead into the handset, and grunted. 'Six-digit pin. I can't break it here, I'll need my proper computer, or if it's what I think it is, I'd need to get my mate Clive to have a go.'

'What – that computer geek in Yorkshire I paid about six grand to last year to bust the dark-web bunch?'

'That's the one. Clive. Clever bugger.'

'Expensive bugger. Does it have fingerprint recognition on it?' said Ross.

Barney looked at the screen on the tablet. 'It does.' He then paused, and looked hard at Ross. 'You're not serious?' he said.

'Pass it over,' said Ross, holding out his gloved hand.

'I'm no expert, but where does this fall in the police crime scene manual?' said Barney, handing the phone back to Ross.

'Under the fucking Ways and Means Act, pal. Which digit do you reckon?'

Barney shook his head, and sighed. 'I'd say left thumb, that's probably most common.'

Ross grabbed Stringer's thumb and pressed the phone's home button firmly.

Remarkably, the phone unlocked on first go. 'Blimey, good suggestion, you're not bad for an old codger.' Ross nodded and handed the phone back up to Barney.

'Most logical, wasn't it? Most people are right-handed but hold the phone in their left, so use left thumb. That's my theory, anyway.'

'So bloody clever, now hurry up, it probably won't stay unlocked for long.'

Barney plugged the phone back into his tablet, and swiped and tapped away for a moment, before nodding. 'Done. Pin disabled, we've free access. I'll get it in a Faraday bag to stop anyone remote wiping it.'

'Look at the last received message before you do anything else,' said Ross.

Barney swiped and clicked again, looked at the screen and grinned behind his mask. He held up the phone, a WhatsApp message displayed. 'Norma was right. Disappearing messages are enabled, and these would have gone in ten more minutes, but I've captured it now, so we're good. It's a three-person group: Shorty, Stringer and the person that sent this message. Here's your inside man, Ross.'

Ross looked at the message, and Barney tapped on the unknown number. The message was short and to the point.

UC COPS.GET OUT NOW!

Ross's eyes hardened. 'Right, let's do the other one and then get Norma working on it all.' He stood up with a grimace and looked at the phone screen again. 'We're coming for you, you scummy wee shite.'

'What now?' said Barney.

'Now, we get back to the office, you secure what's on those devices. Then we check in on Craigie and make sure the bugger's okay, and then we go home. We all need some rest, and then we start again tomorrow.'

56

IT WAS ALMOST 4 a.m. when Max let himself into the cottage, shushing Nutmeg as she fussed around his feet, tail lashing. His temple throbbed underneath the sticky dressing, and he was thankful for his shaved scalp, predicated by his male pattern baldness.

He felt almost as if he wasn't in contact with the scrubbed floor as he locked the door behind him and pulled the blind back down, kicking off his trainers as he did.

He fell onto the sofa, and closed his eyes, images flying around inside his head. The sight of Joe, lifeless on the ground. The sear of pain as the bullet grazed him, the rain hosing down, the flashes from the cop's carbines, Stringer's body twitching as the bullets slammed into him. Max's eyes flicked open, and fell on the sideboard. The bottle of whisky was just sitting there.

A fifteen-year-old malt that he hadn't drank from in years. He'd discovered that his PTSD didn't really mix with alcohol, but this, surely, was different?

Suddenly he longed for the burn of a dram. The numbing sensation of the neat spirit carving a passage down his throat, then seeping into his bloodstream. Surely, just one. It would be almost therapeutic.

He got to his feet and went towards the sideboard, his hand gripping the cool glass bottle, the pale amber spirit almost daring him to pour a shot. Just one. Medicinal, it would be, surely?

'Max?' Katie's voice behind him made him jump, his heart thumping in his chest.

He turned, mouth open, the breath almost ripped from him. She was dressed in her pyjamas, her hair messy and her face creased from sleep.

'God, you almost gave me a heart attack,' he gasped.

'Oh my God, what the hell has happened?' She came up to him, raising her hand towards the dressing. Reflexively he pulled away.

'Max?'

He lowered his eyes. 'There was an incident at work,' he said, in the greatest understatement of the century.

'Incident? What? I went to bed early, as Evie had been so unsettled, and I passed out at about nine. What's happened?'

Max sat down and rubbed his face. It felt gritty and greasy.

'Max, for God's sake, will you please tell me?' she said.

He sighed, and then sucked in a deep breath. He just had to tell her. 'I was on an undercover job. Supposed to be buying drugs from some criminals, and they pulled guns. My partner on the job was shot, and died. His name was Joe.' Max just let it out. There was no way he could soft soap this.

Katie's hand went to her mouth, and she gasped. 'Oh Jesus, and that injury on your head was caused by a fucking *gunshot*?'

'Just a graze,' he said, his fingers feeling the dressing covering the wound that continued to throb.

Katie fell onto the sofa, tears flowing down her face. Her beautiful, kind face.

Max said nothing, there was nothing he could think of to say, so he sat next to his wife, and held her tight. They both wept together, their tears mingling.

57

THE DREAM WAS inevitable. The dream was florid, technicolour and as intense as any he'd had.

The dream tore him from his fitful slumber at eight after just a couple of hours sleep, and he just sat there, in the bed, the sheets sticking to him, breath rasping.

Katie wasn't there with him, but he could hear Evie giggling in the kitchen as they played together.

He picked his phone up from the bedside table, and saw that there were several messages, from Janie, Ross and one from a number he didn't recognise.

He opened the message, and read, his heart pounding. *Hi Max. My name is DC White from the MIT. I'm family liaison for the murder of Joe, and I wonder if you can give me a call. Joe's wife Hettie is asking lots of questions, and she'd like to meet you again. Can you give me a call to arrange?*

Max suddenly felt cold, and the hairs on his neck began to prickle. Any traces of sleep, or tiredness, were blown away by the prospect of seeing Joe's wife.

Or his kids.

But he knew that he had to. Had it been him that had been shot, would he want Katie to hear about it from some faceless senior officer, with his false platitudes, or from the person who was with him when it happened?

He knew then that he had no choice. He had to go.

He felt nauseous. A cloying, rancid sensation that propelled him out of his bed, and into the en suite where he was violently sick, retching, gagging and gasping, until there was nothing more to give. He rinsed his mouth, splashed his face with cold water, and picked up his phone, staring at the message for a full minute before replying to DC White.

That's fine, what time?

The reply came back almost instantaneously. *Thanks, Max. She's really desperate to hear from you. Meet me and DCI McKechnie at Perth Police Station at 11?*

Max sighed, and stared at the words on the screen, struggling to arrange his thoughts. He knew as he sat there, his head reeling, that this was going to be the hardest thing he'd ever done, and just for a moment. Just for one brief microsecond, he wished that he could switch places with Joe.

58

ROSS, JANIE, BARNEY and Norma were sitting in the office, in total, complete silence.

Barney was staring at his laptop, which was in turn connected to the iPad that had been seized from the Mondeo that Stringer and Shorty had been driving.

The sense of shock had dissipated, only to be replaced with a deep, unrelenting sadness that hung in the air of the depressing office like a fug.

Janie's phone buzzed on the desk. She picked it up, and she exhaled, slowly, hissing as she let the breath out between her teeth. 'Shit,' she muttered.

'What's up?' said Ross.

'Text from Max. He's not coming into the office this morning.'

'Don't blame him, the poor bugger. Fucking bullet scrapes the side of my heid, and I doubt I'd fancy it.'

'No, he's on his way to Dunkeld now, meeting with the FLO for Joe's family. Jesus, that's gonna be brutal. Should I go and meet him there?' Janie said.

'Does he want you to go?'

'He's not said.'

'Ask him. His decision, like.'

Janie tapped at the handset, which buzzed in reply quickly.

'He said no. Just no, without explanation. Christ, I'm worried about him, Ross.'

'You know him. He has to find his way to deal with this. I've alerted welfare branch, and they're contacting him directly to offer support.'

'You know about Afghanistan, right?' said Janie, stretching her arms above her head.

'Well, I know he did a couple of tours. He's not talked about it to me. Why?' Ross furrowed his heavy brow, his bushy eyebrows bristling.

'One of his guys died in an IED attack, and he was with him when it happened. I think this will hit him hard, Ross. I'm worried for him.'

Ross didn't reply, and the gloomy silence descended on the office, again.

'Can I talk work for a minute?' said Norma, almost guiltily.

'Kind of why we're here, I hope,' said Ross.

'The number that tipped Stringer and Shorty the wink.'

'What about it? You said it was a prepay burner, with no bank account attached, so we're assuming whoever has it is topping up manually.' Ross yawned, his face lined with fatigue.

'Aye, that's correct, unless we get a specific shop or location we can trace for CCTV, not a lot of use, right?'

'Aye. Go on?'

'Well, looking at the call data it's a wee bit more intriguing. It's only switched on infrequently, and looking at the timelines, it always seems to coincide with significant events. So, it went on around the time of all the murders, sometimes before, sometimes after. It's interesting. It's also thrown up another number, which is even more notable.' Norma tapped at her keyboard, and resettled her glasses on her nose.

'How?' said Janie.

'Well, it's also called into another number that I've cell-sited in County Durham, over the border.'

'How's that notable?' said Ross.

'Well, looking at the azimuth, and timings, I'd say that it was either inside, or close to Frankland jail, a couple of months ago when Stringer was on remand there, and there's something else.'

'Go on,' said Ross.

'It was also cell-sited in central Newcastle, close enough to the Crown Court, on the exact same day that Stringer was formally acquitted of the murder.'

'So not an inmate, then. Maybe a visitor?'

'His prison intel records should be illuminating.'

'Jesus, so whoever this is has been right up close and personal with Stringer, then?'

'Looks that way.'

Ross threw his pen down on the desk and massaged his temples. 'Right, I'm knackered, team. Suggestions?'

'I'll reach out to prison intel at Frankland. Look at visits to Stringer, and who was on his contact list. It looks to me like this whole thing has been in planning for bloody ages,' said Janie.

'Errm, guys . . . ?' said Barney softly, as he stared at his laptop.

'Good idea, Janie. Norma, can you get all the data on a chart, overlaid with the timeline around notable events? There has to be something in all of this. The answer is right in front of us.' Ross was suddenly animated, and he creakily got to his feet.

'Guys?' Barney tried again.

'Good idea, Ross. The key is linking the timeline with the number, and the cell sites. Must be a link somewhere,' Norma said, her enthusiasm visibly intensifying.

'Fooks sake, will you bloody people listen to me?' Barney barked, his eyes flashing and his face reddening.

'What is it, you grumpy old get?' said Ross.

'This iPad belonged to Shorty. I imaged the contents of it, as it was pretty much empty of anything saved, so I couldn't see why they'd have it with them. I sent the data to Clive, who has done a deep dive, and extraction of it all, and he noticed summat odd.'

'Who?' said Ross.

'Oh, shut up. You remember him, proper computer expert I used to work with at Box.'

Ross narrowed his eyes. 'Go on.'

'Right, it's an old iPad, but was totally wiped about a year ago. As far as he can tell it's really only been used for some emails, and not many of those. It's only sent blank emails to a particular address on a few occasions. All shite Gmail addresses with just a few characters, letters and numbers, etcetera. Clive knows his way around this kind of thing, and he recognises the tradecraft. It's draft-folder communication.'

'What, as in just updating a draft message, then the other person just refreshes and reads the message. Nothing sent, nothing to intercept?' said Janie.

'Aye, that's it. Old-school method, but pretty effective. Well, anyway. These buggers weren't as clever as they thought they were. Clive's found the autosaved data deep in the memory of the iPad. Look . . .' He swivelled his laptop around so they could all see. The conversation on the screen was as clear and unambiguous as it was chilling.

> Hi, Cashier. Job we spoke about. It's on. We're ready to transfer Bitcoin to wallet. How much deposit for the contract?
>
> 50 up front. 50 once task completed, as before. Any request for method of despatch?
>
> Spectacular. As spectacular as Daniel Solomon, but maybe a different method. Brains all over the pavement would be nice.
>
> Acknowledged. Identity?

The team all stared, open mouthed at the exchange. A contract had been paid for. Fifty thousand had been paid as a deposit.

'Fucking hell. It's there in black and white about the Daniel Solomon car bomb. This is bloody huge, and we were fucking right all along. Al-Qaeda my arse,' Ross said, his eyes like saucers.

'Aye, a hundred grand contract killing. That's no' gonna be a two-bit drug dealer, when the going rate is only between ten and twenty K.' Janie brushed her hair back with her fingers.

'Cashier?' said Ross.

'It's no' as impressive as The Scorpion or some shit like that, is it? In fact, it's a pish name for a contract killer. Hasn't he seen *John Wick*?' said Ross.

'So, who's the target, then?' said Norma, raising her eyes at Ross's turn of phrase.

'Well, that's the thing. No name given, but at exactly this time, an image was copied from the BBC news page.' Barney opened another screen. It was an image of a distinguished-looking middle-aged Asian man, wearing red-and-black robes and a long full-bottomed wig. The ceremonial regalia of a High Court judge.

'Who the fuck is that?' said Ross.

'Well, the BBC page says it's the Honourable Mr Justice Imran Ahsan, High Court judge,' said Barney.

'Oh my God, I read about this in the intelligence package, not only is the Honourable Mr Justice Imran Ahsan a senior High Court judge, he was the first Muslim to take that role.'

'Other than the obvious reason for a bunch of evil racist bastards, why him? Is he particularly outspoken or something? Why Mr Justice Ahsan?' said Ross.

Janie looked at the rest of the team and sighed. 'He was the judge at Stringer Dent's trial. Has the contract been accepted?'

'Look at the next slide.' Barney clicked on the keyboard. A solitary word came up.

Acknowledged.

'Aye, well, that's as maybe, but whoever this Cashier twat is, he isn't gonna finish the job now, is he? He's just got fifty grand down payment for bugger all.' Ross shrugged.

Barney shook his head, slowly. 'I wish that were the case, Ross.'

'What?'

'I got Clive looking at the Bitcoin wallet, and there's summat very bloody worrying. The balancing transaction of £50k worth of crypto has been set up, ready to go through some kind of online autopay system that I can't fathom.'

'What? Are we saying that it's set up to pay? But how would the system know if the contract has been fulfilled?'

'It doesn't. Clive is convinced that it's set to pay out after a specific amount of time passes. I guess it's a way that the contractor can ensure payment, particularly if the contractee is dead, as in our case.'

'So, you're saying that the Cashier is getting paid, whatever happens?'

'Looks that way. There's no one to cancel the payment. I'd say Lord Justice Sir whatshisname has still very much got a target painted on his arse.'

Ross's head dropped, and he banged his hand on the top of the desk, wincing and cursing as he did. He reached for his phone. 'This fucking job is worse than we thought. Good work, people. I'm calling the Chief.'

59

HETTIE BLAIR COULDN'T have looked more different than the last time he'd seen her, just a couple of days ago with Joe.

Then, she'd been sparkly, full of smiles, her eyes shining and bright with vivacity and fun.

Now she looked broken.

Her skin was sallow, her cheeks pale, and her eyes were puffy and red. She just sat, head down, her fingers playing with her wedding ring. An older woman, who looked almost identical to her, was next to her on the sofa, stroking her hair. She'd introduced herself as Isla, Hettie's older sister.

DC Sharon White was a stout middle-aged cop, with short, severe dark hair and a soft, round face that radiated kindness.

'Now, Hettie, I understand you and Max have met already?' said Sharon.

Hettie nodded without looking up from her fingers that twiddled with her wedding ring.

Isla cleared her throat and dabbed at her eyes. 'Hettie wants to hear it from you, Max. We know it's going to be hard to hear, but she wants to know. All of it.'

Max gripped the arm of the easy chair he was trying to sit upright in. Even though it wasn't comfortable, he didn't feel he could relax.

Max opened his mouth to speak, but then closed it again. He thought about what he was going to say, but he didn't have the words. He felt the familiar grip of nausea, almost as if there was a lead ball in his gut that was itching to be freed. His skin was prickling, and he could feel the burn on his cheeks. 'How much did Joe tell you about what we'd been doing, Hettie?' Max's voice was tight and constricted.

'Nothing. I didn't even know he was undercover.' Her previous confident voice of a few days ago, with eyes full of humour, was gone, replaced by a monotone, flat whisper.

'How much would you like to know?'

Hettie looked up and stared at Max hard. 'Are you married, Max?'

Max nodded.

'What's your wife's name?'

'Katie.'

'Kids?'

'Aye, one. Evie, she's just a year old.'

'What do you think your wife would want to know, if she were me, Max?'

Max looked down at his trainers, his thoughts turning to Katie. His beautiful wife. So funny, so kind and so strong. He looked back at Hettie, the tears brimming in her swollen eyes. He took a deep breath. 'I think she'd want to know the truth.' He felt like he had a golf ball in his throat.

Hettie lowered her eyes, and gripped her sister's hand so hard that her knuckles went white. 'Then tell me the truth. All of it.'

So, Max told her the truth.

All of it.

After he'd finished, Hettie stood up, walked over to Max and touched her fingers to the dressing on his temple. 'Does this hurt?' she said.

Max shook his head. 'It's fine. Just a wee scratch.'

Hettie stepped closer, threw her arms around his neck and hugged him tight. She hugged him hard, her body stiff and rigid as she buried her face into his shoulder, and she remained like this for five minutes. Then she pulled away, looked him straight in the eyes, her face wet with tears. 'Thank you for being with Joe at the end, Max. It means a lot to know that he was with a friend when he passed.' She then turned and left the room with her sister.

The silence that descended on the room was deafening, every tick of the wall clock was like a hammer being tapped on Max's scalp.

'Did I do the right thing?' Max asked Sharon, without looking at her.

'You did the only thing you can ever do, Max. You told her the truth. Some people don't do that, but the truth always comes out. Whether it's at the inquest, or the trial, it always comes out, and if you lie, it will always hurt them more, because then, they feel betrayed.'

'I almost wish she'd bloody screamed at me, or hit me, anything.'

'Some do, some don't. You're a good man, Max, you were brave to come up here, so soon after it happened when you've been through a horrible experience yourself.'

Sharon's eyes were kind, and Max could see why she performed this role. His eyes fell onto a framed family photo on the wall. Joe stood there, a man mountain, grinning widely, all three of his kids in his huge arms, Hettie giggling wildly, her arms around his shoulders. A sudden surge of emotions, all disparate, all fighting, began to swirl in his consciousness.

He closed his eyes tight, trying to clear the fug, but his mind was a mess, a conflict of bouncing, opposing emotions, none of which made any sense, and he began to feel nauseous and dizzy again. He felt like there was a pinball machine inside him, balls bouncing, lights flashing. He began to sway, just a little, and he reached out to steady himself against the arm of the chair.

'Max?' said Sharon, dragging him from his reverie.

He snapped his eyes open, an urge to be alone so powerful it was overwhelming.

'I have to go.' He almost staggered out of the house, digging in his pockets for his car keys, breathing heavily, the breaths rasping as he tried to calm himself.

'Just get in the car, Max. Get in the fucking car, you idiot,' he muttered, as he wrenched the door open and dived in, heart pounding, sweat running down his back, as he pressed the starter button, desperate to be away. To be alone.

He jammed the car into gear, and screeched off, his head spinning.

Within a couple of minutes, he saw the shop on the main street in the village centre. A small local parade of shops on both sides of the road. Pulling over, he jumped out of the car and headed straight for the Co-op, knowing exactly what he was going to do.

Entering the thankfully quiet shop he went straight up to the counter, where the bottles of spirits were displayed behind the till.

'Help you, pet?' said the smiling woman.

Max looked behind her. The bottles were lined up, like soldiers, labels out, all innocent and innocuous, but each offering temporary oblivion. His eyes stopped on the bottle of cheap vodka. It didn't matter what it was, it was what it represented. Escape. To be away from his reeling mind, if only for a short time.

'Bottle of Smirnoff,' he said.

'Here you go, pet,' said the lady, but Max barely heard her. He just took the bottle and tapped his card on the machine.

'That's all gone through.'

Back in the car he sat there for a moment, looking at the bottle lying on the seat next to him, his mind still like a clockwork toy that had been overwound, tears streaming down his face. The image of Joe appeared, his eyes full of panic, gasping for breath as the life force drained from him.

His phone began to ring through the speakers of the car, the display informing him that it was Katie. She had been sick with worry about him when he'd told her he was going to see Hettie, begging him not to go.

'Not now, babe. Please not now, you've been through a horrible trauma, and you need some time to process this. Please just stay here with Evie and me,' she'd implored, with tear-filled eyes. She'd even offered to accompany him, but he'd just shaken his head and left the house without another word.

His hand hovered over the button on the phone, but rather than answering it, he declined the call. 'Not now, babe. Not now,' he said, softly. He picked up his phone, and powered it down, staring at the screen as it went black. Solitude. All he wanted was solitude, and oblivion. He started the engine, and moved off.

He steered the car through the village, over the Dunkeld Bridge until he hit the T junction with the A9. He paused there for a moment, competing thoughts crashing around in his mind, colliding and bouncing. A beep of a horn behind him made him start, and he gasped out loud.

A simple choice. Turn left to head south, towards home.

Or right. Right towards the Highlands, away from Katie and Evie, towards solitude.

Max signalled, and turned right, and headed north.

60

KATIE SHUSHED EVIE as she lay her down in her cot for her post-lunch nap, nerves nipping at her as she patted her daughter's blonde head.

She was so worried about Max. He had barely spoken to her since coming back in the early hours of the morning, and she knew he'd been sick in the en suite. He wouldn't even discuss the whole situation about going to see the poor cop's widow.

She loved Max more than she could bear to think about, but she knew he was complex. She knew he'd had some terrible experiences in Afghanistan and London, and now this. Watching a colleague die, and having to go and talk to his widow, it was enough to break even the strongest of men. And now he wasn't answering the phone?

She crept out of the bedroom and back into the kitchen, where she went to the iPad. She opened up the Find My iPhone app. She frowned. The phone had been switched off straight after her call, when it was in Dunkeld. That was so unlike him.

As she closed the app, she saw a notification from their joint bank account. She frowned again.

A purchase of £18.99 from a Co-op in Dunkeld. She knew then. That wasn't right. Max hated shops, never bought anything, and yet here it was in black and white. Memories flared of Max a few years ago in London after the shooting when he was on the Flying Squad. His disappearing with a bottle of spirits, and half drinking himself to death. She went cold. She dialled again, this time his work number.

It began to ring. It continued to ring, until the voicemail message cut in. '*Hi, this is DS Max Craigie, please leave a message.*'

'Max, it's me. Please call me back, darling, and please don't do what I think you're going to do. Please? For me, and Evie, please don't.' She hung up and placed the phone on the worktop, her stomach churning. She dialled again.

'Hi, Katie,' said Janie.

'Janie, have you heard from Max?' she said, her voice wobbling a touch.

'Not since earlier. He texted me to say he was going to see Joe's wife. Why, is everything okay?'

'I don't think so, no. He was in a terrible state this morning, Janie. Then he left the house before ten to go and see Joe's wife. I tried to call him, but he didn't answer, and now he's switched his phone off. I've just tried his work phone and he's not answering. I'm scared, Janie.'

'I'm sure he's fine, Katie. Maybe he just needs a little time?' Janie didn't sound convinced at all.

'There's something else. He went to the shop in Dunkeld and spent some money. You know what he's like with shops, Janie.'

'Well, that's true, he hates spending money, but surely that's meaningless.'

'He spent £18.99. That sounds like a bottle of spirits to me.'

'Katie . . .' Janie began, but Katie interrupted her, her voice cracking with worry.

'I'm telling you, Janie. I've been through this before. He did this in London once, after the shooting. Almost drank himself stupid, I'm really scared.' She began to weep, the tears flowing down her face.

Janie said nothing for a moment, but Katie could hear muffled voices.

'Katie, you there?' Janie sounded businesslike.

'Yes.'

'We're getting an urgent trace on his work phone, it'll only take a few minutes, as we don't need authorisations, Norma has a hotline to the telephone unit. Hold on the phone a second.'

Katie listened to the muffled voices, all urgency and efficiency, and she was suddenly thankful that she wasn't having to deal with this on her own. Her skin was prickling and her breathing was shallow and quick as she imagined Max out there alone, broken. Her heart lurched at the thought.

'Katie?' Janie's voice was tense down the line.

'Go on.'

'His phone is live, and its GPS is putting it right on Avoch Harbour. Looks like he's right out on the wall, and almost in the sea? Isn't that near Auntie Elspeth's place?' said Janie.

'Yes. Why the hell has he gone there?' she said, her mind racing.

'Old haunts, I guess. Shall I make my way?' said Janie.

Katie paused, her mind chewing it all over, and then it hit her, and her thoughts suddenly cleared. 'It's okay, I think I know what to do. Thanks, Janie.' Katie hung up, and then selected WhatsApp. She engaged a video call. The phone buzzed a number of times before it was answered, and an elderly white-haired lady appeared, squinting through her wire-framed glasses.

'Hello, Katie, my darling. This is an unexpected surprise?'

'Hello, Auntie Elspeth.'

61

MAX SAT ON the harbour wall. He unwound a length of raggy old fishing line, scraped out the contents of a limpet shell, attached it to the hook and lobbed it into the softly lapping sea, just a couple of metres below him. The battered lead weight tugged the line taut, and Max unwound it until it stopped. This was almost a reflexive action that catapulted him back thirty years to when he used to fruitlessly fish here as a youngster.

Avoch (pronounced 'Och') Harbour would never have been described as 'bustling'. It was more serene, and basic, and mostly now used for pleasure craft, or the dolphin-spotting vessel. It was an irregular basin-type structure formed by a C-Plan pier that jutted out into the North Sea. Whilst picturesque, it didn't feature heavily on any Black Isle tour guides' 'must see' attractions. It didn't matter. At this moment, it was where Max wanted to be.

To be alone. To be free of all the external pressures, to have nothing to think about beyond the pointless activity of trying to hook a crab.

Of course it hadn't worked. He closed his eyes and enjoyed the warmth of the sunshine on his face, the only noises were a cry of a seagull and the lapping of the waves against the harbour wall.

The images of Joe swam into his consciousness. The big, beefy cop, his eyes shifting from panic-stricken and terrified, to confused, and then to empty. The gaping hole in his chest, the blood diluted by the pissing fucking rain, soaking the man's huge body. Joe's wife sobbing, then holding him, and then, almost worst of all:

Thanking him.

Her gratitude that Max had been alongside her husband as life slipped away from him was the worst of all. He wanted to feel her anger. He wanted her to scream in his face, blame him for the death of her husband. The father to their three children. The familiar nausea began to creep in, and his eyes snapped open, and his head turned ninety degrees to the right, where the bottle of vodka sat there, still unopened. Taunting him.

He reached out and touched the cool glass, only warmed by the balmy breeze. He tucked the reel of the line under his thigh, and unscrewed the bottle; he lifted it to his lips and drank a little. Just a nip. It was harsh, coarse and fiery, and the familiarity was almost tangible. His brain was filled with a blast of memories, of drunken arguments, of puking, fighting and crying. It offered something, but it could take everything.

He was tipping the bottle to take another swig when a voice rang out behind him. Soft, kind and instantaneously recognisable, tinged with the warmth of the Black Isle accent.

'After you with that, Max. I could use a wee nip.'

Max turned to see his beloved Aunt Elspeth there behind him. Her soft grey hair, shapeless jeans, cardigan and carpet slippers were all crowned with a floppy-brimmed hat. Her eyes surveyed him, sharp, intelligent and kind. She groaned as she sat down next to him. 'Shite the bed, boy. My auld knees dinnae like sitting on this crappy wall. Hand it awa.' She held out her tiny, delicate hand, and Max handed her the bottle. She raised it to her lips, and took a much bigger swig than Max had.

She screwed up her face. 'Jesus, if you're planning on drinking yerself to death, boy, why not with a decent dram of malt, eh?' She lowered the bottle and placed it on the rough concrete.

Max turned to his profoundly deaf aunt, and spoke. She'd been deaf for many years, but was an expert lip-reader. 'Didn't want to waste a decent malt if I was gonna die, no sense on spending forty quid, when less than twenty would do the job. How did you know?'

'Your lovely wifey called me. As soon as she said, I knew you'd be here. You loved fishing for crabs, even if you never, ever caught one.'

'How did she know?'

'Because she's no' daft, pet. She knows you, and she loves you. You turned your phone off, and you spent almost twenty quid at a shite Co-op in Dunkeld. She knows you're a tight-arse, so it got her worried. She called your pal Janie, and they tracked your other phone.'

'Did Katie tell you what had happened?' said Max, looking at the vodka.

'Aye, and I'd heard about it on the news. Sounds bloody horrible, Max. I'm so sorry.'

'I couldn't save him, Auntie E.' Max felt the tears begin to rise again.

'You want another nip of this shite?' She offered the bottle. Max took it but didn't drink from it. He just held it in his lap and looked out to sea. He didn't say anything.

The silence was long, but not awkward. Max had lived with Elspeth for the two years after his parents had been killed in a traffic accident on the A9, before he joined the army. She was way more than just an aunt. She was everything to him.

'Were you actually gonna drink all of this crap, and hoy yerself in the North Sea?'

'I hadn't thought that far ahead. I just wanted away after I told Joe's wife what had happened.'

'Was she scunnered at you?'

'No. She thanked me, but she's broken, Auntie E.'

'Was it your fault?'

'No, we didn't know they were carrying, although it was always a risk, and we certainly didn't expect them to be warned by some bastard.'

'Well, then. It's no' your fault, any more than the time your folks died, and you tried to blame yourself for that, didn't you?'

Max paused, remembering the huge argument he'd had with his parents in the hours before they'd died that terrible day all those years ago.

'I was just a kid. I didn't know what to think.'

'Aye, that's shite, Max. Stop blaming yourself for stuff that isn't your fault. Your mum and dad were killed because a bloody tourist did a stupid overtake on the A9, and Joe was killed because two nasty, violent criminals decided to pick up guns. Stop bloody blaming yourself, and start thinking what you can do to make it right, Max.' Elspeth's eyes blazed, and he knew she was right.

Elspeth was always right.

'I just wanted escape. I needed some space. I . . .' He paused, and raised the bottle to his lips, but then stopped, and lowered it again. He rested his head on Elspeth's shoulder, and she encircled his shoulders with her tiny arm and pulled him in. They just sat like that for a few minutes, not talking, mostly because Max realised that Elspeth wouldn't have been able to see his mouth to lip-read.

Eventually, Elspeth pulled away and looked straight at Max. 'Is everyone caught who had anything to do with this?'

Max shook his head. 'No, there are others. At least one bent bastard.'

She narrowed her eyes. 'Can the team catch him without you?'

'Probably.'

'Will they catch him as quickly without you?' Her voice hardened a touch.

Max paused, an image of Bruce Ferguson suddenly entering

his thoughts. He needed to speak to Bruce, remembering his last words to him. *'Maybe stay in touch, eh? A bit of quid pro quo?'*

Max looked back at Elspeth, his face serious. 'Maybe not.'

'You think you can make a difference?' Her voice wasn't accusatory, rather it was curious. She had a rare gift with people, did Elspeth. A question could become something more. It could become a suggestion, which would become an imperative. It was almost a super-power.

'I guess.'

'You want any more of this shite vodka, or would you prefer a cup of tea at mine? I've baked scones.'

'I don't want the vodka, anymore. I've realised I don't even really like the bloody taste of booze. Cup of tea would be good, though.'

'Come on, then.' She screwed the top of the bottle back on, and stood with a muffled groan.

'Bloody hell, Obi-Wan Kenobi has nothing on you, does he?' Max said, cracking his first smile for some time.

'Eh?'

'Nothing, but your powers of suggestion are a little Jedi-like. Not tipping the vodka out then, Auntie E?' said Max, also standing up.

'I'm no' daft lad. Partial to a V&T, and shame to waste it.'

Max's work phone began to buzz again. He'd been ignoring it, but looking at the screen a slight smile crossed his face.

'Janie?'

'You're not dead, then?' said his partner.

'Not yet.'

'Thank God for that. You still owe me a tenner. Hold up, Ross wants a word.'

'Oh great,' he began, but Janie had already gone.

'Craigie,' barked Ross.

'Aye?'

'Are you no' mad anymore?' Ross's voice was its usual mix of caustic, with an undercurrent of concern, that Max hadn't really experienced anywhere else.

'I'm okay. Just needed a moment or two.'

'Tell me you've no' necked a whole bottle of Smirnoff.'

'How did you know it was Smirnoff?'

'Your lovely wife, who is going nuts by the way – call her – told us you'd spent £18.99 at the Co-op. Only booze at that price in the Co-op I could find was Smirnoff.'

'Very perceptive.'

'I'm a detective, man. Right, are you fit for work?'

Max grinned again, feeling the clouds begin to clear, as his aunt looked at him and smiled warmly.

'Aye, I'm good. I'll drop home first to see Katie, but then I'll be in.'

'Aye, best you do, and make sure you look after my bloody goddaughter. After that you need to do some fucking work, you idle fud. We've had an unpleasant development. The phone work is kicking off, Norma has some leads, and there's a contract killing that Stringer ordered, and that contract is still fucking live. Also, we've no doubt that it's the same guy that planted the bomb in York, it bloody has to be.'

'Shit, are you telling DCS Barr?'

'No, not yet. Those bastards can wait till we've sought corroboration and know a bit more.'

'That's a big call, it could get very political.'

'Dinnae give a fuck. Chief has our backs on this one. We've broken it open, that snidey cockney walloper can wait, and can cop all the fucking egg on his smug face when we prove it was these bastards that blew that poor mannie up.'

'Fair. Who's the target?'

'One of the country's most senior judges is gonna get whacked unless we stop it. Get here pronto, and call Norma for a speedy update when you're en route. However, go and give your lovely wife, who I have to add, you are massively punching above your weight with, a reassuring kiss first. Understood?'

'Aye.'

'Crack on, and say hi to Auntie Elspeth.'

Max smiled, as he slotted his phone back in his pocket.

62

MAX FELT HIMSELF relax as he headed south on the A9, Mogwai, the Scottish post-rock band, pumping their harsh, discordant sounds out of the car's speakers. The music was coarse, but it was mesmeric, and was helping him organise his thoughts. Or possibly to block them out by overwhelming them. Whatever, it was cathartic.

Norma's briefing had been typically succinct and to the point, and it was clear why he was needed back at the coal face.

He knew what he needed to do now.

Being sad, feeling guilty, feeling grief were not helpful for anyone. He needed to make sure that everyone connected to this case, everyone who looked the wrong way, anyone who enabled, assisted or informed would all pay.

Then they could all grieve for their fallen comrade.

Only that would allow it to make sense. His jaw tightened as it became clear what was needed. And if he had to cut corners, or breach protocol to make sure that the right things happened, then that's what he'd do. He pulled the car over and stopped in a layby, and took a deep breath, checking himself in the rear-view mirror. He looked pale and tired, with dark circles around his eyes.

He picked up his phone, selected the contact listed as 'B' and pressed the call button. There were no numbers, just an indecipherable string of characters.

There was no ring tone, and there was no voicemail. Just a number of clicks, tones and beeps until he heard the familiar voice, rich, confident and full of the tones of Caithness. A sergeant major's voice. 'Max. I was expecting your call,' said Bruce.

'Been following events, Bruce?'

'I watch the news. Sorry about your colleague, were you close by when it happened?'

'Aye,' said Max, flatly.

'How close?'

'Close enough,' he said, reflexively his hand went up to his temple to the flat, smooth dressing that was still stuck in place.

'I'm glad you're okay. I take it the reason for your call isn't to tell me that Dent and Shore are both dead, and therefore this inquiry is all completed with a natty bow around it?'

'No. It's not over, not at all. Someone tipped them off at a very inopportune moment.'

'How?'

'WhatsApp message to both men saying we were cops.'

'I'm assuming that you're all over who that is, where the phone's been and timeline issues?'

'Aye, we're working on it. You hinted that Stringer was on your radar?'

'He was, are you willing to engage in some quid pro quo?' Bruce's tone was mildly amused.

'Let's see, Bruce, I'm still a cop, I have to keep to the law as much as I can, but . . .'

'But you also want justice. Proper justice, eh?'

'Aye.'

'Stringer Dent and to a lesser extent Shore were useful idiots. That's all. They were allowing themselves to be used by those seeking to allow others to sow discord in the UK. You'll not be surprised to learn that having a big race war would make certain individuals in Russia happy. In the same way that Brexit suited the Kremlin, so did the murder of Daniel Solomon, and so will a similar murder that I suspect Dent and Shore were planning.

Sow discontent amongst minority groups, polarise the population more, back it up with an avalanche of bots on social media, and they're pissing themselves.'

'What, you mean the Kremlin are actively encouraging attacks like this?'

'Definitely. Using idiots like Dent and Shore give multiple layers of deniability, particularly as they were using their own drug money to fund them. Daniel Solomon was killed using a car bomb with the signature of Islamic fundamentalist terror groups. That severely upped the tension amongst certain sections of society, feeling that the Jewish community is under attack. It's classic Kremlin tactics, and now they get useful idiots not only to plan and carry out the attacks, but to bloody pay for them. No money trail back to Moscow. It's like having your cake, eating it, and then selling it, as well.'

'We have some evidence, but do you have anything that would prove that Dent and Shore, or National Force killed Solomon?' said Max.

'No. We don't always follow the rules, Max. Also, National Force is basically nothing. It's cover. Make everyone believe that Stringer and Shorty are just two-bit yobs.'

'I need to prove it. I also need to prove who's on the inside. We have another problem with another murder plot that they set in place.'

'Surely that shouldn't matter, now. They're both dead, right?' Bruce sounded confused.

'We've found evidence that a contract was paid for to take out a prominent judge. Half down in Bitcoin, the other half securely lodged for payment after a certain period of time. The first Asian Muslim judge in his position. If they succeed in killing him it will be devastating, and no doubt far-right organisations will be blamed.'

There was a long pause on the line, and Max could almost hear the cogs in Bruce's brain turning.

'Bruce?' said Max.

'Aye, just thinking. Are we talking about the Cashier?'

Max froze, mouth agape. 'What? How the hell do you know about that?'

'The Cashier. It's mostly rumour, and I don't know his identity, but he gets used by Kremlin assets to carry out contracts in the UK. How the hell did Dent get to employ the Cashier? It doesn't make sense, a two-bit muppet like that. He was in Frankland, right?'

'Aye, high-security wing.'

There was a long pause before Bruce spoke. 'What did you say the name of the judge was?'

'I didn't, but it's Mr Justice Imran Ahsan. He was Stringer's trial judge before his case got slung after the main witness disappeared.'

There was a long pause again, and Max could hear tapping on a keyboard.

'Bruce?'

'Shite,' he muttered by way of response.

'What?' said Max.

'Why didn't I join the dots, here? I'm supposed to be bloody good at my job,' muttered Bruce.

'Bruce?'

'Mr Justice Ahsan was also the trial judge for Bogdan Volkov.'

'Who the hell is Bogdan Volkov?' said Max, his voice tense.

'Doing life for murder, he shot a Russian journalist in the head a few years ago in Newcastle. He's a Kremlin asset, ex-Bratva, you know, Russian mafia, who was given a licence to commit crime as long as he did the bidding of his paymasters when required. He was sent over to the UK by his Bratva bosses as a deniable asset, ready to spring into action when required, but unfortunately, or fortunately, depending on your viewpoint, he wasn't that competent, and he got caught. He's a direct link, Max. A direct link to those close to the Kremlin. He's the key to this. Target him, and you get your inside man.'

63

BOGDAN VOLKOV WAS in his cell, staring at his TV, watching a terrible programme about some doctors. Despite how awful it was, he tuned in every day finding himself intrigued about what the idiotic medics were up to.

He stood up, and went to his kettle, yawning as he flicked it on. He didn't really need another cup of tea, but it was something to do.

There was a tap on his door, which was ajar, and a head poked in. It was Stevo, an armed robber who wasn't even halfway through his twenty-year sentence. He was thickset, turning to fat, and covered in tattoos of all variety. He'd been a mutual friend of Stringer before he'd got out.

'Boggie, you heard the news, man?' he said in his thick Geordie accent.

'I don't watch English news. All fake, you know this.'

'Aye, that's as may be, mate, but I'd also had a whisper from the out, and it's bloody true. His brother, Charlie, told a mate of mine, and he told me.'

Bogdan narrowed his eyes as he poured boiling water over a teabag. 'Tell you what?' he said, looking up at Stevo.

'Stringer's been killed by the cops, shoot-out in Scotland. Him and his pal Shorty got blazed.'

An icy fist gripped Bogdan's gut. 'What?' he stammered, the boiling water overflowing from his mug. He started, looked down and cursed, setting the kettle back on the table.

'You sure?'

'I saw it on the news, but that just said three killed in a pre-planned police operation, including a cop. Still no more out there, but I'm plugged in, man. It's fuckin' gospel. It's all over the wing. Fucking pigs, eh? Stringer was one of your own, man.'

Bogdan looked back down at his mug, scooped out the bag and tipped a little of the steaming brown liquid into the sink. Wordlessly he spooned three sugars in, and took a sip.

'Are you okay, man?'

'Fine.'

'I know you two were mates, like. Chess, and all?' Despite Stevo's reputation for being a hard man, he seemed genuinely concerned.

Bogdan looked up, and nodded. 'All good, Stevo. Thanks for tell me.' He sat on the bed and sipped his tea again.

'I'll tell you if I hear any more,' and then Stevo backed out of the cell.

Bogdan just sat there for a few moments, thinking about his brother, Stringer. A decent man, if a little too easy to influence. He genuinely missed their chess and conversations, and now he was dead. He felt himself flush as the brief moment of sorrow moved, like flicking a switch, to anger. How the hell could this happen? They were supposed to keep them informed. He placed his tea on the side table, and stood up. Moving to the door, he stepped outside and looked up and down the landing. It was quiet as could be, as no doubt all the screws would be having their post-lunch coffee. He'd not get a better chance than this.

He went back into the cell, shut the door and pushed his chair up against it. It wouldn't stop it opening, but it'd give him a precious few more seconds to sort himself out should a screw come.

Reaching up to his shelf he pulled down an open packet of Weetabix. He removed the plastic-wrapped stack, and went for the very bottom, where he carefully unfolded the plastic flap, and pulled out the bottom biscuit. Quickly, he snapped the rusk in half, and a tiny mobile phone fell out onto the table.

A Long-CZ. Just 68mm long and 23mm wide, about the size of a typical disposable lighter. Cost just a few pounds on the outside, but far more expensive for someone serving a life sentence in Frankland Prison. Not that money was a problem to Bogdan, either in or out of jail. One of his Bratva brothers had arranged it by paying a screw a tasty sum to smuggle it in.

Breathing hard, Bogdan powered up the tiny phone, and then navigated to the SMS function. He just sent a star to the number he tapped in from memory.

His contact would know.

He quickly pocketed the phone, and then swept the detritus from the Weetabix into the bin, and replaced the box on the shelf. Always the same, always with maximum self-discipline. The screws generally left him alone, as he kept such a low profile, but it paid to be careful.

He felt the phone vibrating in his pocket. Pulling it out, he saw that it was his contact. With the tip of his pinkie, he answered the call.

'Yes.'

'You called?' The voice was low, flat, even and anonymous.

'I hear some very bad news from outside, about Stringer?' he said, sotto voce, but almost quivering with suffused rage.

'Yes. Along with his friend and one of the cops. It's mayhem, I can't really talk.'

'You supposed to protect from this. You get paid plenty, so what happened?'

'Undercover sting. I only learned late on, and tried to warn them, but they went blazing away. It's fine. Casualties are the price of doing business. Police have nothing. They think the problem dies with Stringer.'

'Is contract still on?'

'Yes. Money has been paid. The Cashier has pride in his work. Have you spoken to X?'

'No. You have to do this, and explain your fuck-up.'

'Fine. Anything else?' The voice was devoid of any trace of emotion.

'No.'

The three beeps in his ear told him that the contact was gone.

A smile spread over Bogdan's face. Stringer was gone, but in doing so he made the contract even more guaranteed, thanks to the Cashier's foolproof method of making sure he got paid, and also his legendary reputation. Pay the Cashier, and success was guaranteed.

The objective would still be achieved.

64

IT WAS LATE afternoon before Max got back to the office, only to find it a hive of activity, with everyone tapping away, or on phones. Ross was red-faced and sweating in the stuffy office, a phone clamped to his ear.

'Oh, aye. Fucking wanderer returns. You sane?'

'Aye. Well, no more doolally than usual,' replied Max, sitting at his desk.

'Family okay?'

Max nodded.

'You okay, genuinely?' said Ross, more softly this time, his eyes concerned.

'I'm angry, Ross. I want every bastard concerned in this shite in the jail. Where are we?'

'Just had a bit of a stramash with the line room. Turns out they didn't mention the fact that both Stringer and Shorty were packing heat, as the guy listening didn't interpret the term "strapped" to mean armed.' He shook his head in disgust.

'Would it have stopped us doing the job if we'd known for certain they were strapped?' Max said with a sigh, exhaustion only just being chased away by the adrenaline beginning to course through his veins.

'Probably not. We'd pretty much assumed it anyway, but it did mean they feel guilty, so I've managed to get a rapid change for the intercept to add on the number that warned Stringer and Shorty when you were in the car.'

'Nice,' said Max, nodding.

'Better than that, man. I'm just off the phone from them. The number received an SMS. Just a star, and then the number receiving called straight back. Interestingly the number sending the message is right by Frankland jail. I suspect it's an inmate's phone.'

'So why use SMS on the cellular platform, which we can intercept, rather than WhatsApp or some other secure messaging platforms which we can't?' said Max.

'Think about it. Would you want to jam an iPhone X phablet up your bahoochie?' said Janie.

'I guess. A tiny phone is great to hide but has limitations. Did he get a return message?'

'Better than that, pal. He got a phone call, just as the line had come on.'

'And?'

Ross looked down at his A4 book. 'A male caller phoned a bloke with a Russian accent. He asked about details relating to the shootings of Stringer and Shorty. The caller stated that he tried to warn them, but it was too late.'

'Shite, anything about the voice?' said Max.

'Unremarkable, and no strong accent, the line room says. It gets worse. Now I know that the line room is only supposed to summarise, but I played the card and asked for verbatim for the next bit, after their fuck-up about "strapped".' Ross looked down and continued to read. He even tried to impersonate a Russian accent. It was bad.

'"Is contract still on?"

"Yes. Money has been paid. The Cashier has pride in his work. Have you spoken to X?"

"No. You have to do this, and explain your fuck-up."'

Ross looked up. 'We need to urgently find out who the source was contacting in Frankland. Can you get on that?'

Max smiled. 'No need. I know already.'

'What, how?'

'Deduction.'

'Piss off, you're not Sherlock Holmes. How?'

'Does it matter?' said Max.

'Actually, I dinnae give a fuck, we've a judge about to get whacked, and a cop with access to all levels snitching to a villain in Frankland. Just fucking tell me.'

Max told Ross everything, leaving out the source.

'Fucking hell. Why didn't we know this?' Ross rubbed his face, which was pale and lined with tiredness.

'They both had the same judge for their respective trials. Bogdan was convicted, Stringer bust his case. It's not just that, however, is it? Killing the first ever Asian Muslim High Court judge? Imagine the furore. This is just what the Kremlin want, and they get it for free, because Stringer paid for it with drug money. No link back to them, whatsoever.'

'Fuck, this is like a spy book, isn't it?' said Ross.

'Who's X, then?' said Max.

'No idea. Like *X-Men*, or something cool like that. They really go for the dramatic, these bastards, but the tone of that conversation is that he's someone's boss, we need to bear this in mind moving forward, but right now it's all about not letting a judge get whacked,' said Ross.

'What are our priorities, then?' said Janie, standing up and stretching.

'The judge, fucking obviously, did'ye nae listen?'

'Okay, so how are we reacting?'

'The Chief deployed Miles Wakefield to get down to Newcastle Crown Court pronto. Does he live nearby?'

Janie shook her head. 'No, he's London based, but as Newcastle didn't have a judge with a murder ticket, he's come up for the trial. He's tried a fair few cases there, I understand.'

'Where's he staying?' said Max, his hand touching the dressing on the side of his head.

'A city centre hotel, apparently the trial is expected to finish this week.'

'Okay, how about short-term security for him?'

'He's remaining in the court building until we get a chance to make a plan, but we're keeping it as tight as a gnat's chuff for now. Last thing we need is for it to leak, right?' said Ross.

Max frowned and slumped back in his chair. 'Actually, I'm not sure you're right there, Ross.'

Ross looked at Max almost sympathetically. 'Pal, I know you've had a bit of a fucking weird couple of days, have been shot in the heid, and shit, and we're all here for you – you know what a touchy-feely leader I am – but what the fucking fuck are you talking about?'

'Is the judge safe?'

'Aye, well, he's holed up in his chambers at a secure court facility until further notice, then we have people arranging secure accommodation for him.'

'Look. As I understand it, the Cashier is a contract killer whose reputation means everything to him. If he takes a contract, and his terms are met, he will deliver. Every time. We can secure the judge short term, but what about moving forward? We've a chance here. A big chance, but it'll take some balls.'

'That's you fucked then,' said Ross, bristling with sarcasm.

'I've a suggestion. Much depends on the opinion of the judge, but it may be worth a try.'

'Mr Justice Ahsan isn't known for his love of police, is he?' said Ross.

'Well, he was a specialist in actions against the police before he became a judge, and he's not known for his patience with cops giving evidence, but surely he'll listen to reason?'

'You'd hope. Anyway, never mind that, I still say we have an opportunity, and rigid, strict secrecy may not be our best option. Is the Gold Group WhatsApp still functioning?'

'I guess so. I'm in it, anyway.'

'Who else is?' said Max.

Ross fumbled for his phone and looked at it, squinting, a sausage finger held over the screen. 'The Chief, Miles, me, all the SIOs, the MI5 dobber, that walloper Counter Terror DCS from York, that cop from England, Ord, and a couple of others from the intelligence hub. Oh, and the NCA witness protection lead. We're not using that, though, are we? Surely that's way too bloody risky. We should be tight-lipped as an elderly spinster librarian who has just chastised someone for farting.' Ross looked up from his phone, brow furrowed.

'So, half the population of the policing and intelligence community. Perfect.'

'What, we shouldn't be super-secret is your idea?'

'Aye, to a degree, but also some tactical releases of intel may be of value. I've an idea, Janie, Barney, are you free tonight?'

'I'm good,' said Janie.

'I live in a bloody van, and I'm always brassic. What do you think?' said Barney, speaking for the first time in ages.

'Right, then, as I said, I've an idea, but it may take a bit of everyone working their magic.' Max jumped to his feet, with a sudden burst of energy.

'Where are you going, numb-nuts?'

'I'm going to phone Katie, go to the gents, and then get something to eat. I'm famished.'

65

MR JUSTICE IMRAN Ahsan, sitting behind his wide teak desk in his sleek book-lined chambers, looked at Detective Superintendent Miles Wakefield with a baleful eye before moving to the other occupants of his chambers, distastefully. He wore a beautifully tailored blue pinstripe suit, a blindingly white shirt with a stiff collar attached with studs, and a plain blue tie. He removed his spectacles and polished the lenses, thoughtfully.

His usher stood by the door, almost like a bouncer in a Newcastle nightclub. She said nothing, just stared directly at Miles disapprovingly, lips pursed, at what was no doubt a meeting that was delaying her finishing work.

Miles was sitting next to DI Nick Ord from the North-East CT team, and DCI Laura McKechnie. They had discussed the case prior to this meeting, in order to present a united front.

'So, Detective Superintendent, am I to understand that because of leaks in police and intelligence, or wider law-enforcement failings, I'm to trust that I'll be safer with you, than if I looked after myself?' His voice was balanced, as one would expect from a man used to speaking for a living.

'My lord, we have credible intelligence that you're a target for a contract killer arising out of the recent shooting incident in Pitlochry.'

'May I enquire about the veracity and source of the intelligence?'

Miles shifted uncomfortably in his seat. 'My lord, an iPad in the possession of the two males shot in Pitlochry that has been examined. Your photograph was found on that device, along with a conversation in draft folders between one of the men and the person we believe to have been paid to harm you.'

'Mr Wakefield, you do know that this isn't the first time I've been the subject of such threats. I have tried countless murder cases, a number of terrorism cases, and I've never gone into hiding, and now you tell me that there are possibly active malign forces within your own ranks passing information on outside of your organisation?'

Miles adjusted his spectacles, and shifted in his seat again. 'Unfortunately, yes, my lord.'

'Then there it is. I won't accept your offer of protection. I will relocate from my current lodgings, book into a new hotel and will keep my location to myself. Then I will feel safe, at least. I know Newcastle well enough to not be followed, and my car is parked in a secure car park. I've tried many serious cases up here. Now, if there's nothing else, I'd like to prepare to leave. I'm hungry, and I have a great deal of material to read ahead of the trial tomorrow.'

'But, my lord—' began Miles.

'That'll be all, Mr Wakefield.'

'My lord—'

The judge's face hardened, and his eyes turned flinty. 'I said, that will be all. Good day.'

66

THE CASHIER WAS in his cheap, anonymous hotel room, lying on the bed, watching TV and resisting the urge to slip off into sleep. It had been a long drive to Newcastle early that morning, followed by a day scoping out the Crown Court. His disguise was simple enough. He was excellent at covert surveillance, after many years of doing it in locations around the world. Just don't stand out.

Being seen was not an issue. Skulking around, hiding in the shadows were the simplest ways of getting spotted. So, he dressed to impress. A sharp, dark pinstriped suit, with detachable-collared shirt secured with gold studs. A plain and sober tie completed the look, along with subtle braces and black Oxford shoes. He carried a mulberry leather case that contained a gown, wig tin and the latest edition of *Archbold Criminal Pleading, Evidence and Practice*. All perfect camouflage to effortlessly blend into a busy and bustling Crown Court.

The look was finished with a neatly trimmed goatee, and iridescent green contact lenses behind heavy-framed spectacles. His chubby hamster cheeks were the result of two wads of cotton wool he'd tucked in this morning, and his normally pale skin was bronzed after the application of some fake-tan lotion in his hotel this morning. A quick change of clothes, shave, remove the glasses, lenses and cotton-wool cheek wads, wash off the tan, and he'd look totally different.

Camouflage for any occasion. It was why he never failed and was in such high demand.

While he was still in his research and reconnaissance phase of the operation, he'd happily accelerate plans should an opportunity arise. His former career had taught him the value of flexibility. In order to catch your prey, one had to first understand them, which necessitated his current surveillance stage.

He'd understood Mr Justice Ahsan very quickly. He was highly motivated, diligent and a master of his own small empire. He also noted, with a little sadness, that he appeared to be a good, honest man of high morals, if the way he gently dealt with nervous witnesses was any indication as to his personality.

Not that the Cashier cared about that. A target was just that. A target. An objective.

He had sat at the back of the court for an hour, making notes in a blue legal pad. Notes about the trial. Not about anything else. Anyone studying the legal pad would take him for an interested legal observer.

Mr Justice Ahsan was a master of his environment, running the proceedings with practised ease and polished eloquence. The rows of barristers and members of the jury were clearly in awe of the man.

The only people in the room who were clearly unimpressed with Mr Justice Ahsan were the two surly defendants, who looked on with a mix of indifference and sometimes hatred, depending on who was in the witness box.

The Cashier enjoyed the theatre of the trial, but after a while, he decided that he'd seen enough. So, he left. He was hungry, and his hotel in central Newcastle seemed to have a decent restaurant.

He'd decide soon his plan of action, but it felt that Newcastle was the likely theatre he'd choose to strike in. London was too busy, with too much CCTV, facial-recognition technology and armed police on every corner.

Not that they worried him in the slightest.

The trial was scheduled for two more days.

Plenty of time.

67

THE SOURCE LOOKED at his laptop, as he replaced the phone on the desk. He poised his fingers over the keys, and then paused, considering his next move. He was in his office at home, in a respectable suburb; it was a small attic room, far enough from the rest of the house so the TV downstairs was almost inaudible.

The message he'd just received was illuminating, to say the least. Somehow, probably down to lack of communications discipline by the idiots Stringer and Shorty, the authorities knew about the plot to kill the judge. This wasn't ideal but probably wasn't a major problem. The Cashier was hugely resourceful, and it wouldn't dissuade him from the job. Nothing stopped him, his whole reputation depended on it. Plus, Bogdan and X would be expecting success, and he'd take the fucking blame if the Cashier wasn't successful. Bogdan was a terrifying individual, but was thankfully out of the way in Frankland, unlike X. Once again, he cursed his weakness in being caught in a classic honeypot situation. A stunning woman in a bar, too much champagne, possibly with a bit of a micky finn in his glass, and the results were almost inevitable. The diminutive, smiling Kazakh (known as X) had presented him with the photographs, and a film clip of him in the most compromising of positions in a hotel room with the voluptuous woman. Threats to tell his wife, threats to tell his employers. He almost shuddered at how stupid he'd been, but he was on the hook, with no way out.

The intelligence had come through as a secure newsflash

briefing, and his idiotic boss had asked him to monitor it closely. The bosses at Tulliallan had initiated a 'Gold Group' WhatsApp live-feed with intelligence updates sent regularly, and all the key players were kept informed at every stage, this being so high profile. There had been way too many bodies on this one, and he was struggling to forgive Bogdan for recruiting that idiot Stringer while he was in prison. Of all the people to use, he chose a pathetic hooligan-turned-far-right-activist to do his bidding. The bosses were obviously nervous about the consequences of a senior member of the judiciary, a Pakistani Muslim in particular, being publicly murdered so every man and his bloody dog were being asked to contribute.

However, it seemed that he now had an opportunity. The WhatsApp message had made it clear that the judge was refusing protection, which wasn't particularly surprising, bearing in mind he was thought of as being fairly anti-police. It sounded like there had been a confrontation in the judge's chambers, and he'd refused all offers of help, thinking that he'd be safer on his own. To be fair to the judge, he was probably correct, the investigation team being as leaky as it was. The source grinned, mirthlessly. How wrong the man was.

So, there was a chance. The judge was out there somewhere, on his own in Newcastle. He just needed to find him, and the Cashier could do the rest.

And the source was an expert in finding people. He'd been doing it for years, and it had never been easier, if one had access to all the right systems.

And he had access to them all.

Quickly, he shut his own issued laptop and pushed it away. He then opened a drawer and pulled out another, an older Lenovo, with a Wi-Fi dongle attached. This was a laptop that should have been handed in when another member of the team had departed to another role. The computer should have been destroyed, but the source had managed to repurpose it, fake the destruction certificate and then pull it back into the pool, by a bit of jiggery-pokery. IT services were so bloody incompetent, they never even queried it. A new employee was added to the system, an analyst called Margaret McDowell, with a faked requisition chit, and boom. A fake employee, with access to all systems, on a ghost computer that didn't exist on the system.

A VPN engaged to mask where the terminal was logging in from, and he was ready. Ready to do his thing at which he was supremely gifted.

Finding people.

Firstly, he logged into the Police National Computer and located the judge's car. A newish Jaguar F-Pace. He noted the registration mark and checked for any automatic number plate recognition activations. He frowned as he looked at the multiple activations, mostly over the last few weeks in the Newcastle area. It seemed that the car had mostly been in the centre of the city, where he had been staying. However, this evening, the car had travelled west, away from the city and on the outskirts of Newcastle, where it had tripped a camera on the A696 heading towards Newcastle Airport. He pursed his lips as he considered this. The perfect place to hide in plain sight. CCTV, lots of hotels and great road network. It's where he'd go if he wanted to stay off-grid. Worst place to go would be somewhere remote, where everyone stands out.

He navigated to the financial intelligence icon on the desktop. He didn't need to log in, as the single-sign-in system was working perfectly. He entered the judge's details and hit 'search'. The database was intuitive and broadly searched all accounts and cards listed against Mr Justice Ahsan's profile. A smile stretched across his lips. A rarely troubled Monzo credit card had been used to book a room at the Premier Inn at Newcastle Airport, Southside, within the last hour. Excellent. The perfect place to hide, as long as you didn't have an expert looking for you. He quickly looked at the profile of the hotel on the Premier Inn website. A big enough hotel, with multiple rooms, restaurant and bar. He narrowed his eyes as he thought it through. No way would he use the restaurant or bar; that would be way too risky for a man in hiding, surely.

He refreshed the page, and his smile broadened. His lordship may be a clever man, but he'd made a critical mistake. He'd just spent £21 at a nearby pizza delivery joint. Mr Justice Ahsan was clearly being careful, but by being careful he was also being careless, not that he'd know this.

The source looked up the pizza restaurant, noted the phone number and dialled.

'Hello, Pizza-Pizza,' came the cheery voice, the bustling noises of a kitchen in the background.

'Hi there, my name is Mr Ahsan, I've just ordered a pizza to be delivered to the Premier Inn at the airport, but I think I may have told you the wrong room number, can I check, please?'

'One minute, sir.' There were tapping-on-keyboard sounds before he spoke again. 'We have room 256?'

'Oh sorry, my mistake, I was sure I said 526 for some reason, a busy day.' He forced a chuckle. 'How long for the delivery?'

'Twenty minutes, sir. Sorry, very busy tonight.'

'Thank you, very kind.' He hung up.

The source picked up his phone, connected to the VPN-enabled Wi-Fi from the dongle. No hitting cell sites, just a double-ended encrypted message sent over the WWW.

He tapped out a message. *Premier Inn Newcastle Airport, room 256. He's just ordered a pizza, and his car hit ANPR close by.*

Within thirty seconds the response came.

Acknowledged.

68

THE CASHIER WAS relaxed as he pulled his car over in the far reaches of the car park at the Wheatsheaf Farm, part of a pub/restaurant chain in front of the hotel. He looked at the car's digital clock, which told him that it was almost 10 p.m. Perfect timing. If he was going to do the job and immediately flee, he'd have possibly parked farther away, but as the plan was to book into the hotel, he did what any experienced operative would have done. He parked in the car park where he'd be expected to park. He'd book into his room, like any other weary traveller.

He'd noticed with some satisfaction the judge's Jaguar at the opposite end of the space in the dark shadows underneath a large, dense shrub. Mr Justice Ahsan's profile declared, somewhat pompously, that he was 'one of the finest legal minds of his generation'. Not when it came to hiding away, he wasn't, ruminated the Cashier.

He checked his appearance in the car's rear-view mirror. Shaggy, straggly hair protruded from underneath a branded baseball cap. A simple set of upper and lower dental prostheses had totally changed the shape of his face, and his normally blue eyes were now a muddy brown. His complexion was blotchy and reddened with what seemed to be rosacea marks, and there were dark circles under his eyes. There were four hoops in his left earlobe.

He looked utterly revolting, and unlike like his normal, bland appearance. He was certainly nothing like the suave, well-dressed lawyer that was at Newcastle Crown Court just a few hours ago.

Throwing a rucksack over his shoulder, he walked towards the back of the Wheatsheaf, and within a moment was passing through the automatic doors, and into the reception area of the Premier Inn. He saw himself in the security monitor, dressed in the typical attire of a builder. Paint-encrusted work trousers, a raggy old fleece that bore the mark of a plumbing brand. He limped, as if in pain.

'Yes, sir?' said the receptionist, a smiling young woman, whose name badge which hung on a lanyard with her keycard identified her as Lin.

'I've a room for the night, name of Cleeves,' he said, his accent was broad Yorkshire. He gave his widest grin, which displayed his brown, stained teeth.

Lin's smile was a little forced.

The Cashier rested his rucksack on the counter for a moment, before digging into it, as if searching for something inside.

Lin looked at her terminal and nodded. 'Just one night, Mr Cleeves?'

He nodded, still rummaging in the bag. He frowned. 'Do you need my credit card?'

'No, you're all paid for. Will you be breakfasting with us?'

'Maybe. I can decide in't morning.'

'Of course. Well, you're all paid up for one night, breakfast you can pay for if you decide you're hungry. Can you just sign where I've marked on this, please?' She pushed a piece of paper towards him. He scribbled in three places, without touching the paper.

She then handed over two plastic key cards, wrapped in a piece of paper. 'You're in room 262.'

He nodded, 'Ta, love,' and set off to his room, which was on the second floor. He eschewed the lift and instead took the two flights of stairs.

He was satisfied with the encounter. Lin the receptionist would only remember the obvious things. The scraggy hair, the diseased yak-like beard, the bad-taste earrings and the limp. He always remembered the lessons of his years of doing this. When acting in plain sight, only be remembered for things that you want people to recall.

Within a few moments, he was using his room key to enter room 262, a few doors away from his quarry. Just a couple more details to sort, and he could get this done.

As always, the room was plain, basic but functional, the same as a million hotel rooms across the country, but he barely saw it.

Reaching into the bag, he pulled out what looked like a round, dark compact disc, which was attached with a wire to a flat plastic box full of computer chips and circuitry. A card cloner that was attached to a high-frequency antennae, which was in turn attached to a mini laptop computer. The Cashier opened the device, to reveal a white screen and incomprehensible gibberish. A few lines of hexi-decimal string appeared at the foot of the screen, as the RFID tag was copied. It was the ID of the hotel receptionist's keycard that the hi-frequency antennae had captured when he'd put his rucksack on the desk.

Taking one of the cards given to him by Maggie, he pulled out a Sharpie and put a simple dot on the purple plastic, and then laid it on the antennae. He tapped a couple of command lines of code into the laptop, and then that was it. A master keycard that would allow him to move freely through the hotel, and more important, to access room 256.

He reached into the rucksack and pulled out what appeared, at first sight, to be a length of blue steel tubing. That was followed by a small, shaped and ribbed magazine, which he snapped into the side of the tubing. A B&T VP9 silenced pistol.

Based on the Second World War Welrod pistol used by the Special Operations Executive in occupied countries, the newest version was ostensibly a piece of equipment used by vets for euthanising large animals with a 9x19 parabellum. In reality, it was the favoured weapon for despatching a wholly different type of animal, with minimal sound. The Cashier had used it on a number of occasions, and the report was remarkably quiet. Nothing louder than a clap of the hands.

He racked the action, working a round into the chamber, and locked it into place. A big advantage was that there was no auto ejection after it was fired, leaving no evidence behind. The perfect up-close assassin's tool.

He smiled to himself as he pulled on a pair of blue nitrile gloves, snapping them into place with relish. He gripped the pistol tight and pulled the oversized fleece's sleeve over the length of it. He looked at his watch. It was almost 11 p.m.

He really should wait until 4 a.m., the time when the sleeping human was at his deepest phase of REM sleep, but really, was there any need? Every minute he was here, he was exposed to some degree, and he would prefer to sleep in his own bed tonight. So, he decided that now was the time.

He repacked his rucksack, zipped it up and slung it over his shoulders. He stashed one keycard, the other marked with the dot, he held in his gloved left hand. He took a deep breath, feeling the familiar buzz, opened the door and stepped out into the corridor. It was just ten steps to room 256. He paused, listening at the door. Faint sounds of the TV drifted out from the room.

He raised the card, tapped it against the reader on the handle, listened for the click, and confidently, his arm extended, stepped into the room, the pistol out in front of him, aiming at the bed.

The room was empty. The TV was tuned to *Family Guy*, and the remains of a pizza in its box were on the dresser. Silently, he advanced to the bathroom, pistol at the ready, and eased the door open.

Empty. Wet towels were on the floor, a toothbrush on the edge of the sink, a bottle of expensive-looking cologne next to it.

Returning to the bedroom he took stock of the scene. A suit

was hung in the wardrobe together with a crisp, fresh shirt and some underwear, ready to go. A sleek Apple laptop was open on the dresser, a legal document open on the screen. A set of keys, including to the Jaguar, was next to it. He moved closer and read the document on the computer screen. *'In the case of R v Grant and Jameson, before HHJ Ahsan, Newcastle Crown Court.'*

He looked down, a soft leather briefcase was open on the carpet by the chair. It bore a small brass plate with the initials I.A. stamped on it. Imran Ahsan. Peering inside he saw sheaves of legal documents and an identity tag bearing the photo of his quarry.

The Cashier reached into his pocket and pulled out his phone. He dialled.

'Yes?' said the contact.

'He's not here. His suit and briefcase are here, and he's eaten his pizza, but he's not here. Do the checks.'

There was a tapping in the background. 'He's just used his credit card in the Wheatsheaf Farm. In fact, it's the third time he's used it in the last hour. I suspect he's having a couple of drinks, the naughty boy.'

'Acknowledged,' said the Cashier, and he hung up.

He pulled out the chair from the dressing table and sat, facing the door, the pistol in his lap.

He looked at his watch. The pub would close soon, and he'd be waiting.

The Cashier was nothing if not patient. He'd once waited four days in a hide, in a stinking old house in a putrid suburb of Sarajevo, a sniper rifle in his shoulder, pissing and crapping into a bag, and eating cold food. He hadn't missed when the militia leader had eventually shown up.

He could wait now.

He wouldn't miss.

69

MAX AND BARNEY were sitting in a hotel room crowded around the computer terminal screen looking at the image in front of them, the atmosphere as taut as a piano wire.

There was a tap at the door. Max jumped up, peered through the spyhole and opened the door. Janie entered, grinning.

'All good?' said Max.

'Aye, I'm full of lemonade and crisps paid for by his lordship's credit card,' she said, stifling a burp.

'All worth it. He's bitten. Look.' Max tapped the screen.

The scruffy man was sitting in the chair, in front of the open laptop, facing the door, weird-looking pistol with a bulging silencer in his gloved hand.

'Who are you?' said Janie, peering at the man, who looked like a somewhat grimy builder.

'He's smart, I reckon,' said Barney, as he stared at the split screens.

'How d'you reckon that?' said Max.

'Somehow, he's managed to clone an RFID lock to gain entry to the hotel room. He didn't pinch one in reception, but did you see how he dumped his bag right close to the receptionist?'

Max nodded. 'Now you come to mention it, yes.'

'I bet there's some kit in his bag. It's not hard to do, I've done it myself.'

'Also, that's a serious-looking silenced pistol. I think it's a Welrod, like the old spies used to use to eliminate bad guys. I heard one shot, once. Eerily quiet, it was,' said Max.

'Something you want to tell us, Craigie?' said Janie.

Max looked puzzled. 'Like what?'

'Were you pulling the trigger?'

'As if.' Max grinned as his phone buzzed on the dresser. 'Ross?'

'You all ready? Everyone else is set up.'

'I reckon so,' Max said.

'Let's get on with it, then.' Ross hung up.

Max looked at both of them in turn. 'Now, you reckon?'

'Aye, send the bloody message, Barney, and let's watch the fun.'

'Before you do, are you sure about this?' said Max.

Barney nodded. 'All I have to do is press this key, and it'll send the messages to all the numbers in the Golden bollocks WhatsApp group.'

Max shook his head, and grinned. 'Gold Group. It's a cop term. Means a group of senior police officers, or law enforcers, talking shite around a table.'

'I'm impressed. How'd you manage it?' Janie asked Barney.

'Clive showed me. Pretty easy, to be honest, just a bit of jiggery-pokery. Worst bit was getting WhatsApp onto me laptop, then it fires the messages out in a quickfire burst, but each recipient gets a slightly different message, even though that won't be reflected in the group. They'll all think that everyone got the same message.'

'Okay. Send it.' Max clapped Barney on the shoulder.

Barney tapped at the keys, his face rapt with attention. There was a *whoosh*, and he grinned. 'Done.'

70

THE SOURCE WAS in his office, his guts churning with nerves as he looked at his phone, waiting for the fateful message from the Cashier. He was dreading it, but he knew he had no choice. Once this was done, he'd maybe be able to extricate himself from this terrible arrangement. Surely, he'd done enough to satisfy Bogdan and X now.

His buzzing phone made him jolt. He picked it up and scrabbled to open the message. His heart sank when he saw that it wasn't from the Cashier, but instead from the stupid fucking WhatsApp Gold Group that the Chief Constable had insisted on setting up. His heart felt like it had suddenly been immersed in liquid nitrogen.

> *****not for dissemination beyond Gold Group*****
>
> Urgent. Intelligence received. Judge A is booked into Premier Inn, Newcastle Airport. Receptionist reported in when she observed male (described scruffy, builder's gear, beard, walks with limp) on CCTV using keycard to access Judge A room. Believed Judge left room earlier, location unknown. Firearms teams briefing now locally. Await further details. Full investigative response team being scrambled. All members acknowledge.

The source scrabbled, his hands shaking as he dialled on his burner. 'Yes,' came the monotone electronic voice of the Cashier.

'You've been fucking rumbled. They know the judge is there, and the receptionist clocked you on CCTV breaking into the judge's room. Cops have your description. Where are you?' he blurted out.

There was a brief pause on the line before the Cashier spoke, his voice, as always tinny and mechanical.

'Where is the target now?'

'They're just saying "location unknown". They can't know he's in the pub.'

'Acknowledged.' The phone went dead.

Hands quivering, the source picked up his official phone and looked at the message again. How could he have been so bloody stupid? If he could easily find the judge, so could they. Of course, they'd have taken measures to protect and investigate. He needed to make sure that he was personally safe and secure, and he thanked God he'd used his burner, and had dialled using only VPN-enabled Wi-Fi that was also unconnected to him. There'd be no trace whatsoever of him making the calls to the Cashier, even if they got hold of the phone. Disappearing messages were enabled, and he'd scrub his WhatsApp history. Once the Cashier was all secure, he'd ditch this SIM and mobile altogether. He let out a long, slow breath. He was safe, and as long as the Cashier got away, they were clean.

The only real fly in the ointment were those bastards Bogdan and X.

No way would they be satisfied with all this, but they'd appreciate that they couldn't act against the judge anymore.

It was way too risky.

He looked at his phone, willing it to ring and for the Cashier to tell them he was safe. If his reputation was anything to go by, he'd be well away already.

The contact eyed up the bottle of malt on his desk, grabbed the bottle and poured a hefty slug.

It was almost over.

For now.

71

THE CASHIER POCKETED his phone and pursed his lips, deep in thought. The situation was urgent, but not so urgent that he needed to rush without considering the options. He looked at himself in the mirror, taking in the scruffy beard, mottled face, earrings and glasses.

He smiled, pleased with his foresight. He looked at the judge's suit hanging neatly on the rail and made a quick decision. There was no mad rush: the cops would be on their way, they'd be assembling at an RVP, probably away from the immediate area, ready to brief, before they attempted to interdict. He didn't have long, but he had long enough, providing he just got on with it, and didn't panic.

He reached up, pulled off his cap and tugged the wig from his head, revealing short, neat hair. He removed his glasses and plucked all the rings from his ears, all of which were just secured with clips. Leaning his head back, pulling his lower eyelid down, he removed one of the coloured contact lenses, and then followed with the other. He then pushed his fingers into his mouth, removed the dentures and sighed, feeling his face relax as he did.

Reaching into his bag, he took out an empty plastic laundry sack and stuffed all the items inside. He stripped off his crappy fleece and paint-encrusted trousers, and jammed them in the bag, leaving him just in a plain black T-shirt and his boxer shorts. Quickly standing, he grabbed the judge's trousers from the hanger and pulled them on. They were a little big around the waist, but acceptable in the leg. He fastened the belt into place and cinched it tight. He followed with the jacket, which was just a touch too big, but more than adequate.

He moved through to the bathroom, looking at his wispy beard still attached with the light glue. He peeled it off, then cleared all the residue with an alcohol wipe from his bag. A quick scrub with a hotel flannel removed the red make-up and dark circles, leaving his face looking clean and fresh, certainly in comparison to the bespectacled, blotchy-faced builder who had entered the hotel. He looked at himself in the mirror. It was a total transformation. He smiled at his reflection, revealing his white, even teeth. He couldn't have looked more different than the man who had entered the hotel just a short while ago. If anything, he looked pretty sharp in the well-cut suit, with plain black T-shirt underneath.

He checked his watch, seeing that it was just three minutes since he'd received the call from the contact. There was no way the cops would be anywhere near ready, yet, and he was confident that his change of appearance would do the job. He just needed to distract the receptionist from the CCTV screens.

He stood and pulled his plain black trainers back on, dumped all his discarded kit into his bag, and hoisted his rucksack on his shoulder. A quick check around the room to ensure he'd left nothing behind, and then there was just one more job to do before he made his exit. He picked up the hotel phone in his still gloved hand, pressed the button marked 'reception' and lay the handset down next to it. He picked up the Welrod from the dresser, and tucked it into his waistband, opened the door, stripped off his nitrile gloves and stepped out into the corridor, hoping that the ringing phone would be enough to distract the receptionist.

Quickly, but without rushing, he strolled down the corridor and headed for the staircase. Within a few moments, he was pushing out of the rear hotel door and into the car park. He pulled the Welrod from his waistband and held it down by his side as he hurried towards his anonymous car. He blipped the lock, opened the door and sighed as he sat behind the wheel. He was almost there, and there were no flashing lights, no sirens, no shadows skulking in the trees. It was quiet, and peaceful.

In fact, it was too quiet and peaceful.

He reached for his phone, wondering whether a call into the source was worthwhile. Could there be a mistake?

Maybe no one was coming?

Was this a double bluff to flush him out? His heart sank at the prospect.

He reached down, slotted the key into the ignition and turned.

Silence.

Not a murmur from the two-litre engine. It was inert and silent. He was firming his grip on the Welrod when the first laser dot appeared on his chest.

Followed by another.

And then another.

And then another.

He sighed, and strangely, he felt no terror. A smile spread across his face.

And then it was all over. Screams of 'armed police!', blinding torches, and thronging armed cops in body armour and Kevlar helmets.

The Cashier knew enough about police firearms operations to realise that there was no escape, so he didn't try. The Welrod was a great weapon for close-up, one-shot situations, but not now. He tossed it to the floor, raised his hands above his head and closed his eyes.

It was over. His smile widened, as the door was wrenched open and he was dragged out, smashed to the floor and handcuffed. He had known ever since he began, after his discharge from the army, that this day would come, one day.

He'd miss the missions, though. That was why he did it. The

thrill of planning, researching and then successfully executing a mission. He began to laugh, softly at first, his shoulders heaving, before he broke out into a full-throated chuckle.

It was actually hilarious. His eyes streamed, he was laughing so hard, and he barely noticed when one of the cops pressed his fingers to some type of device. They'd soon know. A mobile fingerprint machine.

They'd soon realise just who they'd caught, and they'd forever marvel at the day they caught the Cashier, and they'd probably never know how lucky they really were.

In other operations, when he wasn't just armed with a poxy one-shot Welrod, he'd could have killed the fucking lot of them.

They sat him up, and a bald-headed, lean-looking unarmed cop wearing body armour squatted down next to him; his face was firm, and his eyes were sharp and intelligent. He could immediately tell that he'd served.

'What's your name, pal?' the cop said, his eyes were warm and full of humour.

'The driving licence in my pocket says Curtis Langfield, but that's not my real name, which you'll see when you get the results from your fingerprint machine. I'm Peter Gow.'

'My name's DS Max Craigie. We'll get nae bother from you, pal, eh?' said the cop, eyebrows raised. It was more of a statement than a question.

'None from me. Game over as far as I'm concerned, mate. Nice work by the way, dressing the room to look like the judge was there. Had me fooled.'

'Not my first rodeo.' Max looked down towards where his hands were cuffed behind his back, reached down and pulled the judge's jacket sleeve up.

'Para reg tattoo?' DS Craigie said.

'Yeah. You look like you've served?'

'Aye. Black Watch.'

'Serve anywhere nice?'

'Aye, Afghan, and Iraq.'

He grinned and chuckled. 'I can't believe I got caught by a bloody crap-hat.' He used the pejorative term that paratroopers used for any other branch of the armed services.

'Come on. Let's get you out of here, you're under arrest for conspiracy to murder and murder by the way.'

'You want to know something, Max?'

'Aye, go on,' said DS Craigie, looking at him with curious eyes.

'I'm glad you've caught me.'

72

'GOT HIM,' MAX said into his phone, as he stood at the side of the road, outside the hotel, as the contract killer was bundled into the back of a waiting police van by local uniforms. Rather than there being cops everywhere, there were just two BMW X5 armed response vehicles parked up, with their Kevlar-clad crews watching as the prisoner was driven away.

'Nice work. Who the bloody hell is he?' said Ross.

'Snidey driving licence says he's Curtis Langfield, but that's a load of old shite. Local cops in Newcastle had a mobile fingerprint scanner, and it's been interesting to say the least.'

'Who the shite is he?'

'His name is Peter Gow, and he was discharged from the army ten years ago.'

'Shite, why?'

'Only limited info, as you'd expect, but I'll send everything we have on him to Norma, and she can get cracking. All it says on the record is "discharged services no longer required". Smells like a whitewash, if I'm honest. He looks the real bloody deal, Ross, I can't quite work him out.'

'Was he armed?'

'Aye. A Welrod silenced pistol in the car, and his full disguise kit in his bag. He was serious, Ross. And we have him bang to rights, we need the interview teams right into him, but I have a feeling he won't flip,' Max said.

'Why?'

'Something about him. He smells like Special Forces, Ross.'

'How can you tell?'

'He has para reg tatts, but with his service number tattooed over, and a couple of others obscured. An absolute giveaway. Anyway, I'm not interested in him, right now. We want who he was in contact with. Anything to share?'

'Not really. Norma couldn't get anything from his contact's number, although the phone was active. We can't prove which phone has been contacting him, or who tipped him off. Do you have his phone?' Ross's usual sarcasm had gone, replaced with customary brisk efficiency.

'Aye, Barney's into it. We managed to persuade our man to unlock it.'

'Really?'

'Well, we used his fingerprint while he was cuffed. The number he's been communicating with is the familiar number that has been near Frankland jail and Newcastle Crown Court historically, but it won't have been hitting cell sites with him, as he's been using 4G-enabled data with a VPN to communicate. We need to flush the bugger out. Is the custody site for Gow prepared?' said Max.

'Aye, they're opening a suite especially for him, with a trusted custody skipper somewhere nearby.'

'Incommunicado?' said Max.

'Aye. All rights being withheld, beyond an approved duty solicitor if he requests one. No phone calls, no visitors. Sod all. Miles has an interview team all ready to get straight into him.'

'Perfect. It's vital that this stays under the radar, Ross, until we get a chance to flush his contact out. He's at the centre of it all. What's happening with the Gold Group messages?'

'Nothing yet, what do you suggest?'

'Send out an anodyne message, saying that the hit man is into the wind, but that the judge is safe. Fast moving incident, blah,

blah. We just need to buy time to identify our man on the inside. We can re-evaluate after that. It's absolutely vital that no one knows that he's in custody, so we need the Chief on board.'

'Agreed, but we can only keep the bastard off the radar for a while, not forever.'

'We just need enough time to flush out his contact on the inside. Once that's done, we can decide what to do next. Then the pressure's off.'

'On it. I'll put something out in a while, keep the bastard panicking for a while longer.'

'Cool, it's just imperative that the bent bastard thinks the Cashier is still out there. He'll go to ground if he knows he's nicked.'

'It's time-limited, Max. You know that it will leak eventually, even if not maliciously. All cop shops are like sieves, and it only takes one call.'

Barney looked at Max and waved the prisoner's mobile in the air. It was attached by a lead to his computer, and he even looked animated (for Barney).

'Right, have to go. Looks like Barney has found something,' said Max.

'Aye, probably a quid in his coat he'd forgotten about. Stay in touch.'

*

'What's up, Barney?' said Max.

'This phone.'

'Aye?'

'Not much on it, he's been using WhatsApp for calls, and he's been speaking to our mysterious grass, with the same number we already knew about.'

'Aye, we know this. We just don't know bugger all about who's using that phone beyond the fact that he's supposed to be one of us?' Max looked perplexed.

'I know that, but that's not the interesting bit. The phone has Voicemod installed.'

'Am I supposed to know what that is?' said Max.

Janie had just appeared at Max's shoulder, and she clapped him on the back. 'That's him away now. Jesus, he's a weird bugger. What have I missed?'

'Barney was just telling me that matey-boy's phone has Voicemod installed.'

'Really? Shite, that's interesting,' she said, eyes wide.

'I still dinnae know what that even is?' said Max.

'It's an app that allows you to make calls using an electronically altered voice. Way safer to use that than to text or use messaging services. Leaves nothing on the phone, and data-enabled calls can't be intercepted,' said Barney patiently, as if explaining to a child.

'Yeah, c'mon, Craigie, get with the programme,' said Janie, grinning.

Max paused, and looked between his two colleagues in turn, his eyes narrowing. 'Are you guys thinking what I'm thinking?'

'Well, Gow is going into incommunicado custody, so we have a short window of opportunity, and we need to draw this scummy, corrupt bastard out into the open. Question is, how?' said Janie.

'I think I know,' said Max.

'How?' said Janie.

'Barney, is it set up to use now?'

'Aye, we just have to make the call using the Voicemod app. It's all ready for generic electronic anonymising.'

'So, if we call Gow's contact now, he'll think it's him?'

'Unless he knows that he's been nicked, which we have to hope he doesn't. Even the firearms teams don't know any of the details of who Gow is, but sooner the better,' said Barney.

'Pass me the phone,' said Max.

Janie's eyes widened. 'Are we sure, here? This must require authorisation, isn't it technically an undercover deployment?'

'Well, I'm good for undercover deployment, and I think there will be some residual authority remaining, but failing that, you know how diplomatic our dear leader is at securing retrospective permissions.'

'Och, he's a bloody master, pal.' Janie sniggered.

Max took the phone from Barney's hand. The app screen was open, with a dial button displayed. 'I just press and talk?'

'It's just a phone call, mate. You'll sound just like Gow did.'

Max pressed the 'call' button. It was answered immediately. The voice was soft, crackly and full of panic.

'What the bloody hell is going on, I've been shitting myself.'

Max paused for a beat, and then spoke, evenly and slowly. 'I got away without a problem, cops are floundering around in the dark. How did they find out?'

'I've no idea, but I got warned last second. I think they traced the judge the same way I did, it wasn't difficult. Did you see him at all?'

Max looked at Barney and Janie and smiled. 'No. I don't trust this line of communication. Can you get to a safe phone?'

'This phone is safe. I'm using a VPN, and 4G to call. It can't be intercepted.'

'They could be recording you in your premises. They may have malware on your phone. Get to a call box, send me the number by message, then delete immediately from your handset. I'll call back from another safe line. I can still complete this contract, but I must have secure comms, and I don't trust your tradecraft. Do it now, or I disappear forever.' Max ended the call.

'Jesus, Max,' said Janie.

'That'll work. He'll call back, he's shitting himself.'

'What did he sound like,' said Janie.

'Anonymous, but shiteing a brick. Definitely being careful, though.'

'Not bloody careful enough,' said Barney, looking through the phone, his brow furrowed in concentration.

'Other stuff on the phone?'

'It's deep in there, but I'll be able to access in due course.'

'So, what now?'

'We wait? Nothing else we can do. Miles has sent a reception committee to the police station where Gow is headed, so he's all good.'

'How about the judge?' Janie said, yawning extravagantly.

'Safe as houses, with Miles, and an armed protection team well outside the city. It took a bit of persuasion, but he eventually saw that going out on his own was a daft idea. Then he cooperated fully, handed all his kit over so we could dress the room, and is probably very bloody thankful once he realises that he could have had a nine-millimetre slug in his big legal brain tonight.'

'Ayup?' said Barney, handing the phone over to Max.

There was a one-line message. Just a phone number.

A landline number, with a Newcastle area code.

Max held it up to Janie. 'The bastard's in Newcastle. Get this sent to Norma, now. We need this phone's location.'

Janie tapped at her phone. 'Done. Only take a minute. Are you calling him now?'

'I want to know where he is first.' Max's voice was flat as he stared at the phone.

Janie's phone buzzed in her hand again. 'It's a phone box at the junction of Elswick Road and York Street in Gosforth. How far is that?'

Barney tapped on his phone screen. 'Fifteen minutes away.'

'Right, let's get ready to move.' Max dialled using the Voicemod app.

'Yes?' The voice answering was flat and anonymous.

'I'm keeping my head down for another fifteen minutes at least, there's way too much activity for me to move. Return to the phone box in twenty minutes, and I'll call you again, it's the safest way. I'll use a new handset and SIM, and I'm on a VPN, so they'll never be able to intercept, on any level. I have an opportunity to complete the contract, but I can't move yet.'

'Understood.'

Max ended the call.

The three team members looked at each other. 'Barney, remember that phone jiggery-pokery you did once, making a mobile look like another mobile number when I make a call?' said Max, his face hard.

'Aye. Easy old fraudster's trick,' he said.

'Good, get it set up, with Voicemod enabled, and we need to be able to record the call. We'll make him think that the Cashier has ditched for a new mobile, and is practising solid tradecraft by phoning a callbox. He'll feel secure speaking on that. Barney, we also need a decent camera ready to go, do you have one?'

Barney nodded.

'Excellent. I'm gonna make this bastard stitch himself up like a bloody kipper before we drag him in.'

73

THE SOURCE HAD returned the two hundred metres back to his house to wait the twenty minutes before the Cashier would call back. The streets were almost silent in the middle-class Newcastle suburb of Gosforth, and he didn't want to attract any more attention than was necessary.

He crept into the house, aware that his wife and kids were all asleep upstairs. He went into the kitchen and sat on one of the stools at the breakfast bar, looking at the open bottle of wine on the polished granite. He picked up the bottle and sloshed out a hefty glug into the wine glass next to it that still bore a smear of lipstick after his wife had almost decimated its contents.

He necked the glass in two gulps, and set it back down on the surface, his stomach churning.

His phone buzzed in his pocket. It was the Gold Group WhatsApp.

Update. Suspect has fled the scene prior to police arrival, area searches are underway. Judge is secure, and moving into police protective custody, NCA Protected Persons assuming responsibility. Meeting being planned for tomorrow morning for Gold Gp.

The source sighed and rubbed his shaking hands through his hair, almost sick with relief that the Cashier had got away. Unfortunately, the judge was secure, but it seemed that the Cashier still had a plan to complete the contract. If the target was moving to NCA protection, that'd be a tall order, but nothing would surprise him about the abilities of the Cashier. He knew very little about him, other than the fact that he was ex-Special Forces, and was hugely efficient. If anyone was capable of tracing a person once in protective custody, it'd be him.

Carelessly, he grabbed the bottle again, and sloshed some more into the glass, necking it in one go, relishing the tannin-rich red wine and feeling the familiar numbing of his mucus membranes as the velvety liquid calmed him.

He wondered what the hell Bogdan and, even worse, X would make of this.

He knew for sure that they would not stop, and no way was he off the hook, yet. They'd never let a man in his position walk free. He was too valuable to them, and he had to admit, that the money he got paid was helpful, especially bearing in mind his wife's expensive tastes. He grinned, without mirth, when he considered that he had probably just gulped down about forty quid's worth of expensive claret. Add to that the kids' horrifying school fees, his wife's relentless shopping habit and the massive mortgage, he'd come to rely on the money given to him by X.

He shivered when he thought about X. The diminutive, but terrifying Kazakh who worked for a private intelligence agency in Canary Wharf. He'd never really got to the bottom of it all, but he strongly suspected that he ran a proxy organisation with links to the Kremlin. He knew he should update the man, but he was equally unsure what his reaction would be. He decided then and there, that this was probably better delayed until he knew what was next, after he'd spoken to the Cashier. It may be that he'd complete the contract tonight, and he'd be able to call X with the good news. Yes, that's what he'd do, far better to call when he had firm news, good or bad.

His phone buzzed. A star in the message box. He groaned as

he realised that Bogdan wanted an update. Well, he could fucking wait, as well. The pressure in his head began to pulsate at his temples, the blood almost roaring in his ears. He longed for this whole shit situation to be over, but wondered if it ever would be. How the hell could he escape the clutches of X and Bogdan?

He checked his watch. It was time to go. He took a deep breath, necked the last of the wine and looked around the large, expensively appointed kitchen, and then left, heading back down the peaceful street towards the phone box just outside the convenience store, just five minutes away.

74

BARNEY DIVED BACK into the car, and looked at Max and Janie with a grin. 'Told you it'd be worth the risk, didn't I?' he said, tapping his finger on the iPad that was on the centre console. It showed a pin-sharp colour image of the inside of the dimly lit, empty phone box.

'Too risky, Barney,' said Max.

'Ah, stop frettin', I had plenty of time. It means we don't need to be on top of the phone box. It's tight as anything down here, and if this bloke is a cop, he'll be aware,' said Barney.

They were parked a hundred metres away from the phone box in the quiet, leafy street in Gosforth. The street was tree-lined and packed with cars.

'Are you sure he's not gonna see the camera, Barney? It's a bloody phone box, not Auntie Elspeth's front room. How many bloody hidey-holes can there be?' said Janie.

'Not my first covert camera, love. He'll not spot it, and I've put a microphone in there as well, so we get the whole lot. A good enough image, together with proper sound, plus we can live-stream this to Ross, as well.' Barney adjusted the settings on the feed, which sharpened even further, as he increased the light sensitivity.

'We don't need the microphone, do we? I mean, I'm making the bloody phone call, which you're recording, right?' said Max.

'As I say, not my first gig, lad. If he decides to make another call straight after, we'll at least get half of it. Even if he uses his mobile, he'd probably stay by the box, as its cover. I tell you, it'll be worth it, and it took me a second to hide the microphone. I take it you're nicking him straight off?'

'Probably,' said Max.

'Then we're ready. I reckon he lives nearby, otherwise, why here?' said Janie.

'Inevitably.'

Max's phone buzzed. 'Ross?'

'You all set?' he said.

'Aye. Is the feed clear?'

'Sharp as a pin, pal. I have to give it to the old git, he's good at his job, and audio as well,' said Ross.

'He's worth his exorbitant day rate, then?'

'I would'nae go that far. He's still a malodorous old fud,' said Ross, with a chuckle.

Then, they saw it. A shadow flitted from right to left. 'Is that someone coming out of York Street?' said Janie, pointing down the street.

'Aye, it's something. Standby, Ross. We have movement, I'll keep the line open,' said Max, picking up a small monocular from the door pocket, and putting it to his eye. He focused the eyepiece and swept the area around the phone box.

Then he saw it. A figure tucked into the doorway of a food store, just a dark shadow against the soft lights of the shop.

'What's he doing?' said Barney.

'He's waiting,' said Max, keeping the monocular trained on the shop.

'Waiting for what?' said Ross over the open line.

'For the Cashier to call. Let's not disappoint him.' Max lowered the optic and grinned at Janie. He picked up the phone that Barney had fitted with the recording app and Voicemod, and dialled.

They could hear it. Despite the distance, they could hear the faint ringing wafting in on the warm summer air. Max raised the monocular again. 'He's moving,' he said, as the shadow burst into life, and went straight for the phone box.

Suddenly, the feed burst into life as the dark-clad figure appeared in the box, and just for a moment he stood there, staring at the handset, as the shrill tone rang, spoiling the late-night peace of the neighbourhood. His hand reached out, and he gripped the receiver without picking it up, leaned back in the box, and looked up, giving the camera a full, lurid, hi-def view of the man's face.

'Well, bugger me with a pitchfork,' whispered Barney, as he stared at the feed, recognition on his craggy face.

'You wee corrupt shite,' said Ross, sotto voce over the line.

'Well, come on. Don't leave us in suspense,' said Janie.

'That, my girl, is David Stafford. Senior case officer from the MI5 northern office. The filthy, dirty piece of crap,' said Ross, his voice crackling in the car's speakers.

Stafford looked up, his eyes seemingly fixed on the camera. He looked worn, weary and broken. It was written on every inch of his face.

The car was so silent you could hear a pin drop, as everyone held their breath.

Stafford picked up the handset and raised it to his ear, his eyes closing, almost in a silent prayer, as he did so.

75

'YES?' SAID STAFFORD, his heart pounding in his chest.

'Are you clear?' came the electronic voice, harsh with static.

'Yes.'

'I'm away, but it was too close. What happened?'

'I received a message that you'd been compromised. I think they tracked down the judge and called the receptionist who must have seen you entering his room. Where is the judge now?' Stafford asked.

'I saw him in a plainclothes cop car being driven away, probably into protective custody, now. Can you find out where?'

'I may be able to, but the NCA handle witness protection. They were at the Gold Group meetings, so I imagine that they'll be squirrelling him away. I can't see that he'll be reachable once they have him. The Protected Persons Unit are a law to themselves, and I have no sway over them.'

There was almost silence on the line apart from the faint static hiss. A car drove past, the headlamps bathing Stafford in their glare. He had to resist the urge to duck down, but the car just swept by without pausing.

'Are you still there?' said Stafford.

'Yes, but I have a question.'

'Yes?'

'The job had been paid for by Stringer, but I'm assuming that it wasn't their idea?'

'No.'

'Am I correct in thinking that it was the same organisation that contracted me for the operation in York?' The Cashier's voice was unemotional, even with the flattening factor of the electronic distortion. Stafford shuddered.

'Yes.'

'Would I be right in thinking that it's Stringer's former fellow inmate?'

'Yes. And another member of that organisation, who is on the outside.'

'Well, then tell them I can do this. I have access to resources that you won't be aware of that will locate the judge. Once that has been done, I can complete the contract, but it will require an additional fee to pay for the resources I need to do the job.'

'How much?' said Stafford, his heart jolting at the prospect.

'At least fifty, but in cash this time. I'm concerned how cops managed to uncover this plot, so it'll be cash to a dead drop. You can get it from the clients, and then we'll arrange the details. I will have to pay for certain services from individuals involved in this area of business, and cash will make it faster. I'll contact you about methods, and timings. I need to go now. I'll send you a new burner number by secure message to your phone tomorrow, delete as soon as it arrives, and then immediately call me back on a safe line. Either a brand-new burner, or a different public phone, in the meantime speak to whomever you need to speak to in order to authorise funds for me to complete this contract.'

'Fine. I've a new SIM ready to go, which I'll start using tomorrow after you message me with the new number.'

'Wait for my call.' The Cashier hung up.

The phone went dead.

Stafford sighed with relief. There was still a chance, but he'd need to speak to Bogdan soon, as he'd be going crazy, and he had no choice but to use his current phone, or the Russian would never answer it, if he didn't recognise it. He went to his pocket and pulled out a new SIM card, still in its packet, unwrapped it and laid it on top of the phone base. He pulled out his phone and dialled Bogdan.

The phone rang four times before it was answered; presumably at nighttime, Bogdan wasn't fearing any cell inspections.

'Yes.' His voice was dark, thickly accented and rich.

'It's me. We've had a problem.' Stafford's voice cracked at the end of the sentence. He cleared his throat.

'Problem?'

'Police got wind of the contract, after Stringer was shot, so the judge has gone into hiding.'

There was a pause on the end of the line for a good fifteen seconds, followed by a deep exhale. 'This isn't acceptable. This contract must be completed, what does Cashier say?'

'He says he can do it, but he needs another fifty thousand in cash. Can you arrange this?'

'Not me from jail, but I speak to X, and he call you direct. He's one with money, and he is certain he want this job done. More accurate, his big bosses want it done, so I imagine no problem.'

'You're sure he can come up with the money quickly?'

'Don't say this in front of X, he take it personally. He has access to all the money, only reason we use idiots Stringer and friend is for deniability, but this must be done, okay?'

'I'm changing burner phones tomorrow. Too much activity on this one, is your mobile still secure?'

'Yes, of course.' Bogdan almost sounded bored.

'Write this down then . . .' Stafford read out the new phone number from the SIM packaging.

'Done. Wait for my signal, I speak to X tomorrow.' The phone went dead.

Stafford sighed, feeling something like relief flooding through his veins. Bogdan seemed almost understanding, which was very unusual.

He just hoped that the Cashier could come up with the goods, or they'd all be sunk. He pocketed the detritus from the SIM card, tucked the new SIM in his shirt pocket, ready for tomorrow, and left the phone box towards home, and some peace for a few hours.

76

'GOT THE BASTARD, he's even given us his new number,' said Janie.

'Aye, that's the little bugger all kippered up, lad,' added Barney.

Max just sat there, staring at the windscreen, not talking, his brain spinning. That was Stafford convicted, no doubt. A big collar of a senior British intelligence agent with evidence of his being a major co-conspirator in a contract killing of a Jewish author, and the plan to kill a sitting High Court judge. The recriminations would be huge, and the press would be digging deep into the motivations. Max remembered a course he'd attended on why intelligence professionals betray their country. The acronym MICE was key. Money, ideology, coercion and ego. The drivers for treachery, whether against a fellow villain, or one's country. They needed more; they had to close the whole damn thing down. Max felt his face flushing as he considered the cost of this operation, and like a flash, the image of Joe's big, smiling face popped up in his mind.

'It's not enough,' said Max.

'What?' said Janie.

'Stafford. He's not enough. He's bang to rights, everything evidentially captured, but that's not enough. What about Bogdan Volkov? What about the mysterious X? All we have there will be what's on the intercepts of Bogdan's phone, and we can't use that in court. We need admissible evidence of what both of them are saying, and then we need to nick X, either with recorded conversations or handing over the fifty grand.'

'Max, can't we just go with what we've got?' said Janie. She looked and sounded exhausted.

Max's jaw tensed, as irritation flashed. 'No. No way. We get each and every one of the fuckers, Janie. Let's not forget we lost a friend in this, because of these scumbags. We get every single one of them, from the ones at the bottom to those using Stringer and Shorty to screw the country up. We get them all. The whole damned lot of them.' He looked towards Janie and felt blood pounding in his ears.

The phone buzzed on the dash. It was Ross.

'I got all that, including the new number for tomorrow, line room will get them both setup ready, and they've just given me Bogdan's side of the phone call verbatim.' Ross then relayed the details of the conversation between Stafford and the Russian.

'Not enough, is it?' said Max.

'Nope. Not for the Russians, anyway. Stafford is totally stuffed, but for the others, we need more. Are we up for it?' said Ross.

'You know I am,' said Max.

'Aye, of course I am. Just knackered,' said Janie.

'You've always got me, fellas,' said Barney.

'So, what do we need, then?' said Ross.

'We need to evidentially capture both ends of a conversation between Bogdan and Stafford in an admissible format, and then we need to catch X as he hands over a bag of dosh to Stafford, then we're home and dry. We can do it, guys. If anyone can do it, it's us.'

'One thing, do we know if Stafford has a car?' said Barney.

There was the sound of papers shuffling on the car's speakers. 'Norma has been researching him now, with her typical speediness. Aye, one car registered to him, one to his wife. Her car is a brand-new Audi TT, he has a fairly old Ford Focus. I'll email the details to you all, they live literally a minute from where you are.'

'Can we be sure which one he uses?'

There was a pause on the line, and Norma took the phone. 'What do you need, Barney?'

'I want to be sure which car Stafford uses, maybe need to chuck a quick lump on it, but I don't want to lump the wrong one,' said Barney.

'Isn't it obvious?' said Norma, a smile in her voice.

'No.'

'She'll use the TT. A dowdy spy wouldn't be seen dead in an Audi TT. I think Jeremy Clarkson even said that it's only air hostesses that drive TTs.'

'Fair point, well made, if a bit sexist,' said Barney.

There was a long pause in the car, the crackle of the open phone line with Ross breathing heavily at the other end before he broke the impasse. 'Right, you buggers go and get a hotel nearby, and get your heads down for a few hours. I'll head down early and we'll reconvene in late morning, we all need some sleep, especially you, Craigie. All agree?'

'I'm in,' said Max.

'And me,' said Janie.

'Can I get a posh 'otel, as well?' said Barney.

'Can you fuck. Kip in your bloody van, you freeloading old walloper.'

Barney grinned widely, before rummaging around in his kit bag on the seat next to him, satisfied with what he'd find, he looked at Max.

'Give us ten minutes, I just want to go and 'ave a quick gander at this Focus, just in case I need to do something with it.'

Janie groaned. 'Come on, Barney, I'm hanging on by a thread, here.'

'Ten minutes, maximum, I promise, it may save us ages later.' Barney eased the door open and was gone, melted into the night in the way only a man with fifty years in covert operations could.

77

MAX, ROSS, JANIE and Barney were in the conference room of a hotel in central Newcastle, yawning and drinking thick, strong, bitter coffee that had been served in pots by a smiling porter. They'd hit the hotel late on, and had all fallen into their beds for six hours, before reconvening.

'Not bad, here, is it?' said Barney, sipping at his coffee.

'You'd say that about anywhere with a bloody flushing cludgie,' said Ross.

'Aye well, easy pleased, me. What's 'appening then?'

'Waiting for Miles to come. He's got a liaison officer from Northumbria police. Different rules mean we need a minder, I tried to tell him we'd be okay, but it's "politically sensitive".' Ross mimed the quotation marks.

'I think we're okay, unless there are more bent bastards about,' said Janie.

'Surely we've nicked them all now, not that this is a bent cop case for once, which is a bloody miracle,' said Max.

'Aye, a bent spy is way cooler. Like Phil Kimber, or someone like that,' said Ross.

'Who?' said Janie.

'You know, Phil Kimber. Some posh bastard Cambridge spy, getting tapped on the fucking shoulder, and being corrupt, and living his life oot in Russia. God, no bloody education, you millennials.' Ross shook his head and took a self-satisfied swig from his mug.

'I think you mean Kim Philby, who was exposed as a member of the Cambridge Five spy ring in 1964,' said Janie, stifling a grin.

'Aye, whatever, Poindexter, anyway. Spies and shit, just call me Jackson Pollock,' Ross said, with a grimace.

'It's Jackson Lamb, not Pollock, and have you read the Slough House books?' said Janie, her brow furrowed.

'No. I don't read books, but I saw a bit of the telly show.'

'Then surely you know Jackson Lamb is a bit iffy, certainly hygiene-wise?'

'To be honest, Mrs Fraser likes it more than me, I mostly fall asleep.'

The banter was interrupted when Miles entered the room, accompanied by a woman smartly dressed in a stylish business suit. She had her hair neatly tied back, and an open and smiling face.

'Morning all, can I introduce DCI Heather Mortimer. She'll be acting as local liaison, comes highly recommended, from an impeccable source.' Miles Wakefield grinned, looking sparklingly fresh, unlike the jaded, crumpled members of the team.

Heather nodded. 'Thanks, Miles. He's neglecting to mention that we're actually related. In fact, Miles is my brother-in-law,' she said, with a chuckle.

'Heather is here as a direct representative of the Chief Constable of Northumbria, to ensure smooth liaison and make sure all our powers work, okay?'

Ross stood and shook hands with Heather, who looked at the exhausted, scruffy DI with some alarm.

'Did you get the outline of our plans?' said Ross.

Heather sat down and poured herself a mug of coffee. 'I did. Luckily the Chief is moving heaven and earth to make it all happen as we hope. Surveillance activity is authorised, including property interference, intrusive surveillance, undercover deployments and the like. All good to go, as far as we're concerned, are you sure you don't need more staff?'

'I think we should be fine, but we may need an armed response vehicle later, depending on what happens this afternoon.'

'I've one on permanent standby, centrally located, just waiting for your word.'

'Awesome, then we're action stations,' said Ross, grinning a little too widely.

'Any updates from Norma?' said Max.

'Just prison intel back from Frankland. Bogdan Volkov has only ever had two visitors since he's been inside. One is listed as Geoffrey Clarke, but if we look at the ID supplied for the visiting order, it's very interesting.' Ross held up a sheet of paper, which had a photocopy of a driving licence on it.

It was clearly David Stafford. There were chuckles all around the room.

'Not so careful. How about if he claims he was meeting an agent in the jail?' said Max.

'Well, if he was, it would be recorded within MI5 files, and I'm betting it's not,' Ross said, shuffling the papers before picking out another. 'Here's his other visitor, listed as Piotr Nevalny.' Ross held up another sheet of photocopied paper, bearing a bio-data page of a British passport. The face was Slavic, unsmiling, with swept-back jet-black hair and coal black eyes that stared at the camera with disdain.

'He looks nice,' said Janie.

'Can I see?' said Max.

Ross slid the sheet across the desk. Max picked it up and studied it on his lap. He quickly and discreetly pulled out his phone, and took a snap of the image. He then slid the sheet of paper back across the desk to a perplexed-looking Ross. Max just shook his head, as if inviting no further questions.

Within a second, he had sent the image to Bruce Ferguson, with a single character message attached. ?

'Okay, folks, let's get busy and stay in touch. Our Chief wants updates regularly, and I'm the one doing it, so don't keep me in the dark.' Ross nodded, and stood, indicating the briefing was done.

The meeting began to break up, as people moved towards the door. Max's phone buzzed in his hand. A reply from Bruce.

Call me, urgently.

'Give me a couple of minutes. I'm just going to call Katie,' Max said to Janie, who just nodded, tiredly.

Max left the conference room and went to a distant corner of the reception area, before he dialled.

'Max?'

'Bruce, I don't have long.'

'Where'd you get that photo?'

'He's been visiting Bogdan in the jail, why?'

'You'll not be surprised to hear that Piotr Nevalny is not who he claims.'

'Shock and horror, Bruce.'

'Ah, the mysterious X. His name is Xavier Petrov, and he's actually from Kazakhstan, although he's spent most of his life in Russia. He's a very bad man, Max.'

'Why am I not bloody surprised? We've encountered a lot of bad people recently.'

'So I'm hearing. How about the Cashier?'

'He's in hand.'

'I'm hearing rumblings.'

'Not for phones, Bruce,' Max said flatly, not in the mood for a game of verbal tennis with Bruce.

'You're crap at this quid pro quo lark, Max. Still, that's fine, you've a job to do. Look, X is not to be underestimated. He ostensibly works for a dodgy corporate intelligence company based out of a swanky office in London. In reality he's a proxy spy for the Kremlin, and is no fan of my boss, and the feeling is entirely mutual, to say the least. If you can take him out of the game, you'll be doing me a favour.'

'I'll bear that in mind. Look, I have to go.'

'Max, don't underestimate Petrov, okay?'

'Is he dangerous?'

Bruce exhaled long and hard before answering. 'He's a killer, Max. A brutal, sadistic killer who has the ear of the Kremlin. He's powerful, so take care.'

78

BOGDAN VOLKOV WAS in his cell, a chessboard set up in front of him, along with a book about finishing moves used by the grandmasters over the years.

However hard he tried, he just couldn't grasp how to perform the move called Anastasia's Mate. It just made no sense. He sighed and decided that a cup of tea was just what was needed. He stood up and flicked the kettle on.

A tap on the door made him look up just as Stevo's head popped around the door, his eyes wide with urgency. 'Boggie, man. Cell spins happening now, turbo and rummage teams all over, make sure you're clean,' he said, nodded, and then he was gone.

Immediately, Bogdan's stomach lurched. His tiny phone was in his pocket, ready for the call to come in from Stafford. No way could he lose it now, it would be disastrous.

Shouts and yelling began to emanate from the landing, with noises of crashing and banging as the screws charged up the landing.

Quickly, and without a thought, he grabbed the phone and stuffed it down the back of his trousers, wincing as he slid it between his buttocks. The best he could do at short notice.

There was a banging at his door, and it flew open. A group of three officers, two big brutish men, all gloved up, together with a young female officer. One of the specialist rummage teams they sent in every now and again.

'Volkov, step away from the kettle, it's a cell spin,' said the biggest of the men.

He did as he was asked, stepping into the centre of the cell, his face impassive, and a calm descending on him like a soft blanket.

'Right, shit for brains, anything to declare?' said the biggest screw.

'Nothing, boss,' he replied, smiling.

'Good. Arms out to your side,' the screw barked.

Bogdan complied, raising his arms, as the screw began to pat him down, firstly along his arms, then down his body, down his legs, to his feet.

'Shoes off,' he commanded.

Bogdan complied, kicking his trainers off into the middle of the cell. The female screw picked them up, with a wrinkled nose, pulled out the insole, and carefully checked the soles and under the tongue, before nodding and tossing them on the floor.

'All good, if a bit stinky,' she said, with a sneer.

The big male screw continued his search, with a none-too-gentle feel around Bogdan's bollocks and backside, but fortunately they clearly weren't doing strip searches. Bogdan was thankful that this was clearly a bulk weapons sweep across the whole wing, which mostly arose when the screws got intelligence about someone having a shank. Bogdan felt himself relax.

'Right, Boris, wait outside while we do the spin. You sure there's nothing in here we need to know about? It'll make the difference to any discipline if we find contraband.'

Bogdan smiled widely. 'Nothing, boss.'

'Piss off, then.'

Bogdan complied, feeling light as air, trying not to waddle with the phone jammed between his buttocks. He left the cell to the carnage that was raging on the landing as each and every cell was being torn to pieces by the rummage teams.

He was now home and clear for probably a few days at the least.

British prisons were easy compared to the jail in Siberia.

He chuckled, as he headed down to the association area. A chat with Stevo for half an hour, and then he could get back to his chess.

79

JANIE WALKED OUT of Frankland Prison still dressed in the blue uniform of a prison officer. She crossed the car park and jumped into the back of the Volvo.

'You can piss off,' she said, scowling at him.

'What? It suits you.'

'Double piss off. And don't you chip in, Barney,' she said, as she pulled off the scratchy white shirt, under which she was wearing a vest top.

'I never said owt, love. Any problems?'

'No, piece of piss, as you said. I imagine he'd jammed his phone up his backside, as it wasn't in the cell, that's for sure.'

'How about the kit?'

'I just switched over his extension lead for the one you gave me, like you said.'

'Grand, well done. How about the screws?' said Barney.

'Well, I couldn't hide what I was doing, and they had been briefed, but the DS who runs prison liaison says that they're sound, not like we have much of a choice, is there? Is it working?'

'Yep. Good as gold, sound is crystal clear, and we don't need visuals, so hence it could be the simplest bit of kit ever.'

'Well, we're all set then. No time like the present, I'll send the message to Stafford. I just wish we knew exactly where he was.' Max tapped out the new number into a message and sent it to Stafford.

'He's still in Gosforth, but he's on the move,' said Barney.

'Eh?' said Max.

'He's moving, just left his place on York Street.'

'How did you kn—' Max paused, and realisation washed over him. 'You lumped his car last night, didn't you?'

Barney grinned widely. 'It was dead easy. I emailed Ross late on, and he's sorted authorities out, although he did use DefCon level two swearing when he heard.'

'I bet.'

'Should have heard him when he found out I'd managed to get a bug inside it.' He cackled.

'What?' Max was astonished.

'Tin-shit locks on the old piece of crap, I couldn't resist it. It's only a simple battery-operated thing. It'll give us three days of audio in the car, once remotely activated.'

'Please tell me that—'

'Yep. Ross has sorted it out. We're all above board and legal, as long as no one looks at the timings too closely. I've only just activated them after Ross got the urgent oral authority granted, so we're golden.' Barney looked particularly pleased with himself.

'Christ mate, you playing it fast and loose is gonna backfire one day,' said Max, shaking his head.

'It's been fine up till now. As long as you know what rules you're breaking, you're generally okay.'

Within a moment, the Cashier's phone had buzzed in Max's lap. A thumbs-up emoji with a new number. The same number they'd recorded Stafford reading out to Bogdan last night from the phone box in Gosforth. The same number that was now being intercepted, at an innocuous room somewhere in the UK.

The net was closing.

'Are we ready?' said Max, looking at Janie behind him.

'Go for it, but don't look in the mirror any more, I'm changing my breeks, these ones are like bloody sandpaper.'

Max smiled, and then knocked the rear-view mirror up, so his only view was of the roof of the car. He dialled.

'Yes?' Stafford said.

'Are you clear to speak?' said Max.

'Yes.'

'I've made some enquiries. This can be done, but it will be difficult, and will need the cash quickly. You want me to proceed?'

'How can you?' said Stafford, sounding genuinely perplexed.

'That doesn't concern you, but you know my reputation. It's why you've used me in the past. If I say it can be done, it will be done, but I want payment in advance, there's been too many problems with this job, and I need to pay others to make this happen. This is a challenging mission. Killing a sitting judge while he's protected by the NCA is very hard, and it takes resources. If I wasn't preserving my reputation for hundred per cent success rate I wouldn't take the job.'

'When do you need the money by?'

'Today. This is time critical. My source knows where the Judge is now, but he'll be moved very soon.'

'Leave it with me.'

Max hung up.

'All clear and recording on the probe in the car. Not bad, bearing in mind I put it on in about thirty seconds flat, in the dark, while cream-crackered.'

'You're a genius, Barney,' said Max.

'In't it? Hold up, it's all happening.' Barney swiped his iPad and removed his earbud. There was a crackling from the speaker, tinny and rough, but audible. The sounds of numbers on a mobile phone being pressed.

Janie held up her own iPad. 'If this is gonna work, we should hear both ends of this conversation, always assuming that Stafford is calling Bogdan.'

No one said anything. The silence was overpowering.

Janie's iPad burst into life.

'Yes?' A harsh-edged Slavic voice.

'It's me,' said Stafford.

'Yes.'

'The Cashier says he can do it, but he needs fifty today.'

The speakers crackled as Bogdan sighed. 'Is cheap, I guess. Stringer paid for the hit, so fifty is cheap. It is good that Cashier is professional. I call X now, and he will call to make arrangement, lucky he is north today already because of this job. Where?'

'Newcastle.'

'This is okay, but Cashier must not fail. Ahsan must be dead soon.'

'He says he can do it. We know what he can do, it's a miracle that he escaped.'

'Okay. I call X, and you meet him to collect cash, then you get to Cashier, yes?'

There was a long pause.

'Understood.'

The phone clicked, and the iPads were silent, apart from the faint sounds of engine noises from Stafford's car.

'Where is he, Barney?'

Barney looked down at his iPad, switched to the map view, clicked and swiped. 'Heading south towards town. Or should I say, toon?'

'You probably should,' said Max, laughing.

'Heads up, boys. Bogdan is calling, it can only be to X,' said Janie, removing her headphone jack.

The sound of Bogdan's voice rang out of the speakers.

'*Eto ya. To, chto, my skazali vchera vecherom. Ono, uzhe nachalos, I eto dolzhno, byt' segodnya.*'

There was a pause as Bogdan listened for a full thirty seconds.

'Da,' he replied.

'What's he saying?' said Janie.

'Well, as none of us speak Russian, we're gonna have to wait. I'm hoping he'll do the translating for us when he calls Stafford back. Get Norma on the phone data, we need X's number, and we need live cell sites on it, pronto,' said Max.

'I'll text her now,' said Barney.

They didn't have to wait long. The sound of a phone buzzing was audible from Barney's iPad.

'Yes?' said Stafford.

'One hour. Centre of the Gateshead Millennium Bridge. Money in red bag.'

The silence following the call was long and empty, only softened by the hiss from the iPad speakers.

Max gunned the engine, engaged the gears and began to drive off. 'How long to the Millennium Bridge, Barney?'

'Traffic dependent, half an hour?' he said, swiping on his map application.

'I won't spare the horses, then.' Max floored the car and the streets began to flash by.

'Norma's on X's number. Phone unit are getting the live trace on it now.'

'Are we ready for this?' said Janie.

'Aye, let's get this done, I'll call Ross, and we'll get the firearms teams on standby. We need an urgent tactical plan.'

Max dialled using the car's hands-free. 'Ross?'

The noises of bustling activity were in the background, and Ross sounded harassed. 'Aye, all going on here. Norma is just waiting for the cell site for X to land, which should be anytime now. It looks like the combined weight of two Chief Constables giving it the beans has put a rocket up the arses of the phone companies.'

'That's good. You've heard the meeting site, I suspect. We're on our way, now, but we're half an hour away.'

'Aye, fucking nightmare. Busy footbridge, with shit loads of tourists, and no escape routes if the bugger pulls a gun. We also don't have a surveillance team, as Northumbria's is deployed miles away and will never get here in time.'

'We can manage. It's a narrow footbridge, once you're on it, you're pretty much committed. Firearms?'

'Tac adviser is looking at it now, and drawing up a plan, but there's not really much we can do. We'll need to stake out the bridge, and have a couple of armed cops on foot ready to support. Who's collaring them?' said Ross.

'I'll take X, Janie will arrest Stafford, with support from the armed cops.'

'Fine, I'll update the tac adviser.'

'Is there an RVP?' said Max, referring to the rendezvous point.

'Aye, RVP for the briefing with armed cops will be the car park of the Ramada Encore on Hawks Road, which is just a minute or two away from the bridge. Will you make it in time?' Ross's voice crackled out of the speakers of the Volvo.

'Of course we will, Ross. Have some faith.' Max rang off and looked at Janie in the back of the car, a grin stretched across his face. He pulled the car to the side of the road and said, 'Janie, you're driving.'

'Thank God for that,' said Janie, unbuckling her seat belt.

80

BARNEY STARED AT his screen, a map application open as he watched the pulsing blue blob of the tracker come to a stop.

'Right, Stafford's car is stopped, Baltic Car Park just a two-minute walk to the bridge,' he looked at his watch, 'we're ten minutes early.'

'Right, Janie, let's get eyes on the prize.' Max's finger went to his ear, and he tucked in the wireless earpiece deep and out of sight. His hand went to the covert pressel in his pocket. 'Foxtrot team from Max, about to deploy on foot. Subject one vehicle currently parking up in Baltic Car Park on south side of river.'

'All received, we're holding south side, you'll have one armed foot unit shadowing you from north entrance to bridge,' came the voice of the operational firearms team leader, a young, open-faced officer called Beth.

'All received,' said Max. He turned to Janie. 'Ready?'

Janie nodded, securing her own earpiece in place.

'Anything on CCTV, Barney?' said Max.

'Just searching now, decent of the locals to patch me in to council CCTV, I'll keep you posted, get out there, and get eyes on the car park, okay?'

'On it, keep us posted.' Max and Janie both stepped out of the car, which was parked just a hundred metres along South Shore Road.

Max and Janie set off on foot along the busy South Shore Road, the sun warming their faces as they headed the short distance towards the car park.

Barney's voice crackled in their ears. 'Right, he's out of his car, and he's on foot towards the entrance that's on South Shore Road, he's at the junction, a quick left and a right, and he's turned right into South Shore Road, and towards the bridge. You can move off.'

'Received, Barney.' Max and Janie were standing by a strange metal sculpture, which they looked at with apparent interest.

'Yep, he's moving, and he's now next to the big Joseph Rank building, you have him?' said Barney.

Max scanned, looking down South Shore Road, and there he was. Just as Barney had said. Walking with purpose by a new-looking brick building, emblazoned with JOSEPH RANK LIMITED in block capitals fifty feet up the façade.

'Got him, fifty metres ahead, walking west towards the bridge on South Shore Road. Foxtrot, you receive?' said Max, barely moving his lips, as he and Janie set off, matching his pace.

'Yep, ahead and waiting in cover by the entrance to the bridge,' said Beth.

'Received, still moving, fifty ahead, now passing Baltic Centre,' said Max, as Stafford continued his even stride pattern, eyes dead ahead. A man on a mission, thought Max.

Another voice came on the net: it was Dave, a member of the firearms team.

'Yeah, we have a possible for subject two north side of bridge. Male, late thirties, dark swept-back hair, jeans and a dark shirt, carrying a small red holdall, he's now close to the entrance of the bridge, no looks behind, and he's on. He's on the bridge, and that's now confirmed as a positive for subject two. Confirmed, X is on the bridge.' The voice was urgent but not panicked.

Barney came on the net, his accent as broad as ever, but his delivery was so relaxed that it was almost like he was reading a bedtime story. 'Barney here, that's a double confirmation. X is on the bridge, heading towards the middle, and he's stopped, stopped,

stopped. Leaning on the barrier, looking out over the river. Holdall is on his left shoulder.'

Max felt his stomach clench, this was game on now. 'That's received by Max, closing up now, subject one is on quayside, and he's heading towards the entrance to the bridge, Janie and I will take point, Beth, stay close, stay close.' He glanced at Janie and grinned. 'You ready, pal?'

She returned his grin. 'Och aye, ya teuchter bastard.'

The bridge, a long, sweeping arch of glass and steel that sparkled in the sun, was suspended above the dancing grey waters of the Tyne, which surged past, swollen by high tide and recent rains.

'You know that this bridge can fully tilt upwards to allow ships through?' said Max.

'Trivia? You're giving *me* bloody trivia, after the pelters you give me every time I hit you up with an interesting fact?' said Janie, as they stepped onto the modern structure.

There were two lanes on the bridge, both sleek and smart-looking, and both busy with pedestrians crossing in every direction. Office workers competed with tourists, all taking in the engineering marvel. Max shuddered. Of all the places for a potentially armed and dangerous encounter, this was possibly the last he would have picked.

'We have a meet. We have a meet. Subject one and two are together at the midway point sat next to each other on a metal bench, I'd say you're clear to strike, boys and girls,' said Barney, almost sounding amused.

Max looked through the throng of pedestrians, and there they were. Stafford was on the metal bench, next to X. Stafford's head was down, meekly, as X gesticulated with a finger towards the MI5 agent.

'We're thirty metres away, firearms teams, standby, standby, standby, and move up ahead of us, ready to strike,' said Max.

'Received, Max, let us leapfrog you once in position, you hold back anyone heading towards the centre to get the pedestrians out of the way. Once it's less busy, we strike, Dave, same for you. One hold back, keep pedestrians back, copy?'

'Received,' said Dave.

'Countdown, thirty seconds, we're moving up, radio silence, we are state red, confirming state red,' said Beth, calm and collected.

The radio went quiet. Dead air at the point of a strike.

Time for action, time for silence.

81

STAFFORD ALMOST FELT faint under X's withering stare, the red holdall at his feet. X had come to hand it over, but he wasn't letting it go easily. Stafford's head spun, and he felt nauseous.

X was the most terrifying individual that Stafford had ever met. His eyes were deep set and almost black, and they reminded him of a giant saltwater crocodile. Empty of emotion, but utterly ruthless and deadly. X wasn't a big man, in fact he was possibly smaller than Stafford, but he had a way of speaking that chilled him to his core.

'This is the last time, Stafford. The last time I hand you money, you understand?' X growled, his accent was thick and harsh Russian, and each word was enunciated for maximum menace.

Stafford nodded.

'Those above me do not want these eliminations to be traceable back to them in Moscow, which is why we used those idiots to do our bidding. That's what we do. We exploit those who are malleable to do our bidding, we don't use our own resources. We just light the touch paper and watch as the UK destroys itself, and you have made problems, Stafford. Well, no more, understand?' he almost hissed, like a viper.

'Matters beyond my control . . .' Stafford began to jabber, but X interrupted him, his voice sharp enough to slice fruit.

'I don't care. I don't care even a tiny fuck bit.'

'I'm sorry,'

'"Sorry" doesn't matter. You owe me, Stafford, remember the

video, eh? You fucking that cheap whore in a cheap hotel, her taking a piss on you, eh?' he said, laughing nastily. It was a terrible, evil sound as if he'd been gargling glass.

Then, a sudden movement to their left. A woman running towards them, a pistol in her hands, raised at them, eyes wide with aggression, mouth open preparing to bellow. The shock on X's face was instant as he saw her, but he was much quicker to act, and reaching into his pocket, he pulled out an automatic pistol and was raising it, before someone's shouts made him freeze.

'Armed police!' screamed the woman, and only then did Stafford notice the chequered baseball cap, emblazoned with 'Police'. There was more shouting, from the right. A burly male cop in an identical cap, his body armour visible beneath his unbuttoned shirt, a pistol levelled at them.

'Drop the gun!' the male cop bellowed at X, who had the pistol drawn but not levelled at the cops.

X relaxed and lowered the weapon. 'It's okay, don't shoot. I'll put it down,' he said, as calm as if he was being asked the time.

'Drop it now!' screamed the female cop, her face twisted in aggression, the pistol levelled at X.

Incredibly, X's face softened, he smiled, and he placed the pistol down on the bench, next to Stafford.

Pandemonium raged around them, as pedestrians screamed, other cops were arriving and shoving them away, and the armed officers stood there, faces hard, pistols trained on X, who simply widened his grin and placed his hands on his head. 'I'm no threat, I'm unarmed now, no shoot, eh?' he said, his tone almost jocular.

'Turn around, face away from us,' shouted the cop.

X did as he was commanded, his face suddenly hard and dark as he stared at Stafford, those deep eyes boring into his.

'Stafford, you say one fuck word to the cops, and I kill your kids, you hear. My people will rape your wife, and slit your kids' bellies, you understand me?'

The cops were edging forwards towards X, who looked down at the pistol next to him on the bench. 'Do it, Stafford. Do it, and your family are safe,' he hissed.

'Stafford, stand up slowly, hands up,' said the female cop. She was looking at him, but her pistol was still trained on X.

Stafford sat there frozen, and desolation swept over him like a black wave. It was all over. He knew that. His marriage was dead, his wife hated him, his kids hated him, and now he was going to jail. High-security prison, probably forever. He thought one day he might be able to escape it all and live his days out rich, and in luxury, but now it was just a category A prison cell for life. He was indirectly responsible for multiple murders. He was never getting out, and now his poor kids would always be looking over their shoulders, probably in witness protection. Fat tears began to swell in his eyes and cascade down onto his cheeks.

'Stafford, stand, now!' the cop bellowed again.

He knew what to do.

He knew in that microsecond, with almost laser-like focus, that he had only one option. Without giving himself a chance to change his mind, he did it.

In a flash, he reached for the pistol, lifted it, jammed it under his chin, not hearing the bellows from the cops, and pulled the trigger.

82

MAX, JANIE AND Barney were sitting silently in the CID office at Newcastle Central Police Station, a palpable sense of exhaustion hanging over them like a fug. Beth, Rob and the rest of the firearms team were also in the room, scribbling their notes.

Investigators from the Independent Office for Police Conduct had come and taken initial accounts from all of them, and appointments for formal statements had been made, but what happened was as clear as day. It had all been captured on CCTV.

David Stafford had been declared dead at the scene, and very quickly the world and his wife had turned up, and all those at the scene had been despatched to wait at Newcastle Central while the post-shooting procedures were underway. Max and the others had no idea whether they'd be hanging around here for hours, or possibly days, with the vagaries of their being Scottish cops working in England.

Max decided that now was the time to call Katie. He dialled, and moved to the edge of the police office.

'Max?' Katie sounded worried.

'Aye, you okay, babe?' said Max.

'We're fine, but what's happening? I heard there was a shooting in Newcastle?' she said, her voice laced with concern.

'Aye, it's all underway, but not a cop. A guy we were looking at shot himself.'

'Oh my God, were you there?'

'Aye.'

'God, babe, are you okay?' she said.

'I'm knackered, but I'm not bad.'

'When are you coming home?' she said.

'Probably tomorrow. Thankfully it was all captured on camera, so no suggestion cops shot the guy, but they do things a bit different this side of the border, and it's taking a wee bit of getting used to.'

Max looked out of the window and down into the car park. He saw Miles Wakefield getting out of a car, along with Heather Mortimer, Ross was waiting for them, arms folded, defensively. Max could see that the dynamic between them was somewhat awkward. Something was happening, he could sense it.

'Well, come home soon, we all miss you,' said Katie.

'All?' said Max.

'Of course, me, Evie and Nutty.' Katie sounded amused.

'Aye, of course, look, I'd best go, things are still happening here.'

Max had a funny feeling in his gut as he watched Ross, Heather and Miles striding into the building. Something was up.

'I'd say shit is going down badly, lads,' said Max, as he rejoined Barney and Janie.

'How?' said Janie.

'Vibes, but I think we're about to find out. Heads up, bosses entering the room.' Max nodded towards the door, where Ross, Heather and Miles were coming in. The atmosphere around the three was almost visible.

'What's going on, guvnors?' said Max, in what he hoped was a jocular tone.

'You can fuck off with that bollocks, Craigie. Just because we're in England doesn't mean you can go all cockney on us. We have an update.'

'Go on?' said Max.

Heather folded her arms, eyed Ross suspiciously and spoke. 'Peter Gow, aka Curtis Langfield aka the Cashier, has been interviewed. He refused all legal advice and said absolutely nothing in interviews so far, and I had my best team on him. Charges are likely to be authorised by CPS for conspiracy to murder, firearms offences, money laundering and burglary, and he's remanded to Newcastle Magistrates Court in the morning.' Heather turned and looked at Max. 'But there's something else.'

'What?' said Max.

'He wants to talk to you, Max. He says he'll not grass those that are alive, but he wants to give "context". His words, and he'll only speak to you. He thinks you'll understand. I think it's a military thing.'

'I take it he knows that the tapes will be on, and I'll report everything. I'm not his bloody mate.' Max flushed slightly.

'He knows. CPS are aware, and their view is that their charging decision will be "informed by" whatever he says, even if irrelevant, and they want you to do it. We have plenty of time, as our superintendent has given a twelve-hour extension to custody time limits, and if necessary, we'll go to court for a warrant of further detention. We want to hear what he has to say, Max. Even if it is bullshit.'

'Where is he?'

'A covert custody facility we opened specially for him, it's just fifteen minutes away,' said Heather.

'How about the murder of Fin in Stirling?' said Max.

'No evidence of it at all yet; he's been very, very clever.'

'Laura McKechnie has all the info and is on it. If the evidence is there, she'll find it,' said Miles.

'How about the bomb in York?' said Janie.

'York CT team are monitoring and sending a team. We have what's on the iPad, but that's all. May get something now they know who they're looking for, but they're all going to be long-term jobs, and that's less of a problem now that all the suspects are either dead or in custody,' said Heather.

'What's needed from us?' said Ross.

'Nothing in Northumbria, beyond all the material relating to matters happening in our area, and I believe Yorkshire just want a guarantee of evidential sharing. It's a reactive investigation now, Ross,' said Miles.

'And how about Bogdan, in jail?' said Max.

'There's another conundrum. He's likely facilitated a number of murders because of his dealings with the late Stringer Dent, together with X, also aka Xavier Petrov,' said Heather.

'So, not Piotr Nevalny, British citizen?' said Janie.

'Nope. He's now claiming to be Xavier Petrov, a Kazakh diplomat who lives in London,' said Miles.

There was a long pause in the office.

'A diplomat?' said Max, an empty feeling in his gut. The word 'diplomat' carried significance. It meant only one thing.

'That's his claim. He's requested his embassy in London be contacted urgently, and we have no choice but to do so,' said Heather.

'I hate, and hesitate to ask, but . . . diplomatic immunity?' Max could hardly say the words.

'He says he does, and he's an arrogant shit, but we've not had it confirmed yet, so we proceed as if he doesn't. We have him bang to rights for conspiring to kill the judge, but . . .' Heather paused, her face pale and tired-looking.

'I don't even want to think about this,' said Max.

'Aye, well, until I'm forced, he stays,' said Heather.

A silence descended on the room again. A deep sense of lassitude and frustration was almost visible, like clouds forming in the room.

'This feels like a failure,' said Janie.

'It's definitely not a failure, Janie. You guys have done amazing work as always. Let's not forget that this all started because of one word to Barney from an old colleague, and you've now uncovered, and totally destroyed, a multi-handed conspiracy to cause disaffection in the UK by malign forces. Not all jobs get wrapped up with a big bow on them, do they? The Chief sends his congratulations all round,' said Miles.

'Feels like failure, though. Bogdan was running this operation from his cell, along with X, and there's nothing stopping them continuing, is there?' said Max.

'They'll be locked down, as tight as a duck's arse, Max. Bogdan's already been moved to a new facility, and his mobile has been confiscated. They've failed, Max, you guys smashed this network to pieces. Not all jobs end up neatly finished with successful convictions. Success can be defined many ways, and I'm chalking this as a success.' Miles tried to smile, but it was unconvincing to say the least.

Barney stood up, his face hard, and when he spoke his normal avuncular delivery was full of venom. 'Bullshit. Fin's dead, and he was a good man, that lassie Juliet is dead, as is that lad Billy Mac, and those bastards who did it get away with it by being bloody dead. Now you're telling me that the two Russians that inspired it all just get to carry on regardless?'

'That's the justice system, sometimes, Barney,' said Miles.

'Well then. There's fuck all justice, I'm going for a fag.' Barney stormed out.

The room fell silent again after the uncharacteristic outburst from the normally laid-back Barney.

'You ready, Max?' said Heather.

Max looked down at his scuffed trainers and nodded. 'Not really, but let's go.'

83

GOW LOOKED DOWN at the table, only half listening as Max read out the caution, which was similar to the Scottish version.

Gow was dressed in a grey tracksuit with the sleeves rolled up, gripping a Styrofoam cup in his rough and calloused hand. The wings of the Parachute Regiment were tattooed on his forearm, the motto 'Utrinque Paratus' underneath, but there was a plain black oblong below it. He was remarkably unremarkable. Short, lean to the point of being wiry, but his arms were corded with muscle. His face was worn and leathery, and he looked significantly older than the date of birth on his custody sheet indicated. His eyes were blue, and icy, and they shone with intelligence. These were eyes that had clearly seen way too much.

'What's with the tatts?' said Max, pointing at Gow's forearm.

Gow snorted in amusement. 'Got it done in Aldershot when I was a crow in para depot. Long time ago, mate.'

'Not the first, nor last.'

Gow raised his eyebrows. 'Could've been worse. Some of the lads got Union Jack–clad bulldogs wearing a red beret, or "I'm a killer" and crap like that, the bloody idiots. The training team went mental. I just had the badge and my number, but when I went on selection, I had my number covered up. They were like that in the regiment.' His accent was a soft Cumbrian burr, gentle and soothing, which didn't match the profile of a ruthless killer sitting across the desk.

'SAS?' said Max.

He nodded. 'I passed first time, got badged and then that was me at Hereford. Who Dares Wins, "best of the best".' He mimed quotation marks.

'What did you specialise in?' Max eyed him, trying to push down the feeling of loathing. Not now. Now was time for a clear head.

'Demolitions.'

'Know your way around an IED, then?'

The man grinned, his teeth uneven. 'Yeah. I was damn good, Max.'

'How long were you there?'

'Ten years. Ten fucking years, mostly spent in the Middle East, killing people. You understand?'

'I did two tours, Peter.'

'Then you understand.' A statement rather than a question.

'What do I understand?' Max leaned back in his chair and narrowed his eyes.

Gow sat up in his seat, his eyes glittering. 'The mission. The thrill of the mission.'

'I suspect we had different experiences. I was mostly stuck in a forward operating base scratching my arse.'

Gow's eyes met Max's, and they seemed to bore into his very soul, such was the intensity. 'Somehow, I suspect that's not true, I can see it in your eyes. You've seen shit, Max, we all saw shit, whoever you were, and you'd have been out of your FOB every day. We all saw bad stuff and we all did bad stuff. You know what they had us doing?'

'Tell me?'

'HVT eliminations. High-value target operations. Kill or capture, but mostly kill. Taliban leaders. Smashing down doors, and then killing the fucking lot of them. We were good, Max. We were very good.'

Max sighed, a flash of irritation nipping at him. 'Why are you telling me this, Peter?'

'Context. Everyone is going to be thinking that I'm a monster, and maybe I am, but I want people to know that I wasn't always like this. I had good parents, a nice life in Carlisle, but the army, the SAS and Afghanistan ruined me. It took a decent kid and turned him into what I am now. Context matters. Do you understand?'

'Not really.' Max felt a chill descend on him, as Gow fixed him with a stare, his eyes icy cold.

'Did you kill anyone?' Gow said, his voice low.

'I'm not answering that. This is an interview, Peter, I ask the questions.'

'I'll take that as a yes, then.' He sniggered. It wasn't a pleasant sound.

'Take it how you like. Why've you done this?'

'Done what?'

Max shook his head, dismissively. 'Let's not mess about. You killed people, Peter. Daniel Solomon, Billy Mackee, Fin Smith, Juliet McNamara, and you were in that hotel last night to kill Mr Justice Ahsan. Why?'

'Firstly, I didn't kill Billy Mackee, and I didn't kill Juliet, or whatever her name was.'

'So, you don't deny killing the others, then?'

'I did what I'd been paid to do with Solomon and Smith, and I failed with Ahsan, but I had nothing to do with the others.'

'So, you knew how to make an IED that looked just the same as Islamic State ones?'

'Simple stuff, Max. Effective, but deadly. I learned from the best when I was there on a covert mission. Child's play to make it look like one of theirs, on the basis that they make them so simple. I just updated it enough so I could remotely arm it. Let him arrive at his event in York, and then arm it. Quick wire into the ignition, and boom! Shame about the passer-by.' If he was regretful, he didn't show it. He clearly didn't give a shit.

'Why?'

'Why what?' Peter looked genuinely perplexed.

'Why were they all killed?'

Gow laughed. 'The people who know that are dead, Max. I was just a hired hand. I get paid without even meeting the client. I just do the job I'm paid for, and I've never failed.'

'Why do you think, then?'

Gow just shrugged.

'Who did kill Billy and the others?' said Max, the chill of Gow's easy denial settling like a cold Scottish haar.

He shrugged. 'They're already dead, so it doesn't matter if I say so. Stringer and Shorty killed Billy Mackee, but I didn't kill Juliet. I was in Stirling at the time killing Fin Smith.' His eyes were flat, and as emotionless as if he was describing delivering parcels for a courier firm. Max shuddered.

'You know who did kill Juliet?'

He shook his head.

'Was it all about the money?'

'That kept a roof over my head, but it wasn't that, as you'll see if you find where I live. It's one step beyond a single-man bunk on a shit military base.'

'Why, then?'

He paused, and showed his teeth in a wide grin. 'The missions, Max. All about the missions. The research, the plan, the stalk, the engagement and the executive action. Whether it's a silenced Welrod for the judge, or an IED under a Jewish author's car, it took expertise. It's the one thing I'm good at. The government trained me well. You understand, I think.'

Max shook his head dismissively. 'So, explain it to me, then. I want to understand, Peter.'

'It's primeval, you know this. You're a warrior, as well.'

'I was once. Now I'm a detective. I detect and prevent crime.'

Gow snorted with amusement. 'It's still in you, I promise. The highest of stakes, planning the operation, rehearsing, researching, making sure you have the right kit, the right target, and then executing the mission efficiently. It can't be beaten. It's like a drug.' He grinned, but not one bit of the smile reached his unreadable eyes.

Max shivered again, the hairs on the nape of his neck alive. He exhaled slowly before continuing. 'Why did you leave the SAS?'

'I didn't leave. They kicked me out. After everything I did, they slung me out on my ear after a stupid mistake.'

'Why?'

He sighed and rubbed his face. 'I'd been overseas for a year, under the most intense pressure in Iraq. I came back to Hereford, and I made a bad error of judgement.' He paused to drink from the Styrofoam cup.

'Carry on.'

'A woman. She was beautiful, she was unbelievable, and I was head-over-heels smitten. I had no idea she was working for the Russians. I'd thought she was Bulgarian. Before I knew it, she had me in the palm of her hand. I was obsessed with her, probably for about six months.' For the first time in the interview, he looked reflective as he cast his eyes down, and Max thought he detected some shame.

'Go on.'

'First it was little things. Probing me on the work, and I probably let too much go, trying to impress her, and that. That's when I met X and he hit me with the photos. Pictures of us in a hotel together, lurid, graphic photos.'

'Who's X?' said Max, keeping his face impassive.

Gow shook his head. 'No. That's not why I'm here. I did what I did, and I'll pay the price. I'm a professional, I took the risks, and I'll take the punishment, but I won't take others down. Let's just say he was linked to the Kremlin.'

'Carry on.'

'He threatened to release the photos on social media, tagging everyone and everything. Send them to my wife, to my CO. So, I did what I was told. I passed over secrets, and they were fucking delighted.' He smiled, without humour.

'So, how'd you get caught?'

He paused for a full thirty seconds before answering, his head lowered and his eyes averted. 'They obviously had suspicions, so I got nabbed leaving Stirling Lines with all the tech details on a new crypto device in my bag. I was nicked by the military police, and that was that. They found out from my phone that I'd been with Ivanka, and soon realised she had question marks about her. From that moment, I was finished.'

'You weren't charged, though?'

'They didn't want the bad publicity. They just closed all the doors down, got their stories straight and realised that I didn't really pass anything cataclysmic over. I mean the crypto intel I gave them they could probably have got from the internet. So, they slung me out, SNLR, with no references, nothing. My wife left me, I had no money, I had nothing. I was angry, and in the wilderness, but you know what I missed the most?'

'Go on?' said Max, his stomach tense as he anticipated the reply.

His eyes lit up. 'It was the missions, Max. It was all about the missions. After all those years, planning and executing life and death operations, I was now working in fucking Tesco. Fucking Tesco, Max. I was a fucking cashier in a supermarket, having been in the SAS. The worst day was when a few pals saw me working the till. Me. I used to be a communications expert, I speak Arabic, I used to be able to deploy with a million quid's worth of state-of-the-art kit, and now, here I was ringing up Mrs Bloggs' weekly shop. I'll never forget the laughs and piss-takes from those guys.'

'I can see how that'd be difficult,' said Max, considering for a brief moment the stories similar to this. One minute a soldier is in charge of a ten-million-pound tank, leading a crew of expert operators, the next he's queuing at the dole office for government handouts. 'Go on.'

'So, when X made me an offer, it was a no-brainer. An easy job, a new mission. I had a skillset that was valuable. I could make big money, and I could scratch the itch. No more a cashier behind a till at a supermarket in Hereford.'

'So, you become the Cashier, killer for hire?'

He nodded, his eyes shining. 'You understand, don't you?' He stared hard at Max.

Max felt sweat break out on his back. 'No. I don't understand one bit, Peter.'

'We're more similar than you think, DS Craigie. You understand the lure of the mission, don't you?'

'It's just a fucking job. I do it for a wage to feed my family, I'm nothing like you.' Max felt his face flushing.

Gow pointed to Max's dressing. 'How'd you get the injury on your head?'

Max's hand went to the dressing, before dropping it back down quickly and shaking his head. 'You're not interviewing me here, Peter.' Max felt his stomach clench, and the heat rising in his chest.

'I've seen many gunshot injuries. That dressing covers the wound, but I can see the muzzle flash burn marks around it. I'd say that's a skim bullet wound. You were lucky. Was that Stringer?'

'I'm not playing this game. This interview is over.'

'Yep. You almost stopped a bullet, and yet you're still here, interviewing me, when you should be off on the sick, but you've stayed. Why?'

'That's enough. Interview terminated.' Max jabbed at the recording machine button, his insides boiling with suffused rage.

'It could have been you dead on a slab, rather than your colleague the other day. It could have been your wife widowed, but instead your friend copped it, and yet, you're still here. You're still here, because you feel guilty that it isn't you dead in the morgue, but you're still here. All about the mission, Max.' He sat back and laughed, his eyes full of disdain.

Rage overcame Max, and he exploded out of his chair, grabbed Gow by the scruff of the neck and slammed him down on the desk, wrenching his arm hard up behind his back until Gow yelped in pain, still laughing. A nasty, cackling sound, one step away from madness. Max jammed his forearm hard into the back of the killer's neck. 'Listen. You evil fucking—'

The door bust open, and Heather appeared, face hard and eyes wide. 'Max, stop,' she barked.

Max leaned forward, his face brick-red, his mind seething, dark and full of hate. He wrenched Gow's arm harder and drove his forearm further into his neck. He leaned down and growled through gritted teeth, 'We. Are. Not. The. Same.'

'Max!' Heather's voice had a real edge of steel.

Max stopped and stood, just as a uniformed cop entered the room.

'This interview is over. Get rid of him.' Max turned and marched out of the room.

He stormed through the custody office and into the yard where he just stood there, breathing deeply, sucking in the warm air, feeling the stress begin to leach from his body as his mind roiled.

A noise behind him made him turn. It was Heather. She didn't look angry, as Max had expected, she looked sympathetic. She clutched two Styrofoam cups, wisps of steam drifting out of them.

'He was talking crap, Max.' She handed over one of the cups, and Max accepted it.

'Aye,' said Max, turning away and watching a cop who was pressure-washing a car in the yard. He sipped at the tea and grimaced. It was sickly sweet and weak.

'Seriously. He's a bloody psycho, and you're a good professional cop. You've saved lives, Max. Not just the judge's, but all the others he'd have killed in the future, and you've got justice for his victims. You're nothing alike.'

Max exhaled and smiled. 'He's a bit right, though, isn't he?'

'Meaning?'

'I got shot in the head a few nights ago, and a pal was killed a couple of feet away from me. I had to tell his widow how he'd died. And yet, here I am, working. Fulfilling the mission, rather than being at home with my wife and kid. We're not the same, but we have similarities, don't we?' A sudden wave of exhaustion swept over Max, and he sat down on the concrete, back to the grimy wall of the building.

'It worked, by the way,' said Heather.

'What?'

'That interview. He basically admitted to killing Fin Smith and Daniel Solomon, and plotting to kill the judge. He even mentioned X which is nice to know, even if he is probably gonna walk. Makes the CPS's decision much easier, doesn't it?'

Max sighed again. 'I'd almost forgotten about X walking free. This tea is bogging, by the way.' He tried to smile.

'I thought you needed some sugar. We're holding on to X, but from what I hear, it's almost an inevitability now. The noises from the Home Office, Diplomatic Service, etcetera, are getting impossible to resist. In fact, we'd better get back there.'

'Aye, come on. I want to look the bastard in the eye before he goes.'

84

IT DIDN'T TAKE long for Bruce to catch up with events, as Max had suspected.

As soon as Max got back to the HQ building his phone buzzed, the familiar letter, numbers and characters.

'Heather, I'll catch up with you in the office, I need to take this.'

'I'll get the kettle on.' She winked.

Max nodded, and sighed as he answered the call. It was inevitable that he'd call, the only surprise was that he'd taken so long.

'Bruce?'

'Anything to tell me?' The familiar soft Scottish accent.

'I bet you know most of it already, and I'm assuming you know we arrested your boss's pal.'

'I've heard rumblings, some of which I don't like.'

'Meaning?'

'The Kazakhs are claiming him as one of theirs with diplomatic immunity.'

'Yep,' was all that Max could be bothered to say.

'That's not ideal.'

'Aye, that and the fact that Bogdan Volkov is unlikely to face any more punishment, and in fact has been shifted to a much cushier regime to keep him from the more suggestive prison population. All feels like a failure, Bruce.'

'Ach, dinnae be so harsh on yourself, pal. These things often work out in the end. When's Petrov getting out of the nick?'

'Very soon. A representative from the embassy has been in

already, with a high-powered solicitor, and we've been told we have no choice by the Foreign Office, Diplomatic Service, Home Secretary and pretty much every other bugger. My boss has unleashed a great deal of swearing at almost all of them.'

'Do any good?'

'Nah. Petrov is getting released from Newcastle main custody very soon, and apparently an embassy driver will be here imminently, on diplomatic plates to take him back to London, and then back to Kazakhstan, where he's very much out of reach.'

'You sound gutted, Max.'

'Such is life. Not all jobs have a happy ending, and sometimes the bad guys win.'

'They never do forever, Max. Bad things happen to bad people . . . eventually.'

'Aye, right. Look, I have to go, Bruce.' Max hung up and headed to the custody suite. He had volunteered to sign Petrov out. He felt responsible, and his stomach churned with nausea.

*

The custody suite of the Newcastle Central Police Station was almost empty, all prisoners apart from Petrov being transferred to other stations.

Max looked on blankly as he watched Xavier Petrov snap his Rolex back on his wrist and put his wallet and coins back into his pocket. His solicitor stood there silently, eyeing Max with interest. He was a Slavic-looking man in a sharp three-piece suit, and he was clutching a briefcase.

'Are we ready to release my client, DS Craigie?' said the solicitor.

'Aye,' said Max, not looking at the man.

'How about money in holdall? That's fifty K of my country's money.' His eyes glinted with amusement. The solicitor whispered into his client's ear, and they shared a smile.

'Evidence. Coroner will need it for the inquest, so you can whistle for it, pal,' said Max.

Petrov chuckled. 'Tell you what, Detective Sergeant Max Craigie, of Police Scotland, put it in station fund for police widows, eh?' His coal black eyes glittered with no amusement.

'Aye,' said Max, not breaking his stare directly into Petrov's eyes, feeling his right fist balling and the desire to uppercut the man, smashing his jaw and rendering him unconscious. Instead, he breathed deeply, and smiled. It almost hurt.

'I hear there are lots of police widows, DS Craigie. It's so sad when a police officer dies, eh? Or their family die, eh? So, I donate all money to the worthy causes, as token of esteem for hospitality. Now, I hope I have a car coming to collect me, and take me to embassy in London.'

'Follow me.' Max turned and led the way out into the late afternoon sun.

A sleek Mercedes was parked at the front of the police station, a driver wearing a peaked cap was at the wheel, and the engine purred away. The number plates were unmistakable. Diplomatic plates. Making the occupants of the vehicle untouchable to law enforcement.

'Thank you for your hospitality, Detective Sergeant Craigie,' said Petrov, holding out his hand to shake. Max just stared at it, turned and walked back up the stairs to the station doors. He looked back just as Petrov was shaking hands with the solicitor and then climbing into the back seat of the Mercedes.

Max went back inside, feeling sick.

It was time to go home.

85

XAVIER PETROV WAS sitting in the rear of the Mercedes, reading *The Moscow Times* on his iPad when his phone rang.

It was his contact at the Kazakh Embassy, the normally taciturn Amir, who had some type of role in the building on Park Lane.

'Amir, what gives?' he said, trying to sound bright and breezy. He realised that his popularity may not be particularly high at the moment. He'd caused a lot of people a lot of work, and he was thankful that his contacts in Moscow would be bringing pressure to bear to keep him out of too much shit. He was resigned to being sent back to Astana, probably tomorrow, but hopefully for not too long. He preferred London, but maybe he'd go to America next.

'Where are you?' Amir said without preamble.

Petrov looked out of the window. Rather than the dual carriageway he'd been expecting to see, he saw that he was actually on a quiet road, lined by tall hedges.

'I've actually no idea. Driver, where are we?' he said to the back of the man behind the wheel, whom he had taken absolutely no interest in so far.

'Just a quick diversion, there's an accident on the A1,' he said, in a strange accent.

'Amir, we're on our way, I'm in a limo.'

'Strange, we sent a car, and the driver's just called asking when you're coming out. Are you in a car already?'

'Yes, he was waiting outside the police station, maybe they sent two by mistake?' he said, feeling a chill descend on him, as he saw the driver's eyes flick towards him in the rear-view mirror. They were steely blue and icy.

'Perhaps. Get here fast, the Ambassador is keen to speak with you, as is your friend from Moscow.' Amir rang off.

'Driver, where are we going?' said Petrov.

'As I said, sir, diversion, it'll be quicker in the long run.' The car began to slow down before it pulled over into a passing place, letting a car go ahead.

'This doesn't feel like a . . .' The words died in his throat. The driver turned to face him, a pistol in his hand, trained unerringly at him. The driver was a lean, hard-faced man, with short grey hair visible underneath his cap.

The corners of his eyes crinkled in the beginnings of a smile, and when he spoke, it was in accented Russian. 'Alexsei Demidov sends his regards, Xavier Petrov.' Petrov's mouth gaped at the mention of the telecommunications oligarch, the President's sworn enemy, treacherous friend of the West. Instantly, his heart froze in his chest. The pistol jerked in the man's hands, and Petrov felt a sharp pain in his pectoral muscle where the projectile had buried into his chest. He looked down, seeing the tuft of a dart in his chest.

He reached for the dart, as his surroundings began to swim and his limbs suddenly became impossibly heavy, his vision fading.

86

IT HAD BEEN a proper police funeral.

The church in Dunkeld had been rammed to the rafters with cops in their best blue uniforms, along with lots of CID officers all wearing their smartest suits, generally reserved for High Court appearances. The front pews were packed full of family and friends.

Cops lining the pathway stood to attention as Joe's body passed by in his flag-draped coffin on its journey into the small church.

Max barely heard a word that was said in the funeral service, he just stood there, numb, as the images of that day replayed, vivid and technicolour in his mind. He couldn't speak, and he couldn't look at Joe's wife who was flanked by legions of her family.

But it was Joe's kids. Three sweet, innocent wee toots, sobbing silently at the front of the church. The two twin boys, solid, stocky, the image of their dad; the daughter, blonde, and tiny. They were all broken. So young, so innocent, and distraught, having their dad torn from them. Max balled his fists so tight that his nails almost drew blood. He didn't flinch when he felt Janie's hand come down to his, gripping it. He turned to look down his pew: Ross, Barney, Janie and Norma were all there, solemn and pale.

His stomach roiled at the injustice of it all. The Russian tactics of using the useful idiots Stringer and Shorty, evil though they were, they were just tools. He tried to shake the anger at Xavier Petrov being driven away in a limousine. Even if he hadn't been seen since, Max assumed that he had been squirrelled out of the country. The diplomatic wranglings had continued with expulsions and condemnations. But innocent people were still dead, and for what?

Max just clamped his jaw tight and stared straight ahead, ramrod straight, ignoring the tears that cascaded down his face. As the coffin passed them en route to the hearse, to be driven away for the private family cremation, he bowed his head, his stomach roiling and his mind spinning as if several cogs had worked loose.

Hettie was immediately behind the coffin, her two stocky boys holding her hands, their faces streaked with tears, but they walked upright, square-shouldered and proud. Just like their dad. Joe. A good cop, an even better man.

Hettie stopped when she saw Max and turned to face him, her face pale and shattered. Wordlessly, she reached up and touched the healing wound on his temple. It was pink and puckered, but it was fading day by day. She snaked an arm around Max's neck, and pulled him in tight, shoulders heaving as she sobbed against his blue suit.

'Thank you for trying, Max. I'll never forget you.' She wiped her eyes, grabbed her boys' hands and continued the slow walk out of the church, out into the sun.

Max's head surged, spinning as he closed his eyes. He began to sway and was reassured when he felt Janie's firm grasp.

When the procession had filed out, Max sat and exhaled deeply.

The rest of the team followed suit. They all just sat there as the church emptied.

Chief Constable Chris Macdonald, resplendent in his best dress uniform, approached them.

'Okay, guys?' he said, his eyes soft.

No one said anything.

He tried again. 'Fancy a drink?'

'What would Joe have done?' said Janie.

'As I understand it, he loved a beer,' said Max.

'Then let's go and have a beer, The Taybank is just around the corner,' said Ross.

*

Cops do what cops do at funeral services. They pay their respects, they often weep, they remember their fallen colleagues.

And then they go to the pub. It had always been the same.

A drink to remember your old colleague. You shared the good times, faced the same dangers, laughed at each other's jokes, and if it went well, or even if it went badly, you dealt with it together.

And when one of you shuffled off this mortal coil, you went for a drink with those who were left behind, after the thin blue line became just that little bit thinner.

The team all stood together, clutching drinks in silence. No one seemed to know what to say, as was often the case until alcohol had loosened tongues, as the emotion of the service began to fade.

Max took a sip from his cranberry juice and felt his phone vibrate in his pocket. He pulled it out and looked at the screen. It was Katie.

Hope it went well, babe. I'm almost packed up, and excited about tomorrow.

Max had booked a week away and they were flying to Portugal in the morning. He knew that they all needed a total break.

His phone buzzed again, this time the familiar string of numbers, letters and characters. There was a video clip attached. Max felt his skin prickle, as he clicked on the play button. It took a moment to realise what he was seeing: it was the inside of a helicopter. The camera swung around and stopped on a short, lean man with black swept-back hair, who was slumped, unconscious in the seat next to an open door, the wind buffeting his hair.

It was Xavier Petrov.

Max knew what was coming. Bruce Ferguson wasn't one to let bygones be bygones.

A hand grabbed the man by his jacket, heaved him up and tossed him out of the door, a length of heavy chain following him out into the abyss below. The camera followed the man out of the door, giving a view of Petrov cartwheeling, the chain glinting, as he headed towards the grey sea a thousand feet below.

Then the camera footage went blank.

Max continued to stare at the phone in his hands, a slow smile spreading across his face.

'What's so fucking funny, Craigie?' said Ross.

'Nothing, just Katie excited about going on holiday tomorrow.'

'Aye, about time you took my goddaughter on holiday, you tight fud. All the overtime I pay you, least you can do, eh?'

Epilogue

Three months later

BOGDAN VOLKOV LOOKED up as Mr Jamieson, one of the friendlier screws, popped his head around the door of his cell.

'You okay, Boggie?' he said, raising his eyebrows knowingly.

'Of course.'

'Present for you, from an admirer on the outside, pal. He slipped me a few quid to get them through, said his name was X, and he was very insistent that I get it to you. He said you'd know why.'

'X? You're sure?'

'What he said, Russian fella with black hair.'

Bogdan couldn't believe it. He'd been led to believe that X was going to be sent back to Kazakhstan, but he had disappeared on his way back from Newcastle and hadn't been seen since. Bogdan had suspected that X had kept his head down, secured a new identity and had carried on regardless with the business. This was good news.

Mr Jamieson was one of the more approachable screws on the wing, and could occasionally be relied upon to get a little contraband through.

'Don't leave me suspended, then. Hand over?' he said, his excitement rising.

Jamieson entered the cell, pushed the door shut, held out his hand and dropped two miniature bottles of Beluga Gold vodka onto the bed.

'He apologised for sending miniatures, but it's not easy smuggling this shit in. For fuck's sake don't get caught with it.' Jamieson grinned and left the cell.

Bogdan looked at the precious spirit, almost with awe. It had been so long since he'd experienced the five-times filtered, natural malt spirit from select grain, and the purest of Siberian water. His mouth almost watered at the sight of the spirit.

He opened the first of the small bottles and tipped it into his plastic mug. He smelled the clean, fresh spirit. No sipping. No Russian would sip a vodka, so he downed it, in one. Initially harsh, but then mellowing out on his tongue, with slightly sweet flavours of vanilla, oatmeal and honey, and a spicy finish on his palate. He sighed, the memories it evoked of happier times.

Suddenly sleepy, he lay down on his bed, a feeling of exhausted euphoria beginning to wash over him, which was unusual but expected after a four-year abstinence. He yawned and closed his eyes, drifting off, barely aware of someone returning to the cell and retrieving the bottle. He tried to move, to object, but his limbs were too heavy. Just so, so very heavy. Like the alcohol was withdrawing all of his energy from his sinewy body.

And then there was nothing.

Acknowledgements

Once again, I've come to the end of a book.

I mean, woo-hoo, right? A great job by me.

Well, no. Not really. I'm only one part of the equation. The idea is mine, as are the words on the page, but if we published it after what I've done alone it would be really rubbish. It's a team game, with lots of other folks playing a huge part in making my daft stories into something that you, the reader, will actually enjoy and someone may want to buy!

So, with that in mind all my heartfelt thanks go to the following.

To all the staff at my tremendous publishers at HQ. My editor Georgina Green, your championing of the series, and putting up with my daft questions are vital to keeping me on the straight and narrow, and means that the books get finished. Felicia for all the PR, Lou for the marketing genius, John for the line and structural edits, and Eldes for the copyediting. All vital in taking my gibberish and making it work. Big thanks to the gaffers, Manpreet and Lisa who both have my back, and laugh at Ross's daft jokes.

My agent, Kerr Macrae, for all the advice, soothing words, beers and laughs. I'm so happy to have you in my corner getting these stories out there.

My writing pals, Colin Scott, Tony Kent, Ed James, Sir Ian, and all the others who keep me writing and laughing.

My fabulous kids, Alec, Richard and Ollie, you guys are my inspiration.

Clare. Forever.

All my crazy family, who are my biggest cheerleaders.

To all my former brothers and sisters in blue. I know what you do that the public never get to hear about. You save lives, and keep us safe.

Of course, to all the booksellers, bloggers, grammers, and champions of books and writers.

And of course, you. The reader. It's kinda pointless without you guys.

Neil

Discover more thrilling books in the DS Max Craigie Series . . .

Dear Reader,

We hope you enjoyed reading this book. If you did, we'd be so appreciative if you left a review. It really helps us and the author to bring more books like this to you.

Here at HQ Digital we are dedicated to publishing fiction that will keep you turning the pages into the early hours. Don't want to miss a thing? To find out more about our books, promotions, discover exclusive content and enter competitions you can keep in touch in the following ways:

JOIN OUR COMMUNITY:

Sign up to our new email newsletter: http://smarturl.it/SignUpHQ

Read our new blog www.hqstories.co.uk

X: https://twitter.com/HQStories

f: www.facebook.com/HQStories

BUDDING WRITER?

We're also looking for authors to join the HQ Digital family! Find out more here:

https://www.hqstories.co.uk/want-to-write-for-us/

Thanks for reading, from the HQ Digital team